Blood Feud

S.J.A. Turney is an author of Roman and medieval historical fiction, gritty historical fantasy and rollicking Roman children's books. He lives with his family and extended menagerie of pets in rural North Yorkshire.

Also by S.J.A. Turney

Tales of the Empire

Interregnum
Ironroot
Dark Empress
Insurgency
Invasion
Jade Empire
Emperor's Bane

The Ottoman Cycle

The Thief's Tale
The Priest's Tale
The Assassin's Tale
The Pasha's Tale

The Knights Templar

Daughter of War
The Last Emir
City of God
The Winter Knight
The Crescent and the Cross
The Last Crusade

Wolves of Odin

Blood Feud

BLOOD FEUD

S.J.A. TURNEY

CANELO

First published in the United Kingdom in 2021 by

Canelo
31 Helen Road
Oxford OX2 0DF
United Kingdom

A CIP catalogue record for this book is available from the British Library.

Print ISBN 978 1 80032 128 1
Ebook ISBN 978 1 80032 127 4

Look for more great books at www.canelo.co

Printed and bound in Great Britain by Clays Ltd, Elcograf S.p.A.

1

For Tim Easton, an extraordinary teacher
who inspires like no other.
May Odin always have your back.

In addition to his twin ravens, the Allfather was
accompanied by two wolves by the names of
Geri (the Ravenous) and Freki (the Greedy)

A Note on Pronunciation

Wherever possible within this tale, I have adhered to the Old Norse spellings and pronunciations of Viking names, concepts and words. There is a certain closeness to be gained from speaking these names as they would have been spoken a thousand years ago. For example, I have used Valhöll rather than Valhalla, which is more ubiquitous now, but they refer to the same thing. There is a glossary of Norse terms at the back of the book.

Two letters in particular may be unfamiliar to readers. The letter ð (eth) is pronounced in Old Norse as 'th', as you would pronounce it in 'the' or 'then', but in many cases over the centuries has been anglicised as a 'd'. So, for example, you will find Harald Hardrada's name written in the text as Harðráði (pronounced Har-th-rar-thi) but it can be read as Hardradi for ease. Similarly, Seiðr can be read as seithr or seidr. The letter æ (ash) is pronounced 'a' as in cat, or bat.

Prologue

In the Days of Gods

'Night comes. The ceremonies are almost done,' Prince Onund murmured.

Yngvar looked up. Clouds the colour of slate scudded across a dull sky, the pale, watery sun closing on the end of its downward arc. The ancient sacred clearing still gleamed, though, in the lee of the longhouses and surrounding woodland.

'The king will need to be persuaded. He will not want to risk angering the islanders,' Onund added, nodding at his father.

The gathering of karls and jarls before them was the largest of the year, and the throng filled the two great ship outlines, marked by time-worn stones before the great mound. Voices carried to them on the wind as each man in turn spoke the words of allegiance to their king, who responded from atop the mound with the ritual acceptance.

Yngvar's eyes played across the throng, his disapproval rapidly turning to spite. The loyal Geatish delegates from the south filled the larger of the two ritual 'ships', the northern Swedes the other. Off to the side stood a smaller, less impressive example with but few men standing therein. Insular Goths from their island. His lip wrinkled. Twelve men were missing.

Yngvar shook his head. 'Those isolated throwbacks cling to their heretic ways and God will judge them in the end if my sword cannot. But whether they pray to God or no, they should take the oath to your father.'

Oaths of allegiance complete, King Olof Skötkonung threw his arms wide and announced the feast, a time for joy, relaxation and all manner of hedonistic delights in the numerous longhouses at the periphery of this ancient site. The hum of conversation came in waves, rising as men who saw one another only once or twice a year made deals and exchanged news, and then dying down as the king on the mound spoke before rising and cresting once more.

Gesturing to his companions, Yngvar slapped the reins and dug in his heels and the riders walked their horses out from the treeline, emerging from shadow into pale late-afternoon light.

'Still, it is a foolish man who stamps at the ice he walks upon, looking for cracks,' young Onund said, sagely. 'Father will not wish to press too hard, in case it gives.'

'One or two figures missing from a ritual ship is normal, Onund. It is to be expected. Some will be attacked on the road, killed or have turned back. Some will be ill. Small absences might be explained. Those Goths, though… Twelve missing is too many to explain away so easily. Twelve can *only* be deliberate.'

Onund Olofsson nodded, keeping his own counsel as they arrived at the rear of the great mound, coming to a jingling, snorting halt a respectful enough distance away to keep the king's guards happy. King Olof himself was making his way down, surrounded by his senior jarls, his law speaker, the itinerant skald, Óttarr Svarti, and his favourite priest, Sigfridaer. The king's eyes fell upon the group awaiting him.

'Onund, my boy, and Yngvar Eymundsson. You will sit at my table, of course.' He smiled, pointing ahead to the longhouses.

'The Gottlanders fail in their duties, King Olof,' Yngvar replied without preamble.

The king shifted uncomfortably within his heavy cloak, shrugging the garment into place. 'Their numbers were lacking, but they are an island people, Yngvar. Most men have to brave only roads and fields to get here; the Goths must cross open waters. The deficiency may be merely unhappy accident.'

'The Goths can sail a dragon boat as well as any Swede or Geat, King Olof, and some of their number made it. This was a deliberate sleight.'

'The Goths have always been loyal, Yngvar. They hammered their shields and travelled the whale road with us against the Norwegian king. They sailed with us to the land of the Wends. They are loyal.'

Yngvar shook his head. 'The Goths cling to the old ways. They see the bishops and missionaries at your court and they sneer. They see the churches rising in your lands and fear that soon this will be another Daneland or Norway, that their ways will be extinct. They will not take your oath, for they see you as an enemy.'

The king's expression grew troubled. 'There are many who still deny the church, Yngvar,' he replied, 'especially in the inhospitable North or on the islands, cut off from the world. But the Swedes, the Geats and the Goths are a proud lot. If I drive the blade of Christianity down into the ice as you would wish, I fear I would see the land split and whole regions drift away like icebergs.'

'You cannot rule a land of men who would rather pray to a heathen idol than give you their oath. How could you rely on them to fight?'

King Olof sighed. 'If we want a land united under the cross, it will be a long and careful business. Still, there is truth in your words: there is wisdom in securing their oaths. You wish to visit the Goths?'

'The only way to assure yourself of their loyalty is to challenge them, my king. Let me take a force to the island and determine the problem.'

Still the king stared into space for a while, before finally scrubbing at his neck and nodding. 'Go with grace, though, young Eymundsson. Go with the wisdom of the sage, not the ire of the warrior. You will leave in the morning? After the feast?'

'I see no reason to delay, great king. If we leave now, we can get to Västra Aros and be aboard my ship with everything stowed by nightfall. It will save us half a day of gathering hungover men from under tables in the morning.'

The king snorted. He looked into Yngvar's eyes once more, unsettled by the hard certainty he met in them. 'Go, then, but remember that you represent me, not God.'

Yngvar bowed his head and turned, but the king held up a hand. 'Not Onund, though.'

'Father?' the prince turned, brow furrowed.

'Your place is not with Yngvar Eymundsson visiting Gottland. It is here, where the people gather in my honour. A king needs his sons by his side in the sight of all the jarls.'

Onund threw his father a rare petulant look, and for a moment the king thought he might object, but then he nodded and waved a farewell to his friend, slipping from his mount and handing the reins to one of the thralls as he fell into step beside his father.

Yngvar did not look back.

–

'We have a chance here to bring light to the darkness.'

Yngvar glanced sidewards at the young priest, Hjalmvigi, a pale and reedy man in a white robe who might have been lost in any crowd but for the fire of zealotry that burned in his eyes.

'You heard the king. I am to be careful and not press the cross upon them.'

'Things go wrong,' the priest shrugged. 'Sometimes trouble is unavoidable.' The man gave him a knowing look before letting his mount drop back once more among the other armed horsemen as they approached the village. Over a week ago they had landed at Visby and overnighted there, secure in the knowledge that the jarl who ruled his lands from that place, the largest settlement on Gottland, had been one of those who had turned up at the Thing and hailed his king.

For nine days since, they had travelled around the island, visiting each man who had not put in an appearance and securing their oaths. The task had been distasteful to all of them, for these fools really did belong to a lost age. They clung to false gods and heathen ways and had the temerity to look at Yngvar and his men as though *they* were the ones at fault. Still, each jarl and karl had taken in the swords and axes of the visiting warriors, and the look of determination in their leader's eyes, and had bowed their head as they swore the oath.

'One last visit,' Yngvar said to himself.

Along the churned, filthy track they rode, past two pairs of houses facing onto the road, and then over a small but well-constructed timber bridge crossing a narrow stream that spat and gurgled and danced on its way to the sea. The village was small and simple, an open space surrounded by peasant houses. Off ahead and to one side, the eaves of the forest were visible encroaching on the village. Other than houses, the only landmarks were a pair of standing stones, one close to the bridge, covered in runes and likely commemorating some long-since fallen raider or trader, the other at the far side, close to the trees and considerably larger.

No church, Yngvar noted. No cross. Just signs scratched into doorframes to ward off elfish magic. Throwbacks and pagans all.

As they rode, house doors opened and suspicious faces appeared, men and women stepping outside to watch this display of power, something that had probably not happened here in their lifetimes. Reaching the open space that was the heart of the village, Yngvar reined in, his men gathering around him, but did not dismount.

'Who speaks for this village at the Thing?' he called.

Several doors opened and more folk came out to stare. A man who was busy feeding a small bonfire in his garden near the stream threw an armful of cut bushes onto it and then stumped over towards them, lurching with a gammy leg. There was a pause, and a big Goth with a grey beard and an ancient tattoo above one eye stepped forwards on his porch. There was a heavy, bearded axe at his side, Yngvar noticed; he could not decide whether to take that as a veiled threat. No, the man was old, though had clearly once been a warrior of note.

'I am called Vigholf,' the old warrior said, simply and with no sign of deference. Deserving of respect, Yngvar judged, even if he was misguided and outdated. After all, the kingdom of Olof needed warriors as much as the Kingdom of God. A quick glance at Hjalmvigi, however, revealed only an expression of anger and hatred at such pagan ways.

'I am Yngvar Eymundsson, the voice of your king. No representative appeared at the Thing this month to take the oath. Your absence was through illness, perhaps?'

'I recognise the king, but have no wish to take an oath in the presence of his pet priest of the nailed god,' the old man rumbled, throwing a look of distrust at Hjalmvigi, who returned it with a glare of hatred. Yngvar was beginning to regret bringing the priest along, yet the respect he'd been willing to show the man was crumbling in the face of such a lack of deference. He took a deep breath, calming himself.

'Idols of Satan,' spat Hjalmvigi, drawing up beside him and pointing across the square. Yngvar's gaze followed the priest's finger, alighting upon that large standing stone near the trees. The monolith was taller than a man and covered in patterned *ringerike* work, dotted with images, runes and a stylised image of a warrior on a horse with eight legs. An unmistakable sign: Odin riding Sleipnir.

'Go with the wisdom of the sage, not the ire of the warrior, Olof Skötkonung said,' Yngvar murmured to the priest, deliberately keeping his hand away from his sword hilt, in case he was tempted. He gestured to the old villager. 'The king insists on the oath from all his jarls and freemen. You will take the oath, and the offence of your absence will be absolved.'

The villager nodded sagely, wordlessly. Something about him was making Yngvar irritated, though.

Hjalmvigi reached across and gripped Yngvar's elbow. 'Before we leave, pull over that hideous stone. Let their demon see only earth with his one good eye.'

'No,' interjected the greybeard, stepping down from his porch and to the dirt of the village square.

Yngvar had been considering whether or not the priest's idea contravened the king's orders, but while Hjalmvigi might be pushing things, further defiance from this heretic was not to be ignored.

'You do not command us, old man,' Yngvar said angrily, gesturing to his men, three of whom began to walk their horses towards the monolith.

'Nor you I,' the old man snapped. 'I will take the oath to the king, but not when his men do such things. I will not allow it.'

Yngvar snorted. 'There are twelve of us, greybeard, and I have fifty more at Visby. You have an axe and a village of farmers with sticks.'

'Yet we have honour, where you appear to have none.'

This time, Yngvar did not stop his hand going to his sword hilt. 'Watch your words, old man. I promised the king this would go smoothly.'

'Then you are an oath-breaker too, for you will not impose your nailed god upon this place.'

'Yngvar,' called one of the three men who had ridden over to the stone. He glanced in their direction, fingertips still dancing lightly on the leather hilt wrapping of his sword. The warrior near the stone was pointing into the trees. Yngvar could see nothing but the shadowy shapes of trunks and branches. Gesturing for the old man to stay where he was, he walked his horse over to the stone. As he closed, he saw what his rider had been pointing to.

Animals hung from the trees, pale and lifeless, suspended by their hind legs. The ground beneath was richer coloured, darker than the rest of the packed earth. Yngvar felt his gorge rise. How were these appalling spectacles allowed to continue? But that was not the worst of it. Among the grisly shapes his disgusted gaze found the one thing he could not accept. The body of a man hung by the feet, grey-white, with an ugly second mouth opened across his neck.

'Savages,' spat Yngvar, urging his horse closer. 'Is it not enough that you refuse your king's summons, but you must murder his subjects?' He'd not realised that Hjalmvigi had ridden after him until he heard the priest hiss in fury. He'd been trying to ease the zealot's temper thus far, but sights like this were too much. The body in the trees was naked and unadorned, he could see no signs of tattoos or markings. Something glinted among the white hairs of his beard, and Yngvar tilted his head curiously, trying to make it out.

'A cross,' Hjalmvigi snarled, pointing at it.

'What?' Yngvar frowned, squinting at the gleaming metal.

'This man wears a cross around his neck. He was a man of God!'

'He was a blacksmith and no lover of your Serkland nailed god,' the old man from the porch said. 'What you see is *Mjǫllnir*, the hammer of Thor, not your weak man's cross.'

'Lies,' Hjalmvigi spat. 'All lies and heresy, all evil and witchery. You deny your king and you deny the Lord God while performing your demonic rituals and murdering good men.' The priest glared a challenge at Yngvar, who felt himself teetering. The king's peace or the Lord's grace?

He turned to his riders. 'Pull over that stone and cut these creatures down. This poor soul we will take to Visby, and find a good burial ground for him.'

'You will do no such thing,' snarled the old man. 'Nine bodies were given and nine bodies will hang for nine days, for we cannot afford a poor harvest two years in a row.'

'Do it,' barked Yngvar, pointing at the stone. Two of his riders had produced a rope now, and moved over towards the monolith.

'No,' bellowed the old warrior, hefting the axe at his side.

'I warn you, Vigholf: interfering will get you killed.'

The old man looked this way and that, and Yngvar followed his gaze to see that half a dozen other men had stepped from their houses with axes or spears, one with a rusted pitchfork. The threat was tangible, and though the danger they posed to the well-equipped riders was laughable, Yngvar couldn't help but acknowledge that this could have gone better. The king would be furious. The moment's silence was broken by Hjalmvigi, whispering a litany at the hanging body, urging Yngvar to action.

'The gods are easily offended,' the old man said, taking another step forwards and hefting his axe. 'Your nailed Christ will not save you. Do not do this.'

Hjalmvigi's chanting rose in volume, and Yngvar's gaze was drawn once more to the sacrifice in the tree. He snarled at the old karl and waved a hand to his men. The two with the rope threw it around the rough-shaped monolith and pulled it taut.

'No,' called the old man again, lifting his axe threateningly and starting to stride purposefully in their direction. Yngvar hauled on his reins, turning his horse to follow the man, and only that same preternatural sense that had saved his life during the debacle collecting tribute from the Semgalls saved him once more. He turned his head just in time to see the weapon coming for him and to loll back in the saddle, the spear point slicing through the air a hand's breadth from his face.

Yngvar spun in his saddle, hauling out his sword even as the farmer pulled back his spear for another thrust. The man was quick for a nobody, and the sharp point plunged towards the horse's neck fast enough that Yngvar had to urgently knock the blow aside. All the riders had their shields on their backs or strapped to horses' harnesses; it was when some crazed heathen was trying to sink four inches of ironwork into your side that you regretted not having the shield to hand.

Yngvar pulled his foot from the stirrup and kicked out at the man, sending him sprawling back into the dirt, his spear clattering to the ground. He turned, taking advantage of the momentary freedom to examine their situation. Despite the fact that they outclassed and outnumbered the villagers, the suddenness and ferocity of their reaction had taken its toll already. One of his men was on the ground with a spear standing proud from his chest, while the peasant responsible had drawn a sax, a long-bladed fighting knife, and was circling another rider, snarling like a wolf. Over by the monolith, the rope lay on the ground, one of its owners lying nearby, a great wound cleaved in his side, pouring torrents of dark blood into the dust. The old man, his bloodied axe whirling expertly in his hands, was facing off against the other rope man, who was, understandably, being cautious, waiting for an opening to strike.

The menfolk of the village were divided, half were attacking the riders, while the rest had disappeared into their houses. Of the women there was no sign, nor of the majority of the village children, though a small group of young faces were just visible beneath the porch of another house, peering out, terrified, from their place of safety.

It would not be safe for long. These peasants had damned themselves by their own actions. Through gritted teeth, Yngvar issued orders to those of his men not already engaged in the fighting. Two hurried over to the bonfire and selected burning logs, pulling them from the flames by the dark, untouched end, and carrying them towards the timber buildings.

The spearman Yngvar had knocked down was reaching for his weapon now, readying himself to stand once more. Yngvar's lip wrinkled at such resistance from the man. If only they would understand and bow to the cross, what warriors for the king they would make. With a sigh, and the knowledge that examples had to be made, he pushed forwards and walked his horse across the struggling spearman, cracking bones and crushing organs. He turned the beast on top of the stricken man, then rode slowly towards the clash by the great stone. The old karl, Vigholf, now displayed a red gash across one shoulder. It did not seem to be impacting on the warrior's ability to swing his axe, though, for blood sheeted down Yngvar's rider's left side.

The old karl heard Yngvar coming and managed to extricate himself from his current contest in time to leap aside and dodge Yngvar's swiping sword. As Yngvar hauled on his reins to turn his mount and face the greybeard, the old man took an unexpected opportunity to cut the front legs out from under the other rider's horse with a mighty sweep of his great axe blade. The beast howled in agony as it fell to the ground, thrashing and shaking, throwing its rider. The horseman, dazed and panicked, hit the ground hard and struggled to rise to his feet, only to meet the old man's axe as it descended.

The blade slammed into the rider between neck and shoulder and bit down so far that his arm peeled out away from the body. The man's screaming was lost beneath the feral, bestial howl of the old warrior.

'Odin!'

Yngvar leapt from his horse, storming towards the old man. Any hopes of a peaceful resolution here were now lost. The old warrior's violence had been his undoing. His last blow had been so hard that the axe was jammed in the bone and innards of his victim; his muscles rippled with effort as he worked to pull the weapon free.

He never made it.

Yngvar's sword swept down and smashed into the arm gripping the axe. The bone broke in several places and the arm was almost severed, and despite everything Yngvar was impressed: the man, ruined now and facing inescapable death, kept his grip on the axe haft and continued to tug only until it became clear that his arm would tear in two before the weapon came free. Instead, the old man accepted his lot, held the blade in his dying grip and turned his face, contorted with pain, towards his killer.

Yngvar stepped forwards again and raised his blade. 'Repent of your heresy, and perhaps you might yet find God's grace in the world beyond.'

Vigholf, his face folding into a grimace, growled. 'I die in battle with axe in hand. I go to the afterworld with honour. I shall be chosen and sit beside my forefathers in *Valhöll*. I go safe in the knowledge that I will never see you there.'

Yngvar nodded once and thrust out, his blade slamming point-first into Vigholf's chest, beside the breastbone and into the heart. With effort, he put all his strength behind the blade and drove it on until it emerged from the man's back. The old karl was whispering something with his dying breath, though Yngvar neither heard it nor cared what it was. Planting his left boot on the dying man's shoulder, he heaved on his sword, pulling it free. The ageing warrior collapsed, his arm miraculously still gripping the axe haft.

Yngvar straightened, blade held out to the side. The other villagers were all dealt with now, barring that last man with his sax, who was wounded and was circling defensively, surrounded by three riders. Several of the huts were on fire, and their occupants were fleeing the village, slipping across their gardens and running for the trees.

Even as he turned back towards that obscene pagan stone, Yngvar's attention was caught by a cry of unholy fury, and he spun to see a woman hurtling out of a burning hut, cleaver in hand, charging straight for him. Teeth gritted, he readied himself and, as the woman reached him, raising her cleaver to strike, he stepped neatly aside and swung his sword, hacking deep into her midriff. She stumbled to a halt, staring down in surprise at the mortal wound. Blood escaped her mouth in gobbets as she sank to her knees.

He straightened again. For some reason he simply could not think of an appropriate prayer, if ever there could be an appropriate prayer for this place and its heathen populace. He watched as the last man was felled, his sax falling away into the dust, and turned slowly. The village was aflame. The children lurking beneath the porch were still there, but even as he looked at them they withdrew into the darkness.

'Throw the bodies into the burning houses along with the animal corpses. Save the poor bastard hanging in the tree, though. We'll take him back to Visby for burial.' He glanced at the priest, whose face shone with righteous victory. Damn the man, but this was as much Hjalmvigi's fault as his own, yet now he was committed, he might as well finish the job. 'Pull that fucking stone down. I have no desire to gaze upon that demon and his twisted horse.'

Turning his back on the scene, he walked towards his horse, pulling a rag from his belt and wiping the viscera from his blade before sheathing it. It was going to take all his powers of persuasion to make the king accept this. But then Olof Skötkonung was too accepting sometimes of his people's failings. Hjalmvigi would talk to the king's favoured priests and smooth things over.

With a sigh, Yngvar son of Eymund pulled himself up into the saddle and prepared to leave the godforsaken island. As the riders crossed the small bridge once more and departed the burning village full of bodies, sobbing women and white-faced men emerged from hiding, some rushing to the stream with buckets, others falling to their knees beside the burning buildings containing their loved ones.

Four children, carrying wooden swords and brightly coloured shields of wicker, slunk from the shadows of one of the few buildings not aflame and crossed the square. Two burst into tears and ran to find their parents. Vigholf's son and his friend crossed to the conflagration that contained all that was left of his father. Tears would not come to Halfdan for he was not frightened, and nor was he sad. He was *angry*. His gaze slid from the fiery doorway to the disappearing horsemen and he looked down at the birthmark on his arm, the entwined serpents of Loki. He had always been lucky, and this day he and his friends had survived a massacre. But something had been born amid the blood and flames of violence.

'Yngvar,' the boy said, trying out the name, testing how it sounded, how it felt, tasting the bitterness of it. He was too young to address a Thing and seek the righting of this wrong, but one day... *one day*.

Part One

ᚹᛟᛚᚡᛖᛋ ᛟᚠ ᛟᛞᛁᚾ

The Warrior and the Witch

Chapter 1

Uppsala, ten years later

'Breath of Hrimgrimnir, eh, young 'un?' the toothless old man across the table muttered, pulling his cloak about his shoulders.

Halfdan grunted a non-committal reply, but he had no great desire to converse right now. The wind did indeed whistle through the cracks in the rough-hewn timber wall like the breath of a frost giant. It bore a few flakes of snow inside, which danced and eddied through the air, landing on the table in front of Halfdan, where they swiftly settled into tiny puddles to be lost among the stains of old ale, mead and sour milk. The fire-warmed surface felt good under his hands after an aggravating and fruitless day in the royal town of Uppsala, plagued with failures.

'New to town?' the old man went on, conversationally.

'Yes,' he replied, hoping a simple acknowledgement would shut the man up, and pulling down his sleeve a little to hide the birthmark that might draw unwanted attention.

'Biggest place I ever did see, Uppsala.'

Halfdan sighed. 'Huge.' As a boy he had not known that places larger than a village even existed, and certainly no *building* larger than Thorfin's mead hall. Never before had he thought that such a place as this might exist: a tavern, a sort of mead hall that served anything to anyone in exchange for silver or coin, and with no need to be oath-sworn to the owner.

'You a country boy? Nah… islander, I reckon.' The man was determined to talk.

'Gottlander, from Visby.'

Well, not originally from Visby, but a lot had changed since that day, when Halfdan had hidden beneath the house of his friend and watched their village butchered and torched by the cross-wielding bastard who had gutted women and torn down the powerful Odin stone, egged on by his pet priest. Since the day he had watched his father roar like a wolf and die like a hero in the ancient sagas, cut down in the village square, bellowing his loyalty to Odin to the end. He shivered, and not from the cold of the breeze.

'Left the island to see the world, did ya?'

'Something like that. I was stuck there 'til my uncle died.'

That day, just seven summers old, Halfdan had picked up a bloodied sword from the dust of the wrecked settlement and stood amid the charred embers of his life vowing revenge, and death upon the man called Yngvar Eymundsson. He would have raced in pursuit of the riders and sold his life cheap in an attempt to gut the son of a dog had not Ømund's surprisingly strong mother held him back until the riders were long gone, and then delivered him to his uncle in Visby.

'No love for your uncle, then? And no father?'

Why wouldn't the old man shut up?

'My father died when I was young. I was fostered on my uncle, who worked me hard and made sure I stayed put. He was not a bad man. Ran took him down to her realm when he was tipped from a fishing boat a month ago.'

He frowned. He'd not meant to say so much, but the old man seemed to be drawing his past from him. Arriving at his uncle's, he'd begged the old man to attend a Thing and announce a blood feud with this Eymundsson, but the man would have none of it. Instead, Halfdan had found himself in virtual thraldom. He'd grown to adulthood in the outskirts of Visby, had begun to learn the art of carving, and had dutifully set to every task his uncle had given him, the model foster-son. All that time, the flame of revenge had burned deep in his heart, hidden within black coals, but glowing, like an ember that could reignite with a single breath. His uncle had made his position clear from the outset: there was no profit in revenge. It was a hollow and costly thing. Halfdan had nodded his understanding, but kept the sword from the village safely hidden. He had practised with it whenever his uncle was away. Nothing official had been declared at a Thing, for Halfdan had been but a boy, yet a blood feud it was, and a blood feud it would remain.

Halfdan was subtle, and clever, and both beyond the expected limits of his age. He had grown strong from his work and his swordplay, and he had learned everything he could from whomever he could. Only in the nighttime hours, when the scene of his father's death replayed itself over and over in chilling detail, did he give way to the fear, anger and sorrow, always alone, in the dark. When his uncle had died, Halfdan had mourned only with lip-service as he packed his possessions and lied and tricked his way onto a ship that would take him to the mainland.

'So you came to Uppsala to make your name? To make a fortune? Many come. Few succeed.'

Halfdan shrugged. 'I'm searching for a man.'

He had arrived that morning, and wandered around Uppsala for a few hours, gradually becoming soaked and freezing cold, uncertain of where his path might lead, unable to find anyone among this reticent populace who would speak of the man he sought. Dejected, he had discovered this place quite by chance. The ale here was good, flavoured with bog myrtle, sour and heady, and in truth Halfdan had already had more than enough of it for the maintenance of good sense. The sun had slid quickly from the sky, and darkness settled as he sat in the tavern and fretted. Nightfall had brought new customers, including the old man.

'Who do you seek? Rikvald knows everyone, you see. Rikvald talks much, but sees all.'

The crease in Halfdan's brow deepened. He felt a touch of old *Seiðr* magic in the air. Had the Norns brought this man to him? Was he part of Halfdan's fate?

'I'm looking for Yngvar, son of Eymund, a jarl with ties to the king, and who I assumed to be in Uppsala where the king dwells, but I can learn nothing for no one will speak of him.'

The old man snorted. 'He is long gone from here, boy, yet the son of Eymund is still a bad name to throw around. Folk will not easily discuss him with anyone, for he became unpopular with the king. They say that Yngvar saw himself as a greater king than Olof or Onund could ever be. He left years ago, before he was driven out, gone east, they say.'

Halfdan shivered. He felt a curious mix of exhilaration and despair. At last he had learned of his father's killer, only to discover that he had gone far from here and long enough ago that the trail had probably gone cold.

'Where in the east?' he asked.

The old man shrugged. 'I hear he sailed many days across the icebound sea, to the court of Jarisleif of Kiev in Rusland.'

'*Rusland?*' Damn it, but the man had never seemed further from his reach. It had been a great journey just from Visby to Uppsala, and he could hardly imagine how he could travel so far as to visit another land. Luck and will only got a man so far. He had little in the way of silver, and no realistic way of following. He sighed and sagged back, reaching out, dipping his forefinger into a puddle of snow water and drawing designs on the table, old designs that the nailed god would detest. Signs of a time when Northmen were men to be feared and respected. Another swig from the mug, and he slapped the flat-bottomed thing back to the timber with a crack.

How would he get to the lands of the Rus? He could perhaps talk or trick his way onto a ship if he could find one, but the journey across the Eastern Sea in winter was hazardous, and the northern reaches could easily form into ice solid enough to walk a cow upon, or so it was said. Only a brave and shrewd sailor would try for Rus lands at this time of the year. Finding passage would be difficult.

He was trying to draw a rudimentary map in spilled drink on the table, using his limited geography, when suddenly the door to the street slammed inwards, smashing back against the wall, scattering dust from the rafters. The freezing wind intruded immediately, with myriad snowflakes swirling and raising curses around the tavern.

The old man shrank back into his seat with a spat oath and pulled his cloak tighter around himself. A stranger in a russet tunic tumbled into the room, swearing like a smith with a slippery hammer, staggering back and miraculously managing not to fall. The man stopped and lurched to steadier feet, his face bloodied, his nose broken, and the russet of his clothes darker in places where the blood had soaked in. But he had clearly given as well as he'd received, for the blood on his bunched knuckles was not all his own, and a flash of white looked as though a tooth had become embedded in the back of his hand.

With a roar, a second figure hurtled into the room, and Halfdan's eyes widened. This newcomer was, quite simply, the biggest man Halfdan had ever seen, massive in height and broad across the shoulders with a chest like a barrel. He wore a chain shirt, and an axe hung unused at his belt, gleaming in the firelight as he advanced on the russet fighter. But it was neither his dimensions nor his warrior's garb that almost took away Halfdan's breath. This man might have been Thor himself, had his colouring not been so wrong. His beard was thick and full, divided into a fork and braided to the ends, his hair wild and long and unfettered, but his skin was so pale as to be almost ivory, and his hair and beard the colour of fresh-fallen snow. Four lines of old wounds crossed his nose and cheek, leaving furrows in his eyebrow, and a piece of his ear was missing. Whatever had done that had not been human, and old tales of trolls and monsters surfaced unbidden in Halfdan's mind.

The pale warrior roared and turned, and it was then that Halfdan realised another man was clinging to his back, one arm around the neck and almost hidden by folds of cloak, trying to throttle the life from the big man. The white warrior seemed largely unconcerned by the man recovering in front of him, grinning broadly with a mouth full of blood and a telling gap in his smile.

Bunching his hand into a fist, the big warrior drew his arm forwards and then jerked his elbow back sharply as he turned to face the room once more. There was an explosive exhale and the man around his neck let go, dropping to his knees, heaving in breaths, winded.

'Fucking cross-humpers,' snarled the big man as he stepped forwards once more and, almost casually, picked up a stool by one leg, swinging it back and forth like a club.

Halfdan watched, fascinated, as the warrior advanced on the first man. Moments later, even as the big white man and the bloodied stranger moved further into the room, the winded man recovered and, with an oath in a Daneland accent, ran at the pale giant. He had been anticipated, however, and the big man simply stepped left and let the man career past. Now he was grinning again as he advanced on the pair.

'Take this outside,' bellowed the proprietor, though there was clearly little chance of that. The two men in colourful tunics stood side by side, preparing, making fists and breathing deep. The big man stopped and watched them hawkishly, ready for their next move. So intent was he on his twin opponents that the big man failed to notice their eyes flick up for just a moment, over his shoulder.

Halfdan did *not* miss the move. His head turned as a fourth figure came running through the door, a sword gripped in his fist, face twisted into a mask of hate and fury. Halfdan was instantly certain that the newcomer was a third opponent of the big man, and no ally, and while the big warrior with the unused axe was clearly seeing all of this as little more than a punch-up, the newcomer had a more violent end in mind. The two near the bar ran at the big white fellow now, bellowing, keeping his

25

attention on them, distracting him from the death blow approaching unseen from behind.

Halfdan couldn't say why he did it. This was none of his business, and certainly not his fight, yet somewhere deep within him he knew that he couldn't let the big man die so ignominiously. As the newcomer ran at the great white warrior's back, Halfdan stuck out a leisurely leg and tripped him.

With a squawk, the swordsman fell full length along the rush-strewn floor, his mouth filling with filth and dirt, sword clattering out of his grasp. The ghostly coloured warrior turned with a frown, took in the scene in a heart-beat and grinned afresh before turning back to his original foe and smashing the stool in his hand against the head of the russet tunic'd man.

Leaving the big warrior to his business, Halfdan rose, scraping back his stool as the prostrate man coughed out muck and straw, spitting curses between the filth. With a slight shake of the head, the young Gottlander delivered a powerful kick to the fallen man's cheek. His head snapped back and cracked against the floor again, and he went still. Calmly, Halfdan rounded the table, and picked up the sword. It was a good blade. Nothing fancy, no decorative work or silver inlay, but a solid warrior's blade. Better than the ancient, pitted thing Halfdan had brought from the village. He drew his own sword and compared the two for size. They were quite close. Hopeful Halfdan sank the new blade into his scabbard and smiled with pleasure as it slid home snug and firm. He kept the old sword too, though. No point in throwing away potential loot. He had a long journey to fund, after all.

As he stepped back to his original side of the table, he smiled to see the russet man staggering towards the door, clutching his head and moaning. The big white warrior let out a roar like an ice floe sliding into the sea and turned, the splintered remains of the stool still in his hand as the third man ran for the door, one arm hanging limp. Since the big man did not seem to be giving chase, the pair bent to grab an arm of their unconscious third conspirator each, eyeing Halfdan warily as they did so, then dragged him out into the street.

Calling the three injured men several unkind things, another patron stomped across to the door and pushed it closed, shutting out the icy wind and the flurries of snow.

'Why d'you bring your arguments in here, you great hairy heap?' the owner of the tavern snapped angrily. 'Look what you've done to my furniture. And there's blood all over the floor. I hope you've a purse full of hacksilver.'

The big man looked a little apologetic, an expression most comical with his bloodied mouth and missing tooth. Before he could say anything, Halfdan was approaching them, holding out his old sword.

'It's no jarl's blade, but it's solid and well balanced. Worth more than a stool and a quick scrub of the floor. Maybe even worth an evening of ale?'

The owner's eyes narrowed as he took in the blade being offered. Clearly it would be a very advantageous trade, yet while a Svear might be a warrior or a craftsman, fisher or farmer, first and foremost he will always be a trader.

'Four ales,' the man said, still eyeing them up carefully.

Halfdan smiled. 'Done. For four ales each.'

As the owner blustered, claiming he'd never said 'each', Halfdan placed the sword on the counter and returned to his table. The other chair sat empty, the talkative old man

27

gone during the scuffle. After a pause and with a furrowed brow, the big man stomped after him and sank into the recently vacated seat. A moment later the owner was there with two more mugs of sharp ale and no further argument. He might have been outmanoeuvred in a barter, but he had still got the better deal, and he knew it. The sword would more than pay for an evening for these two.

'Your help was timely,' the big man said finally.

'A fight's a fight, but murder's different,' Halfdan said simply, taking a pull of his ale.

The big man nodded and followed suit. 'Christians,' the white warrior snorted quietly, though not quietly enough, for several heads turned and regarded them warily for a moment before returning to their own conversations. 'They cannot let a man worship his own way. Everything has to be crosses and eating their god's flesh and drinking his blood. I don't care what foul things they do in their temples, but I'm not eating the flesh of their nailed god. They say he's a thousand years old. How rotten will that flesh be now?'

Halfdan chuckled. 'Our sort are not popular these days, my big friend.'

The big man's eyes narrowed. 'Except where you come from, I think. I know a Gottland accent when I hear one. I'm Bjorn, who they call "Bear-torn".'

'Halfdan. Who they call Halfdan.'

'Tell me, what brings a young Gottlander to Uppsala?'

'Only if you tell me what brings you here and how you got into a fight with those three.'

The big man grinned again, and sucked the blood from around his pink teeth. 'It is a long story, and a very tedious one, though it involves more than one unfortunate death and I fear if I do not leave Uppsala in a hurry, these will not

28

be the last angry men who find me.' He laughed, as though being hunted were but a small thing. 'Let me instead tell you how a bear once almost took my head off while I was having a shit in his cave.'

Taking a pull of ale, Bjorn began to weave his story as the fire danced and the air fugged.

Time rolled on as Halfdan listened to tale after tale of Bjorn's exploits, some of which may even have been true. Halfdan had fully intended to be reticent for his part, listening expansively but giving away little in return. The reason for his eventual outpouring was twofold, a combination of the simple acceptance and friendliness the strange albino exuded, and the regular flow of heady ale that, before the evening ended, had far surpassed the four for which they had bartered, and had dug into the funds in both their purses. He told Bjorn everything, in low tones and making sure that each time a name was uttered it was done carefully and unnoticed by any other occupant of the low room. He spoke of his father and of the jarl who killed him. Of a blood feud that could not be declared in public. Of a childhood of servitude used to learn and to acquire the cunning of a wolf. He even let the man see the twined snake mark on his arm that some thought a curse, while others thought it a source of luck.

'And so my uncle died,' he finished, sitting back heavily and slugging more ale. 'I saw no reason to wait any longer. The murderous bastard is out there, and I'll find him.'

'And you mean to kill him.'

'Of course. The old ways still hold in Gottland: a blood debt is still a blood debt, whether declared at a Thing or not.'

Bjorn huffed through his teeth, bloodied spittle landing on the table before him. 'Your uncle was wrong.'

'What?'

'Your uncle. When he said there is no profit in revenge.'

Halfdan leaned forwards, folding his arms. 'What do you mean?'

'Oh, he's right that there is no profit in revenge, but he underestimates it. Revenge is not only profit free, it is a costly thing, also. It's not simply a case of walking halfway to Ásgarðr and sticking a blade in someone, then dusting off your hands. You know who you're talking about here?'

'Of course,' Halfdan replied, tone lowering in case of wagging ears.

'Your prey is no ordinary man. Not even an ordinary jarl. He is of royal blood himself. He is at the court of the King of Koenugard, and do you know why?'

'Because he seeks new enemies to convert and new temples to tear down?'

'Because he made too many enemies *here*. Because he is almost as powerful as the king and his son. He demanded to be recognised as a king in his own right, and Olof Skötkonung would hear nothing of it. He went east because he is too powerful to stay here and not contest the rule of men. He went east to found a new kingdom for himself. This is the man you plan to impale? It will be no easy task.'

Halfdan sighed. 'Of this I am rapidly becoming aware. But I cannot believe that Odin will deny me revenge. There is Seiðr at work here. The Norns sent me an old man who pointed the way and I will travel to Rusland, no matter the cost.'

'First, we will need others. This is not a task for two men alone.'

'Two men?' Halfdan said suddenly, sitting upright once more. 'You would come with me?'

Bjorn grinned that bloody grin. 'For battle and glory and a chance to kill a king? What warrior could argue with such a thing? I am heartily sick of this place where men are like women and women are like sheep. The nailed god has sapped the spirit from the North. And,' he reminded Halfdan, 'there are a few bodies bearing my mark for which I will be hunted as long as I stay. There may be no profit in revenge, but neither is there in being a steady target.'

'Where will we find others for such a journey? I have little to pay them.'

'The sort of men you seek are not the sort who would work for pay. You seek those who see the future as a hoard of silver ripe for the taking. And more than that, unless you plan to wear through a foot of boot leather hiking halfway across the world, we'll need a ship.'

'Now you talk in dreams. I have a half a purse of poor hacksilver and a sword. Beyond that I own nothing. Not even the house back in Visby, which by now will be in my cousin's possession. A ship? I am a freeborn farmer, not some great jarl with a longhouse full of coins.'

Bjorn gave him a smile again. 'Jarls are only jarls because they fought harder than others and took more silver. Jarldoms are stolen, not found. And I know where we might find a ship, just a day's travel from here.'

Halfdan found himself nodding slowly, marvelling at the weavings of the Norns. Just hours ago he had been forlorn and alone, all hope of finding his murderous prey in this place torn from him, at a loss as to how to go on. Now here he sat drinking sharp ale with a man in whom Odin himself would find great value. Was it possible that the wisest of gods had sent Halfdan this man to propel him forth on his path?

He looked up into Bjorn's eyes, seeking a flash of untruth, an intent to betray. Instead he found in those strange icy blue-pink eyes nothing but certainty and openness. Bjorn, it seemed, was not a man to whom deceit came easily.

'Then...'

His words trailed off as the door slammed open and snow flurried in again, gusting through the room and drawing fresh shouts of anger. Shapes appeared, and it took Halfdan only moments to recognise the man whose head he had almost stoved in such a short time earlier. Behind him came his friends once more, and more besides. Bjorn's assailants had returned in force, and now they were wielding stout ash clubs.

The big white warrior across the table glanced at the door, shivered in the cold and then grinned at Halfdan. Returning the toothy smile, Halfdan rose from the table.

'Come on, then. Who's first?'

Chapter 2

'Don't get your hopes up,' Bjorn said, eyeing Halfdan as the younger man took it all in.

'What? I thought you said we could get a ship here.'

The big man snorted. 'I said "might". And not in *these* yards.'

'I don't follow you.'

Bjorn's finger jabbed out in the grey, and Halfdan's gaze followed it. The town of Sigtun, nestled on the northern shore of a vast freshwater lake, seemed largely given over to shipbuilding. The yard Bjorn indicated, though, had a plain and rough-sawn timber cross proudly displayed by its gate, carved with runes that spelled some unfamiliar foreign name. Halfdan shuddered. No, he would not trust a ship made by such men, for Ran's daughters would surely tear at the timbers and pull them apart in the cold waters. The sea was no lover of the nailed god.

'Why are we here, then?' he asked, glaring suspiciously at the yard and realising now that the melody that rose from a gaggle of ruddy-faced women sitting in a circle as they put the finishing touches to a great sail was probably one of their dirge-like god tunes.

'Because these are not the only ships in Sigtun.'

They walked on around the edge of the lake, further and further from the town, as the first snowflakes started to fall.

'Piss-poor weather,' Bjorn muttered, scrubbing his hair irritably as snow settled upon it. 'Much more of it and I'll concede the end of the world might lie beyond the next corner.'

'The snow will be gone soon, my friend. *Årsgång* was held in Visby before I left, and the Year-walkers said even then that warmer days were near. This cannot last much longer.'

Bjorn merely grunted in unconvinced reply and led them on in silence. Where they could be going was beyond Halfdan, for it seemed that the town, and even its peripheral industry, was petering out to rough woodland and lakeside mud. Bjorn suddenly gestured and turned left, away from the water's edge and up into the woods along a rough track.

'Come meet an old-fashioned craftsman,' the big albino grinned.

Halfdan's eyes widened in surprise to discover that another yard lay concealed within the trees at the track's end, much smaller than the others and with considerably less work going on. A single ship lay at its heart, held upright with great timbers driven into the ground on either side. As they moved into the clearing, he realised that the ruts in the track were the result of keels being manhandled down to the lakeside, leaving furrows even with rolling logs beneath.

Bjorn was saying something knowledgeable about shipbuilding but Halfdan had stopped listening, for something else was calling to him now. He could feel it in his blood, the song of the sea drawing him in as it could do only to an islander. The *ship* was calling him, summoning him.

'…a lighter frame than the Daneland ships I used to see…'

Bjorn walked on and talked on, unaware that his companion was no longer paying any attention. Halfdan instead drank in every aspect of that ship. This was no trader, but the ship of a hunter, and it was no child of the nailed god, but a true ship of the North. The prow rose to an intricately carved figure of a howling wolf's head. No detachable dragon here, to be affixed for battle, removed for trade: the wolf's head was as much a part of the ship as the keel and mast. This ship was a predator, pure and simple. All along its gunwales, the timber was carved with the skill of an artist into intricate designs curving in upon themselves and creating clever knots. Hidden within those designs were scenes of gods and men and monsters, their freshly painted forms announcing eloquently that the ship had been recently completed.

'Craftsman' was the truth…

Halfdan was breathless at the sight. His hand went to the purse at his belt, acutely aware that it was small and its contents pitiful. How much might a great jarl pay for such a vessel? As he rounded the bow and his eyes slid along the sleek hull, he became aware that he was being watched, and his gaze snapped to a man by the trees. The figure was enormously tall, more so than Bjorn even, but narrower and lither. Still, he cut an imposing figure. His head was shaven and his beard trimmed to a narrow point, black as the halls of Hel beneath glittering, dangerous eyes. He wore a black tunic and grey trousers constrained with black wrappings above black boots. His cloak was grey, and a sword hilt gleamed at his belt, an axe on the opposite hip. The monochrome man seemed almost ghostly.

'Eyes off her,' he said in a thick, foreign accent, his own eyes narrowing at Halfdan as he walked past towards a horse tethered to a tree, its saddlebags bulging. Even the horse was black. Halfdan turned away from the strange man and continued to circle the ship, passing the stern where the keel came up into a delicately worked spiral. As he returned to the far side, he spied the workers, clearly thralls, sitting on a log bench while a man of squat build in a thick fur cloak stood talking to Bjorn, hands flapping this way and that in expansive gestures.

'Ah, that's where you got to,' Bjorn grumbled, waving Halfdan over. 'Tell this tricky little bastard that we need a ship.'

The tricky little bastard shot a momentary glance at Halfdan, apparently sizing him up in a heartbeat, and then turned back to Bjorn. 'It's not going to happen, old friend. I've agreed a price with the Icelander for this one, and there will be no other. I tell you it cannot be done.'

'All right, Ulfr, so you've sold this beast, but why can you not make another? How long can it possibly take? A month? Two?'

The smaller man glared at Bjorn, no mean feat given their difference in height. 'You fool,' the shipwright spat. 'Even a ship this size – and it might be a thing of beauty, but it's still small – took me six months. I don't have a labour force like the other yards. This is all the work of me and a couple of cousins, and the thralls, of course, but you can barely trust that lot to saw wood, let alone carve a strake or fashion an oar.'

'You could do me one in four months,' countered Bjorn.

The small man's brow furrowed. 'It would be possible given the silver in advance, but I know you, Bjorn Beartorn, and unless your young friend here has a golden leg, there's no way you're buying a ship from me. Besides, I cannot get the materials. It would take me four months to build a new ship, but four more just to get the timber.'

Bjorn stared at the man, his hand coming up slowly to point at the dark mass of trees that surrounded the clearing. 'You dozy fuck. I could get you the materials in a day.'

The smaller man bristled. 'Don't shout about what you don't understand. There are fair few trees of use in these woodlands, true. They might be all right for ribs, and a few in the deeper woods might split to make good strakes, but there's no oak here, and no pine taller than four men. If you want a ship, you need a strong keel. If you want a strong keel, you need oak.'

'Then get oak, Ulfr. I walk past oak trees from time to time. How hard can it be?'

The little man sighed with exaggerated patience, as though trying to explain complexities to a child, snow settling heavier upon both of them with every passing moment.

'Small oaks, yes. Or you'll find oaks with too much curve. The big ones, the straight ones, they are all taken as soon as they're found. You can buy them at an inflated price, but the bastard merchants won't sell to me. They only sell to the bloody Christians. They look after their own, that lot, and they don't like our sort. They've been slowly running me down and pushing me out of business for half a decade now. This beauty is the last ship I'll ever build here. I'd leave Sigtun and set up somewhere else, but the nailed god is everywhere these days, and at least here I have a few friends.'

'One less if you don't help us.'

Halfdan cleared his throat. 'You just sold this ship?'

The pair turned to him, and the smaller man nodded. 'Just about. I've agreed a price. It was built for some minor lord, but he died in an unfortunate accident involving two cousins, an axe and a succession crisis. This place is flooded with Christians these days, and they wouldn't buy such a ship. I was lumbered with it, until the Icelander found me.'

'The Icelander in black?'

'That's him.'

Halfdan nodded thoughtfully, then turned and looked back beyond the prow of the ship. The man in black was tightening straps on his horse, readying himself to mount the beast.

'Hold there, Icelander.'

The man paused, turning to look over his shoulder. 'What is it, boy?'

'I can't let you walk away with my ship.' Seiðr was in the air once more, that intangible crackle of old magic. A path was being woven for Halfdan, and he could feel it in the very air.

The black-and-grey-clad giant turned fully now to face him, and he pulled back his hood, letting it fall so that the snowflakes began to settle on his shaven scalp. 'You have a big mouth for a small man. This is *my* ship, and I pay with precious silver taken by blood and sweat from a dozen Irish lords. The seas will soon begin to clear, boy, and there's good raiding to be had. Say farewell to her, for she will next be seen by terrified Finns.'

He made to mount the beast again, and Halfdan, stepped closer. 'Wait.'

The black-clad man's hand went to his sword hilt. 'Don't push me, boy.'

'The ship is mine, not yours. She calls to me. Can you not hear it?'

'Horseshit.'

Halfdan turned to the shipwright, Ulfr. 'Whatever he's offered you, I'll match it and more.'

Bjorn's eyes bulged. 'We've little silver, boy,' he hissed.

'But the promise of more.'

The Icelander was glaring now, eyes narrowed. 'Ignore him, Ulfr. The boy has no idea, and probably no money. I have good silver.'

'But you go to raid the Finns, and they are poor. We are bound for the lands of the Rus, where it's said Serkish silver flows like waterfalls.'

A fantasy, that, but an enticing one. Enticing enough that Ulfr's ears pricked up.

'Business has been slow…' the small man said, quietly.

'Don't be swayed by these fools,' the Icelander snapped. 'Remember that I have silver.'

'But not quite enough. I was selling cheap. Now there is competition.'

The Icelander stomped over towards them. 'Competition? Between my real silver and his imaginary coins?'

'And a place in the ship and a share in the prize,' Halfdan added quickly. 'We will need a helmsman, and who better to know a ship than the man who built her?'

He smiled as he watched the greed going to work on the small shipwright.

'It's tempting.'

'Let the gods decide, then,' Halfdan announced, folding his arms. 'I'll play you for her.'

'What?' the man snapped, his brow wrinkled.

'A wager. I'll play you at any game you choose. If you win, Bjorn and I shall sell ourselves into thraldom and you can do what you like with us.'

'Now wait a fucking minute…' the big albino snarled, rounding on Halfdan, but paused as the younger man held up a hand to stall him, and continued to address the Icelander.

'But when I win, I get the ship.'

'Don't be ridiculous. I have good silver.'

'But Ulfr here has no future in Sigtun, and with me he has a future and the chance of great wealth. With you he sells his ship cheap and is stuck in a world of Odin haters. I wonder how long a man sitting on a pile of silver will last in a town that hates him?'

Again, Ulfr was nodding. The Icelander stared in disbelief at the shipwright. 'You're *listening* to him. I cannot credit it, but you're actually considering this.'

'And when we take it,' Halfdan added, addressing the Icelander now, 'you and your men should come with us. You'll sail with us and fight with us. You'll see no Finns but perhaps a waterfall of Serkish silver in Rusland.'

The Icelander stared at him in disbelief. 'What kind of a fool do you take me for?'

'You choose the game. The odds are all in your favour. If you win, you get two free thralls each worth more than any you've ever taken.' He looked carefully at the Icelander, noting the pendant on the thong around his neck. 'And when I win, you'll know that Odin watches over me, while your nailed god cowers.'

The man in black frowned, then looked down and held out the heavy pewter cross. 'This? You think I bow before the craven Christ?' With a deft flick, he tipped the cross over, so that it was upside down and back to front, and now it was clearly Mjǫllnir, the hammer of Thor. 'When doing business in this modern world, it does a man well to hedge his bets.'

'So you *are* a betting man.'

'You've some balls on you, boy, I'll say that.'

Bjorn grabbed Halfdan by the back of the neck and hauled him round. 'I'll be no man's thrall,' he hissed quietly. 'I like you, lad, but not enough to sell myself.'

Halfdan gave him an odd smile. 'There'll be no risk. I know his game, and there is no master I cannot beat.'

'What?'

'I saw the board in his pack. *'Tafl*. With Loki's blessing, I will sweep this ship out from under him, mark my words.'

Leaving a worried and unconvinced Bjorn, he turned and shrugged. 'So how lucky do you feel, friend?'

'Ketil,' said the tall man in black, eyes still narrowed. 'My name is Ketil. You are serious?'

'I am.'

For a moment the Icelander rummaged in one of his bags, and then produced the slab of wood Halfdan had seen the corner of, poking out, and a large leather pouch. 'Very well, since the dwarf over there is smitten with your offer and I'm left with little choice, I shall take your wager. *Hnefatafl* is the game, and I get the first move. Let the gods decide, as you say.'

Halfdan nodded seriously as the Icelander wandered over to a space where the low branches at the edge of the clearing had been cut back to create a sheltered spot, a large tree stump forming a makeshift table with log seats around. The tall man swept the stale and soggy bread and the cheap cup from the surface and slapped the wooden game board down, untying his pouch drawstrings and letting the grey and brown pieces tumble out onto the sodden stump.

Halfdan sank onto a seat opposite the man, Bjorn and the shipwright still clustering close behind him, the former with a face full of unbelieving worry, the latter simple fascination.

'How do you play?' Halfdan asked.

Bjorn almost exploded. 'This is stupid and I shall not—' but Halfdan gave him a secretive sly grin, silencing him.

'The wager has been set,' Ketil the Icelander said quietly. Oddly, there was no sign of overconfidence in him, as Halfdan might expect in the ridiculous circumstances, just an air of calm concentration. The Icelander looked deep into his face. 'This is your jarl,' he said, holding out a carved grey shape. 'He sits at the board's centre. He has a war party of ten men around him. To win, he must reach the board's edge while my warriors, twenty-four in all, must stop him. All pieces move only in straight lines, and to capture a warrior, you must surround it on two sides. Do you follow?'

'Simple enough,' Halfdan nodded. 'I played something similar as a boy. My friend was good at it.' The something similar being precisely this game, and for all his uncle's provinciality as a poor fisherman, there was not a man in Visby who could beat him at 'tafl. Or there hadn't been until Halfdan came along…

Ketil busied himself settling the pieces in position, and once they were all in place he sat back. 'The game begins.' Gripping one of the small brown pieces around the board's edge, he moved it laterally, ready to cover some of the open space.

Halfdan took a long breath, peering at the board and frowning. Finally, he reached out and picked up one of the pieces. Moving it forwards into a gap, he let go.

'Once you touch a piece, you are committed,' the Icelander added, shifting one of his own to flank the jarl's grey man.

Halfdan tapped a second warrior and slid him out, parallel with the first. Ketil looked at him oddly, as though he were an idiot, and moved a second piece, surrounding Halfdan's first and plucking it from the board.

'I will be no thrall,' growled Bjorn behind him, earning a cutting look from the Icelander.

'Merely testing the water,' Halfdan said calmly, then took a second piece and slid it next to the one that had so recently enjoyed victory, now surrounding it himself. With a smile, Halfdan lifted Ketil's warrior from the board.

'Very good,' muttered Ulfr the shipwright behind him, 'but remember that the Icelander has twice as many pieces as you. A war of attrition is a guaranteed loss.'

Halfdan simply nodded and watched as Ketil moved a second piece. Frowning, and keeping all his concentration on the board without once looking up, Halfdan moved again. With little delay, Ketil countered. And so it went on, a swift game with hardly a pause. Halfdan played a careful strategy, moving his pieces to keep them from harm, always short journeys, always staying close to the jarl, and when he lost a piece, Bjorn swore and growled and smacked the young Gottlander in the back. Halfdan was taking the Icelander's warriors, but not enough to stand a great chance in this battle. Bjorn appraised the board: the reduced clustered heart of Halfdan's position had not moved, the main thrust of his diminishing forces concentrated on one side of the board, where they were fighting a seemingly impossible battle, two stray pieces fruitlessly guarding openings elsewhere.

'You will owe me for life when you cock this up,' grunted Bjorn. 'I might even carve my price out of your hide.'

Ketil smiled as he plucked one of the remaining grey pieces from the board, destroying Halfdan's attack. The younger man leaned back. 'You are a good strategist, Ketil the Icelander,' he said, 'but what you claim in wits, you lack in observation.' Leaning forwards again, he reached out and gestured to one of the two stray pieces that had seemingly been guarding openings on the untouched side of the board. Ketil had been slowly manoeuvring his pieces from that area, leaving enough to hold it, but concentrating his men at the main fight. Only now as he peered down at the piece Halfdan was indicating did he realise with widening eyes that the piece close to the edge was not one of the warriors after all, but the jarl himself. He glanced back at the board's centre. Inevitably, where the jarl had sat, now a simple warrior waited. None of them had seen it, and Ketil had been so intent on destroying Halfdan's attack that he'd not noticed the switch being made.

'How did you do that?' Ketil breathed as Halfdan calmly slid his jarl in a short straight line to the edge of the board and off into his hand.

'I waited until you were busy with the main fight. You were concentrating so hard on it that you missed moves at the far side of the board. You had already decided they were unimportant. I did not cheat,' he added in a defensive tone. 'In two simple moves, I had the jarl out towards the edge and a warrior sliding into his place. It was all a matter of making sure you were distracted.'

Behind him, Bjorn started to belly laugh like a man possessed.

Ketil stared at the board as Halfdan carefully deposited the jarl back onto the table. The snow had begun to settle on the pieces and the Icelander silently began to wipe them with his scarf before dropping them back into the pouch. Doing the same with the board, he lifted it. As Halfdan reached out to push himself upright from the stump, the Icelander's hand shot out and gripped his wrist, turning it, palm upwards.

'Loki,' he muttered.

'What?' The others behind him craned forwards to see what had so drawn the Icelander's attention.

'Your arm,' Ketil hissed.

Halfdan looked down. The birthmark on the inside of his forearm that he habitually kept hidden had slipped out from the cuff of his tunic: a strangely symmetrical marking in the colour of wine, shaped almost like two intertwined serpents. 'It is nothing,' he replied, pulling his arm free and letting the sleeve slide down. 'A mark from birth.'

'It is a sign of Loki cunning,' the Icelander breathed. 'No wonder you won. I could no more have beaten you at 'tafl than I could walk across the clouds.' The man shivered and lurched back. 'The ship is yours. I shall not hold it from you, Loki-born.'

Halfdan shook his head, a smile gracing his lips. 'Consider yourself fortunate, Ketil the Icelander. Had you won, you would have a ship and a crew, but you would be bound for poor Finnland with an empty purse to refill. But you lost, and so now you still have your silver. I offer you and your crew that same ship, with a first-rate steersman, and better than any Finn, the silvery world of the south. Come with us. We need you, and you need us.'

Ketil, the board tucked under his arm, looked long and hard into Halfdan's eyes. Finally, seemingly defeated in some private battle, he sagged. 'When do we sail?'

Halfdan turned to Bjorn, who was still chuckling and grinning. The big man turned to the shipwright. 'Ulfr?'

The little man looked up into the falling snow and then out across the lake. 'No time like the present. If we wait for perfect weather, it could be months. In two days we could be through the lakes and canals and out into the Eastern Sea, which even now will be clearing.'

'We?' Bjorn said, frowning.

'I believe I was offered the position of steersman on a ship led by a son of Loki? This I have to see. Bjorn, my big friend, we live in a world of the flat and mundane, where the nailed god rules everywhere. This young Gottlander is a relic of the days of adventure. The gods move through him. There is nothing here for me with the Christians pushing me out of business and no new commissions of value. Perhaps we will find somewhere I can begin again.' He dropped his voice to a whisper and spoke behind a hand. 'Besides, most of the thralls actually belong to my cousin, and he's a bastard.'

As Bjorn laughed, Ketil the Icelander nodded. 'Then I shall find my warriors and bring them here. We sail on the morning tide, Gottlander.'

'Halfdan,' the younger man said, thrusting out a hand.

'Halfdan,' repeated Ketil, taking it.

'Halfdan *Loki-born*,' whispered Ulfr the shipwright, watching him carefully.

Chapter 3

'This place feels unfriendly,' Halfdan murmured, glancing left and right as they made their way through Hedeby's busy streets, enthusiasm and excitement over this strange new world vying with the dull aura of mistrust he could feel all around.

'Just keep your Loki sign hidden, look unobtrusive and keep that ready,' Ketil the Icelander muttered, jerking a thumb at Halfdan's newly painted shield. He'd had one of the thralls in Sigtun emblazon it with three black wolves, a design inspired by the prow beast of their ship, which had been named *Havsvarg*, Sea Wolf.

The Icelander continued to cast sidelong glances at Halfdan as often as the residents of Hedeby did. He may have acquiesced at the shipyard, but Halfdan felt the mountain yet to climb before he could trust the black-clad foreigner. Still, he had begun to realise that he must come to rely on others now. Ulfr, for one.

They had cut their way south from Sigtun across the churning waters, passing just within sight of the black shore of Halfdan's home, then rounding the tip of the land of the Geats, bound for Daneland. He had argued against the plan of travel, though only quietly, and with Bjorn and Ulfr. Why, he'd demanded, would they journey south and west when his prey lay to the east? Ulfr, a man more familiar with the whale road than any Halfdan had ever met, had been straight with his answer.

'It is still late winter, my young friend, and the Eastern Sea will swallow unwary ships whole. The open water carries waves as high as the highest trees, and the northern reaches will be frozen and treacherous. If you wish to travel east, we follow the trade routes south to Daneland, then across the coast of Wendish lands from there until we reach the Rus. It is the only way that is remotely safe. At Hedeby we can gather supplies that will see us past the Wendish coast.'

Landing at Hedeby, Ulfr and four of the crew had gone to find traders near the waterfront, having pooled all available silver, including a small portion of Ketil's fortune. Bjorn instead, having visited the place before, had brought Halfdan and the Icelander into the heart of the settlement, looking for an alehouse to while away the time. The three of them moved through the streets, the younger man looking about himself with careful interest, the general populace watching them sullenly as each man and woman went about their business silently.

'Watch yourself here,' Bjorn murmured, leaning close. 'Danes can only be trusted so far. The whole race are driven by the love of silver. Almost as bad as the Icelanders,' he added, jerking a thumb at Ketil.

'Why the Icelanders?'

'Because that whole bloody lot are driven by their hearts alone, which makes them unpredictable to a man.'

'All of them? Danes are all greedy and Icelanders all unpredictable? Don't forget, my big friend, that my mother was a Dane. The clue's in the name. So what about the Norse, then?'

'Driven by the sword. Fierce, but not too bright.'

Halfdan gave a small chuckle. 'So what about Svears and Geats? What drives you?'

Bjorn turned a frown on the younger man for a moment, then grinned, grabbed his crotch and made thrusting motions. Halfdan burst into laughter, which drew a disapproving look from Ketil, and the pair quietened down once more. 'Everywhere in Daneland a church,' the Icelander grunted as they passed a tall wooden building with a large window and a neatly carved cross above the door.

Bjorn nodded and leaned close to Halfdan again. 'Nearly all the Danes follow the nailed god. More so than the Norse. It is a place where even the warriors are but cattle, though cattle can still be dangerous in sufficient numbers. See, though, how a few brave ones cling to the true ways,' he added, pointing ahead. It took Halfdan a moment to pick out whatever Bjorn had seen, but when he did, he realised how defiant it looked in the midst of this vastly Christian world.

Outside one building, tightly packed in with its neighbours, dirty and rambling like the entire town, stood a sharpened pole with a ram's head jammed down onto it, tendrils hanging from the neck and a dark stain below from the blood that had dripped free. A sacrifice to one of the gods proudly displayed by the owner despite the church nearby and the overwhelming presence of the Christian religion. As they approached, Halfdan watched with nervous fascination as the streetfolk of Hedeby passed the house and showed their hatred. Men, women and children spat at the door as they went by, though none of the spittle reached the timbers, for no one would come close to that pole, and the tide of humanity flowed along the opposite side of the street, giving the place a wide berth.

'Brave to show devotion here,' noted Ketil. The Icelander had turned his Thor hammer over to resemble a hanging cross, and even Halfdan and Bjorn had tucked their own pendants away inside the folds of their clothes, out of sight of the Danes.

'I seem to remember a passable tavern up ahead,' Bjorn said, pointing off along the street as they half walked, half waded across the slushy ground. The snow had held off for some time now, and the further south they had come the more temperate the weather had been, though the sky was still the colour of undyed sheep's wool.

Halfdan continued to watch the house with the sacrificial display as they neared it, Ketil steering them to the far side of the street along with the rest of the population. Thus it was that he was looking directly at the door when it creaked open and a pale face emerged from the darkness within. Halfdan stopped walking, staring at that doorway as the woman stepped into the light. She was but a few years older than he, and striking. Smooth, porcelain features around a pink bow of a mouth, green eyes that glittered like emeralds in clear water, and ash-blonde hair that hung wild, braided only at the temples and tucked behind the ears. She was bareheaded, forgoing the cap that seemed to be the norm for women here. Her garb was at odds with the shabby structure she inhabited, for her gown was of the same bright green as her eyes, clean and seemingly very expensive, as was the white fur mantle that hung about her shoulders.

Bjorn and Ketil had walked on a few paces before realising that their companion had stopped, and turned, taking in the scene. Halfdan felt his throat become dry in an instant as the handsome woman crooked a finger, beckoning to him. He took a hesitant step forwards, and in a heartbeat his two companions were there, unusually in accord, each with a restraining hand on Halfdan's shoulders.

'This place is dangerous,' the Icelander murmured.

'And women like that doubly so,' Bjorn added.

Yet the woman continued to beckon and stepped back into the gloom, leaving the door wide. Halfdan frowned. She could be no Christian, given the signs, and her garb said she was no whore or thrall. There was definitely a hint of danger in the air, but he could not quite define what it was or where its source might be found. One thing he was sure of, though, was that it was not from the woman.

'We need to go in.'

'No, we don't,' Bjorn grunted, but Halfdan shrugged from their grip and trudged forwards, across the street, making straight for that door. The other two shared a look, and cast their gazes about. They were being eyed suspiciously by the Danes all around them. Weighing up the comparative dangers of entering that house against the peril of being identified as pagans by the people of Hedeby, the two men heaved a sigh and followed Halfdan through the door into the dark, hands on the hilts of their weapons as they did so.

As Ketil, the last of the three, entered, the door closed behind them, shutting out what little light had intruded, and the fact that there appeared to have been no one there to close it sent shivers across Halfdan's skin, prickling the back of his neck.

'Seiðr,' breathed Bjorn, and Ketil made noises of muted agreement. Halfdan could feel it again. The magic filled the place, running like water up, down and across every surface. It made him shiver. He'd only seen the one Seiðr woman in his life, an old crone in Visby who'd lived like a queen, respected and supported by the whole of Gottland for her gifts. She had been powerful and wonderful and wise, and yet her presence had felt as nothing to the sheer power in this place.

The building was unaccountably warm, and smelled of roasted meat and cloying smoke. Candles sputtered into life at the far side of the room, illuminating a richly carved wooden seat draped with pelts and piled with cushions, upon which sat a woman with a face like a long-dead falcon, a beak of a nose and parchment skin drawn tight over sharp bones. Her hair was as white as Bjorn's, tied in intricate braids and designs, and her robes were even richer than those of the girl who had beckoned them. As Halfdan's mind recalled that first figure, so she stepped from the gloom to stand beside the old woman as though he had somehow summoned her from the shadows.

'Greetings, *Völva*,' Ketil said, with a bow of the head. Bjorn made polite rumblings, as Halfdan simply took it all in.

The old woman leaned forwards in the seat. 'What drives you, young warrior?' she said.

The others remained silent. The question had clearly been for Halfdan alone.

'I carry a blood debt and must kill a man,' he said simply. There was no dissembling here. No need, he was sure. Truth was everything to the Völva.

'Not just *any* man, I think,' the woman said, eyes narrowing, her fingers closing on the silver-adorned ash staff in her hand and jerking it forwards towards him. 'A powerful man. A king?'

'Of a sort.'

'Your path will be long and perilous. I can see it stretching before you like a dawn shadow, reaching out. I can see this even without the song, but a shadow hangs over it.'

A frisson of power once more crackled across Halfdan's flesh, making it pucker into goose bumps.

'Sing the wyrd-song, Gunnhild,' the old woman commanded. As the three men stood watching, the young woman spread her arms, then folded them across her chest and began to sway back and forth. As she did so, her voice rose and fell like waves against a harbour wall, a quiet melody rising into a powerful song, then falling into whispers only to rise again, higher every time. All three men could feel it now, the Seiðr in the air, all around them. As the song faded and Gunnhild let her arms fall and stepped silently back into the shadows, the old woman dropped from the seat into a crouch like a hunter's, something that seemed unlikely, or even impossible, given her age and apparent frailness. Yet she hunched there, glaring at the floor for a long pause before looking up. Rheumy, pale blue eyes lit upon Halfdan, making him shudder again.

'This man you seek has a doom written upon him. The powers have woven his life, though he follows the false god and so he pulls against it, trying always to unstitch his fate. His path is entwined with yours, I see, like the serpents upon your arm.' Halfdan frowned in fascination. His sleeve covered the mark, she could not have seen it.

'The same shadow hangs over you both. It obscures what will be, though his doom remains clear. His end is... complex.'

'It will be I who kills him,' Halfdan said quietly. 'It must.'

53

'This I cannot see, for there is another who pulls at him and who brings the shadow that obscures my sight. All I can see clearly is that he is woven to end badly. It may be that this other is to bring the end about. It may be that this shadow foretells your own end. All I can see is that your prey's journey is long, its conclusion unclear, but through it, his end will be vile. Of you and the shadow I can say no more.'

Halfdan nodded uncertainly. He was grateful that this woman, whose very essence was power and the will of the gods, had confirmed that Yngvar would die, yet more than a little unsettled to learn that another could interfere and that it might not be Halfdan's fate to wield the blade. A blood debt unpaid hung over a man for ever, even one not given law at a Thing.

'Your prey's path is long,' the old woman repeated. 'The threads weave off into unseen distance before the shadow falls. You and he have many dangers to encounter before his doom can find him. You will face dragons and giants, and *draugar* at the very edge of the world before his threads can come undone, and only then can he end in such a manner that the gods sneer at his memory.'

'I will kill him,' Halfdan said again, 'but I cannot delay. My father sits in Odin's mead hall, and he watches the world, waiting for me to avenge him. He has waited too long already. It is a blood debt.' He paused, a thought striking him. 'I will kill him before this shadow falls and things become uncertain.'

'You cannot,' the old woman hissed. 'It is your *urðr*, your fate, to ride this path to its conclusion. Do you think yourself a greater weaver of fate than the Norns? No, your prey, driven by his nailed god, pulls against his weaving, though he does not realise it. It is this shadow that works to unweave the path. You cannot end him swiftly, young warrior, you cannot kill him yet. Indeed, you must keep him to his weaving and see that this other does not end him before his time.'

'I cannot wait.'

'If you defy the Norns and your fate in this, he will win and your blood debt will be nothing, for you will give the man a hero's end, sending him to sit beside your father.'

Halfdan stared, shivering. 'You cannot ask me to do this.'

'It is not my place to ask you anything, nor to command you. I simply tell you what is, and what could be. The prince you seek belongs to the nailed god, but Odin is fickle. He is not choosy. Freyja will not take this man into *Sessrúmnir* for the afterlife, and I know this, but Odin is as unpredictable as all men. Even as a disciple of the nailed god, Odin might still bring the prince to his mead hall if he deems him worthy.'

Again, Halfdan shuddered, picturing Yngvar seated beside his father in Valhöll. The image made him angrier than anything he had known since that day he had lurked beneath the house and watched his world ripped from him. Would Odin really take a man who had torn down a stone sacred to the Lord of Frenzy? But the woman spoke true. Odin *was* fickle. He *was* known to break his own rules with wild abandon. And when the day of the final battle came, it would be the mettle of the warriors in Odin and Freyja's halls that counted, not their origin. He felt his plans slipping away as a pit of darkness opened beneath him.

'He must not fall in battle,' the old woman said. 'If he is slain as a hero, Odin will decide his fate, and may take him. If he dies in the water, then Ran might give him to Hel for her underworld. If he is to end as you would wish, then he must face the pattern that has been woven for him. He must fight giants and dragons. He must reach the edge of the world and find the wraiths that live there. Only then can his doom be sealed.'

Halfdan felt hollowness fill his being. Not only must he put off his plan to kill Yngvar Eymundsson, but *follow* him? The very notion filled him with anger and dread. He felt it brimming, boiling over. It must have shown in his face, for the old woman rose now like some shade from a grave mound and stalked towards them, circling him and the other two. 'You are like the wolves of Odin, all hunger and purpose, but you must also display wisdom if you are to succeed in life. I see in the three of you the raw power of Thor and the cunning of Loki, the virtue of Tyr and the deep thought of Odin. What you lack is the wisdom of Freyja.'

The younger woman took a step forwards now from the edge of the room, her brow creasing in consternation. 'No, Mother.'

'Yes, Daughter. Your place is not with me. It never was. You have the Seiðr flowing through you just as I, but your fate is not to sit as a Völva, a last bastion of power in this world of crosses. As the goddess herself rode with Hyndla to seek the truth of Ottar, so you will ride with this warrior to keep the weaving of his enemy true.'

'I cannot leave you,' the girl said, flatly. 'Every day the threat grows that the children of the nailed god will burn us as they do their witches. Without me you will fall, Mother.'

The old woman turned a strange and eerie smile on the girl. 'That is not to be my end, Daughter. You think I have looked along the threads of time for others and not once questioned my own future? I know my end, and I accept it. You must also accept what the Norns weave for you, every bit as much as these three men.'

Now the girl stepped forwards again, into the brightest light. She really was striking, Halfdan thought, watching her even as she fought against her own fate.

'Daughter,' the Völva said quietly, 'how can we expect men to accept the will of the Norns if we cannot do so ourselves?' She turned back to the three visitors. 'Wait outside.'

With a bow and a clear sigh of relief, Ketil backed towards the door and, reaching out, pulled it open, admitting the cold white light of Hedeby and a chilly draught. Bjorn bowed and followed, and Halfdan brought up the rear, his eyes on the girl until the moment the door closed and she was lost to sight.

'I knew this was foolish,' Ketil grunted. 'In Sigtun I tried to walk away, but you pulled me back with an offer I could not refuse and now I am bound to some quest that is none of my concern. You heard the old woman. Giants? Dragons? Draugar? These things are monsters of the old times, creatures that even the *gods* fought with difficulty. I have no wish to visit the edge of the world and throw away my life following a man just so that he can die badly. I came east to plunder, to take a ship and a stout crew and raid the lands of the Finns and the Wends.'

Bjorn shrugged and draped an arm across the Icelander's shoulders. 'On the bright side, it's a long journey into the unknown, and the further we get from the crosses of the nailed god, the easier I will sleep. We are the sons of Thor...' He smiled, recalling the words of the old Völva. 'No, better, we are the wolves of Odin. Wherever we go there will be plunder and battle to sate our hunger. This world is becoming too small and too peaceful with the cross on every corner. There are few places left for a man to make a name for himself and to show his mettle for Odin on the battlefield. I, for one, welcome such an adventure.'

'And that labels you an idiot more than anything else I've seen so far,' grumbled Ketil.

Halfdan turned to them, noting as he did the looks they were receiving from the Christian passers-by in the street. 'It might be better to save such talk for a more private place. For now, I would have you remember that you have merely agreed to come on a voyage, while I have been commanded to watch over the very man I seek to kill.'

'Only so that he can die badly in the end.'

Halfdan paused. The image of him driving a blade through Yngvar's heart as the shade of his father cheered from Odin's mead hall was enticing. But there was more going on here than he could have imagined. He could *feel* the magic in that house. The Völva had known about his birthmark, which was impossible. The gods were guiding this now, or perhaps the Norns. One thing was certain: his part in this was now to walk his path, just as others must. No child of Odin could deny the power of the gods.

'Still, it is no easy thing,' he said with difficulty, 'and if I can manage this, then I'm sure you can, too.'

The Icelander gave him a withering look, but still he nodded his agreement. Bjorn grinned. 'And we are to have a shield-maiden with us, too.' A thoughtful look passed across his almost translucent features. 'Do you think when Freyja chooses her slain she does it herself, or does she have maidens like Odin's to scour the battlefield?'

'The way you smell of old fart and rotten cheese,' Ketil grumbled, 'you would be lucky to be chosen by a hog, let alone a god.'

Bjorn grinned. 'Healthy smells. But I admit that I'm due a bath. *Lørdag* has been and gone while we were aboard ship, and I could do with a wash.'

Whatever pithy comment the Icelander muttered in response was lost to them as the door to the house opened once more and the young woman stepped out into the street. She now carried a stout staff carved with flowing designs and runes, a gleaming multi-faceted green gem bound to the top. She gave them all a look that made it clear that, though the decision had been made, she still was not pleased with it.

'Take me to your ship. We leave Hedeby this day.'

Ketil shook his head. 'The crew is maintaining the ship and seeking supplies. This will take time, and we will undoubtedly still be here at nightfall. We sail with the dawn.'

The Seiðr-woman raised an eyebrow and fixed the Icelander with a bladed glare. 'If all of us are to follow our weaving, then you must do also. This was not a statement of desire, it was a statement of fact. We leave Hedeby this day.'

Bjorn frowned. 'That might not be possible. Why the urgency?'

Gunnhild stepped back and looked this way and that, gripping her staff tightly, a question in her gaze as it settled upon them once more. Along with the other two, Halfdan looked about him. The number of people in the street had increased dramatically, and only a few of them were still hurrying about their business. Many were standing some distance away, their eyes upon the four figures outside the house, close to the offering-post. They did not look friendly.

'I take your point,' Ketil acknowledged, moving closer to the others.

'To the ship,' Halfdan said. 'Time to look for the edge of the world.'

'And the wraiths that live there,' added the Icelander with a shiver.

Chapter 4

'This,' Ketil grunted, 'has been a most tedious and uncomfortable journey.'

'Maybe if you spent more time pulling oars and less time complaining, it would pass faster,' Bjorn said with a sly grin.

The Icelander's eyes narrowed. 'I pull my weight as much as any man. More than you, you pale sack of pig lard.'

Ulfr's eyes rolled. These two had been at one another for so long now that it had become a game of one-upmanship. 'I will take tedious over exciting any day,' the shipwright said. 'Exciting gets men killed and ships sunk.'

Halfdan was only half listening, standing beside the wolf head at the prow. To him, the journey across the Eastern Sea had been a heart-stopping and breath-stealing voyage into the unknown. Not only was this the furthest from Gottland the young warrior had ever been, but every breath of icy wind and every stroke of the oars brought him closer and closer to his goal. Thus, while the rest of the crew grumbled about the hardships and the uncertainty, for Halfdan it represented progress.

Progress towards *what* was a question he felt ill-equipped to answer, but he felt certain that the old woman must have misread something. He would kill Yngvar. He had to.

'Men die,' Bjorn shrugged. 'Ships sink. It is the way of things.'

'Not *my* men,' snapped Ketil.

'And not *my* ship,' added Ulfr meaningfully.

As Halfdan had watched the world slide by, the short shipwright had taken the helm and guided them past the unfriendly coastal lands of the Wendish tribes and into the east. They had beached the ship and alighted somewhere on the coast each night of the journey to make camp, but forage was sparse and the various settlements of Wends they had seen had each been too large and well defended a proposition for simple raiding. Having been unable to restock the ship properly, they had eked out their meagre supplies, hoping that in the friendlier lands of the Rus they might provision once more.

They finally left the sea at the lands of the Semgalls, who hated Svears and Geats with the passion that only a regularly subjugated enemy could achieve, and so the crew had been watchful as they pulled into the mouth of a wide river. A settlement Ulfr called Ringa had grown up there, and wary eyes followed them as the ship slid by.

From here, a river flowed against them from the south, and Halfdan had queried their route with Ulfr during a pause in the strenuous rowing.

'This is the river that takes us to Kiev?'

Ulfr snorted as though he'd asked if the sky was green. 'Hardly. This is the Dvina, and it flows *from* the south. Kiev is on the great Dnieper and it flows *into* the south.'

Halfdan's face must have openly displayed his confusion, for Ulfr gave a sigh and a sympathetic look passed across his face. 'Not familiar with portage, are you? No, I'd guess not, being a Gottlander. Not much need for it when you're on an island surrounded by sea.'

'Portage?'

'The Dvina flows our way, the Dnieper the other, but they come close to one another, perhaps a day's travel apart. We have to get the *Sea Wolf* from this river to the other, and we do it with brute strength and a little bit of Odin's wisdom. We beach the ship and lay out timber runners as a track, greased till they gleam. Then we push poles across the ship from rail to rail and push and pull her along the track until we reach the Dnieper, where she splashes down into the water and we're on our way again.'

Halfdan's frown had deepened. 'Do we have enough muscle here to move the ship?'

Behind him, Bjorn roared. 'This ship? She's a looker, but she's small, my lad. I could carry her on my back. You should see the size of a ship I once helped portage across the Orkneyjar. Big as a mead hall and about as sleek. There was this bear, too...'

Halfdan stopped listening as the inevitable bear story entered the conversation and peered ahead, trying not to think of the backbreaking labour coming.

Finally, after eight days of labouring against the current and watching the banks for Semgall raiders, making use of the strong gusts and employing the oars during the day whenever the wind dropped, the steersman warned them that they were closing on the portage site. When the flow they followed finally turned north-east, they beached the *Sea Wolf* on the left bank, and even Halfdan's inexperienced eye could tell that this was a common site for 'portage'.

'Keep a watch for bandits,' Ulfr warned them as they heaved the ship up onto a riverbank that had long since been torn up with the keels of vessels and now resembled a shallow stony beach.

'Bandits would dare attack a ship of armed men?' Halfdan asked.

'Portage sites attract such things,' Bjorn advised. 'Groups of raiders tend to gather because they know the crews will not be at their best during portage. We must all be on our guard, even lazy Icelanders.'

'I thought you told me Icelanders were unpredictable?' Halfdan smiled as Ketil shot both of them evil looks.

'They are. He is being lazy now, but when we really need him to settle, he will do something stupid, mark my words.'

'I'll mark your fucking hide if you keep this up,' Ketil growled.

'Let's all shut up and pull, eh?' Ulfr gasped from where he hauled on a rope.

As men grunted and heaved and occasionally cajoled or threatened, Halfdan hauled on his rope, but continued to watch the surroundings, half expecting a horde of slavering Semgall riders to emerge whooping from the nearby treeline.

Still, in little time, they had the *Sea Wolf* up onto dry land and propped upright with timbers taken from a huge discard pile of logs and beams, evidence of earlier vessels' passage.

Once the ship was secured and the men stood around, heaving in breaths, Ulfr sent the crew off upriver some way to secure more good timber. Halfdan could have waited with the ship, he was sure, but if he was ever going to lead men properly it was important that they saw him doing everything that they did. As such, he helped cut timbers where they found the best trees, muscles bunching with every swing of the axe, shoulders aching as the blade bit deep into the bark.

A nervous night on the bank ensued. Halfdan, as had become his norm, slept on the periphery, facing away so that when the nightmares came, no one would see his face twist in anguish and his murmurs would go unheard.

Despite Ulfr's warnings, the night held no unexpected visitations and when the sun arose, the crew woke with it and set to the morning's labours. A single day, Ulfr said. That was all it would take if they worked hard. And so at the shore they emptied the ballast from the *Sea Wolf*, lowered the mast and secured it, and then planed down the poles they had cut until they were the right size to fit through the apertures in the ship's gunwales fashioned for this very purpose. Seven beams were slid through, while other men worked on the larger boles that were to be used as runners. These were greased from the ship's store and carefully positioned as a track ahead of the keel.

The day that followed was one of the most strenuous in Halfdan's life, and no man escaped the labours as the full crew heaved beneath the poles, lifting the ship until the greased beams could be slid beneath it. Then six men were placed in charge of those timbers, carrying them round from the stern to the bow as the rest heaved and slid the ship slowly forwards. Tedium reached new heights that day, and even banter died away as men expended all their breath on their work. Finally, as the sun slid towards the horizon in a melting pot of gold and bronze, the glittering course of another waterway came into view.

Another night on a riverbank passed, though this time with little nervous wakefulness. Danger was just as acute here, but the efforts of the day had been sufficient to lay every head down for blissful slumber, and watches were kept short and light.

'What river is this? It is the Dnieper?' Halfdan said as he wrapped his blankets around him against the chill and settled in.

'Shit if I know,' Bjorn admitted. 'Rivers all look the same to me. Wet.'

'We sailed the Dvina upstream, remember?' Ulfr murmured from his tightly wrapped blankets. 'So yes, this is the upper reaches of the Dnieper. From here, the water will carry us downstream all the way to Kiev.'

'Where you can kill your prince and then we can get to the real business of easy women, shiny silver and punching the shit out of people we don't know,' Bjorn sighed happily.

'It will not be that easy,' Ketil said. 'Remember the words of the Völva. Our young warrior cannot kill him before his time, and something else interferes. A shadow.'

'The Norns be damned,' Bjorn snorted, raising a heated debate on the nature of fate, respect to the Norns and Bjorn's level of intellect. Halfdan half smiled as he rolled over, away from them, and waited for the dream to come.

The next morning, they dropped into the water with immense relief, pushing the *Sea Wolf* out into the current until it no longer ground on the riverbed, and clambering aboard with cries of triumph. Within the hour they were moving at speed once more with a good tailwind, and by the end of the next day the shallow and narrow river had become a more consistent and impressive flow. From there, they kept watch with growing anticipation, and when the first settlement they spotted by the riverbank sported familiar-looking boats of northern construction, it became clear that they had made it to the lands of the Rus at last.

The days passed easily, each bringing new settlements, each of which seemed larger than the last, all of which accepted the visitors without comment, and all of which were willing to trade. That there were churches in the settlements put Halfdan on his guard, but the crosses here seemed to be ornate affairs with two, or sometimes three, crossbars, so perhaps the people were not the same as the nailed god followers in the North. No one aboard seemed to know what the difference was, even Ulfr, but equally no one seemed inclined to ask, lest they bring trouble upon themselves, and so they moved slowly south. By the fifth day, the river was a broad and fast flow, and as they rounded a wide sweep in the current, everyone marvelled at what lay ahead.

Just as Halfdan's youth-town of Visby would have fitted in a mere corner of Uppsala, so even the Svear capital would have fitted into a corner of Kiev, but it was neither the scale nor the huge population that drew the breath from each of them.

'It's amazing,' Halfdan breathed.

'Looks like the very rock of the earth rose up to form houses,' Bjorn agreed.

Only occasionally had Halfdan heard mention of the use of stone for constructing buildings. None of the settlements on his native island held any such wonder. After all, why would a man spend so much effort carving out the ground to make a house when the gods gave him trees that seemed made for the purpose. Timber could easily be repaired and replaced, was easy to come by and relatively easy to fashion, and it maintained a warmth in the winter that stone would surely lack. It was said that the Franks and the Saxons had built whole towns from rock, and whispers of fabled Miklagarðr said that the whole city was formed of shining stone as smooth as a babe's skin, yet Halfdan had always brushed aside such tales as more fantastical than any dragon.

'This cannot have been made by man,' Halfdan murmured, taking in the wonder before him. 'Is this Ásgarðr?'

'This is Kiev,' Ulfr confirmed. 'No gods here. Just men who've forgotten what it is to be a Northman.'

Kiev gleamed in the weak late-winter sun. A massive, powerful gate in stone faced the river, and the visitors could just see similar structures away inland, all linked together by a defensive wall that would dwarf those of any northern fortress, formed of timber rising up on a rampart of immense proportions. A church protruded above the roofs in the heart of the city, and it was of a size Halfdan could never have imagined, and of a strange construction, all domes and tall turrets with latticed windows, the whole thing made of some golden-red stone and fashioned in an impressively decorative way. While the bulk of the city still seemed to consist of closely packed timber buildings, other stone structures were visible here and there, often churches.

At the river's edge, the Kievans had constructed a port, but again on a scale that would shock any ship-wright in the North. Scores of vessels worked in that great harbour, jetties and wharves reaching out into the water like welcoming arms. Most impressively of all, beyond the port they could see the shape of dozens of northern-style warships gathered by the left bank like a fleet of predators awaiting the call to hunt.

'Odin's beard,' Bjorn marvelled quietly at Halfdan's elbow. 'What world is this?'

Halfdan simply nodded and stared. It was well known that the Rus were the children of the North, that mere generations ago Svears and Geats had come here with a will to conquer and had forged a great land along this river. What magic had they encountered that had allowed them to do this? Where was half the world quarried away to build such impregnable defences and such monuments to the nailed god? The very notion of finding one man in such a place seemed impossible.

'Anyone for a raid?' someone called from halfway along the ship, raising a chorus of jeers and cheers.

Halfdan stared, the scale of his task suddenly brought home to him in that view, the monumental quest upon which he had set out. Shaking his head, he reminded himself that he was far from alone in this, at least, and that the Norns had woven a path for him that must take him to Yngvar, for the old Seiðr woman had been certain of that at least.

'You need to be sure of our path,' murmured Bjorn, as though Halfdan's thoughts had been carved upon his face for all to see. He turned a questioning look on the great pale bear of a man, and Bjorn shrugged. 'In half an hour we will be at one of those jetties. For now, you are the leader of these men, for all your youth, my friend. But remember how easily leaders are pushed aside. You must be confident and full of action. You must have your path laid out.'

Halfdan nodded slowly. But how? One man in that great sprawl. A thought struck him as he took in the larger stone structures amid the smaller timber ones beyond those ramparts. Yngvar was said to be with the king of Kiev, Jarisleif, and a great journey was coming. In a place like this, a king would not be content with some fine mead hall. If the King of Kiev was willing to build such a great monument to his god, then surely he had built an even bigger monument to himself.

'Bring us into the harbour,' he said to Ulfr, loud enough to reach the crew as though by chance. 'When we dock, take a third of the men and what goods and silver we have and secure supplies. We may be here for days, so be shrewd. Another third of the men will stay aboard the ship. We do not know if we can trust these Rus, and the ship must be guarded. The final third I will take into the city.'

'Where are we bound?' asked Ketil the Icelander, clearly presuming he would be one of the latter.

Halfdan turned to him. 'The man we seek will be in the palace, for certainly the ruler of this place will have a palace.'

Ketil nodded without his usual frown of suspicion, and Halfdan silently thanked Bjorn for his timely warning. Bjorn and the others were here by choice, but Ketil, and the crew who had come with the Icelander, owed him nothing, and he would need to win their trust if he was to rely upon them in the coming days.

'Have you given thought to what you will do if we gain access?' the Icelander asked quietly, coming closer.

'I am no closer to a plan, if that is what you mean.'

'You cannot simply make this up as you go along, young warrior. We cannot walk into the palace of a king and demand that his noble visitor accede to your wishes. Plan, man, plan.'

'He is going upon a great journey,' Halfdan said.

'What?'

'Those ships, they are not part of the city. For all the time Yngvar has been here, he cannot stay forever, and I believe he is preparing to leave.'

'What? Why?'

'If Yngvar left home because he would be a king there, he will have the same problem in Kiev. If he would be a king, he must go somewhere where there isn't one already. Those ships are his. I'm sure of it.'

'This Yngvar has an army, then, Halfdan. You are not encouraging me.'

'Those ships are ready,' Ulfr noted. 'Poised for departure, low in the water with supplies.'

Halfdan nodded. 'Look at them. They're prepared to leave at any time. I say again, they are Yngvar's ships and he is setting off upon a great journey. Remember what the Völva said. Yngvar and I share an entwined path and it is a long one that will stretch to the edge of the world. You are seeing her words made flesh and timber before you.' At the notion of an entwined path, he instinctively pulled down his sleeve over the serpent birthmark on his arm.

'So this offers you a plan?'

'We can do nothing against Yngvar while he is in the court of the king, so we must be with him when he travels into the wild. We will join his army. Join his expedition.'

Ketil sagged. 'I sacrificed my mastery of this vessel to you, and now you offer it to your enemy.'

'As a means to an end. We offer our swords to the jarl for a chance to use them on him.'

'Loki's cunning runs through your veins like blood, my friend. I don't know whether to cheer you or fear you most of the time.'

Halfdan stood silent, watching the great city as they slid through the inky waters towards the wharves. The *Sea Wolf* moved slowly and easily to the side of a free jetty under the expert guidance of Ulfr, and Halfdan took part alongside the crew in tying the ropes and tethering the vessel to the shore. Once all was done to Ulfr's satisfaction, he let his gaze play over the crew and picked out a third of the men, jabbing a finger at each as he counted off under his breath. The criteria for his choice were specific and simple: they were in essence the most powerful and fierce-looking men of the ship, the best armed and armoured, and the most visibly scarred. First impressions counted for much, and with this selection they would be as unlikely to encounter trouble in the street as they would be likely to draw the eye should they gain access to the palace.

Bjorn, Ketil and Gunnhild gathered around. Somehow, somewhere during the voyage from Hedeby, the young woman had reworked her staff, for now, rather than the impressive green stone at its tip, it bore a gleaming and sharp blade. She gripped a spear like a true shield-maiden.

'Where did the jewel go?' he murmured under his breath.

'Somewhere safe,' Gunnhild replied, with an arched brow. 'Keep your raider's hands to yourself.'

Halfdan turned, slightly abashed that she'd overheard his musing, and looked at their destination. Biting his cheek in trepidation and with a last nod at Ulfr, who would take care of things around the ship, Halfdan stepped from the gently swaying vessel and onto the hard ground of Kiev. Keeping close together and with eyes straying across their surroundings, constantly alert, they moved towards the heavy gatehouse set back from the riverside. The gate itself was as tall as three big men and wide enough to admit two carts side by side. The earth bank supporting the ramparts rose to the same height as that high arch and, above that, two storeys of stone with arched windows loomed, the immense and heavy timber walls stretching off to either side. Two men stood on guard by the doorway, and despite the strangeness of this alien world, Halfdan was relieved to note that either man could have passed without comment in Uppsala, so northern did they look.

'Familiar, eh?' Bjorn nudged him as they approached the guards. 'We could be at home among men like that.'

Halfdan nodded. 'The Svears who settled here might have taken on a few new and strange ideas, but they clearly cling to their roots in other ways.'

The guards hardly glanced at the small crowd of visitors as they passed inside the city, which took Halfdan by surprise, and he drew closer to Ketil. 'Surely a crew of Northmen armed for war is enough to raise at least an eyebrow?'

'A development that leads me to suspect the city crawls with such sights,' the Icelander warned as they passed through the shadowed tunnel and out into Kiev.

Inside the walls the scale of the streets and buildings once more struck Halfdan and, judging by the craning necks and wide eyes of the others, he was not alone in his amazement. The noise of the place insisted itself upon them immediately, and as they walked, uncertain of their path, he listened carefully, trying to cut through the general din and pick out individual voices. The Rus, it seemed, had formed something of their own tongue in this place, yet though he had to concentrate to catch anything that was being said, most of the words were mere twistings of sounds he recognised from the North. Their tongue was almost his own, and though they might be foreign in many ways, he felt confident he would be able to understand most of what was said here.

They passed into a wide square filled with mud and stalls, hawkers and noise, colour and smells of every kind, animals both familiar and new, and the whole group pulled a little tighter together without any order being given. Moving as if in a dream, they passed through the great market, and made for what looked to be another gatehouse, albeit of a less grand nature, ahead.

As they emerged from the crowds and stalls into an open space with fewer bodies, Bjorn muttered beside him, 'Thor's balls, this place is huge. How will we find what we need?'

But Halfdan had stopped and, realising as much, Bjorn pulled himself up short and turned, stepping back to where his young friend stood, peering off to one side. The group moved to a halt behind them, and every hand went to the grip of a weapon, for something about Halfdan's posture spoke of trouble, and everyone felt it.

Clearly Odin was watching over them, and Halfdan had felt that odd shiver as the Seiðr magic writhed across his skin in warning. He'd stopped dead, knowing that something important was happening, and sensing the presence of the gods in that moment. Still twitching with the feel of it all, his eyes scanned the open space and fell with certainty upon a small procession on the far side of the square.

'What is it?' Bjorn murmured, and the quietness of his voice, the very reverence in it, suggested that he now felt something too.

'The boar walks unwitting towards the point of my spear,' Halfdan hissed.

'What?'

'Yngvar Eymundsson, the nailed god's pet murderer, walks calmly across the square in front of us.'

Bjorn squinted. 'Are you sure? Everyone looks alike here to me. He doesn't *look* like a prince.'

But Halfdan was sure. More than a decade might have passed since he had last seen that face, and it had picked up a few lines and was framed by more grey now, but he would never forget that visage, those eyes, which he had committed to memory over the body of his father. Yngvar the killer was here, marching confidently across the square as though Kiev was his own mead hall's yard.

'It is him. He has only six men with him.'

'They're warriors,' Bjorn noted, 'but they're few.'

Halfdan's fingers tightened on the hilt of his sword, knuckles whitening. He realised that his jaw had clenched and was set firm, his muscles all bunched like a twisted rope, tight and ready. All his instincts were at work now, preparing him. His blade slid just a finger-width from the mouth of the scabbard as his hawkish gaze followed the seven figures across the square as they moved towards that smaller gatehouse.

'Come on. The old woman was wrong. This can be ended early after all. There will be blood this day,' Halfdan growled, the blade inching free a little more as he turned to move off at a tangent, making to intercept that small group, his gait that of the hunter in the forest, stalking the deer.

'Halfdan,' hissed Gunnhild at his shoulder, and he turned to see a look of careful concern upon her face.

'What?'

'Remember what you were told.'

75

Bjorn, listening in, snorted. 'Seven of them. I could kill seven with my dick alone.'

'But it would take weeks for the disease to carry them off,' laughed Ketil, earning a black look from the big albino.

Halfdan saw Gunnhild's eyes darting this way and that, though, and his gaze followed them. He'd not noticed the other armed men, for they were unobtrusive and immobile, but now that she'd drawn his attention to them, he could see pairs of guards, the same as those at the gate, on corners and in doorways. The King of Kiev, it seemed, had an iron grip on his city. With a nod to her, his sword slid back into his hilt.

'We can take them,' grunted Bjorn.

'What use is settling a blood debt if I get us all killed in the process. There are Rus guards all around us. By the second blow against Yngvar we will be overcome.'

Ketil heaved a sigh of relief. 'Sometimes your cunning pays dividends, young Halfdan.'

Gunnhild set the pace and they walked on as she spoke. 'You show wisdom, Halfdan. As the serpents of Loki twine and merge on your arm, so does your weaving and that of Yngvar writhe and fuse. You untie his threads and not only do you give him to Odin and betray your father, but in severing them, you will break your own. Your fate is long and golden, but it can be cut just as you would cut that of your prey. There will be other times.'

Halfdan peered ahead at the seven men striding towards another large, defended archway, and turned to Bjorn. 'The palace must lie beyond that gate. Where the murderer goes, we follow.'

Bjorn gave him an encouraging grin. 'Come on, then. I've never met a king before.'

Chapter 5

'Say nothing. Just look businesslike.'

Halfdan and his companions fell in behind the seven men as they stepped into the gateway. Yngvar and his half dozen warriors simply nodded to the men at the gate, who treated them almost as old acquaintances. As they passed inside, Halfdan and his small war band drifted through in their wake, admitted without comment.

'Who needs a fortress this size?' Bjorn murmured as Yngvar and his men turned and angled away from the gate.

'A king is bigger than other men,' Ketil replied, 'because he stands on a plinth of self importance. The bigger the fortress, the more honoured the king.'

This compound *was* huge. Larger even than the impressive fortresses Halfdan had seen in Danish lands on their journey, it was occupied by no fewer than two churches and a dozen halls big enough to make any Jarl envious. Most importantly, it held a great complex of both stone and timber bearing banners of a three-headed spear depicted in gold on a rich blue background.

'The king's hall?' Bjorn muttered, looking at the place.

Halfdan felt a moment of worry at the sight of those banners. He was rather out of his depth. Kiev was a land of wonders far beyond his ken, and this was clearly the hall of a great lord of immense power and lands. He had his own rich banners and a city that Odin himself might covet. Strangest of all, Halfdan could see that the whole compound was packed with warriors.

'The king's army looks like a warband of Svears,' Bjorn said.

Halfdan shook his head. 'The ships we saw were Yngvar's. Many ships mean many warriors.'

'You think these are Yngvar's men?'

'I fear so. The king's men would be in halls, not camped like this. These men are ready to leave. Still, my enemy is well protected.'

Many hundreds of warriors trained and lounged within the compound, some sparring with one another, their shields rapidly splintering, some sitting and eating or drinking, playing dice or beating one another to a pulp in a good-natured manner. One man was busy rutting with a thrall by a water trough in full sight of all, a tangle of arms and legs. Around the southern edge of the compound, halls of immense size seemed to breathe men in and out in a constant flow.

As Yngvar moved among them they all acknowledged him, many bowing their heads like thralls. Halfdan glanced sideways and realised that Ketil had flipped over his Thor hammer once more to look like a cross, while Bjorn had hidden anything that might give him away. Only Gunnhild stood straight, almost daring the warriors to criticise her.

'If I am to get to him,' Halfdan said in low tones, 'we must join these men.'

'Perhaps we could just anchor the *Sea Wolf* among their vessels,' Bjorn said. 'And then stay here with this lot. Maybe we don't need to go into the hall at all?'

'Afraid, big man?' Ketil smiled wickedly.

'Want me to tear you a new shitter?' the albino snapped. 'I'm just thinking of the easiest way.'

'No,' Gunnhild put in. 'Yngvar leads a fleet, so he will have a council of skippers from each ship and will know them all. If we are to be part of this, we cannot slip among them as we did at the gate. We must be open and acknowledged.'

'You realise that every man in this city is a Christian?' the Icelander pointed out. 'If you intend to be open and travel with them, there will be trouble. We cannot disguise who we are among that lot. I for one will not sing their Christ-dirges. And if our devotion to the old ways is revealed, we will hardly be popular.'

'Then if we cannot be desirable companions for them,' Gunnhild replied with an arched eyebrow, 'we must prove indispensable instead.'

Ahead, having paused to speak to some of his men, Yngvar marched on purposefully towards the door of the palace, and Halfdan and his companions followed. They had slipped into the compound unnoticed in the wake of Yngvar, but with the warriors from the *Sea Wolf* escorting them, the same would not be readily possible when moving into the palace itself. Halfdan gestured to the others.

'Styrmir, Eberg and Kalevi, you're with Ketil, Bjorn, Gunnhild and me. Everyone else, stay out here, move in small groups and speak to people. Learn what you can without starting fights and meet back at the gate.' As the bulk of the group moved off in response, the remaining six hurried, keeping pace with Halfdan, on the heels of their prey.

Yngvar and his companions strode through the palace doorway and between the two glowering guards without comment, and as their pursuers moved close at heel, they simply slipped in behind, assumed to be more of Yngvar's entourage. Moreover, the jarl himself was intent on his goal and not bothering to look back, and neither were his men, so they remained blissfully unaware that their number had suddenly doubled.

Once inside, Halfdan motioned with a flattened hand and they slowed, allowing Yngvar and his men to move ahead down a wide, torch-lit passage. Bjorn surreptitiously checked their surroundings and, satisfied there was no one close by, spoke in a low voice.

'I know you're committed to this, lad, but I might point out that we're in the palace of a king. There'll be riches here that would make the Svear king mad with envy, and we have fourteen strong arms and a ship waiting.'

'Bjorn...'

'I'm just asking you to think about it,' the pale giant added defensively.

'No. We are here to follow Yngvar and that is what we will do. Pull out the pendants and signs you have hidden from view, it is time to show them. We must be seen for what we are, if we are to proceed.'

As he fished for his Thor hammer, Halfdan realised that the enemy had slipped out of sight ahead, though they could not be far away, for he could hear conversation that had to be them. Hurrying as they revealed their pendants, tattoos and birthmarks, they dashed forwards to catch up. It was a foolish rush, Halfdan realised in retrospect, as they had passed through a doorway at speed and emerged into a huge hall before they realised what they were doing.

Halfdan's heart beat in his throat suddenly.

They had walked blithely into the king's court.

Benches all along the edge of the huge room held men and women in expensive-looking garb, and more were clustered in groups at the bottom end of the hall. Warriors stood here and there, impassive and watchful. Yngvar and his small entourage had stopped a few dozen paces away in front of a huge dais upon which sat a great carved chair covered in furs. The man seated upon it could only be the king. Bedecked in gold and silver and wearing a blue tunic that glistened and gleamed like the surface of a river as he moved, Jarisleif bore curled hair the colour of two-day-old ash, and a beard slightly whiter still. He looked old and bored, and yet even as Halfdan glanced at him, he realised that the man's eyes were shrewd.

A man with long, black, braided hair waited close to the king, fingering an axe blade absently as he looked on, scratching his beard with his free hand. He too was dressed in expensive garb, though a step down from the king's.

The ruler of Kiev had been in mid-sentence and fell suddenly silent, turning to look at the seven mismatched northerners who had just stumbled into the room.

'More of yours, Yngvar?' the king asked in a barbed tone. 'Kiev is beginning to sweat under the weight of your men.'

For the first time in more than a decade, Halfdan heard Yngvar speak, as the jarl turned and looked at the seven of them.

'Not mine, sire. I would remember such a group.'

The king was still looking at them. 'What have you to say for yourselves, then? And briefly. My guards can skin a man in less time than it takes to sink a mug of ale.' Almost as though that were a command, men around the hall began to move in their direction.

Halfdan could feel his companions tensing as they bristled, ready to defend themselves, fingers touching hilts and hafts. He stepped a pace forwards and nodded a head at the king, a gesture of respect, but with no fear, and no suggestion of fealty.

'Great king, we came seeking to sign on to the jarl's fleet.'

The king's mouth turned upwards at the corners and his eyes twinkled. 'Hear that, Yngvar. A pup and his friends have managed to penetrate both the outer and inner walls of Kiev and the palace defences, walking right into my audience chamber as brazen as anything. I've half a mind to have my guards scourged for their stupidity. Yet this is merely the latest in a very long line of infractions over the time you have been within my halls. Despite our blood ties, men I trust warn me that you have a reputation. You are seeking a kingdom, and every month your army here builds. A more nervous king might worry...'

'Majesty,' Yngvar said, nostrils flaring. 'You know I seek only to build a fleet sufficient for my journey, and that we are now on the cusp of departure.'

'Thirty ships,' the king said, conversationally. 'Near a thousand men.'

'Majesty, we sail in two days.'

'I know,' the king sighed with a strange smile. 'I have enjoyed your visit, kinsman, but I would be lying if I said I was not looking forward to your departure even more.'

Halfdan suddenly felt ignored. The prince and the king had seemingly picked up where they had left off before the interruption. He waited, not sure that interrupting a king and a jarl was a bright move. It was only as the two returned to their exchange that the black-haired man close to the king broke the routine, taking a step forwards and gesturing at Halfdan.

'Your interlopers await your word, Yngvar Eymundsson.'

The jarl turned now, eying the newcomers, and as he stared at them, a second familiar figure stepped up beside him. Halfdan was suddenly transported back to the last day of his childhood, when his family had been torn from him. He recognised instantly the priest who had accompanied Yngvar, who had urged him on.

Hjalmvigi the priest fixed the seven of them with serpent's eyes. 'These men are pagan scum. Look at the pendants they wear in fealty to demons. You have no need of such animals, Yngvar. They should be peeled and hung from a high tower as a warning to their kind.'

Steeling himself, Halfdan stepped forward, bearing his Mjǫllnir pendent in clear view. Two guards moved to intercept him, but the king wore an indulgent smile once more and waved his men aside. Halfdan settled before his enemy.

'I care not whether I sail with Christians,' he lied glibly, for both Odin and Loki were masters at the art of the untruth, after all. 'I seek silver riches and battle fame for my ship and my men. You will need our swords, and you can trust me on this.'

'Seven heathens are of little value to me,' Yngvar replied with a brief glance at Hjalmvigi, whose lip was wrinkling in disgust as he glared daggers.

'*Forty* heathens,' Halfdan corrected him, 'all battle-tested and with the fastest ship on this river.'

'Were it four *hundred* heathens you would not be welcome,' the priest spat. 'Yngvar Eymundsson and his fleet wear the armour of God, and your presence offends us. Begone before you are flayed.'

'Do not speak above your station in my court, Priest,' the king snapped, and Hjalmvigi bowed his head and fell silent, though he trembled angrily.

The black-haired man near the king stepped a pace forward. 'Yngvar, my cousin, you are too short sighted for your own good. Do not be guided by the acidic piety of your counsellor. Do not forget that while you worship the Church of Rome, we here follow the rule of Byzantium and its Patriarch. Were we to worry too much over heresy, we might have had you ejected from Kiev the week you arrived. The world is a large and dangerous place, my friend, and refusing forty strong sword arms is foolish, no matter your reasoning. Time and time again we in Kiev have allied ourselves with heathens for the greater good. Sometimes you have to look beyond the threshold of your church for strength. You are being offered a ship full of warriors, and Svears at that, if I do not miss the mark. Don't be a fool.'

The king chuckled now. 'My boy is right, Yngvar. *Take* the heathens. Their swords will help you in such dangerous lands, and God knows I don't want them left behind in Kiev to cause trouble.'

'You *cannot* take them, my jarl,' the bitter-looking priest hissed, moving closer. 'They are godless. They will bring ill fortune to us all. Have I ever steered you wrong?'

Yngvar turned to him. 'Wrong? Perhaps not. But you have steered me into difficult waters time and again, old friend. Look to my other skippers. Æskil and Nænnir are strong, but their loyalty will hold only as long as my luck, and men like Gorm fill the ranks but cannot be relied upon to forge ahead in battle. I cannot afford to pass up forty strong blades and a fast ship.'

He turned to Halfdan. 'Your value would have to be high for us to dilute our godly fleet with your presence.'

Halfdan had been entirely unaware that someone had been moving until they struck. His head snapped round in surprise, though it seemed at least someone had been better prepared. One of Yngvar's warriors, who had remained near the door, had moved slowly up behind them, lifting a bow with an arrow nocked. Tellingly, the king's guards had done nothing to stop him as he had moved quietly between the gathering of bodies until he reached the open space close behind them while they talked. Unfortunately for him, as he pulled the string back, fingers straining, ready to release at a word, Ketil took a single step to the side, grasping the arrow even as it strained in the bow. The surprised warrior stared at him as Ketil neatly gripped the arrow where it intersected with the bow and delivered a middle-knuckle punch to the hand gripping the string. The man let go with a gasp of pain, and for a second it seemed the arrow would fly. Then the weapon and missile alike collapsed and fell, Ketil grabbed them as they dropped, turning, and, with a speed even Halfdan had not expected, drew the bow himself, resting the tip of the arrow just under the surprised archer's chin, his own fingers now straining on the string.

The room was completely silent as the warrior in front of Ketil began to sweat uncontrollably, death resting lightly against his throat.

'You make too much noise drawing,' the Icelander said quietly, and pulled the tip of the arrow away from the man's throat. He turned and loosed the missile in a fluid movement, a shock to everyone. Halfdan watched, eyes wide, as the arrow whirred across the room between bodies and then over heads, where it lodged directly in the centre of the tall wooden cross that stood on the far side of the room. The entire hall turned to stare at the missile, all breath held. This was unacceptable. Gazes drifted then to Jarisleif on his great throne, his own eyes wide as the arrow sat silent and still, wedged deep in the human-sized crucifix. Then, suddenly, the king roared with laughter.

'For the love of God, Yngvar,' he bellowed, 'take these men away from my city.'

Ketil held out the empty bow now and Yngvar's man took it sheepishly and backed away towards his lord, who looked less then pleased. The jarl narrowed his eyes at Halfdan and his companions. Then, at a clearing of a throat, he turned to the priest, Hjalmvigi, whose expression remained one of revulsion and undying hatred. Another look at the king and at the black-haired man beside him, and Yngvar straightened.

'Your ship is welcome on our journey,' he said with an expression that rather belied the words. 'You will be treated as any other warriors in my *hirð*, though I will not have your heathen ways in clear view where they can offend others. Keep your devilry to yourselves.'

Not trusting himself to speak without issuing a challenge, Halfdan clenched his teeth and bowed his head in acceptance. He glanced to the side to see Gunnhild nodding slightly at him, a look of sympathetic satisfaction on her chiselled features. As Yngvar tore his gaze from them, Halfdan glanced back towards the king, though his attention was drawn instead by the black-haired younger man, who was grinning.

'I for one will be happy to sail alongside such men,' black-hair announced. 'We are far removed in Kiev from the lands of our ancestors. Heathenry or not, I should like to hear told the tales of old. Our journey will be long and the nights cold and dull, I fear.' He took another step forward. 'I am Valdimar, son of Jarisleif. Welcome to Kiev, brave sons of Odin.'

Had hate been a blade, the look Hjalmvigi shot the prince would have killed. Ignoring the quivering priest, Yngvar turned towards his companions and singled out a man in good-quality garb of middling expense and with an ornate hilted sword at his side.

'Leif, go with these heathens and settle them in. Somewhere far from my hall.'

The man, a warm and moon-faced fellow with golden hair and a neatly trimmed beard, smiled and bowed his head, scurrying across the floor towards Halfdan and his companions. As he closed on them, he spoke in low tones. 'Come. Swiftly.' And with that he swept past them and out through the door. They followed on, emerging once more into a wide and smoke-choked hallway. As they left, Halfdan bringing up the rear, he glanced back. The priest was still glaring at him. The man was not only trouble in the offing, but, fed by memories of that day in the village square, Halfdan could see the priest wielding Yngvar in place of a blade.

Once the talk in that great room had become little more than a hum in the distance, the man called Leif took a deep breath.

'I heartily recommend that you keep yourselves out of the jarl's view unless you are willing to kiss the cross for him. That was bravely done, but Yngvar listens to Hjalmvigi, and the priest will not blink at ordering your death if he thinks he can get away with it. And Yngvar and his priest are not the only danger: a dozen other arrows were trained on you throughout that meeting from the rafters of the hall. Jarisleif has not reigned for thirty years by putting himself at risk, you know? The faster and the further you get from that room, the safer you will be.'

Halfdan nodded and turned to the man. 'You do not need to find us accommodation. We will stay on the *Sea Wolf* until the jarl is ready to depart. Thirty ships is a lot. Where are we bound?'

Leif gave him calculating look. 'You came to sign on to Yngvar's expedition without knowing even where we are bound?'

Bjorn laughed and leaned in between them. 'An opportunity for plunder and glory presents itself. Does a man worry too much about its source?'

'A *clever* man does,' Leif replied quietly.

'Cascades of silver,' Ketil rumbled quietly.

'What?'

'Remember, Halfdan? Poor Finns or the lands of the south, where silver flows in waterfalls?'

Leif gave the man a strange frown, then shrugged. 'The journey will be a great one, but full of danger. We sail south and east down the Dnieper, past the great rapids and out to dark Svarthaf. Fabled Miklagarðr, the Constantinople of the Greeks, lies on the western shore of that black sea, though we instead travel east, and there seek the mouth of the middle of three rivers. We will move into lands rarely seen by Northmen. Perhaps the opportunities for glory and plunder will be great. Certainly the opportunities for a grisly death will present themselves often. For me, though, the draw is the unknown. Like skalds of old I seek new inspiration, for the lands of our home have become dulled and mundane. Of what tongues do you have command?'

Halfdan frowned. 'Mine.'

Leif laughed easily. 'Then much of the south will be anathema and mystery for you. Fortunately for you all, I am a man of both letters and languages. In my younger days I served with Jarisleif's father, Valdimar the Great, as part of his regular embassies to the emperor in Miklagarðr. I shall take much pleasure in bending your tongues and minds alike to the learning of Greek – *Grikkjar*, as you know it – during the long days of our voyage. You may find it of great value, and in return you can shelter me from these men of the Roman Church. You may be throwbacks to a lost age, my friends, but I suspect you will be much more interesting than Yngvar and his men.'

'I think you might find that a difficult task,' Halfdan smiled at the thought of Bjorn trying to wrap his tongue around a new language. 'And what of Valdimar? Why would the king's son journey with Yngvar?'

Leif's face took on a troubled expression. 'Valdimar is a good man, better even than his father, and like the king himself, I am not sure how far I trust Jarl Yngvar. Were it not for Jarisleif's strength, I fear the jarl would have attempted to wrest his throne from him over the three years he has been in Kiev. Indeed, I fear the reason young Valdimar travels with us is to ensure that we make it far beyond the borders of his father's lands to where Yngvar can do him no harm.'

Halfdan nodded as they walked. So, they had signed on to an expedition that would take them far from Rus lands…

To the very edge of the world, he thought, remembering the Seiðr woman and her prophecies. He hadn't realised that the Loki mark on his arm was itching until he noticed he had rubbed it pink with scratching.

Part Two

ᚠᛟᚱᚠᛖᛋ ᛟᚠ ᛟᚾᛁᚺ

The Enemy and the Friend

Chapter 6

'I do not understand.' Bjorn frowned at Leif, scratching his chin.

The ship lurched alarmingly, though neither man seemed to notice as the Rus smiled indulgently. 'It's about the more fantastical edges of your old tales,' he said. 'I can understand the heroes and their exploits, but you have to understand that giants and dragons are simply metaphors.'

'No,' Bjorn said, shaking his head as though the man had suggested that up was down. 'Giants are big fuckers, and dragons are great wyrms that can eat your head.'

'They are not,' Leif said with exaggerated patience. 'They are reflections of the human understanding of evil, passed down by our forefathers and given beastly shape in the telling.'

'No,' Bjorn said, still shaking his head, 'they are vicious bastards that will pull off your arm and beat you to death with the wet end.'

Leif sighed. 'There is a long way to go before you are ready for astronomy, my friend.'

'This is not the time for another of your argumentative Things,' Halfdan barked, Ketil nodding avidly at his elbow. 'Prepare yourselves.' Turning back from such idiocy, he paid attention to the churning river ahead. All the way down the Dnieper, Leif had been prising tales from the big albino, filtering them through his knowledge of the nailed god's story and then feeding them back in lifeless, prosaic and dull pieces. That Bjorn had not already given up and tipped the man overboard said more about his own ability to bear nagging than of Leif's oratorical skills. But still, there were times and places for such discussions, and the place was definitely not in the midst of the ship-killing Dnieper rapids, and the time was *most* definitely not now.

'Gods, but that sound!' someone shouted over an incredible roaring, the likes of which none of the crew had ever heard, as though the world wolf himself had reared up from the river ahead to devour them. This was the fifth rapid, the worst of the lot, by repute.

Halfdan rose in the prow of the ship. She was the smallest vessel of the twenty-nine in the fleet, but she had already proved on the first four rapids that bulk and power in a vessel had their drawbacks. *Sea Wolf* had demonstrated the speed, manoeuvrability and portability of her narrow hull time and again. At the Sofeigi, the first rapid, the ships had pulled in to the right bank for portage round the obstacle, and Halfdan and his men had managed to beach the *Sea Wolf* and had begun to unload the portage poles they'd kept from their first voyage before even Yngvar's vessel had ground to a halt.

As part of the crews of the other great ships had set out their own trackways of smooth logs, other men unloaded the temporary cradles in which the keels would sit to keep the ship upright during portage. Not so the *Sea Wolf*.

Æskil, skipper of the *Sun Chaser* and a sharp, argumentative men who had spent most of the voyage far ahead of them, had now beached his ship beside Halfdan's and as the two crews had worked, the older warrior stepped closer, frowning.

'You've no cradle, boy. Did it fall overboard or something? We cannot hang around while you fashion a new one.'

Halfdan opened his mouth to reply, but it was Ulfr, nearby, who leaned in and spoke. '*Sea Wolf* is light enough for a crew to move without a cradle, and so we do.'

The dour skipper grunted something non-committal and went back to work with his own men, occasionally glancing with a reluctant nod of appreciation at the speed and ease with which *Sea Wolf* moved without a cradle.

Their decision to work without a cradle had surprised several skippers, and yet the choice was somewhat vindicated as the ships gradually beached and began to move, for the cradle of Hrafn's ship broke suddenly. Work all around stopped as men watched, wide-eyed, the whole thing toppling over to one side, killing a dozen men and suffering serious enough damage that it had needed to be left behind. A disconsolate Hrafn had reluctantly split his crew among other ships.

By the time Jarl Yngvar's ship had passed the Sofeigi rapid and plunged into the water once more, Halfdan and his men had been waiting for them for an hour, and cheered at the great warship's arrival. Similar successes had earned them considerable envy over the next three rapids, though the fifth was set to test them all.

'I wonder if anyone ever tried to sail it?' Bjorn mused as they closed on the roar.

'Don't be an idiot,' Ulfr replied.

'Bollocks, *I'd* do it. Shit, I'd ride that thing on a shield just to say I'd done it.'

Ketil glanced over from the far rail. 'I've seen men go white as a sheet facing rapids smaller than that. Mind you, we'd probably not notice with you. When you get scared, do you go pink?'

'Piss off. I don't *get* scared. People get scared of *me*.'

'Given the smell, I'm not surprised.'

Halfdan smiled, but took a deep breath and waved at them. 'Come on, concentrate. This is important. We've four down, and five yet to go.' He looked across at Ulfr, who was busy fretting over every splinter and mark on his vessel. 'You built a fine ship.' Halfdan smiled.

The short Svear looked up suspiciously. 'A fine ship that's starting to look ten times her age with the way you lot smack her about. If she was a woman she'd have left you by now.'

'If she was a woman he'd be riding her harder,' roared Bjorn, eliciting howls of laughter from across the rowing benches, and a glare from Gunnhild, though even her eyes quickly softened and her face slid into a smile.

Nine rapids plagued shipping along the Dnieper, though traversing them had become a regular feature of travel, and sailors they had met in the port of Kiev had supplied excellent information and instructions. The first four cataracts had been easy enough, though this one, the Eyforr rapid, would prove a great deal more dangerous, for this time the terrain demanded that they beach and portage the ships on the left bank.

'What's so dangerous about the left bank?' Halfdan had queried as they dropped back in at the previous rapid.

'The right bank is under the rule of Kiev and well patrolled,' Leif replied. 'The left is nominally Kievan, but close by lie the lands of violent horsemen and even though we crushed them a generation ago, there have been increasing reports of raids once more.'

Halfdan had nodded, remembering Ulfr's warnings about raiders around portage sites many days ago. His hand danced on the pommel of his sword as his eyes raked the bank.

For a mile, since first hearing that distant rumble, they'd listened to the roar growing ever louder until it became a deafening din, and finally the lead ship gave the signal. The worst of the rapids was now in sight, and the fleet began to pull in ready.

'Everyone knows what to do,' Halfdan bellowed above the roar of the white water. 'No heroics this time. We don't rush ahead and then wait for the others while drinking beer. We move with the fleet.'

The men shouted their assent and the ship turned, along with the rest of the fleet, making for the left bank, above which a high green slope awaited. Halfdan held tight to the carved prow and watched the land come closer and closer, braced himself, and then clenched his teeth as the ship crunched up onto the shore.

Bjorn came bounding along the deck. With a nod at Halfdan in passing, the big man reached the bow and leapt from the ship onto the gravel. Behind him, the rest of the crew shipped their oars and hurried forward, some leaping to the bank while others untied ropes and threw them to their shipmates.

'Come, fierce raiders,' Bjorn bellowed, earning irritated looks from the crews of the nearest ships. 'Come and face Bjorn Bear-torn. I want to rip you all a new arsehole!'

Ketil slapped the big man around the back of the head, earning himself a narrow-eyed glare as Halfdan dropped to the beach with a crunch and stomped his way up to the grassy bank.

'I'll scout,' he told the others, moving off ahead of the crew as they worked.

The difficulties facing them were clear, for he could see the ground levelling off to good portage terrain more than a hundred feet up the slope. Getting the ships up there was going to require effort, and a great deal of persuasion and bribery for the men, but it could be done. Indeed, it *had* to be done. The alternative was to try and portage closer to the shore, but with the many undulations of the shoreline and streams cutting down to the bank, that would prove a great deal more difficult. Leif, who had discussed the rapids with the travellers, had advised them to pull inland at the Eyforr and head up the slope to where good, flat ground could be found.

'A hundred and *fifty* feet,' Halfdan said to himself, revising his estimate. One hundred and fifty feet of tortuous slope, then two miles of rolling the *Sea Wolf* across good ground, and then back down a slope on the far side of the rapids, attempting to hold the weight back as they descended and not simply let the ship roll down the hill to smash into kindling.

Once they were in position and everything was ready, all eyes settled on Halfdan, standing ahead a little, up the slope. He turned to look at the other ships. Many were now anchored mid-stream, waiting for space at the bank, or still coming up from the north. Four ships were lined up, Yngvar's own just off to the left. Halfdan cursed as he realised that the bastard was also ready to move. Damn it, but what if the jarl reached the top first and fell to the arrow of a passing raider? Norns be damned, but his blood debt would remain unpaid then. Someone else would have to reach the top first, and it was clear that that was going to have to be the *Sea Wolf*.

Chewing on frustration, Halfdan waved his hand up the slope.

'Off we go, lads.'

To the left of the ship Ketil shouldered his rope, along with nine others, while Ulfr led the rope team on the right. Unlike portage along the low ground, as they had managed so far, this occasion would involve a steep slope, and so the ropes had been broken out to help. Halfdan couldn't help but smile at the sight of the lead men, for Ulfr might be twice as wide as Ketil but he was little more than half as tall. What a pair!

'All good,' came a voice from the rear, Bjorn giving the wave that he was ready, along with his five men preparing to retrieve used logs and haul them round to the front in an ever-moving track. The remaining crewmen, nine to each side, all held ropes attached to the rowlocks or clutched the poles jammed through the side of the ship, prepared to both heave the great weight forwards and also to keep her upright without the need for the cradle that would add extra weight and time to the journey.

Bjorn's voice rose with the work song, his voice louder than most and not contained behind clenched teeth as he pulled on a rope.

'Olof walks along the cliffs.'

Heave, grind, curse, strain

'And there he's led astray.'

Heave, grind, curse, strain

'He stills himself by the house of an elf.'

Heave, grind, curse, strain

'Where a red flame burns away.'

Heave, grind, curse, strain

And so the portage began, each man heaving in time with the old song. With satisfaction, Halfdan watched the two ships that were ready to move. Yngvar's gave an initial lurch and three false starts before its enormous bulk began to crawl ponderously up the slope. *Sea Wolf*, on the other hand, moved immediately and relatively swiftly.

Halfdan stepped slowly back up the slope, watching his ship creep towards him, accompanied by the strain of ropes and timbers, the grunting, panting and cursing of the crew and the rhythmic boom of Bjorn's song. His gaze slipped across to Yngvar, the architect of this entire expedition, and by chance, the old jarl's eyes slid across to him at the same time. The look the tall, fair warrior threw him was not encouraging, but that was hardly a surprise. Halfdan kept his gaze on the jarl for a while, until Yngvar turned away, then smiled wickedly to himself. He returned to watching the ship then, Bjorn and his men hurrying a great log forwards and finding a position where it would stay in place until the ship slid onto it.

Leaving them to it, Halfdan gripped the hilt of his sword and turned, jogging up the slope towards the good flat land above that they'd seen from a distance. Puffing and grunting, he crested that rise carefully, eyes scouring the land from left to right, taking in everything before him under that cold, leaden sky. The tales he'd heard of head-takers and horse archers had filled his imagination with dangers, and he'd half expected to reach the top and find an army awaiting him. Instead, green meadows stretched away to the horizon, copses and patches of scrubland scattered around. The view was clear for at least a mile.

When the noise came, he was so intent on watching for trouble that his gaze searched ahead all the keener for its source for precious moments before he realised that it had actually come from behind him. Concerned for the *Sea Wolf* and its crew in an instant, he spun to look back down the slope, and couldn't identify the problem, until further shouting instead drew his attention across the rise to Yngvar's ship.

'Hold her, you hapless sons of dogs,' bellowed Yngvar as he danced this way and that, pointing and waving, sending men to where they could be of most help.

Something had gone wrong, and Halfdan could see the strain of the men on the ropes, desperately gripping their burden, holding the vessel where it was while others rushed around to solve a problem. One of the beams the ship was sliding along had developed a weakness, and the weight of Yngvar's great vessel had broken it as it passed across. The ship had rocked in its cradle, and almost careened back down the slope, and only the quick thinking and professionalism of the crew had prevented it, staggering to a stop and bracing themselves to take the entire vessel's weight and prevent it descending the slope once more, where the next ship was already out of the water below.

'Don't let it slide,' someone bellowed, rather redundantly.

Halfdan watched with interest. There was no danger to Yngvar, who was up the slope ahead of the ship and snarling oaths at his men, and so Halfdan felt no need to intervene. As he watched, two of Yngvar's crew ducked beneath the ship's stern to try and pull the broken timber free, shouting at their shipmates to haul the vessel forwards. There was a curse from further up among the ropes, and a series of panicked shouts, and Halfdan winced for a moment, knowing already what was coming.

He watched with just a twitch as the ship lurched back down the slope, the ropes slipping through men's hands and burning their palms as it slithered free. To their credit they managed to grip them again and arrest the descent, but only after it had slid some eight or ten feet back. The two poor bastards who'd been trying to prise the log free hadn't stood a chance. The massive bulk of the dragon ship simply rolled over them, crushing them in an instant. The sound was horrible, though thankfully it was instantly drowned out by the shouting of the other men.

Hjalmvigi the priest was there suddenly, making his cross shapes over the crushed men and chanting his dirges. Yngvar ran and grabbed at the rope to help his men, turning to Hjalmvigi.

'Get your soft hands from your book and onto a rope, Priest, or there'll be more bodies to pray over yet.'

The white-garbed Hjalmvigi shot the jarl a look of surprise, but at the sight of Yngvar's expression, he did as he was bid. The ropes were hauled again, and the ship slid up the slope a little. At Yngvar's bellowed command, two more men, looking nervously at one another, ducked down behind the ship and edged that damaged timber free, trying to ignore the smeared remains of their crewmates on the ravaged grassy slope. With the trouble that had befallen the great ship, the next vessel at the shore had been delayed, the men standing around and waiting to move, while the *Sea Wolf* was already almost at the top of the slope.

Yngvar let go of the rope and stepped back, watching his own men with satisfaction now that the ship's portage had begun once more. The jarl's pet priest also abandoned his rope now that his meagre aid was less important, and walked alongside the big ship chanting his monotonous Christian dirges. The jarl's crew worked silently beneath that nailed god litany while, by comparison, the *Sea Wolf*'s crew sang bawdy songs and argued as they heaved.

'You should be up at the top of the slope with Halfdan,' Leif was saying to Gunnhild, their voices now audible as they drew close.

'Why?'

'This is not a woman's work.'

'It's not a fat bookworm's work either, but you seem to be doing just fine.'

Halfdan smiled.

'If she wants a woman's work, she should be up the slope *on top* of Halfdan,' Bjorn laughed, and followed this up with a sharp curse as the shield-maiden behind him in the rope line kicked him hard in the calf.

Halfdan, and the rest of the crew, were rapidly coming to realise that Gunnhild was not just a Seiðr woman, but that she also had as much strength, both of body and of will, as any of them. A Völva in training, yes, but a shield-maiden in practice too. Woe betide the man who tried to treat her as anything less, for he'd already seen her punch Bjorn in the crotch one evening for naught but a minor insult.

The sense of relief was palpable as their ship crested the rise and runners were laid on the grass to slide her forth, away from the slope. Halfdan gave the horizon one more check and, satisfied that they were alone, he turned back. Yngvar's ship was coming close now, and a second ship was already partway up the slope behind Halfdan's. He recognised the sail as belonging to *Snow Hawk*, the ship of Valdimar, the son of Jarisleif, and one of the few men in this fleet that Halfdan placed any trust in. The man might be a Christian, but he seemed to have an open mind and spoke sense as a matter of course.

The crew of the *Sea Wolf* propped the ship up with beams to rest after their efforts and to catch their breath. As

Halfdan listened half-heartedly to their various jibes and banter, his eyes picked out a lean warrior jogging across the slope from the direction of Yngvar's crawling ship. He waited for the man, who came to a halt before him, breathing heavily.

'The jarl says that there has been enough work for this day, and he has two men to bury. Take your ship seven hundred paces south along the slope and settle it for the night and make camp. The fleet will cluster and the crews will sleep here and move on past the rapids in the morning.'

'Agreed.' Halfdan nodded his understanding, though as the man ran back to his master, he looked up into the sky. There were several hours of light left yet. These Christians were clearly weak. Halfdan would have kept moving until dark fell. With a sigh, he turned and passed on the information to the others, and as the jarl's ship crested the slope at last, Halfdan gathered his crew and they began to move the *Sea Wolf* again the short distance to their camp site for the night.

––

'All done,' one of the crew reported, and Halfdan nodded his thanks as the man ambled off to find his mates.

The light had begun to fade by the time the last ship was atop the slope and being manhandled into place for the night, and Halfdan was forced to concede that perhaps it had not been so foolish to camp now after all. This way, the jarl's entire fleet of twenty-nine ships, with all their crews, were in one place, and not strung out along the hillside. Twenty paces from the *Sea Wolf*, the crew had gathered dry wood and set up their fire for the night.

Supplies had been broken out and the crew lounged around, some sat on the grass, chatting, others wrapped in blankets or busy rubbing balms of beeswax and herbs into sores and rope burns. He could hear Bjorn and Leif engaged in another of their discussions, and smiled to himself.

'It's a simple concept, you great oaf. Sacrifice and reward. A man abides by the code of God in this life and in return, Heaven can be his, a place of ease and glory, where hurt and anguish are unknown. How can a man deny that?'

'Because I don't want ease, you feeble-arsed cross merchant. I *want* hurt and anguish in my afterlife. I want to be in Odin's hall and I want to eat and drink and fuck and fight until the last day, and then I want to earn it all by falling at Ragnarok. And if there are downsides to that, the upside is that while I'm still here I can live as I like.'

'Sacrificing your tomorrow for a brief today?'

'You've no idea how close we are to the end of days, little man. My tomorrow might be even briefer!'

'There really is no arguing with you. Your brain is like a rock. It cannot be changed and nothing gets in.'

'And you, little friend, are a trader in misery, trying to sell me a boring life so that I can have an even more boring afterlife. No thank you.'

Halfdan chuckled at that. In broad terms he agreed with Bjorn but, like Prince Valdimar, despite Leif's clinging to the nailed god he seemed a good man.

Ketil was busy cooking up some recipe from the salted pork they'd carried, assisted by two of his friends, preserving their precious fresh meat, bleating nearby on the end of a rope, for other occasions. Ulfr was busy looking over the ship, checking for any damage or weaknesses from its journey up the slope, though the lack of grumbling and cursing suggested that everything was fine. Gunnhild was busy smacking the shins of one of the crew with her spear as the pair sparred in the open ground nearby.

Halfdan had set himself apart, though. He sat on one of the discarded logs at the edge of their encampment, looking out over the flat ground and the other campfires dotted in the gloom between the black shapes of ship hulls. The noise was like the hum of a busy market, hundreds of warriors filling the landscape, each engaged in their own business. Halfdan could see Yngvar, his ship the furthest inland, set slightly apart as if to mark his rank.

The bodies of the two men who'd been crushed by the ship had been gathered up and wrapped in cloaks nearby. Holes had been dug in the ground, and the bodies were laid by the side of them. The jarl and many of his men had gathered as Hjalmvigi rattled on in his indecipherable tongue, carrying out some sort of funeral ceremony. The possessions of the two men had been laid out on the ground on a blanket.

Halfdan watched with bored interest, running the whetstone up the blade of his sax knife, his eyes flicking back and forth between the jarl, the priest and the graves. He jumped a little in surprise as a hand landed on his shoulder, and he turned to see Ketil sinking to the seat beside him. The distance between the two of them was gradually closing, and he'd felt it happening. While he couldn't yet say he would place his life in the Icelander's hands, the man was no longer treating Halfdan as if he'd cheated him out of a ship.

'It's not your turn on watch,' Ketil said quietly.

'I'm not watching for enemies. Or not *new* enemies, anyway. Look at the jarl. He accords two of his men honours hours after heaping curses on them for failing to stop the ship, just because they pray to his nailed god. What honours did he give my father, the village's headman and a renowned warrior, as he ran the old man through? Or any of the men and women of my village? They were thrown into burning buildings like refuse just because they did not bow to his cross. I had to wait for the buildings to turn to ash before I could take what I could find of my father's corpse away for burial myself, or with my friends, since by then he was little more than a couple of armfuls of charred bone and burned meat. He was a warrior loyal to the king, but Yngvar left him to burn just because he trusted in the Allfather.'

Ketil nodded. 'Do not distract yourself, Halfdan, and I pray that whetted blade is not meant for the jarl. Remember the old witch woman and trust in the weavers of fate.'

'You think I will bring trouble if I interfere with his fate?'

'I think if you sink a knife into him in front of his crew we're going to greet the sunrise nailed to one of their beloved crosses.'

Halfdan snorted and turned back to watch in silence as the bodies were lowered into the holes and men began to push and kick earth in over them. Others picked over the goods on the blanket, taking what they fancied and slipping it into purses and bags.

'Why do they not bury them with their goods?' he mused. 'What will they use in their next world?'

Ketil shrugged. 'They have strange ideas of what happens when you die. They seem to think that men are taken up into some kind of other world where their god lives and where everything is peaceful and made of clouds and sunbeams.'

'Bjorn is right. The Christian afterlife sounds dull as shit.'

The Icelander laughed. 'That's because you're young, my friend. When you get older and your bones start to ache in the winter, peaceful starts to become more and more attractive.'

Now Halfdan chuckled too. 'Their Christ songs always sound like cattle lowing to me. There is no joy to be heard in any of them.'

'Do you feel defiant?' Ketil said suddenly, rising.

The younger man turned a frown on the Icelander as he also came to his feet. 'Almost always. Why?'

'Because it would be fitting to thank the gods for a good day today, and ask their blessing for the day to come.'

'That would infuriate the jarl. His priest has expressly forbidden us from following the old ways in his presence.'

'Hence defiance.'

Halfdan grinned now, and the two moved back to the campfire. Ketil gave a simple nod to the two combatants over on the turf, and they lowered their weapons, limping back to the group. Gunnhild, seeing the Icelander gripping his Thor hammer amulet, frowned. Hurrying across to her bags, she pulled something from them and began to work frantically. Within minutes, her staff was no longer a spear, but now bore a carved figure atop it instead of a leaf-shaped blade. The form was of a woman – Freyja, Halfdan presumed, given Gunnhild's Seiðr connection. As she jammed the pole into the ground the gathering went silent, watching expectantly. Ketil looked across at

Halfdan. 'They're my karls, but they're your *crew*. This is your duty.'

Halfdan took a deep breath and crossed to the tether post close to the ship. Three small goats shivered there, still wet from the river spray that had battered them through the journey south. Bjorn had acquired the beasts in Kiev, though there had been five of them then. Two had gone into pot stews on the voyage, and the other three were destined for the same fate, to give the crew an occasional break from the salted and preserved meats they carried. One could be spared, though, for the favour of the gods.

Untethering it, he brought the goat out across the grass. Without needing to give any order, men rose and brought three poles over, forming a triangular frame and tying the top together with a leather thong. Once it was in place and with their help, Halfdan lifted the struggling, panicked goat and tied another cord around its hind legs, then fastened it, suspended from the centre of the frame, one of the men placing a large soapstone bowl beneath.

'Odin, hear me,' Halfdan said loudly, enough to carry across to the jarl's camp. 'We give thanks, Allfather, for a successful day and for harm to neither ship nor men. We give thanks for our comfort and wellbeing, and we ask that you watch over our portage these coming days so that nothing ill befalls us.'

All around their camp, men had drawn carved figures of wood or stone or bone from their pouches and were gripping them, each honouring Odin, and each their own god too, while many bowed their heads in respect to the figure of Freyja upon the staff. Gunnhild's lips were moving in silent prayer of her own and, satisfied that all had been done properly, if in brevity, Halfdan pulled out his sax and neatly cut the goat's throat, ending its mournful bleating. The blood ran in a thick torrent down and clattered and spattered into the bowl, slowly filling it. Bending, Halfdan dipped three fingers into the warm pool and ran them down his face, drawing three crimson stripes from his hairline to his jaw. As he stepped back, others came and daubed their faces or arms with the blood.

'What is this obscenity?' barked a voice from nearby above the increasing sound of drumming feet.

Halfdan's jaw set firm as he turned to see Hjalmvigi hurrying towards them across the open grass, accompanied by two of Yngvar's karls.

Straightening, Halfdan prepared himself. 'I don't know what you or your jarl calls it,' Halfdan replied with an easy smile. '*We* call it dinner.'

The priest's face dropped into a frown. 'I heard you intoning your chants to your demons, Heathen. I am not easily fooled.'

'You are readily mistaken, though,' one of the warriors with him said, pointing across the camp. 'They've been eating goat before. We all have. They have a cook fire, and the men have plates.'

Halfdan's gaze ranged across the camp. In the blink of an eye, as the priest had come running, each of them had covered their favoured gods once more, no idols were in clear evidence, and the Freyja figure had gone from Gunnhild's staff.

Hjalmvigi glared at them all, fully convinced that they were in the midst of some ancient ritual. Without any evidence, and holding no mastery over them but through the jarl, he was impotent to do anything about his suspicions. He growled like a hungry beast.

'Keep your heathen ways away from the rest of us,' he snapped, and turned, stamping angrily back towards his master.

'Sit and eat,' Ketil said to Halfdan as they watched the figure diminish into the gathering gloom. 'Bjorn will take the next watch.'

'He might want to watch our own people, let alone the horizon,' Halfdan said quietly.

'All will be as it has been woven.'

But Halfdan's gaze was still on the retreating figure and the crew to whom he returned. The edge of the world and the fate to be found there could not come soon enough…

Chapter 7

'No!'

It was the same dream. He was jumping from the fence rail with his wooden sword, and Trygve was holding up his homemade shield to block the blow, when the thunder of hooves drew their attention and they turned, their game forgotten, to see the horsemen drumming their way along the road to the village. Turning in his sleep, cold sweat stinging his brow, he forced himself out of the dream as always, pushing himself to wakefulness before the nightmare descended into terror, yet knowing that he was only delaying the inevitable. As soon as he slid back into sleep, the dream would resume seamlessly and he would watch his father die.

His whispered cry of anguish still echoing in his mind, his eyes snapped open. Something was different this time. His blood was pounding, his brow prickled with sweat and his stomach filled with icy lead, but that was normal. The dream did that, another reason beyond the blood debt why Yngvar had to die, so that perhaps the dream would stop coming.

But it *was* different. Something had changed.

His gaze slid across the slumbering forms of the crew. Snoring, some talking in their sleep, the usual sounds of nighttime and nothing untoward. He could see Ketil on watch at the edge of the camp, which meant it was late, but all was peaceful and quiet. Just the sounds of the night with a gentle breeze soughing through the leaves of the scattered copses, almost lost beneath the distant noise of the river.

Nothing out of place, so was it something to do with the dream?

He realised suddenly that the distant thunder of hooves had not stopped with wakefulness, and in a heartbeat he was on his feet, yanking his sword from the scabbard that had lain next to him as he slept.

'To arms,' he bellowed across the camp. 'Stand to.'

As men blearily reacted, blinking and frowning, looking this way and that, Ketil rose from his log and turned, forehead creased in incomprehension.

'What is it?'

'Riders,' Halfdan replied breathlessly. 'Can you not hear the hooves?' Stooping, he swept up his wolf shield.

Now men in other ship encampments were starting to rise at the commotion, looking about themselves in confusion. Ketil cocked his head to one side. 'You're hearing things, young friend. That rumble is the river rapids.'

'No, it isn't.'

And then Ketil frowned, turning and cupping a hand to his ear as he peered off east. His eyebrows suddenly rose, eyes widening. 'Odin, but you have sharp ears, Halfdan.' And then Ketil was running, sword pulled free, bellowing for the camp to rise. Valdimar's crew were also rising at the alarm, and a couple of the other camps nearby, though most of the sleepers had yet to realise what was happening, including Yngvar's, encamped furthest from the bank and therefore closest to danger.

The rumbling was clearer now, no longer mistakable for the thundering of the water below. Still, many had not awoken fully, and Halfdan's crew was the only one fully mobilised and armed as they moved to the edge of the encampment and shuffled into a line. Most were armed with axes, a few of the better-off with swords, and five of them gripped spears in a gleaming challenge.

Bjorn, hefting his heavy war axe, looked to Halfdan then, and the young warrior understood with a drying mouth that they were awaiting his shout. That realisation brought a shock of worry, and his mind whirled. Realistically, Bjorn had to be the man with the most battle experience here, yet the big man was looking to him, and he remembered Bjorn's advice on the ship when they had first reached Kiev. *You must be confident and full of action. You must have your path laid out.* Halfdan would have to lead this, for all his inexperience.

'They will hit the jarl's camp first. Run.'

It was simple, but it was all that was needed to get them racing for Yngvar's men, who were now stirring and rising, calls of alarm going up everywhere. They could see the enemy now, emerging from the dark horizon like a plague on a thousand equine legs. They were coming at a charge, and a forest of lances spiked the night ahead of them. Some were armoured in steel that gleamed in the light of the stars. One he spotted encased in glistening metal from scalp to toe. The whirr and thrum of arrows announced that not every man carried a lance, and even as the crew neared Yngvar's camp, he watched warriors smashed back with shafts jutting from chests and shoulders, faces and legs.

As Halfdan ran alongside the others, he became aware that Gunnhild was at his left shoulder, shouting at him.

'Odin's maidens watch the battle, Halfdan. Should Yngvar fall, he could be claimed by Odin in defiance of the Norns.'

Halfdan nodded at her timely reminder, and at that moment he saw Yngvar stomping furiously through the camp in the direction of the enemy. Off to Halfdan's right one of his men suddenly cried out in pain, an arrow buried in his thigh, and he collapsed to the damp grass.

'Run,' he bellowed. 'The enemy are upon us.'

The riders crashed into the gathering crew of Yngvar's ship like a winter tide against a badly lashed jetty. The horsemen burst through the hasty shield wall in three places, racing into the camp, hacking and spearing, cutting down men even as they looked for shields. Many, however, had found themselves unexpectedly halted by the sheer power of the Svears locked together in fierce denial. Sections of the jarl's crew had fallen beneath those charges, ground beneath hooves, but already the rest were fighting back.

There was no quarter given by Yngvar's men. Axes swung wildly with roars of fury, hacking into the legs of the horses that had barged into them, in some cases managing with brute strength and razor-sharp blades to sever legs, sending the beasts screaming to the ground, where their riders became instantly vulnerable.

Halfdan waved his men in as they reached the edge of the camp. 'Take the ones to the left,' he bellowed, gesturing with his sword towards those horsemen who had broken through the shield wall and who were now within the camp behind it, whooping and ululating as they killed and looted with impunity.

All along the hillside the other crews were moving now, though only Valdimar's, given adequate warning by Halfdan's shout, were anywhere near close enough to help. Halfdan left the rest to it and, with Bjorn at his right shoulder and Gunnhild at the left, spearpoint once more gracing the tip of her staff, he fixed his sight upon Yngvar, who had waded into the press and was now swinging his heavy sword at a rider clad in more armour than Halfdan had ever seen on one man.

The three of them ran towards that clash, teeth clenched, and Halfdan tried to bite down on his fear, not a fright of danger or wounding, but the very real worry that he would become unmanned somehow in this, his first true battle. He tried to estimate the enemy numbers but failed dismally, for it was too dark and too chaotic. Enough to cause serious damage, though. He decided then that this was a raid of opportunity rather than an attempt at complete destruction. There were insufficient riders to win a full battle here, once all the crews were committed. They would lose in the grand scheme, which suggested that battle had never been their true intent. They had planned to raid the camps, coming unexpected out of the night like ghosts, killing with ease and taking all they desired before the crews could react. Halfdan's warning had changed all that.

Indeed, those riders who had broken through the lines were more intent on sweeping up what stores and posses-sions they could and racing away before they could be stopped than on killing any further.

'They're after supplies and loot, not a victory,' he bellowed.

'Just raiders,' Ketil agreed.

'Just?' Leif said in exasperation as he ran, axe in hand. 'These are Pechenegs! An ancient enemy of our people.'

Halfdan couldn't see a way to get in to join the fight, for Yngvar's crew had closed up in the wall once more, their leader part of the line, now. As they reached the scuffle, however, he realised that the man at the jarl's sword elbow was wounded and staggering, close to falling, and so Halfdan did the only thing he could. He grabbed the chain shirt of the man beside Yngvar and hauled him backwards out of the way. The warrior fell with a squawk and Halfdan leapt into his place, sword raised and coming down hard. It bit hard into the thigh of a rider, who howled in agony and wheeled his mount, lurching away. Some of the enemy were on foot now, having been unhorsed at the first clash, though many were still ahorse. Gunnhild's spear lanced out over his shoulder, smashing into the neck of a rider who had pushed through to the front, only to die in agony on the shield-maiden's blade.

'Father of battle, give me victory!'

The furious intonation in an Icelandic accent behind him told him that Ketil had now joined them too, the tall man trying to find a way to push through Yngvar's crew to get to the riders. The man to Halfdan's right suddenly gave a squeak of alarm and vanished backwards; in a heartbeat Bjorn was there in his place, swinging his axe with consummate ease and neatly dispatching another of the enemy riders, Ketil falling in beside him. For half a hundred heartbeats then, Halfdan lost sight of everything but a succession of enemies trying to kill him as he swung and thrusted, taking a series of hard blows against his shield, his arm swiftly numbing with the repeated impacts. When he finally found a moment to look around, he found his albino friend bellowing beside him with a wide grin.

'I killed three,' Bjorn roared.

'Two,' Ketil bellowed back, 'one's getting back up, look.'

'*Three*,' Bjorn snapped irritably as he stamped down on the fallen rider's foot and hewed an axe blow deep into his neck.

Halfdan realised that his moment's grace was the doing of Bjorn, whose victim and horse had created a tangle that prevented anyone else coming at them. His gaze rose to take in the scene, and the weaving of the Norns was never clearer than in that moment. Had he not managed to find a place right here beside the jarl, and had not Bjorn immediately killed that man in front of them, then Yngvar's doom would have changed. He would have died in the darkness here by the Dnieper rapids, a warrior hero for all his villainy, and sought by Odin.

The world slowed for Halfdan. A rider ten paces back, behind Bjorn's victim, had an arrow already in place in his small bow, the string pulled back to near his cheek, his aim clearly on Yngvar. Even as Halfdan saw the danger, the Pecheneg rider loosed his missile, which whipped and winnowed through the night air, seemingly in impossibly slow motion. Halfdan was shouting as he turned.

'Yngvar!'

The jarl was looking the other way, along the line of his warriors, bellowing something about their nailed Christ. He had seen nothing of the danger. Halfdan's shield was beside Yngvar, and he reacted on instinct. There was nothing else he could do, and no time to think. His arm shot out straight, the shield sliding in front of Yngvar, covering his chest and neck. That meant that Halfdan had showed the inside of the shield to the enemy, and his own arm, gripping the boards, was exposed. He accounted himself favoured of Odin in that moment, as the arrow thudded into the wood little more than a finger-width from his forearm, punching through to emerge beyond the tanned sheepskin face.

Yngvar turned suddenly, aware only that something was happening directly in front of him, and the jarl's eyes widened at the arrowhead jutting from the board less than a foot from his neck. The man swallowed in shock, his sword drooping suddenly as his eyes came up to meet those of Halfdan, realisation dawning. Halfdan was busy now, though, and tore his gaze away and back to the fight, ignoring whatever it was that Yngvar shouted as he pulled his shield back and used his sword to hack off the protruding shaft by his arm, rendering the thing useful once more.

The archer had gone, lost from sight, but more warriors were coming into the press on both sides, and this raid was rapidly turning into a full-scale battle. Yngvar had disappeared from the line now, staggering back, still wide-eyed, and Ulfr slid into his place. Halfdan felt the pride of a jarl himself then, with the immensely tall, black-clad Icelander and the white-haired bear of a man to his right, the icy and beautiful Gunnhild and the diminutive but powerful Ulfr to his left.

Even Leif, the loquacious Rus, was here fighting like a Viking of old though he bellowed to his Christ.

They hacked, stabbed and hewed, striking at men and horses indiscriminately, simply killing whatever got in their way. As a man fell, almost taking off Halfdan's arm with a gently curved sabre in the process, a new figure suddenly emerged in the enemy press.

'Look,' Halfdan called, pointing with his sword at the new arrival.

This fresh foe had been unhorsed already, though it was hard to tell for he was so incredibly tall and broad that he was almost of a height with the men still mounted. Even in the dark, Halfdan could see how rich the man's clothes were, in deep reds and mustard yellows, and his armour was ornate, gilded. If he was not their leader, then he was certainly a noble of some sort. The man had a long, curved blade in his left hand and a spear in his right, with a red streamer trailing from just below the head. This was the first time Halfdan had managed a clear view of the enemy as anything other than a frenetic blur with a blade. The Pecheneg monster was huge and his face was oddly flat and deeply tanned, with a wide nose, narrow eyes beneath thick brows, and a moustache that drooped to either side of his mouth. His scalp was hidden beneath an ornate piece of headgear that seemed half-hat, half-helmet, steel in places but brightly coloured in others.

The man roared in some dreadful, strange language and stomped across the wreckage of one of his men, heading for the northerners. Halfdan bellowed his faith in Odin and prepared for the attack, but was immediately distracted as another warrior appeared before him, pushed aside by Bjorn as the big man tried to fight three at once. Cursing at the ill luck that took the enemy leader from his sight, Halfdan lifted his shield and took a blow from the sword of this new warrior. He was impressed immediately at the qualities of these enemy blades. The curved edge seemed to carve rather than smash in the manner of northern swords, and the edge of the Pecheneg's weapons sliced deep through the painted hide of his shield, gouging an impressive furrow in the timber. Two or three blows like that and his shield would be little more than a pile of useless boards.

Roaring, he knocked the blade aside and threw his sword out in an attempt to jam the tip into the man's gut, though the dismounted rider slammed his own shield in the way, a small and circular metal disc, painted with gleaming enamels. Halfdan's sword clanged off the shield and fell away. Again and again the two men hammered at one another, each of the Pecheneg's blows carving holes in Halfdan's shield, each of his leaving scrapes and dents in that metal disc.

Finally, the young warrior shifted slightly and held off, allowing the Pecheneg to strike at him twice in quick succession, and in the inevitable pause that followed as the man pulled back for a third blow, Halfdan struck. His sword came up in a slice, and though the man was agile and managed to lean back away from the worst of the blow, the tip of Halfdan's sword caught him on the chin, smashing into his jaw and cleaving it in two, pulverising his face as it tore free. The man made a horrific gurgling noise as he fell away, lurching in agony.

Halfdan looked this way and that for the next foe, and realised that they were thinning out. Indeed, only two remained close enough to strike at: a man upon whom Bjorn was venting his frustrations in blood, and the huge leader who was locked in a struggle with Ketil, the two men battering at one another frantically. It was like a war of giants, Halfdan mused as he watched, for Ketil stood a head and a half clear above Halfdan, and almost a head even above Bjorn, and yet this Pecheneg leader towered over the Icelander. He was good, too, for his sword continually whipped at Ketil, keeping him fighting back, while his red spear lanced out again and again, forcing the Icelander to throw his shield in every possible direction and to duck and weave and dodge constantly. Even as

Halfdan realised that the battle was all but over, he saw that spear tip carve a neat line along Ketil's forehead above his eyebrow, calling forth a bellow from the Icelander.

'Bastard!'

Then strange-sounding horns were blowing, and the Pecheneg leader's head turned at the noise. A roar went up among the riders, as they broke off the battle. Even as Ketil lunged at that giant, and Halfdan leapt to join him, arrows whipped out of the darkness, forcing the northerners to hunker behind raised shields. Shafts thudded into wood, and Halfdan jumped as one punched through his shield, close to the hole left by the previous one. His own shield was now all but useless, yet he continued to crouch behind it as he looked up to see that another of the riders had swung past with a spare horse. The giant Pecheneg vaulted up into the saddle like some acrobat, and in a heartbeat they were racing away into the night.

Halfdan straightened, breathing heavily. Bjorn was nodding at him in approval.

'A good scuffle,' the big albino grinned. 'How many did you kill?'

'I was too busy to count,' Halfdan gasped.

Bjorn roared with laughter. Did the big man know that this was in truth Halfdan's first battle? His first real test of arms beyond small personal scuffles? He felt a small flow of pride that he had not flinched, that he had held his own in a true battle with a fierce adversary, and he found himself looking askance at Yngvar and his crew. How could a man follow the nailed god when he could feel the fury of a hundred generations of Odin's sons burning through his veins in the press?

He turned, slowly, heaving in the cold night air. The enemy had not fled through fear but through simple expediency. The other crews were here in force now, hundreds of fierce northerners armed and angry, and the Pechenegs would have been hopelessly outnumbered. What had begun as a raid had become a battle, and the moment it tipped towards disaster, the riders had cut their losses and fled with what goods they had managed to take.

Bodies littered the grass, men from both forces, and horses, too. A few of the beasts had survived unharmed, to wander the scene aimlessly, but the ground had become a carpet of mangled bodies, many of whom were still only partway along the path to death, moaning and hissing in agony. As Bjorn moved among them, killing them all, men of either side, Halfdan felt eyes upon him and turned slowly, searching the field of exhausted warriors and writhing bodies. Yngvar was standing alone now amid the carnage, his eyes on Halfdan. The man's eyes slid from the young Gottlander's face down to the damaged shield in his grip, and Yngvar gave him a single curt nod and then spun away, bellowing angrily at his own watchmen who he now threatened with death for their failure to notice the horsemen before it was almost too late.

Halfdan looked at the sad remains of his glorious shield, the painted wolves barely recognisable beneath the chips and splinters of a dozen sword strikes, the surface pock-marked with arrow damage. Sighing, he cast it to the ground, though Ulfr tutted and swept it back up straight away.

'It's done,' Halfdan breathed.

'Shows how little you know of the carpenter's art. I can put this back together in a few hours. And I'm damned if we're wasting all the time I spent painting it for you.'

123

The small shipwright wandered off with the broken shield, and Halfdan slowly became aware of a tense silence at his shoulder. He turned.

'This is not over,' Ketil snarled, wiping blood from his slashed brow.

Halfdan frowned at the tall Icelander, whose face was washed with crimson from the cut. The big man's eyes were almost glowing with fury.

'We'll never catch them,' he replied. 'They have horses. That was just a raid and they won't be back. Not now that they know we'll be ready for them. It's just a cut. Not even enough for a healer to look at, Ketil.'

'That big bastard isn't done, and neither am I. It's not over.'

Halfdan grabbed the Icelander's elbow and pulled him round to tear the man's gaze from the black horizon and to his own dark eyes. 'Leave it, Ketil. It's done.'

Bjorn leaned close, appearing as if from nowhere. For a noisy giant, he could move surprisingly quietly when necessary. 'Remember what I said about Icelanders. Unpredictable.'

Halfdan, nodding, turned to walk away and found Gunnhild standing nearby, leaning on her spear. She fixed him with an odd, knowing look.

'What?' he said.

'The path of our journey unfolds before us, the weave becoming clear.' When she was met only with confusion from Halfdan, one of her eyebrows rose meaningfully. 'Draugar and dragons and—'

'Giants,' breathed the young warrior, almost reverentially, turning to look into the quiet dark after the vanished horsemen. He felt the Seiðr all across his skin again then.

It had begun.

Chapter 8

'He was a good man, your father,' Ømund's mother said sadly as Halfdan, young and hollow, terrified and furious, stooped to gather a piece of charred femur, not entirely sure whether it was his father's or not. Who knew if other bodies had turned to ash in that house.

'He was my father, and a blood debt is owed,' his young voice replied, darker than the carbon-scored bone in his hand.

'You are too young to appear before the Thing, Halfdan, and your uncle would not do such a thing. You cannot claim a blood debt like this.'

Halfdan straightened amid the remains of his father. He thought deeply for the right words, for they had to be words of power, like a warrior addressing his jarl. 'Then I declare it to a higher power than Thing, or even the king. In the name of Tyr and of Odin, I name Yngvar Eymundsson the slayer of my father, and I say in the presence of the gods that one day, I will take my price in blood.'

The nightmare had come once more, drifting wickedly over him like a leaden blanket as soon as Halfdan's weary head hit the blankets, the fight having drained him of energy. This time he had watched in the dream village as Yngvar and his riders butchered the innocent men and women without a sign of remorse, the priest goading them with his acidic piety. He had watched with his sleeping eyes as his father looked up at the cold jarl and spat defiance to the last. He'd watched as Yngvar plunged the sword into him and then stepped back, yanking it free.

The passage of time had dulled the pain of the memory a little, even with such regular reminders, but it was not just the *death* of his father that drove him on, for all that it still burned within. Men died, and in truth, Vigholf had fought back and died like a warrior. But the old man had died on his knees, dispatched in the name of the nailed god, while the white robed Hjalmvigi danced jigs of hatred behind. He had been despised as he died, and had been cast into the flames without his weapons for the afterlife as was his right. It had not been an end worthy of him, but the end of a thrall.

And so Halfdan, tossing and turning and moaning in his sleep, lived once more through the horror and even the final indignation of gathering the steaming, smoking pieces of bone and gristle from among the black timbers of the house. Only then did the nightmare release him and, still tired and bleary, he awoke, shivering, looking up into a sky of low clouds that promised imminent rain. Though he had lived through sickening hours in the dream, he somehow knew that in the real world, time had not passed so fast, and it was still the middle of that same night, probably not more than an hour or so after the fight had ended and the crews had fallen once more into slumber.

He frowned. Once again, he could sense something amiss, and once again it took a few moments for the reason to sink in. He sat up and his gaze roved across the camp and the sleeping warriors. He saw the shapes of men as mere lumps in the grass, the black silhouette of the *Sea Wolf* rising behind them, the edge of the slope where the river ran a hundred and fifty feet below, gurgling and rumbling, and he could see the shapes of Valdimar and

Yngvar's camps, as well as the others behind them. The remains of fires guttered and flickered in the dark, barely illuminating the closest figures now as they faded. One thing was missing from that scene, and it made him rise immediately.

There was no one on watch.

'Where are you, Ketil?' he breathed to himself.

There could be so many reasons for this, of course, from treachery and murder all the way down to the Icelander simply disappearing behind a tree to relieve himself. But not only was Halfdan already sure who it was who wasn't there, he was fairly sure he knew why, too. Just to be certain, he padded around the sleeping camp until he came to Ketil's blankets. They lay bunched up, cold and empty. It was still the Icelander's watch, as he'd thought, probably less than an hour since they had returned to sleep after the battle.

'Unpredictable,' he cursed to himself. 'All Icelanders are unpredictable.'

He rubbed his hand wearily down his face. He should have seen this coming, really. He had to do something, but shouldn't wake the crew. They had fought harder than most this night and on the morrow they would move a ship miles across land, so they would need all the rest and strength they could get. But he couldn't simply leave Ketil to his fate. He bloody well *should*, but he couldn't. He might have won the right to the ship squarely, but the man had come with him and given him a crew when he'd had none, and had stood by his side in the hall of Jarisleif. He could not be left to his fate now. Drawing his sword and cursing the Icelander once again, he danced quietly through the slumbering shapes until he found the bulk that was Bjorn, rumbling quietly, wrapped in blankets and a cloak. Crouching, he put a hand on the big man's shoulder gently, opening his mouth to whisper him awake, and was rewarded with a punch in the jaw before Bjorn's eyes even opened.

'What the fuck are you doing?' the hulking albino snapped by way of apology, raising grunts of irritation from the sleepers nearby as they rolled over to face away.

'Ketil is missing. Come on.'

As the big man rose, grumbling irritably, Halfdan moved on until he found Gunnhild, which was easier than he expected, for she sat up as he approached and looked directly at him, as though she had been waiting for him. Some days he wondered whether Gunnhild was truly human or was something more, perhaps even Freyja walking among men, for it was said that she did so from time to time. Gunnhild rose and nodded without having to be told anything. As Halfdan turned, he saw Leif also rising in his blankets.

'What is it?' the Rus murmured.

'Ketil has gone.'

The man nodded and stood.

'It is hardly a surprise. His eyes were filled with anger and the urge for revenge from the moment the fight ended.'

Gunnhild sighed. 'He nursed the cut on his brow as though blowing on a dying flame. We should have been watching him. You are not the only one who clings to blood debts.'

Nodding to the others, Halfdan quickly swung by Ulfr and told him what was happening, setting him in charge of the camp, then the five of them hurried off to the heavy log where Ketil had been sitting on watch. Halfdan stopped there and looked about. There were the scuffed mud marks of a man who had spent bored hours in the same place. He tested the log, but there was not a hint of warmth to it. Ketil had been gone for some time. He could see men on watch at the other camps, and they would be alert after what had happened earlier. They had to have seen Ketil go, but it wasn't worth checking with them, for Halfdan had no doubts whatsoever about what had happened.

'Where did he go?' Bjorn said, frowning into the darkness.

'To get even.'

'What?'

Halfdan sighed. 'He took that cut on his face from the Pecheneg leader personally. He's gone hunting.'

Bjorn stared at him, eyes wide. 'You're joking?'

'I'm not. He's gone to even the scales with the Pecheneg. He fears that in the morning we will move on and he will have no opportunity to avenge himself.'

'He is mad,' Leif spat. 'He cannot fight the whole Pecheneg tribe on his own.'

'I think you underestimate the Icelander,' Halfdan hissed. 'I should have had someone watching the man on watch. We all had half a mind something like this might happen and yet I can hardly blame the man for seeking vengeance. I'm crossing half the world and fighting wars for Christians just to bring down my own prey, after all. His revenge is costing him a lot less. We have to save him, though.'

'Why?' Bjorn rumbled. 'It's his problem. He'll die, but he'll die like a Northman, looting and fighting, and he'll end up in Odin's hall when he fails, which is as much as any of us can hope for.'

Leif shook his head. 'You don't want to be taken by the Pecheneg. That's not a Northman's death, as we in Kiev have learned over the decades. They make drinking cups from their enemy's skulls, and they are said to begin the process while the previous owner is still awake, just for the fun of it.'

Halfdan shrugged. 'Ketil is a grown man. He can face his own consequences, but I have to save him anyway. He did not have to come with us and to bring his crew. Without him we would still be in Hedeby looking for sailors.'

'How do we track him?' Leif asked quietly as they started to jog out across the flat grassland away from the river, and the others turned as one to look at him oddly. 'What?' he muttered irritably. 'I can't track. Are any of you hunters?'

Gunnhild shook her head. 'He's followed the Pecheneg back to their camp. A blind fool can follow the tracks of a hundred horses.'

And that was precisely what they did. Crossing the open turf, they followed in the presumed tracks of their friend until they intersected with the churned, muddy turf of the riders' retreat. The swathe of tracks headed roughly southeast towards a line of trees, and the four of them pounded across the grass, keeping their breathing tight to preserve their stamina, their muscles still burning from the strain of the fight. The turf was light and springy beneath their feet and the running easy, with sufficient starlight to see where they were going, though that looked set to change with clouds drifting together from the west. They ran with weapons bared, each knowing that they could come across their enemies at any time.

As they left the noise and light of the camp behind, Halfdan felt his first moment of doubt. They were chasing after a man straight into the camp of a vicious warband. A small part of him rolled its eyes at his lack of common sense, and he was acutely aware that, despite the fight that night, battle was still very much a new thing for him. A glance around him was reassuring. Bjorn was a comforting figure to have beside you when facing danger, and despite having only known the man for a matter of months, there was no one he felt he could rely upon more. Apart, perhaps, from the woman at his other shoulder. As though sensing his nerves, Gunnhild gave him a look loaded with confidence. Even Leif, the smallest and most peaceable man among them, had a face set in a grimace of determination. And so they ran on.

They followed the track past a small copse and down into a low and wide gully, the approach that had allowed the Pechenegs to come so close to the camps without being seen too early. It had been the echo of their hooves in this ditch that had woken Halfdan in the first place, he realised. As they moved, the clouds continued to gather threateningly from the west, and a fine drizzle began, soaking them all, gradually increasing as they closed on their prey. For perhaps a quarter of an hour they jogged, their pace slowed by a combination of visibility and tiredness, and finally Halfdan rounded a hedgerow and then ducked back, holding up a hand to stop the others. As they came to a halt no one spoke, though all eyes fell upon their young leader expectantly. He poked his head around the hedgerow once more and beckoned to the others. Each of them crept forwards to look, ducking back quickly.

A hundred paces or so away sat the Pecheneg camp in a low hollow. This was no one-night stay for the nomads, clearly, for they had erected a dozen giant tents, each circular and colourful, made of hides and woven sheets and held taut with many ropes, with the largest at the centre. Off to one side a corral had been formed from what appeared to be wicker fencing, their horses wandering calmly within, eating the fresh, damp grass. A large fire roared at the heart of the place before that large tent, continually fed with timber from the various copses in the area, as well as dry horse dung, as Leif had told them was the custom. The riders were largely out of sight, presumably within the tents, and only an odd figure here and there sat watch, a dark shape in the night.

Of Ketil there was no sign.

'What if he's not here?' Leif murmured. 'What if he actually just went down to the river for a piss and we got him wrong?'

Halfdan remembered the look on the tall Icelander's bloodied face as he'd watched the Pecheneg giant racing away, and he shook his head. 'He came here.'

'He is *still* here,' Gunnhild added, and the rest turned to her. 'Listen,' she said, changing her grip on her spear, flexing knuckles, apparently anticipating danger. Halfdan shivered once again, feeling the Seiðr at work in the air about them. Freyja indeed...

They stood, though, listening. There was no sound but the gentle hiss and patter of rain, the distant crackle of the fire...

And a bellow of rage from somewhere deep in the camp.

'Shit,' Bjorn grunted. 'That doesn't sound hopeful.'

'Wait,' Gunnhild said now, watching intently. The small party peered off into the darkness, watching the collection of tents. The men on watch were moving now, reacting to the shout as they turned back into their own camp and began to walk hurriedly towards the fire, drawing weapons.

'There,' Leif hissed, pointing, and all eyes slipped to the left, following his gesture, picking out the gangly shape of their friend hurtling at speed away from the tents and off to the undergrowth. The Icelander was cradling something in his folded arms as he ran. The crafty bastard had slipped out between the sentries as they ran to find out what had happened.

'Do we go after him?' Leif muttered.

'He will have to come this way if he wants to return to the ship.'

Sure enough, as they waited they twice caught sight of the shape of Ketil rustling through the scrub, heading in their direction. Periodically they turned back to the camp, which was now in an uproar. Briefly, Halfdan caught sight of the giant noble near the fire, towering over his warriors, throwing out an angry arm this way or that, and the Pechenegs ran all around, searching the area. Clearly no one yet believed that Ketil had managed to get away. That, at least, might buy them vital time.

As the tall Icelander emerged from the scrub and ran across the open space to the shelter of the bushy hedge behind which they lurked, he spotted the figures waiting for him and faltered for a moment, uncertain whether they were friend or foe until the big pale shape of Bjorn beckoned to him. He ran again, then, into the shelter of the bushes.

'You just had to go and blood their leader, didn't you?' Halfdan spat.

Ketil gave him a wry smile. 'I'm no Svear like you lot. Battle is not the god of my heart, and I can get my own back in many ways.' The smile slid into a wide grin as he proffered the bundle he'd been carrying. Halfdan looked down and his eyes widened.

'Is that…?'

Ketil grinned. 'Their leader's personal collection. I think he's a little irritated.'

Four cups sat within Ketil's folded arms. They were at one and the same time fascinating and horrible. They had been formed by removing all the flesh from a human head, boiling the skull clean and then sawing it at eye level, leaving just the bowl of a man's head, which had then been lined with silver to a good thickness, more silver and a little gold worked decoratively into the outer surface. Quite apart from their probable sentimental value to the Pecheneg giant, they represented a small fortune in silver and gold.

'You're a fucking idiot,' Bjorn snorted.

'I'm a *rich* fucking idiot,' corrected Ketil.

'He's not going to let you get away with it.'

'He has to catch me first,' replied the Icelander and, turning, he began to run along the hedge in the direction of the river. The others paused only long enough to look back at the camp and see that a number of riders were now in the corral, gathering their horses, then they too turned and pelted away through the deepening rain after the fast, leggy Icelander.

It would have been impossible to keep pace with the rangy, black-clad man, had he not kept slowing to allow them to catch up before racing off ahead again. As they caught up, Halfdan, breathing heavily, cleared his throat.

'You know you've brought trouble down on us again?'

'I'll not leave a debt unpaid,' the Icelander replied.

'I know. And I understand, but we're in trouble. We're all tired, and it's half an hour's run to the ships. The Pechenegs are already preparing their horses, and once they're mounted they'll outpace even you. There's no chance of reaching the others before we're overrun by horsemen.'

'Let them come,' Ketil said with an air of hunger.

The man had sealed their fate with his revenge theft, for Halfdan could not imagine that giant nobleman retreating from battle this time. He knew little to nothing of the Pechenegs, but all men had their honour and their pride, and the giant would be driven by both now until he'd added Ketil's skull to his silvered collection.

It was as they turned into that long gully, now slippery and thick with mud in the wet, that they heard their pursuit closing, the drumming of hundreds of hooves audible even over the hiss of the rain. Halfdan peered ahead as he listened carefully. There was no chance of them getting to the far end of the gully before the riders were on them, let alone reaching the ships. If they did nothing, not only would the five of them be easily ridden down and butchered, but very likely there would be a repeat of the earlier attack, this time with no warning from Halfdan to save them.

'Up the slope,' he barked, pointing up the slippery, muddy side of the gully towards the trees and bushes clinging to the edge above them.

'What?' said Bjorn.

'We can't fight them and we can't outrun them. We have to hide and let them pass.'

Ketil gave him a calculating look. 'I can make it back.'

'No, you cannot. You're not as fast as you think you are. And this is your mess anyway, so there's no way you're legging it to safety with your silver heads and leaving us here in the mud.' To add weight to his words, Bjorn moved next to him and drummed his fingers meaningfully on the top of his axe.

With that, Halfdan began to scramble up the slope, the others following suit. As he did so, he thought back, trying to judge the distance from here to the ships. Not too far. Too far to run in time, but not too far for a warning to travel. After all, he'd heard the horses from this distance. As he slipped and scrabbled in the rain, he cupped his hands around his mouth and drew a deep breath.

'Odiiiiiiiiiiin!'

'What in the name of God are you doing?' boggled Leif.

'Warning the ships. They'll know it's us shouting. No one else in this entire strange land bows to the Allfather. That should get our crew moving at least, if not Valdimar's and Yngvar's.'

'And bring the riders down on us.'

Halfdan shook his head. 'To them it will just be a shout ahead, mostly inaudible over the horses. They'll assume it came from the camp.'

Ketil grunted his irritation as he juggled the silvered skulls in his grip, and wasted precious moments pulling a sack from where it was tucked into his belt, slipping the skull mugs into it and then looping it behind the belt again. Halfdan rolled his eyes. Why had the idiot not done that earlier, while they were running, and not when trying to get into hiding before they were caught and cut down? Finally, though, Ketil was clambering up with the rest.

It was muddy, tiring and difficult work, their muscles complaining after the strain of the night thus far, but within a minute the five of them were pulling themselves in among the twisted and gnarled boles of old trees and sprawling bushes at the top of the gully side.

They were just in time. Dust and pebbles were still scattering down the muddy slope from Bjorn's scrabbling boot as the horsemen came into view.

'Quiet,' Halfdan breathed to the others as they clung on above the gulley.

The enemy rode in absolute silence, no shouts or songs or whooping. They rode to war, ready to take their enemy by surprise. The five fugitives clung to branches and trunks, watching scores of horsemen racing past beneath them, the thunder of their hooves amplified tremendously by the narrow shape of the gully. A thought occurred to Halfdan and, despite the danger of moving at that moment, he let go of the tree to which he clung and lurched to his left. He'd been right to do so, and just in time too, for as Ketil's hand came up gripping a large stone, his eyes scouring the riders for the giant among them, Halfdan's own grip closed on the Icelander's wrist. Ketil turned an angry look on him, and Halfdan shook his head – a warning and a command. For a moment, the Icelander looked as though he might argue, but finally with a sullen nod he allowed the rock to fall away into the undergrowth, just another short rustle amid the hiss and patter of rain among the leaves.

They watched as that giant warrior rode past in the midst of his warband, the five of them clinging tight to the wet trees until the last rider had passed. As the thunder of horses and the jingle and rattle of equipment faded, Halfdan could hear the distant sounds of the camps by the ships stirring. His cry had alerted them.

Heaving a sigh of relief, he gestured to the rest, and they slowly and carefully lowered themselves back down the slope, slithering and slipping half the way until they were once more at the bottom, stamping their feet and squeezing the rain from their hair. Ketil was the last to drop, his gaze playing across the trees and the gully for long moments before he finally dropped to the ground with them.

'What now?' Leif said.

'The fleet is fighting the Pechenegs again. That's where we need to be.' He tried not to pay too much attention to the strange look in Ketil's narrowed eyes that presaged trouble, and instead turned and started running for the ships.

Chapter 9

'We're in time,' Halfdan breathed with relief as he jogged free of the gully, rounding a small stand of lush green pines, the others at his heel. The cold and insistent rain hissed through the night air and ran down his face, soaking his hair.

'*Almost*,' added Leif, peering out ahead.

Across the wide swathe of green they could see the shapes of some hundred or so riders, already engaging with the crews, the sounds of battle muted yet audible over the rumble of rain. This fight would be far more of a safe wager than last time. Given the surprise attack earlier in the night, the watchers were more alert now, and with Halfdan's call the warriors had risen and assembled into a wall of flesh, wood and steel in time to face the Pechenegs.

In response, rather than charging the Northmen as they had last time, the riders had adopted a more defensive tactic, racing to and fro along the line, staying out of the reach of their enemies while the archers among them peppered the line with arrows. That situation could not hold for long, though, for Yngvar's crews had archers among them also, and even as Halfdan squinted into the darkness, through the curtain of rain, to see what was happening, bowmen took places along the shield wall and began to return the compliment.

'The riders are better archers,' Leif said sourly as they ran.

'But there are fewer of them,' Bjorn put in. 'Numbers will tell in the end.'

Indeed, as they set off across the springy wet grass, careful with every footfall not to turn an ankle in one of the many deep hoof prints, Halfdan watched the tide turn. The horses began to pull back just a little, and the shield wall of northerners began to bow as men lurched forwards, hungry for battle. Any moment now the boar-snout would form and the crews would charge.

'We could be hip deep in the shit any moment, young friend,' the big albino grunted. 'Trapped on the wrong side of the enemy.'

Halfdan nodded, for he had counted on joining in the battle with the other crews and making the Pechenegs pay for all of this, but the Northmen were already getting the better of the scuffle, and unless the riders were either monumentally stupid or suicidally brave they would break and flee at any moment. And they would be fleeing this way.

'Where is Ketil?' he said sharply, counting his companions in the dark.

'He's not with us?' Bjorn said, confused, head turning this way and that.

Stumbling to a halt, Halfdan turned, the others running on for a few steps before stopping and frowning at him.

'Surely he wouldn't be idiotic enough to head for the enemy camp again?' Leif muttered.

'No. He saw this coming. He's preparing in the gulley, but the idiot should have said something, instead of just slipping away again.'

Bjorn gave him a patient look. 'What did I tell you about Icelanders? You cannot count on them.'

'He's clever, but he needs to work *with* us.' Halfdan took a deep breath. 'Are you all prepared to meet Odin's maidens?' he said quietly to the others.

Nods were accompanied by faces of concern, though each of them fingered the weapons at their belt or back or gripped them tighter. Whatever was coming, Halfdan intended to fight, and they would stand with him.

'They've lost too many. There's only a score left, and they'll break any moment and come this way.' Halfdan fancied he could hear the Icelander working even over the noise of battle: faint rhythmic thumps.

'We'll be ridden down,' Leif said. 'You know that.'

'No, we won't, because Ketil has already seen to that.'

Running back into the gully, slipping in the rain-sodden mud, he could see nothing for the first hundred paces or so until the defile curved around to the right, the first of three zig-zagging bends. With the others still muttering their concern behind him, he hurtled along the gully.

'Hurry. We've not got a lot of time.'

Rounding the curve, it took him a moment to see it, but as he did his arm shot out and he turned, racing for the slope at the northern side and scrambling up it with difficulty, slick mud sliding and slipping away around his feet. With the others following, realisation finally dawning on them, Halfdan made straight for where Ketil worked feverishly. One particularly large and unwieldy tree had grown out at an angle, looming over the gully, and the Icelander had his hand axe out, hacking feverishly at the thick bole two feet above the gnarled roots.

Halfdan had only a sword, which would be of little use felling trees, but there were still ways he could help, for he could already see the Icelander's plan. Instead of working to cut the thing down, Halfdan jumped up, catching hold of a slippery, wet branch and using it to haul himself up into the tree. There, he moved out across the gully among the branches, looking down at the wet, gritty ground some fifteen feet below. Edging out as far as he dared, grateful for a childhood of tree-climbing, he settled himself where the branch beneath his feet was thick enough to take the punishment, and then began to jump and stamp down hard, timing his activity with the thuds and grunts of Ketil's axe blows.

'You should have shouted,' he bellowed between thuds.

Ketil looked across with a frown as he worked. *Thud.* 'I wasn't intending on us all making some great stand, Halfdan.' *Thud.* 'I was just going to trap them when they ran so that the fleet could finish them.' *Thud.*

'Horseshit. The others might think you're happy with your skull cups, but I understand blood debts, and you and I both know that you still have your sight set on their leader.'

'Do not think to understand me, boy. I was carving out debts from enemies across Iceland when you were still clung to you mother's teat. You think because you have some nebulous, unofficial blood feud you know me? You do not know me, Halfdan Loki-born, stealer of ships.'

Halfdan gripped his sword pommel, fingers whitening. 'You're wrong, Ketil of Iceland, and you know it. I understand you better than you think. I took nothing the gods did not send my way, and while I could not declare my feud at a Thing, I have made it an open matter, for all to see and understand. What lies in your past and drives you so remains hidden and troublesome, but it cannot be allowed to ruin others.'

Ketil said nothing, but went back to work, wood chips flying through the thickening rain.

As he worked, Halfdan became aware of the others joining in. Bjorn had pulled his own axe from his belt and was stomping forwards, brandishing it, the blade gleaming wetly in the rain. Halfdan had seen enough axes in his time to know what he was looking at. Some men set such stock in the quality of their axe as a reflection of their own status that the weapon was a work of art, etched and silvered with runes and images of war and victory. Most men, too poor to contemplate such a thing, made do with a pitted blade that had belonged to their father before them. Some men clearly could have had any axe they desired, yet had settled for something plain and straightforward, opting for balance, strength, sharpness and efficacy over anything else. Bjorn's axe was different, not a thing of beauty, but simply a weapon designed to kill.

On this occasion, he was to kill a tree.

Ketil grunted his irritation as the big white warrior all but pushed him out of the way, swinging his great blade, biting deep into the timber with each blow, pulling it free with a snarl and almost braining the Icelander as he pulled it back behind his head each time. Ketil moved around the tree, muttering unkind assumptions about the big albino's ancestry as he found somewhere else to work. There, he settled into a rhythm that complemented Bjorn's, striking on his companion's backswing so that the two axes never met in the wood.

Leif and Gunnhild grabbed branches, adding their weight to that of Halfdan. The pine gave a warning groan and Halfdan felt it judder under his feet. The young warrior looked up, peering between the branches and trying to see into the distance. It was futile. Even without the foliage, the sheeting rain made vision difficult beyond a few paces, and the gully curved out of sight anyway. Settling, he stopped stamping for a moment, clinging to the trunk as he listened intently.

He could hear it then, the rumble of horses. Not the same as the first time he'd heard them that night. Then there had been many. Now there were but few, though still enough to create a thunder of their own, echoing along the gully.

Taking a deep breath, he turned. 'They are almost on us. Finish it quick!'

The two big men glanced at one another, nodded, and both began to hammer at speed, each chipping shreds from the bole without care for the weapon of the other. It was the work of Odin that the two axes never met as they smashed and bit, chipped and dug. The others heaved and stamped, Halfdan watching that bend in the gully with growing tension.

The tree came away from the bank suddenly, with a huge groan and a crack that sounded like mountains splitting. The whole thing tumbled down into the gully with Halfdan riding it like a great beast, filling the ditch easily and neatly sealing it against any rider. As the two axemen straightened, heaving in deep breaths, Gunnhild and Leif both teetered over the drop, the shield-maiden managing to regain her feet, while the Rus missed his footing and half fell, half slithered down the slope. Aware that he was on the wrong side of the tree for safety, Leif quickly scrambled up and over the fallen pine, coming down on the far side just as Halfdan, feeling the aches and bruises of the fall, extricated himself from the tangle of branches and joined him.

'They'll give no quarter,' the young warrior bellowed. 'They've fucked up by attacking the ships and they know it. Now they want to get away and when they realise they're trapped they'll fight like bears.'

'While we shall fight like wolves,' replied Gunnhild.

'Bears kill wolves,' Leif said, meaningfully.

'Not always,' Bjorn grinned. 'And whatever wolves do, *Bjorn* kills bears.'

Halfdan drew his sword and essayed a couple of experimental swings with it, testing his bruised and aching shoulder. He would manage, but he also knew this would have to be the last fight for some time. He was drained already, exhausted from interrupted sleep and seemingly endless running and climbing, and he had already fought one battle this night. He would need to recover and see to a lot of small injuries after this.

The first of the Pecheneg riders suddenly burst into view, hurtling round the bend in the gully. The man was looking back over his shoulder and, as he turned forwards once more, let out a panicked cry in his strange tongue as he realised a fallen tree blocked his path and he had insufficient time to react. His horse barrelled into the branches even as he tried to stop it, and with a terrified squawk the Pecheneg was thrown from the beast's back. He crashed and cracked through small branches, taking cuts and bruises as he passed, rolling to a halt close to Halfdan. The young warrior turned, implacably, and slammed his blade down, aiming for the space between the collar of the chain shirt and the man's chin. The tip of the blade sank into the neck and slid through, and Halfdan grunted in irritation as he felt it bite into the hard ground beneath. That would be a chip in the blade he'd have to polish out over many hours. Straightening, he pulled his blade free. Other riders had rounded the bend now, but were more prepared than their friend and were capable of stopping before disaster befell them.

'Odiiiiin!' Halfdan bellowed, a call swiftly taken up by the rest.

As the young warrior pulled his way up into the branches where he could manage a swing at the nearest of them, Leif scrabbled up the lowest part of the slope to give him sufficient height, yanking the axe from his belt. Peering across the branches, he chose a target from among the milling riders and pulled the axe back alongside his head ready to throw, only to watch the rider upon whom he'd set his sights plucked from the back of his horse by Gunnhild's spear and thrown to the murky ground where he was churned beneath the hooves.

'Balls.'

Looking irritably up the slope at the woman for a moment, Leif grumbled, then chose another target. Careful to grip the small axe near the end of the haft and to give it a flick as he let go, he watched the weapon sail through the air, wheeling as it went, to thud satisfyingly into the back of a rider.

With a bellow of rage, Bjorn dropped from the gully top like some dreadful monster, howling his belligerence and with his axe gripped in both hands. He fell some twelve feet, the weapon coming down vertically from over his head as he did so and smashing into the shoulder of a rider. The sheer force of the blow, combined with Bjorn's weight and the distance it had fallen provided sufficient strength to smash straight through the shoulder blade and a number of the ribs, the rider's leather shirt affording little protection. As the man fell almost in half, issuing a blood-curdling scream, Bjorn simply rolled in the wet muck and rose in a smooth movement to hack at the leg of another horse, which shrieked and fell, pitching its rider forwards.

They were butchering the enemy, though Halfdan knew full well that their initial success was largely down to the panic and unpreparedness of the Pechenegs. As soon as someone took control, they would begin to fight back more effectively, and then the five of them could be in real trouble. The important thing, then, was to keep them in confusion.

'Take their leaders,' he shouted as he looked around for signs of organisation. One rider was waving his sword meaningfully at his companions and shouting at them. He couldn't be allowed to mount an adequate defence, and Halfdan threw himself from the tree, smashing into the rider's back and throwing him forwards onto his horse's neck. There was no room to swing his blade in such close quarters, and so as the man lurched and shouted, trying to turn on the man sitting behind him, Halfdan smashed down with the pommel of his sword, hearing the crack of bone from the man's skull beneath his colourful hat.

The man gurgled and shook, and was easy enough to throw from the beast's back. As Halfdan pulled himself forwards onto the saddle, he looked around. There were less than a dozen horsemen left, after their disastrous attack on Yngvar's fleet and the few deaths they had already encountered in the gully. Leif was clambering across the tree now, drawing his sax to inflict further mayhem.

Gunnhild had effectively disarmed herself by throwing her spear, though she was picking up rocks and throwing them into the press of Pecheneg riders. Bjorn was moving like a pike in a stream of minnows, delivering blow after blow to animals and riders, ducking and moving in the chaos so that he was never in the same place for two strikes. Only Ketil the Icelander had yet to commit, the man standing up on the bank with his axe in one hand and sword in the other. He was simply watching, and Halfdan knew precisely what the man was holding out for.

Sure enough, the last three riders rounded the corner, one of them the giant who had led the warband throughout. Halfdan saw Ketil tense then, and move a few paces closer, ready to jump.

'He's yours,' Halfdan said, 'but when this is over, you and I need to have this out.'

Turning back, the young warrior caught a sword on his own blade just in time, knocking it aside and then delivering a punch to the wielder's face with the fist wrapped around the hilt. The man yelped and swayed back in the saddle. As Halfdan finished the man off, Leif was suddenly among the horses, his sax jabbing up into the unprotected underside of the animals.

The fight was already all but over. The Pechenegs had never stood a chance, already routed and panicked, fleeing the battle at the ships only to ride headfirst into an ambush with no chance of escape. As the men and horses alike fell to Bjorn's axe, Leif's knife or Gunnhild's rocks, their leader roared and pointed up in fury at Ketil.

The Icelander leapt at him and, though the Pecheneg giant tried hard to bring a weapon to bear in time, Ketil smashed into him from the side, carrying him from the saddle to fall to the wet ground in a heap. Halfdan lost sight of them for a moment, then, until they rose like the *jötnar* of old, giants locked in god-like battle, both covered in thick, wet mud, swords out as they bellowed and roared, swiped and hacked.

As Bjorn moved among the last few riders, butchering them with impunity, Halfdan, content that it was over, sat and watched the titanic struggle between the two big men. The giant Pecheneg was good, but Ketil had the edge. Perhaps on another night, in another place, the rider would have been ascendant, but tonight he had already fought and lost two battles, seen his warband destroyed in its entirety, and the anger and fear that flowed through him was sapping him of reason. The Icelander, conversely, was sombre, tightly controlled and given to economy of movement.

'I want his hat,' Bjorn said, wandering over with a dripping axe, eyes on the struggle.

'It wouldn't go around that massive head of yours,' Halfdan said without turning.

'I want it as a cock-warmer, but then it still might be too small…'

As the Pecheneg roared and swung, a blow that could cleave a rock, Ketil simply slipped to his left, allowing the blade to whisper past, and slashed, delivering a small but effective cut to the man's arm below the elbow. The Pecheneg turned, sword swinging in a blur, though the Icelander was already gone as the blow came, ducking low and slashing at the giant's leg. The blow caught his hamstrings and, though it was not forceful enough to sever them, the Pecheneg lurched and almost fell, the pain and instability almost overtaking him.

As the fight went on, blows were traded back and forth, with the Pecheneg constantly delivering killing strokes that failed to land, and the Icelander issuing small and tight cuts that merely wounded. Halfdan became aware that the rest of his companions were gathering around, watching the fight as though it were some sort of village competition.

'Come on, Ketil, finish him.'

'Go for the eyes.'

'He's weak, man.'

'I still want his hat.'

Halfdan smiled at his friend as he watched with appreciation Ketil fighting with skill learned over decades. The Icelander knew precisely what he was doing and, though once or twice the Pecheneg's blows almost met with his flesh, he managed to duck and dance out of the way of each, still delivering neat and economic cuts, each time to the less-protected areas of the body. Halfdan could see what was happening, for with every passing moment the giant was turning gradually red, blood from a dozen wounds starting to soak him through, and with every fresh wound the giant's strength drained that little bit more, sapped from his body along with the precious lifeblood.

It seemed to come as a complete surprise to the Pecheneg when he brought his sword up in two hands ready to chop down, and suddenly discovered he lacked the strength to complete the strike. He let go of the sword with one hand, allowing it to droop down at his side, and brought the empty hand round to stare in confusion at his empty palm.

He was still staring at it as Ketil slammed his blade into the giant's throat, driving it deeper until a metallic ding signalled that it had passed through the neck entire and touched the inside of the man's hat-helmet. The giant simply stared in incomprehension at his killer, gouts of blood spraying and cascading around the blade until Ketil planted a foot on the man's midriff and hauled the sword free.

'Ach,' Bjorn snorted. 'Now his hat'll be covered in brains. I don't want it any more.'

The Pecheneg giant folded up and collapsed in a heap, and the Icelander took the opportunity to spit on the fallen man. Halfdan stood silent in the aftermath of the fight, for all was quiet now bar the constant hiss of rain and the heaving of many relieved breaths. The distant sound of approaching men suggested that someone from the ships had decided to follow the fleeing riders, but Halfdan had another battle to fight, right now.

Ignoring the others, he marched between the fallen bodies of men and horses, straight to Ketil. The Icelander was standing above the fallen Pecheneg, rain battering at them both, but turned slowly, his glittering eyes meeting Halfdan's.

'You are a warrior of the *Sea Wolf*,' the young warrior said, quietly but forcefully. Ketil's face remained neutral, but Halfdan kept his voice low, tight, controlled. 'You are one of the crew. We are brothers now, each and every one of us. If we wish to survive this journey, we work *together*, as a crew must. That means not leaving your watch post. That means not finding enemy camps and thieving from them. That means that when you come up with notions such as this—' he pointed his sword at the tree for clarification '—you work *with* us on it, rather than slipping away to do it on your own. This was a clever idea, but you should have told us first, and we'd have been better prepared.'

Ketil glared at him now. 'I came east with a crew *I* had gathered and a ship *I* found, to make myself rich. *I* was to be the master of the *Sea Wolf*. The sale had been agreed before you set foot in the shipyard with your silver tongue. You with your Loki tricks robbed me of all of that, and of the easy raiding of the Finnish coast. And for what? Where are your cascades of silver, Halfdan Loki-born? Where is your treasure for us all to share? Now I am to obey you? Bear in mind, Halfdan, that you are still a pup.'

Halfdan's eyes narrowed. 'Any time you wish to try and take the ship, I will oblige you, Ketil. All you have to do is challenge me and we'll see who walks away with the *Sea Wolf*. Though bear in mind that I might be a pup to you, but my blade has been bloodied more than once, and the weavers have my path set out for a while yet. Until you decide you must challenge me, you work *with* us.'

The Icelander opened his mouth but Halfdan turned away before he could speak, his ears picking up the sound of many boots tramping along the gully. He was shaking slightly. He shouldn't have reacted so sharply, but he'd been pushed by the Icelander's words, and that last had been dangerous. Ketil was a dangerous man, and a challenge might be readily accepted and could certainly be fatal. As he stepped forwards with Leif and Bjorn beside him, Gunnhild gathered up her fallen spear and crossed to the trembling Icelander, speaking to him in low tones that Halfdan could not quite hear. While he would love to know what she was saying, Halfdan's attention was required elsewhere.

Yngvar was the first to round the bend, sword out and colourful shield on his arm, his men gathered around and behind him. Valdimar was close by with his own warriors, and other lesser jarls and karls behind. Fully half the fleet seemed to have come for the gully. The leader stopped at the sight of the fallen tree and the impressive butchery before it.

'You have cost this fleet,' Yngvar Eymundsson barked, pointing his sword expansively at the lot of them.

'We did what must be done,' Halfdan replied in an even voice.

'You brought on a battle that we did not need, and now we have dead men to bury, and exhaustion from a night with no sleep. This is not how I expect my hirð to behave. Had you not stood by my side in the shield wall like a true karl, I would spit you now for what you've all done.'

Halfdan, mind racing, formed his words carefully. He was speaking to a jarl, and lives hung in the balance. This was no time for wavering uncertainty or shrinking away.

'This was unfortunate, but it has happened, and it is a victory. Your fleet needed a test and they have had it. They needed to wake up a little to the dangers around us. That has happened now. There will be no surprise attacks any more. And now that the riders are gone, we can begin portage tomorrow without fear of further raids while we move.'

Valdimar nodded and stepped forwards. 'He's right, Yngvar. And the Pecheneg are supposed to be cowed these days. My father and his father in turn have crushed them to make this so. If they are moved to independence and violence again, then it is well that we have crushed that spirit. My father would thank us for it.'

Yngvar's lip twitched as he looked back and forth between the two men, and finally he snorted. 'You want this man with you, Prince of Kiev, then–you have him. Take their heathen ship under your wing and out of my sight.'

As the jarl turned and walked away, Valdimar crossed to Halfdan, a warning in his eyes. 'Twice now I have stepped forth in your defence, young warrior. I may not do so a third time. Watch how you go. I have influence with

Yngvar, but only so much. Stay out of his way and avoid causing trouble for a while.'

As Valdimar walked away after the jarl, Halfdan turned back to his companions.

'That could have gone better.' He focused on Ketil. 'Are we going to have any more problems?'

The Icelander shot a quick look at Gunnhild, then turned a resigned expression back to Halfdan.

'No.'

'Has anyone seen my axe?' demanded Leif in a voice laden with irritation.

Chapter 10

'Will he challenge me?' Halfdan murmured to Gunnhild as they hauled the ship up to the bank for the night, men sweating and swearing all around them. Ketil was on the far side of the vessel, something that seemed to have become the norm.

The portage had been a struggle, if an uneventful one. Miles of terrain to circumvent the worst rapids, followed by a hair-raising descent to the river once more. The ships had finally dipped back into the water on the other side of the ship-killer with relief, forging on down the Dnieper towards the unknown.

'I do not believe so. I have sung the songs and tried to find such answers, but the spirits of this place are too alien. Odin only sees us here through the flights of his ravens. But I have given the Icelander cause to settle and he seems to have accepted it. You must give him time.'

The atmosphere aboard the *Sea Wolf* had changed, though. The crew had come to understand one another as only men confined to a forty-foot floating timber cell can do, and the Icelander had bowed to Halfdan, yet in some unspoken way Ketil was still their leader. Since the fight there was a new strain and distance between the two men, and it was reflected in the crew.

'What did you say to him in the gully?'

'That is between me and the Icelander,' she said archly. 'He is something of a capricious man, Halfdan. He still resents your taking of the *Sea Wolf*, though even he will admit that there was no cheating involved and he acknowledges that the gods seem to have gifted it to you. His anger will fade. It has already begun to do so, and everything you do that redresses the balance will help. But other wounds are fresh. There is in his past some tale, I think, of being blooded and failing to achieve revenge for it and this is why, when the giant rider wounded him, he would not rest until he had taken his price in blood. You of all people must understand this.'

Halfdan nodded slowly. 'I had thought as much myself. He is a private man, Gunnhild, but beneath his cold armour, he is a good one, I think. If only he felt more with us than apart.'

'The crew respect a proven warrior with confidence, Halfdan, but a good leader also understands his men and treats them accordingly. If you wish all aboard the ship to function as one, look about you and see what can be done to achieve that. If the sail does not hold wind, find the rips and stitch them.'

Halfdan laughed humourlessly. 'For a warrior you are wise, Gunnhild.'

'No one ever said I was a warrior. I am a woman. If you understood women you would know that we are *all* wise, but we can all fight when we must.'

Again, he chuckled. 'Perhaps I should set Leif on the Icelander?'

They turned to look at the Rus, who had paused in his labours to gesticulate wildly at Bjorn, who was watching his windmilling hands with a deeply creased brow.

'Oh, I don't think so,' Gunnhild smiled wickedly. 'Some things are beyond cruel.'

As the Seiðr-wrapped enigma that was Gunnhild walked away about some new, unknown business, Halfdan slapped his hands together to remove the worst of the watery muck from them, and listened with interest to the conversation nearby. Bjorn and Leif's arguments might not be of great importance to ship unity, but they were invariably interesting.

'So where do they go?' the Rus said.

'I have told you a dozen times,' the big albino snapped irritably. 'Odin's maidens take them to Valhöll to await the end. Or Freyja takes them to her hall in *Fólkvangr*. That is all.'

'But their bodies remain on the battlefield.'

Bjorn sighed. 'A worthy man does not always die in battle.'

'You are missing the point, as usual,' Leif said as he picked up a rope and began to coil it. 'If their bodies lie rotting on the battlefield, with what do they fight the final battle? How do they sit in the hall, and how do they eat or drink?'

Bjorn frowned. 'You ask too many questions, little man.'

'It is only with questions that we learn, my friend. This is why the ancient ways are fading, and why the new Faith takes such a grip on the world. There are too many holes in old thought. A man in Valhöll has left his body behind, yes?'

Bjorn rounded on the man, dropping an armful of timbers. 'All right, fart-face, if you're so clever, what happens to Christians when they die? You have your own afterlife, don't you? With clouds and flowers and women's pursuits?'

That last earned a sharp look from Gunnhild, but Bjorn did not notice, jabbing a finger at Leif. 'So your bodies are left behind while you go to the afterlife. How is this any different? Answer me that, clever bones.'

'When we die, we leave our corporeal remains. It is our spirit, our eternal soul, that ascends to Heaven. Or descends to Hell, of course.'

'We have Hel too. She can be a bitch.'

Leif rolled his eyes. 'So you see there is sense in our ascent to be with God, for we are incorporeal.' He saw incomprehension flood the big man's eyes. 'Body-less,' he explained.

'Bollocks. I have heard the story of your draugr god. He was nailed and died. They buried him, but he walked back out of his tomb a few days later. What about *his* eternal spirit, then?'

Leif sighed, patiently. 'But he is the son of God and not some ordinary man.'

'So he ascended *with* his body?'

'Ye-es,' replied Leif, frowning, uncertainty wavering in his tone.

'What kind of a god takes his own body with him but makes his people leave theirs behind? Our gods are fairer.'

Leif almost exploded with exasperation. 'You, my big friend, are going to get a surprise when death comes for you.'

'Not as much of a surprise as death will,' grinned Bjorn, fingering the haft of his axe.

'While you two argue, the real men here are working so that we can settle for the night,' snapped Ulfr, walking past with an oar in one hand and one of Ketil's silvered skull-cups in the other, a dark liquid sloshing about in it.

Leif cast a disgusted look at the container. 'Do you have to drink out of that? It has to be unhygienic.'

'What does that mean?'

'Unhealthy.'

Ulfr snorted. 'It was unhealthy for its original owner, that's for sure. I bought it from the Icelander. Fetching, eh?'

Leif gave him another wrinkled-lip look of disgust, and walked away.

'These Rus are strange,' Ulfr noted, eliciting a nod of agreement from the big pale warrior.

Halfdan smiled to himself. Unity had to be possible. Even with the gulf of religious division between them, Bjorn and Leif were fast becoming friends. Very irritating friends who could do nothing but argue, yet friends still. If two men as different as they could work in concord, then it should not be difficult for Halfdan and Ketil, who were almost reflections of one another. The Icelander was odd and unpredictable, but they were driven by similar goals.

'Finns,' he said, musing.

'What?' grunted Bjorn, close by.

'Oh, nothing. Just thinking aloud.' *The Finns*. Ketil raised a crew to raid the Finns. To take silver and goods from them, and thralls, too. In some ways, he represented the very essence of the Northman of old. He had planned to embark upon raids in the traditional manner. Instead, Halfdan had tricked him out of the *Sea Wolf* and dragged him halfway round the world on a mission of revenge, all the while helping a Christian jarl seek to carve out a kingdom for himself. As changes in plan went, that was fairly fundamental, and so Ketil's immediate problem could only really be resolved by making that change desirable.

As the ship was settled for the night, he continued to think on the issue. Camp was set, a fire started and food cooked. Men sat and ate quietly in groups and finally, as he accepted a cup of *blaand*, Halfdan made a decision. Spotting Leif sitting slightly apart from the others, he wandered over to the log and sank onto it beside him. The Rus was muttering in some strange language Halfdan had never heard, and running a knotted rope of black wool through his fingers as he did so.

'Can we talk?'

Leif continued to mutter and feel the rope slide between his fingers, but held up his free hand, motioning Halfdan to wait. Finally, after what seemed like a tedious eternity, the small Rus stopped murmuring and pushed the rope away into his pouch.

'Devotions to the *Theotokos*,' he explained as though that clarified everything. He smiled at Halfdan's blank look. 'The mother of God. I have been meaning to teach you all Greek, but we haven't had the time as yet. That was the tongue I spoke, you see, Greek. Most ancient of all languages.'

'Anything that helps bind the crew together,' Halfdan nodded. 'I wanted to ask what you know of our voyage to come. You have been to Miklagarðr, I remember. Is that near where we are bound? I've heard the men talking of Miklagarðr as a land of gold and marble. Many riches to be had.'

Leif sighed. 'Miklagarðr is both more than that, and yet less. It is a rich land, yes, but those riches are bound up into life in the city and jealously owned. The city is incredibly complex and dangerous, like a giant game of 'tafl. You find yourself in the heart of the place and just managing to get out to the edge without doing something to upset a powerful lord is difficult. The men of Miklagarðr do not even trust each other, let alone outsiders. And the women are worse, believe me. No, try not to think of Miklagarðr as a source of riches. It is a source of trouble.'

Halfdan sagged. 'I had hoped for better.'

'Fear not. It is not for Miklagarðr, or Constantinopolis as the Greeks know it, that we are bound, my fearless young leader. This great river empties into a wide black sea. If we followed the coast west we would reach that great and dangerous city, but long-established empires are of no use to Yngvar, who seeks to carve out his own. Instead, we will turn east across the Svarthaf waters and make for the Caucasus mountains. In their shadow we will find a jumble of lands that are almost as old as the empire, with their own kings and armies, and beyond their borders lie tribes who have warred and invaded one another since before the days of Miklagarðr. It is there, beyond the Georgian Kingdom that Yngvar intends to find his new land.'

The edge of the world, where the draugar would be found.

Halfdan nodded and then took a swig of the fermented milk, which tasted both sour and sweet, smooth as a woman's kiss and as sharp as a spear point both at once. He took another for good measure. Who wanted to lie for sleep on a cold ground wrapped in stinking blankets while they were sober, after all?

'So you might say that these lands are a source of untapped riches?'

Leif frowned. 'I wouldn't rule it out, but tales are few and far between, and I can confirm nothing.'

With a smile, the younger warrior clapped a hand on Leif's shoulder. 'A possibility is something I can work with.'

Rising and leaving the man to his thoughts, Halfdan singled out another solitary figure in their camp. Gunnhild was not alone through division or anger, though. It was simply her way. She stood leaning on her spear-staff in the gloom at the very periphery of the firelight, looking out into the darkness.

'What do you see?' he murmured as he approached.

'Difficulties that come in shoals like tiny fish. Have you made a decision about Ketil and the others?'

'I have. And I need your help. They will listen to me, but you have the Seiðr ways, and they will trust your words.'

'You want me to lie to them?' she said, eyes closed to almost slits, an anger beginning to bristle within her.

'No. Not lie. Perhaps encourage? Come.'

He walked back to the camp with Gunnhild at his shoulder still looking suspicious. As he neared the fire, he drained the last of his blaand and lifted the cup, smacking it three times with the hilt of his sax, drawing the attention of the crew. All eyes slid towards him, some figures shuffling to see around the blazing campfire.

'I know some of you still feel unhappy with your lot, and some are uncertain about this voyage. Most of you signed on with Ketil to raid easy Finns and get rich, and are not content with where we now are and what we are enduring. We have fought hard against the river and against the riders who would have raided us, and as yet we have nothing to show for it but the few cups Ketil took. I ask for your patience. We journey across the Svarthaf to an ancient and rich land and to tribes laden with silver and gold. Why else would the jarl want to go to the edge of the world to find his new kingdom?'

The logic of this brought nods from men who had looked unsure. 'No journey is without dangers,' Halfdan added. 'But we are Northmen, and danger is our trade. No treasure worth finding is without peril. So I ask you to sail with me as brothers, for even Gunnhild here with her god-born sight sees great treasure in our future.'

He gestured to the woman beside him, who graced them all with an easy smile and a nod.

'Every man and woman aboard the *Sea Wolf* will have an equal share in anything we take, but you all know why I am here. I have made no secret of it. Our precious jarl will not live to enjoy those riches, which will mean all the more for you. My vengeance is my prize, and so I give my share to you all.'

This raised a few eyebrows, for if his words rung true and their destination was laden with silver, Halfdan's shared could be worth much more than the ship. He saw the Icelander peer across the flames at him. The man's expression was unreadable, but his eyes had narrowed in thought. Good. He had made a start. He'd found the holes in the sail and picked up his needle. Now they needed to find some silver thread.

As conversation resumed he spun to walk away, and Gunnhild turned with him, her eyes flashing angrily. 'You lied *for* me.'

'It was not a lie,' he countered carefully. 'It was an estimation. A belief. A hope. You do not know there is no treasure where we are bound.'

'I know that for what there is we will find a great deal more death and pain. That is the last time you speak for me, Halfdan.'

'With luck it will be the last time I have to. Whatever I must do to make the crew one, I will do.'

Part Three

ᛈᛆᚱᛏᛋ ᛆᚠ ᚢᚾᛁᛏ

The Queen and the Priest

Chapter 11

'That's not one fire,' Ødger murmured, peering through the trees.

Halfdan nodded. '*Many* fires,' he added. 'Perhaps even as many as our own. The Dane underestimated them.'

Valdimar shrugged. 'The night has darkened much since the Dane was here. It may be that the glow was yet small half an hour ago. I fear we must be cautious, though.'

The glow that arose beyond the small wood could only be the result of a sizeable group when seen from this close.

'Do we check closer?'

The Kievan nodded. 'I want an estimate.'

Signs of life might have gone entirely unnoticed altogether had it not been for a curious Dane from one of the nearest crews who had gone far from the firelight for a quiet shit. As the purple light of evening descended across the land, the Dane had lowered his trousers and crouched over a ditch in a small stand of pines. Once he was done with his business, he rose and picked out the glimmer of light to follow back to camp, only to emerge from the wrong side of the wood. The firelight he had followed had not been his, indeed was not that of any of Yngvar's fleet. He had emerged from the inland edge of the forest. Heart in his mouth, he'd hurried away, skirting the woods and rushing back to the huge camp by the beach. From there, he had ascertained that the distant firelight was hidden from the beach by a low hill and woodland, which meant that the same was almost certainly true the other way around.

Once his findings had been reported to Yngvar, the jarl had decided that they could not simply ignore the potential offered by the fire. If it turned out to be some small heathen tribe then perhaps there would be good pickings and supplies to be had, and so the command had been given. Valdimar was the nearest thing to a local here, so the Kievan prince was told to go and investigate.

Valdimar, never a man to take chances, had sent for two crews he trusted to join him as he gathered his men at the edge of the fleet's camp. Halfdan answered the summons, leaving half his crew at the ship under Ulfr's watchful eye, and taking the rest. All in all, with Halfdan's twenty, the small force led by the Kievan prince counted seventy – a small enough band that they could move quickly and quietly, yet large enough to handle themselves in a fight, though such a thing was to be avoided for now. They were only there to scout.

Ketil, at Halfdan's side, chewed his lip. 'I am beginning to question the wisdom of this.'

Halfdan nodded. 'Me too. *Anisychia*,' he added, proud of his new word.

It was comforting to have the Icelander working with him once more, rather than coldly separate, and in fact the entire crew of the *Sea Wolf* seemed to be cleaving together better now, which was partly the doing of Leif. As they'd set off once more down the ever-widening Dnieper, the small Rus had begun to teach them all the tongue of the *Grikkjar* each night, with varying levels of success, and Halfdan found himself fascinated with the notion of a language that could be written on skins, with each shape made up of many separate tiny sounds.

'I don't know that word,' the Icelander grunted.

'Worry,' translated Valdimar nearby.

'Ah. Quite.'

Worry had been largely absent from the *Sea Wolf* as they had emerged from the river into the great black sea, for every man felt good to be back on the open water. Now, on the fourth day of sailing southeast along an easy and forgiving coast, the fifteenth since they passed the Dnieper rapids, they had put in at a white, sandy beach. The fleet was lined up neatly side by side, stacked along the beach almost like a shipyard, the very end place taken by the ship of Gorm, probably the only crew less popular with the jarl than Halfdan's. Gorm seemed to be plagued with ill luck, his crew suffering from some sort of bowel illness, his ship holed three times quite by chance, their sail torn, and Gorm himself becoming lame in the right leg during an incident at the last portage.

'Gorm's luck' had become a common phrase now, and Halfdan could only hope that they would avoid Gorm's luck tonight. The number of fires awaiting them suggested otherwise.

'Do they have nomads here?' Halfdan muttered. 'The Pecheneg? Will we find more riders?'

'I am less than familiar with these lands,' Valdimar admitted, 'but I would say we are beyond the Pecheneg now. We are not far enough south for the Greeks or the Serks, though we may already be in the lands of the Georgian kings. There are other lands and tribes in this region too, though.'

Halfdan turned to look back the way they had come. Somewhere back there the rest of the force waited with

Leif, while Valdimar had brought the other two skippers forwards to scout with just a few warriors from each ship.

'Come on. Let's get a count,' Valdimar said, setting off again down and into the trees.

This time they moved low and quietly, holding onto the swords and axes at their belts to cut down on the clonking and rattling of weaponry. Halfdan peered at the intermittent glow as they moved through the sparse woodland. It really had to be quite a sizeable camp. As they neared the edge of the wood, something made the hairs prickle on the back of his neck, and he slowed. With a low, quiet whistle, he drew the attention of the others, and the entire dozen-strong scouting party slowed with him. Valdimar looked over in his direction with a questioning frown, but Halfdan ignored him for a moment. He couldn't see what was wrong, but he could feel it. Something was tense, silent. The silence of something deliberately being quiet.

He stopped and motioned for the others to do the same. Still uncertain, Valdimar and the others did so, the Rus's eyes demanding an explanation. Halfdan could just see a shape moving through the woods ahead. He couldn't hear anything over the rustle and whisper of the wind in the leaves, but the shape of a man moving carefully was sporadically visible against the golden glow of those fires beyond the trees. Like a hunter downwind of his prey, Halfdan thanked great Odin for the fact that he could see the man against that light, while his quarry would remain oblivious of Halfdan and the others, for they would be lost in the darkness of the woods.

He pointed at the man and drew a line across his throat with his finger. Valdimar peered off and, spotting the movement, nodded and pointed back at Halfdan.

The young warrior was about to draw his sax and sneak forwards when he heard an odd creak off to his left. His gaze snapped around to reveal Ketil pulling back the string of a bow. He'd not even realised the Icelander had brought it, for he usually kept the bow in the ship. Ketil looked over in his direction, arrow settled in the weapon, string straining. Valdimar nodded.

There was but a moment's pause as the Icelander waited for the shadow to move once more and adjusted his aim, and then with a subdued 'thunk' he let the missile fly. The arrow whispered through the woods, its course impressively true, and there was the briefest of gasps as the shape suddenly disappeared from sight. Ketil kept his bow in hand and drew another arrow from his side, ready to nock if needed. All twelve of them peered towards the glow now, watching carefully. After a few minutes with no further movement, they began to creep forwards again. The edge of the woods was coming very close, and the light from the fires was sufficient to throw illumination into the undergrowth at their feet.

Swiftly, Halfdan found their victim. The man lay on his back in the undergrowth, an arrow shaft jutting from his left eye, buried deep. They paused then, as Halfdan waved Ødger and Valdimar over. They peered down at the figure, sizing him up. The man had long, brown hair and a neat moustache, though both were now stained with mud and the blood and mucus that had oozed from his fatal wound all over his face and head. His features were not so flat and broad and dark as the Pechenegs had been, but it was not such matters that drew their attention.

'He's no Pecheneg, for sure,' Halfdan whispered as quietly as he could.

The man was armoured in some sort of thick coat and dressed in baggy trousers with high, solid boots. He carried a spear that held a narrow and gently tapering head, and at his side was a sword that hung straight and ended in a bone handle that was intricately carved. While he may have been stalking something in the woods, his ensemble was far from designed for camouflage. His clothing, boots, scabbard, scarf, and even the shaft of his spear, were of bright red, given counterpoint with accoutrements of deep black. Though he was clearly some kind of hunter or scout, his gear was impressive and, Halfdan was willing to bet, expensive. He crouched and pulled the blade from the sheath at the man's side, looking it up and down.

It was shorter than his own sword by almost a foot, and of a totally alien manufacture. The blade was much narrower than his own though just as straight, and instead of holding much the same width throughout and then coming to a point near the tip, this one tapered gently throughout. The hilt was indeed of bone, and the grip had been carved into a hexagonal shape, worn comfortably smooth through long use, the pommel fashioned into the shape of an eagle's head.

He stared at the thing. It was a work of beauty. He held it up to Valdimar, their leader in this, as to him went the right of first refusal. Valdimar shook his head, and so Halfdan turned and offered it next to Ketil, a man to whom his debt was already large. The Icelander also shook his head and whispered some disparaging comment about toothpicks. Halfdan shrugged and swiftly unbuckled the sword's sheath from the dead man's belt. It too was a work of art. Sliding the blade home with but a whisper of wool and wood, he smiled. Dropping the sword he had taken in the tavern of Uppsala, he swiftly belted on this new weapon. It would take some getting used to, but he couldn't just leave it.

Gunnhild picked up the man's spear and hefted it for a moment before shaking her head and dropping it again. Ready once more, they moved off through the trees, heading for the dazzling golden light ahead. As they reached the last few trees they slowed again, each of them keeping close to a trunk or low bush to disguise their shape from any watcher.

Halfdan felt the breath catch in his throat. These most *definitely* were not Pechenegs. Hundreds of figures moved about a large camp with a dozen great fires. The tents they had set up were not the round nomad affairs of the riders they had encountered in the north, but rigid rectangular things of plain leather, set in ordered rows and radiating out from a centre like the spokes of a wheel. At the heart of the camp sat a single tent on its own, larger than the others.

'Tell me you see what I see?' Bjorn whispered.

Halfdan did not answer, peering at the gathering. It was no nomad tribe, but more like some grand army on the move. He could see a corral of horses off to one side, so they had riders, but there were not enough beasts to mount every man there, so they had infantry too. He could see even from this distance that they all wore those red and black colours, a uniform of some kind. Whoever they were, Halfdan immediately decided that only a suicidal idiot would try and raid them. Instinctively his eyes slid to Ketil, but it seemed that even the impetuous Icelander was not prepared for such an attack this time.

'Halfdan,' hissed Gunnhild. 'Look to their banners.'

He frowned now, scanning the camp and looking for flags or suchlike that his eyes might have missed on their first pass. It took just moments for his gaze to fall on the standards rising from the ground near that large, central tent, and when it did, squinting to see the detail at this distance, his eyes widened. Two types of banner rose around that tent, but both drew his startled gaze equally. Tall spears bore hanging banners in black with a single red stylised design upon them, while the others made that design more clear, for they were long staffs, mounted at the tip with an ornate metal dragon head, a long tapering sock of red trailing off behind them. Both standards bore dragons.

'Odin,' he breathed quietly and reverently.

Ketil stepped across to them and bowed his head to Gunnhild. 'Woe betide any who do not trust your sight, woman, for the Seiðr flows about you like a *malström*.'

Halfdan turned to Valdimar then, a thought rising. Their path was woven, and Gunnhild had told him from the start that Yngvar would face dragons. Taking a deep breath, he gestured to the Kievan prince. 'This is not good. The dragons will fight us yet.'

'No,' Valdimar replied. 'We leave now. Quietly. They are not aware of us. We will be long gone before they even learn they were not alone.'

But Halfdan shook his head. 'It is our weaving to face them. We can run, but we cannot outrun the Norns.'

Valdimar gave him a hard look. 'I'm willing to accept your old pagan ways, my friend, but there is more to destiny than three old women stitching the path of *my* life.'

They all fell silent and dropped behind cover at the loud crack of twig nearby.

'Yašpa?' called a deep voice. 'βγr, Yašpa?'

The twelve scouts held their breath as a new figure appeared against the golden light now, wandering towards the treeline from the camp. Curse the man, Halfdan thought irritably. He was looking for the other hunter, and there was no way he was going to find him without walking through the dozen watchers. He looked over to Ketil, who nodded and nocked that second arrow now. With the low creak of bending ash and tightening string, Ketil tracked the approaching figure and released. The second figure fell back with a gentle squawk. He was out of the woods, in the open, but apparently alone. The twelve remained still and silent, watching.

Valdimar finally let out a low hiss of expelled air. 'That was close,' he grunted.

But Halfdan knew better, and so did the others. Gunnhild was already moving, heading back through the woods, hissing the word 'run' at them all.

He turned just as a call of alarm arose. Five men stood on the slope before the camp, silhouetted against the golden light, pointing into the woods and waving their arms.

'Shit,' Valdimar said with feeling. 'I hope your Norns wove us a path all the way back to the ships.'

And with that, they were running.

Chapter 12

'Why do the Norns weave the same pattern time and again?' huffed Halfdan as he ran, leaping over undergrowth and ducking the lower branches.

Beside him, Gunnhild, managing an easy loping pace with little apparent effort, spoke without turning to look at him. 'A weaver makes a garment with patterns, does she not? A pattern is the same shape time and again, the warp and the weft in a rhythm. Have you ever owned a shirt with no repeated pattern upon it?'

The young warrior grunted a non-committal reply, but he still felt that the three great jötnar who wove the fate of men and gods were playing with him. Against the Pecheneg they had been forced to run from a camp, back towards the ships, being chased as they went. Admittedly last time it was all because of Ketil while now there was no blame to be assigned to any but the Norns, yet still here they were once more, running from an enemy camp back to their ships, and once more they were being chased.

'I was taught that old gods are just demons trying to tempt us from the path of Christ,' Valdimar gasped as they ran. 'This is doing little to change my view.'

Gunnhild fixed him with a look. 'The Norns weave for neither good nor ill, but for what must be, Prince of Kiev.'

'I wish they'd weave me a fast horse, then,' Valdimar retorted, looking back.

There was no clear sign of pursuit yet, but none of them were in any doubt that it was coming, and by Halfdan's mental calculations they would be extremely lucky to get to the ships in time. It was perhaps a mile back to the beach and the camp, and the dragon warriors had horsemen, who should be able to outpace them at speed.

Moments later they emerged from the seaward edge of that thin woodland and hurtled across the open grass, beginning to shout to the others waiting at the stream. There was no need to attempt secrecy now, after all. In response, as they neared that stream, the others rose from the dip, waving them on. It was a little relief at least to be reunited with the small war-band that had left the ships with them, and Leif's worried face was most welcome. Heaving in air, Halfdan paused for breath at the lip of the defile, the others stumbling to a halt beside him as they re-joined their companions. Most were breathing hard from the breakneck pace, hands on knees to recover, though Ketil, making light work of the distance with his great strides, and Gunnhild, who Halfdan had never yet seen fazed by events, both breathed calmly, alert and ready.

'Trouble?' Valdimar's second asked, eyeing the distant glow.

'You might say that. It's a fucking army,' the Kievan spat. 'We need to get to the ships and get ready for a proper fight.'

Halfdan reached out and grasped Valdimar's wrist, causing the Rus to turn sharply, hand coming up reflex-ively, ready to react. He stayed the blow when he realised who it was, but pulled his arm away irritably anyway. 'What?'

'Listen.'

They fell silent, ears straining, but in moments they all heard what Halfdan had caught in a moment's lull. A strange, shrill keening sound, like an animal caught in a toothed trap, but more than that, with an eerie edge that chilled to the bone. Worse, that call was not alone, for other sounds joined it, similar ones, a horrendous cacophony of shrieking and wailing.

'What the fuck is that?' Bjorn muttered, staring off into the darkness.

'That is the sound of dragons coming,' Gunnhild said flatly. As they watched, a shadowy force emerged from the darkness behind them, spread out across the open land in huge numbers. The enemy did indeed have riders, arrayed in two wings at the flanks of the force, moving forth at a steady walking pace, while rank upon rank of warriors marched in lines between them, banners streaming. They did not seem to be giving chase to raiders so much as marching to war, which struck Halfdan as odd.

'Why so much fuss? They had to know we are few, so why not just overrun us with the riders? We only killed a couple of hunters, why bring out the army?'

'I don't know,' Valdimar replied, 'but I've no particular urge to find out, either.'

As the enemy came closer, slowly but inexorably, they could see those dragon-headed staves being held aloft, waved this way and that, the long, tapering tubes behind them fluttering in the wind. It was the dragon staves that were making that awful noise, Halfdan realised. He turned to Valdimar.

'We can't fight them. Not this time and not even at the ships. Not while we're not ready.'

Valdimar's face creased in surprise. 'What? Why?'

'Because they are dragons. Can you not see?'

'Halfdan has Loki cunning,' Ketil said quietly. 'You need to listen to him.'

Gunnhild, beside them, nodded. 'A fire drake is not an enemy to take lightly,' she said.

Valdimar harrumphed, peering over her shoulder at that host moving towards them like a dark red sea in the gloom. 'I am a reasoned son of the Christ and of the *Theotokos Pammakaristos*, woman. I give no credit to such legends as fire drakes.' His twitching gaze suggested otherwise, however.

'We cannot win this,' Halfdan pressed. 'The fleet must put to sea. The dragons have no ships, and unless they are true drakes with wings, then the fleet will be safe there.'

The Kievan rounded on him. 'You are being a super-stitious fool. These are but men, not fire-breathing monsters.'

'Be thoughtful,' Halfdan argued. 'Use the cunning of the Northman that is in your blood and not the limiting tales of the nailed god you serve. If we run now and they do not release their horses to chase us, we can beat them to the ships and get out into the water. If we do not, mark me, Valdimar of Kiev, this expedition is over.'

'*Dragons*,' grumbled the Rus dismissively as he watched that host, though now his fingers were drumming nervously on his sword hilt, belying his confident tone. As they waited in the ditch by the stream, Halfdan glaring expectantly at their leader. If they didn't go soon, they might well run out of time. They were woven to fight the dragons, for the old Völva had said as much and she had not been wrong so far, but perhaps how and when remained to be seen. Better to be all together and prepared than but a few running men overwhelmed by them. As he waited, twitching, there came a new noise.

All eyes turned back towards that army once more as the strange sound joined the din. A 'whoop, whoop' that was oddly reminiscent of the wheeling of a sling, though louder and more ponderous, heavier somehow.

'What is that?' Valdimar said quietly.

'That is death and disaster,' Gunnhild answered.

'Time to run and move the ships,' Halfdan urged, though the Kievan was still staring at the approaching force, somehow stunned into immobility. Halfdan turned at some inner warning, just in time for the whooping noise to end as three small black shapes rose into the air, high and hurtling in their direction. He grabbed Valdimar's arm again and hissed at him. 'Run, you fool.'

The Kievan was the last to move, staring in wonder at the enemy, though Halfdan had sufficient view over his shoulder as he ran and missed nothing that Valdimar caught. Those small missiles crashed to the ground not more than a dozen paces from the stream's bank. As the first one struck the earth, it exploded in a shower of pottery shards, releasing a blast of searing flame that sprayed like heavy, sticky golden water in every direction. But this was no ordinary fire. Halfdan felt horror grip him as he realised that wherever it landed it clung to the damp grass and burned on. Worse still, a few drops had landed in the stream where they continued to burn even in the water as they were carried off downstream.

Moments later, as Halfdan's gaze returned to his destination, Valdimar was beside him, having caught up with remarkable swiftness. 'Dragons,' the Kievan said again, though without a hint of derision this time.

'What kind of fire burns on water?' Ketil boggled at Halfdan's other shoulder as they ran.

Leif spoke through heaving breaths. 'It is said that they use such a thing in Miklagarðr, on their ships, though I have never seen it myself.'

'If we don't get back fast, you might see a lot of it, and very soon.'

Every man was running now, as fast as he could, any cohesion of the warband entirely forgotten in the face of this dreadful development. No man of any crew in the fleet was going to back down from a proper fight, but fire that burned on water and clung to things like ship caulk was another matter entirely. No one in their right mind would fight such a thing. No man *could* fight such a thing.

Ketil was easily pulling out ahead with his long stride and Leif, the smallest man there, was miraculously keeping pace. They could see the low rise now, beyond which lay the camps and the ships, a sight that spurred them on through their weariness. A cry of surprised alarm led Halfdan and the others to look over their shoulders, though not a man slowed his pace in the process. One of Valdimar's warriors had stumbled in a rabbit hole and fallen. No one seemed inclined to go back and help him, for that dark mass of red-clad dragons was close behind and moving at speed now. The unfortunate warrior staggered to his feet and tried to run, but his ankle immediately gave way and he toppled once more. A man next to Valdimar slowed, turning, but the Kievan prince grabbed at him. 'Leave him. He's done for.'

Halfdan ran on, but turned to look back again as he heard the fallen man calling out desperately for help. The man had managed to stand, but could only limp forwards. The whooping noise had begun again, and Halfdan saw it happen then, something that was sure to haunt his dreams for months to come.

The unseen throwers were clearly masters at their art, for two more pots of burning liquid death smashed to the grass close on the heels of the runners, while the third crashed straight into the struggling, lurching figure of the unfortunate Northman. The fire seemed to splash on him, rippling around his shoulders and across his hair like a tide, and where it went it burned bright gold, droplets falling to other parts of him where they continued to burn. He screamed, a sound of untold agony the likes of which Halfdan had never heard before, and continued to lurch forwards even as his skin crisped and sloughed away in the inferno.

Halfdan tore his gaze from the horror of the dying man and found unexpected reserves of strength, pumping his leg muscles that little bit faster as the entire warband now picked up the pace, running for the fleet, and Halfdan knew beyond doubt he had been right from the start. Safety was only to be found out at sea, for no ship could withstand such a weapon.

'Do you give credit to such legends now?' he asked Valdimar bitterly as they ran, though the Kievan was too busy heaving in breaths to answer.

They crested that low rise to see the fleet, where already men were moving, the camp a hive of activity triggered by the sounds of running and marching forces and that eerie wailing of the dragon heads. Outlying watchmen had seen what was coming, clearly. Ketil was the first to crest the rise, a good distance ahead of the rest, and as he ran he was bellowing warnings. Not to stand

and fight, though. 'Make sail,' was all he shouted again and again.

Chaos gripped the camp. Some crews were gathering into shield walls, preparing to face whatever threat this was, while others had already heard and begun to gather at their ships, knocking away timber supports and pushing hulls.

Halfdan glanced back once more. The terrifying force continued to follow them, though they maintained a steady marching pace, unhurried and implacable. Unless they decided to release their cavalry, the ships should be safely out into the water by the time the dragon warriors reached the shore. As the runners crossed that hill and temporarily lost sight of pursuit, the three crews among the warband began to separate, each running for their own ship, every man bellowing a variation on the command to put to sea.

Now, the gathered warriors in the camp had begun to move in concert, chaos forgotten. In response to the shouts, the hastily assembled shield walls had broken apart once more and the crews were busily gathering what supplies they needed and knocking out supports, ready to slide their vessels down the beach and out into the black waters of the Svarthaf.

'Good luck,' Halfdan bellowed to Valdimar and Ødger as he and his companions hurtled towards the *Sea Wolf*. Already Ulfr was busy by the ship, gesticulating and ordering the crew about as they began to heave and haul, pushing and pulling the sleek vessel out into the water. As they neared, Halfdan realised with relief that they would make it. The bigger ships to either side were still only just moving, but the narrow and light *Sea Wolf* was already being lapped by water as she slid easily out. Ketil was there even as she left the sand, grabbing the side and pulling himself up. Halfdan and the others were close behind, hauling themselves into the ship with difficulty, given the weariness they each felt from their disastrous expedition.

Even as Halfdan straightened in the prow while his men ran out oars ready to move into the dark water, he could see the mass of the enemy crossing that rise. They were closer now – too close for comfort – and he could see their uniform reds and blacks, the cavalry on the flanks, archers in pockets among the footmen, and three figures moving ahead, gripping cords in both hands as they swung those heavy yet fragile pots with ease, the whooping sound especially chilling to those who had watched their comrade die from such a weapon.

The other ships were moving, though many not fast enough. One of those pots was suddenly released, and Halfdan watched it arc up into the air, heading for the beach and the ships. They had not quite the range yet, and the pot fell among the campfires, where it exploded and sent liquid fire in every direction, igniting discarded blankets and stacks of firewood. All along the beach, crews watching in shock and horror as that fire oozed and blazed, igniting everything it touched.

Unsurprisingly, the work to get the ships into the water doubled in speed, and men who had ignored that task in favour of finding their less important gear from the camp suddenly dropped everything that was not critical and put their shoulders to hulls. The fleet slid out into the water at speed, ships splashing to freedom and running out their oars in an effort to make sure they were well out of range. Halfdan could understand the desperation. Just one hit from a pot of that horrifying fire and a crew could kiss their ship farewell, for there could be no dousing a fire that burned even on water.

'We're clear,' Ulfr called in a relieved tone.

Halfdan felt the ship slow and fought the urge to suggest they move further out, for Ulfr knew his business and had seen those firepots thrown. The man could judge for himself. Still, if it were Halfdan at the tiller, he'd have given them a few dozen paces more.

The fleet was almost out as Halfdan's gaze slipped sideways and he saw disaster beginning to unfold. Gorm the unlucky was living up to his name once more. As his crew had driven their ship, the *Iron Arrow*, out into the water along with the rest, yet another accident had befallen them, for the rudder had caught on a submerged rock. The man gripping it had been thrown bodily across the deck by the impact, and the entire top end of the apparatus had broken with a crack. More unfortunate still, the lower two thirds of the rudder was still attached to the ship and still wedged in the sand by the boulder under the water. Men rushed over to try and move it, but with the top snapped off there was little they could do. Someone shouted an order and the crew began to heave their oars like fury, attempting to break free, but the decision only pushed them further into the disaster. The water was still extremely shallow there and most of the oars to starboard caught the submerged sand, knocking their rowers about. Off to the larboard side the oarsmen were having more success, though all this did was begin to turn the ship so that it slowly angled side-on to the beach.

The deck was now filled with panicked men, all yelling at one another in a futile attempt to be heard. Halfdan shook his head sadly.

'Gorm is doomed this time.'

Ketil appeared beside him, peering out at the nightmare. 'No escape for them.'

'I suppose at least his run of bad luck has come to an end,' Bjorn muttered.

Gorm himself seemed to have come to the same conclusion. Even as his crew argued and panicked, the ageing karl climbed to the top strake close to the stern and threw himself into the water. His luck had not changed, though, for he was tired and clad in a heavy chain shirt. The water there was perhaps a foot deeper than Gorm was tall, and for a few strokes he swam before disappearing beneath the waves. He reappeared briefly and made a spirited attempt to stand and then to swim again, but with a weird shout that sounded almost like a sigh of regret he disappeared once again, to rise no more. It was odd, though, since he was only a foot beneath the surface and Halfdan could see the drowned man, still standing beneath the water, swaying this way and that eerily with the current as he waited for Ran to gather him up.

Still Gorm, for all his unpleasant fate, fared better than his crew. Inevitably, as that massive force of red-and-black-clad soldiers drew up at the top of the beach, the three slingers swung fresh pots of death and released with expert precision, all three missiles smashing into Gorm's ship, thoroughly dousing it. The liquid fire washed across the ship and its crew, exploding and racing like a tidal wave. It climbed the mast and ignited the sail which turned into a conflagration of its own in an instant. The deck was afire, oars were burning, and splashes that had fallen over the side of the ship were even now burning the very surface of the sea.

Fiery shapes of screaming men plunged from the burning ship into the water, but found no respite there.

As they sank beneath the waves the fire was extinguished, but desperation immediately forced the men to the surface once more, and into a lake of fiery death. Halfdan swallowed hard on his rising gorge at the sight. He shivered.

'Thank God we made it out to sea in time,' murmured Leif, coming to stand at the bow beside him.

Halfdan shook his head. 'This is not the last we shall see of the dragon, my friend.'

The Rus frowned. 'But we're free?'

'For now. We are fated, though. We will face the dragon again yet, for the Norns have woven us a battle, I am sure.'

The little man shivered. 'I hope we're better prepared next time, then.'

All about them now, the twenty-eight remaining vessels in Yngvar's fleet were making sure to backwater just a little further, ensuring that they were out of range. The confirmation of their success came when the three slingers fell still. The gathered army of red and black now parted at the centre and a rider emerged, walking his great black mount forwards to the water's edge, where he stopped.

A king, Halfdan decided, looking at the man, or at least a noble of some sort. He wore a shirt of bronze scales the shape of birch leaves, which was clearly of enormously high quality. His beard was forked and knotted into braids, and his long grey hair held back by a simple circlet of gold, though other than the coronet, he was attired not unlike the rest of them, in crimson and black. He cleared his throat and then issued a short sentence in the same oddly glottal and smooth tongue Halfdan had heard the scouts in the woods use. When there was no response from anyone on board the ships that sat glowering at him, the man spoke again. What he said this time might still be beyond

Halfdan, though he had spent enough time now learning the basics from Leif that he recognised the language of the Grikkjar when he heard it.

When he had finished, the voice of Jarl Yngvar called out in reply, in that same tongue. Frustrated, Halfdan nudged Leif. 'What did they say?'

'The king, Jakulus, I think he is called, says that we have trespassed on their land and that we have earned a blood debt.' The little Rus winced. 'I think the man we killed in the woods was his sister-son.'

Halfdan nodded wearily. He'd half expected something like this. 'And what did Yngvar reply?'

'He told the king he would have to swim well to collect such a debt.'

The young warrior shook his head again. 'The fool. We are moving into their lands, I think. Pushing them is unlikely to lead to good things. I wish we spoke the tongue better.'

The Rus was waving him to silence, as well as Bjorn and Ketil who were similarly grumbling about their incomprehension, and Halfdan realised now that the king was speaking again.

'What did he say this time?'

'I don't know,' snapped Leif. 'I was too busy listening to you lot complaining about how you couldn't understand them to hear.'

Now the exchange was over, even the jarl's final retort unheard as they talked. Halfdan sighed. 'Do we know who these dragon people are?'

Leif nodded, still irritated. 'I think they are the Alani, a mountain people from this region. They have served the Greeks of Miklagarðr over the years. I suspect this is where they learned their fire, for it is a closely guarded secret.'

Across in the lead ship, Yngvar's steersman shouted the order and the fleet began to turn and assemble.

'We'll sail through the night tonight,' Halfdan told them, 'for there's no safety to be found on land. Only when we're far from the king of the dragons – of the Alani – can we rest.'

As the *Sea Wolf* joined the rest of the vessels in slowly turning and pulling away into deeper water, Halfdan turned to Leif.

'I think it is time you increased your lessons. I had not realised until now just how important your Greek tongue would be.'

Chapter 13

'*Ouranos*,' Leif said loudly and with deep timbre as he jabbed his hand over his head, pointing up into the fresh, grey-blue morning and sweeping it from horizon to horizon.

'Sky?' Halfdan asked.

'Yes. And?'

'*Ouranos*.'

'Correct. Easy to remember if you know your ancient history, for Uranus was the most ancient god of the Romans, and the sky was his domain.'

'Can we stick to the language and not the history lessons.'

Leif looked momentarily taken aback. 'A man should learn all he can learn. Even your favoured Odin sought wisdom endlessly, did he not?'

'Hmm.'

Leif turned to the rest of the crew and pointed up to the sky once more, cupping a hand to his ear.

'*Ouranos*,' called the crew with varying degrees of accuracy. Still, the Rus nodded his satisfaction, drawing his sword and pointing at it.

'*Spathi*.'

This one everyone got without question, and Halfdan echoed with the crew the response. '*Spathi*.'

The small Rus now moved to the side of the ship and pointed down. '*Nero*. Water. *Nero*.'

The crew echoed it once more, and Leif, nodding, shouted across the ship. 'Sky: *Ouranos*. Sword: *Spathi*. Water: *Nero*. Three words. Keep repeating them and committing them to memory. To date that takes your vocabulary to fifteen words. Not much, but it's a start.' Halfdan looked down at the *nero* as the *Sea Wolf* swept through it. It *was* water, though this was *new* water.

For days after that fraught episode with the dragons they had sailed warily, sleeping aboard once more against the possibility of the fire-wielding soldiers coming across them in camp. Chary eyes had scoured the coastline day and night as they sailed first southeast and then south, around the great dark sea. At one small town the jarl had decided to put in six ships only with the rest of the fleet anchored out at sea. Deals were done and trades concluded, the fleet's diminishing supplies restocked and news sought of the dragon-Alani. The locals clearly feared Jakulus and his army, yet there was no word of them in the area, thank the gods.

'We are in the lands of the Georgians now,' Leif said as they loaded the supplies. 'I have never been here, but I have met Georgians in Miklagarðr, and they are a civilised people.'

'Civilised?' Bjorn grunted, heaving a sack past them and pausing. 'What do you mean by that?'

'They're no *barbaroi*.'

'Another word you've not taught us yet, runt,' the albino snorted.

Leif sighed. 'They teach and learn, they read and write, they have ordered towns and governments. Civilised.'

'Then I'm happy being *barbaroi*, whatever that is,' the big man grunted again and stomped off with his burden as Leif shook his head in resignation and Halfdan smiled to himself.

Throughout the three days around the coast of the sea, Leif had instructed the crew in the basics – the *mechanics* – of the Greek tongue. Everyone was more interested in learning the words for silver, ale and whore, but Leif had been insistent that they would do this properly, and as it became more and more clear that wherever they went in this strange southern world they would only be able to communicate if they spoke the language, the crew relented. Thus Leif got his way, and his students actually paid attention as they worked. By the time they reached the mouth of the great eastern river on the third day's evening and made camp near the shore on the north bank, the little Rus was content that they had mastered the core forms of the language.

Still, for the next two days they had gone over it time and again as they had laboured up the sluggish, wide and snaking river. While it was important they be able to manage the basics of a conversation, Leif was insistent that they know how to string the words together before they knew what those words actually were.

It was only by the middle of the previous afternoon that he'd relented and begun to walk them through some of the more useful words. At the end of the day, as they'd sat round the campfire, Leif had every man in the crew forming a basic sentence from the words he'd learned. It had made Halfdan smile to see the pride flourish among their faces when they had asked him for water or bread in a new language. He'd not seen such beaming smiles of triumph even after they had smashed the Pecheneg raiders.

Now, on their third day along the river, they were learning new words, and even as they rowed, Halfdan could hear men trying out those words in brief halted sentences amid the grunts of effort.

'Sword in water' raised applause until one of the men, grinning, grabbed his friend's sax from his belt and tossed it overboard, repeating the phrase until he was thrown back on his seat by a vicious punch to the jaw, which erupted into a minor brawl cheered on by laughing crewmates.

'This Georgia is a flat place,' Ketil said, leaning on the rail during a break in the rowing, while the sail carried them steadily north and east from the black sea.

Halfdan nodded, yet his gaze was drawn to the land ahead and he pointed. 'Plenty of high peaks to come. Make the most of flat, for I think we're bound for the mountains.'

'Hard to row over a mountain.'

Halfdan nodded. 'Still, we're bound for the edge of the world, my friend, and those mountains must lie between us and it. Mark my words, no matter what Yngvar finds here, we will cross those mountains yet.'

His gaze slid to the flat lands of the northwest riverbank. No matter how far they had come, he still half expected to see those dragon banners hove into view at any moment, spitting fire and menace. They were not done yet with Jakulus and his dragon army.

By Halfdan's estimation they had travelled sixty or seventy leagues since that encounter, looping south, east and then north, yet they might only be as little as thirty or forty leagues away from it as the crow flies. He was no expert rider, but with the fleet having taken six days since the fight it seemed highly likely that horsemen could have covered that distance in the same time.

Still, his eyes slipped once more to the sight that had thrilled the crew for the last half hour. Ahead, the river curved around a low hill, bearing east once more, but on the western bank rose another hill, and that which adorned it had captured the imagination of every man aboard from the first moment it slipped into view.

A town, a *city* in fact, surrounded the hill, climbing its lower slopes like a stone forest, while upon it stood two great structures the likes of which none aboard had ever seen, barring the loquacious Leif thanks to his expeditions to the Greek Empire. A great, gleaming white building with towers and almost glowing green roofs rose atop the hill. Beside it, a fortress of gleaming white stone dominated the eastern slope, looming above the river. Both structures were surrounded by a heavy wall of a similar stone, all of it standing out against the green of the hill in the early spring sunlight. The buildings, even at such a distance, were the most impressive thing Halfdan had ever encountered, smaller than Kiev had been, but so much more grand and delicate.

'How can men create such a thing?' he breathed.

Ketil nodded. 'This is surely the work of gods.'

Halfdan had heard men in the crew muttering the name 'Ásgarðr' since the place had come into view, fearing they had come upon the domain of the gods. He could see why.

'So long as Ásgarðr has whores and ale, I'm happy,' Bjorn laughed.

As they neared the city, Halfdan spotted between two of the ships ahead an impressive riverside facility, a heavy stone dock marching off along the west bank for perhaps a quarter of a mile at the edge of the settlement below the hill. A few merchant vessels and ships of strange foreign construction were already tied up there, one with an unusual triangular sail. There would be far too little space at the dock for twenty-eight ships, and so Halfdan had Ulfr angle the *Sea Wolf* to the riverbank early, so that they were ready to beach when the call to anchor came, relayed from ship to ship. Yngvar and his closer karls would dock at the city, but the majority of the fleet would have to make use of the bank and stay out of the way.

Once Halfdan's sleek vessel was grounded, the first in the fleet to do so, he gestured to Ulfr.

'Take charge of the ship.'

As the shipwright nodded, Halfdan jumped ashore.

'Bjorn, Ketil, Gunnhild and Leif, with me.'

The five of them hurried along the riverbank and past the rest of the fleet still only coming in to moor. The outlying structures of the city were low wooden buildings of poor construction. A little further on they passed what appeared to be a church of the Christ, its cross of a new variety, the crossbar sloping down to each side as though wearied by the weight and misery of the dour and self-righteous Christian attitude. The building itself was small and narrow, though tall and with a delicate round tower crowned by a dome and that weird sloping cross. To find such a building sitting among the rude timber houses was something of a surprise.

As they moved into the town and began to skirt that lower slope of the hill, Halfdan drank everything in. The houses now were mostly of stone with timber uppers, though they had been ingeniously built into the slope of the hillside such that they only really required a front wall. The people of this place clung to the edges of the street or slunk into their homes as the Northmen passed. They wore brightly coloured clothing, some of it expensive looking. Their skin was of a similar tone to the men of the Kievan Rus lands, and their hair was dark, cut short and trimmed neatly into beards for the men, tied back under head coverings for the women. That strange drooping cross was in evidence around many necks, confirming its importance here. Halfdan made a mental note not to invoke Odin too loudly.

Moving around the lowest slopes of the hill, they made for a growing gathering on the dockside. Three ships of Yngvar's fleet had put in there, one of them Valdimar's, and the more important crewmen were massing in a group along with the Kievan prince. The jarl himself was still aboard his own vessel, shouting angrily at someone.

The ship with the triangular sail they had seen from a distance sat moored a little further along the dock, and a strange sight was occurring there. As Halfdan and his friends came to a halt close to Valdimar and his men, the young warrior peered across at the assembly.

Three swarthy men in black, knee-length robes with intricate belts of rich red and some kind of headwear formed of a length of cloth wound around and around the scalp were performing a strange ritual on the dockside. Each man had a small mat of woven material and knelt upon it, all facing some unknown entity, repeatedly rising to sit upon their ankles and then prostrate themselves, arms outstretched. Each movement was accompanied by rhythmic utterances.

'That is not the *Grik* tongue,' Halfdan whispered to Leif as he watched the performance with fascination. The locals had pulled back to allow a wide circle of space around the three men, though Halfdan could not tell whether it was a gesture of respect or of fear and mistrust. Christians, in his experience, tended to both fear and mistrust anything that didn't bear a cross.

'They are Serks, from the south,' Leif said quietly. 'I have seen them in Miklagarðr, for they have a trade enclave there, though I've never seen such a strange dance. They follow the same god as the Christians, after a fashion, though Christians consider them apostates.'

Halfdan frowned at the display, wondering what an apostate was but not wanting to display ignorance by asking.

'Trouble,' Ketil murmured, nudging them and pointing towards the houses against the slope of the hill. A small group of armoured men in a red and white uniform and with narrow-bladed spears and colourful shields were emerging from a side street and fanning out along the edge of the dock, close to the houses.

At that moment, Jarl Yngvar tramped down the ramp from his ship, still angry, his lip curled with distaste as two of his crewmen cowered at the vessel's rail. The jarl stepped from the sloping timbers to the stone of the dock, registering for a fleeting moment the presence of his gathered men, and then his eyes slid to the Serks with their odd rituals and narrowed.

Behind him, Hjalmvigi was coming down the ramp, his own gaze on that strange ritual and his face puce with fury and pious hatred.

'The priest will start a fight,' Halfdan said, watching carefully, hand near his sword.

'Not without the jarl's agreement,' Leif noted.

Almost as if on cue, the priest crossed to Yngvar and spoke to him in low tones that they could not hear. All could guess what he was saying, though, from the spite on his face, long before his jabbing finger pointed at the three kneeling men.

The jarl shook his head, but the priest was avid, hissing hatred into his master's ear, and Halfdan could feel Yngvar wavering. He'd seen this before, long ago. The jarl knew what trouble violent interference might bring, yet he was clearly already angered by something and with Hjalmvigi pushing, urging, it was only a matter of time before Yngvar snapped and did something precipitous.

Like kill an old man and burn a village…

He turned to Valdimar. 'You need to stop this.'

'It's not my place,' the Kievan replied quietly, 'to intervene between heretics and priests.'

'Then you're going to watch a disaster.'

Sure enough, Yngvar started nodding at whatever bile Hjalmvigi spewed, his own hand dancing near his sword hilt. Taking a step forwards, the jarl gestured at the kneeling Serks.

'Get these animals out of my sight,' he snapped.

'My lord?' one of his men asked, frowning at his jarl.

'Now,' barked Yngvar, and a dozen of his warriors surged past him at speed, bearing down on the three Serks. Hjalmvigi's rictus of righteous victory was as hateful as anything Halfdan had ever seen, and his fingertips bit into his palms as he gripped his hands tightly, watching the display. He took a step forwards angrily, and looked down in surprise as a hand closed on his arm. Gunnhild was there.

'This is not your fight. Do not interfere.'

He nodded at her wisdom, yet he felt hollow hatred watching the jarl attacking men for refusing his cross. History played out once more. Another repeated pattern in the weave. He took another step forwards, but this time it was Ketil's hand gripping his other elbow that stopped him.

'Look,' the Icelander hissed, pointing towards the town. Halfdan's angry eyes slipped that way, and he could see that the red-and-white-garbed soldiers had doubled in number and were formed into a square around a group of riders in rich clothes. A strange box with curtains was being borne aloft by strong men in drab tunics. Halfdan's impetus to surge forwards waned.

Yngvar's warriors reached the three kneeling men, and the first of them placed his boot on the hip of the nearest Serk and pushed, sending him rolling onto his side away from his mat, his eyes wide with shock and fear. Halfdan registered in that moment the fact that the three Serks might be wealthy and important, but they were no warriors, for the only weapons they bore were short, curved knives in sheaths they had laid beside their mats while kneeling.

The whole dock went silent suddenly at a loud crack, the retort echoing around the houses. The line of soldiers had opened up at the front and a man in a long robe with a hefty staff shod in iron had smacked its butt against the stone flags to draw attention. Yngvar's blistering gaze swept that way. The second of his men was busy pushing over another kneeling Serk as one of his mates hurriedly grabbed him by the shoulder, turning him to point at the staff-wielder.

The curtains were drawn back on that strange mobile box to reveal its occupant. Halfdan stared. The woman being borne on a seat of gold wore a blue robe of some exotic material that gleamed like metal and shimmered as it moved, threaded with enough gold to furnish and crew a dragon ship. Around her neck hung necklaces of that same precious metal, dotted with glittering blue stones, and gleaming bangles hung from her arms. But the dress, sumptuous though it was, paled beside its wearer. The woman was quite the most beautiful creature Halfdan had ever seen. With a skin of warm hazel and eyes of piercing green, her nose was small and narrow above lips full and dark. Her hair had the colour of a night sky in deep summer and was long and straight, pinned back with yet more gold. Halfdan ogled even as the woman spoke in a tone like steel lined with honey, directing a command in Greek at Yngvar.

'If you drool, I shall stamp on your foot,' hissed Gunnhild at his side, and Halfdan felt an unaccustomed chill of embarrassment at the comment.

'What did she say?' he muttered.

Leif pushed closer. 'She commanded the jarl to stop and withdraw.'

'Good for her,' growled Halfdan. Pretty *and* powerful. *There* was a combination of which to be wary.

He had almost forgotten that the jarl was fluent in the tongue and his head snapped round as Yngvar replied to the woman in cold tones. Silently Halfdan cursed and made a promise to push Leif to teach them faster. He needed to be able to understand at times like this.

'The jarl told her that these men are an abomination to all Christians.'

Halfdan nodded as the rich woman leaned forwards in her seat, eyes glittering dangerously. As she spoke, Leif continued to translate. 'She says that these Serks are from the Emirate of Tpilisi and are allies to Georgia in some war or other. I missed part of that as her accent is strange. It seems she is the queen of this place.'

Again, Halfdan nodded. That fitted with her dress and manner. Leif continued with his translation as Yngvar riposted. 'He is surprised to find a Christian woman allying herself with such animals. She replies that her husband the king is away to the east fighting… yes, I think it is a civil war, some fight between brothers. The Serks are supporting her husband.'

Yngvar, his anger slightly muted now, the colour fading in his cheeks, barked a command to his men, who stepped back from the Serks, then rattled off again to the queen in the Greek tongue. 'He asks that the fleet be permitted to anchor in this place for a few days, to trade for supplies and to seek information about the journey ahead.'

Halfdan noted the look in the queen's eyes. She did not seem entirely pleased with the notion. After a short pause, during which she conferred with the man bearing the staff, she sat back and swept her hand out in a magnanimous gesture. Leif picked up his translation again. 'The Queen, Borena of Georgia, agrees to host the jarl's fleet, but they must camp outside the city and there will be no fraternisation between the crews and the people of the town. Yngvar and a picked escort will be permitted to trade and to approach the palace on the hill, but no one else. Any infraction of that rule will be dealt with harshly by her guard.'

Bjorn, leaning close to them from behind, chuckled darkly. 'You realise that if the king is away fighting in the east, those men around the queen are probably all there are in the city. We outnumber them, and just look at that gold. She's a plum ripe for picking. A plum wrapped in gold!'

Halfdan rolled his eyes. The big man was, he had to admit, observant. He was also a man of simple tastes and ambitions, and often failed to identify the potential long-term effects of his decisions.

Gunnhild, on the other hand, was more astute. 'One wrong step here, and we could find ourselves facing an entire kingdom and their Serkish allies, Bjorn Bear-torn. Do not trouble that pea of a brain of yours with such concerns. I am wondering at this queen. Something here troubles me.'

As Bjorn gave her an irritated look, Halfdan watched the exchange between the two leaders come to an end. The queen's curtains were drawn once more and the contraption turned and slowly retreated into the street that climbed the hill towards those glorious white buildings, accompanied by the riders and perhaps half the soldiers. In a telling move, the rest remained by the dock, lined up and watching Yngvar and his men, accompanied by the official with the face like a kicked dog and the staff of office.

Glancing across at Yngvar he realised why the ire had drained so readily from the jarl. It had been replaced by something else that was struggling to take hold of the man's expression. Halfdan would never have claimed to be good at reading people, but if he had to put a name to what he saw in Yngvar just then… it would be *lust*.

Behind the jarl, Hjalmvigi was almost shaking with anger, glaring at the Serks.

'Let us hope our time in this place is brief,' Halfdan murmured, 'for it is unlikely to be easy.'

Chapter 14

'Two weeks,' grumbled Bjorn, dipping his cup in the large earthenware container they had acquired and pulling out a sizeable measure of the local heavy, amber-coloured wine. It was not a drink Halfdan had come across before, and he had discovered quickly that it swept the legs out from under a man much faster than ale. Bjorn seemed to be able to handle it in the same relaxed manner as beer, of course, though it was often hard to tell when the big man was inebriated anyway.

'Two weeks too many,' Halfdan nodded, his eyes lifting and his gaze playing across the other figures in the tent. They were all similarly frustrated and becoming fractious. Two weeks was a long time for any man to spend in a tent, especially a man born to wander the gaunt lands beneath the cold northern skies.

But stay here they had. Not once had even Halfdan ventured beyond the encampment, for Queen Borena had made it perfectly clear that the fleet was not welcome in her city, which was Kutaisi, the capital of this land. He could hardly blame her, in truth. With her husband and his army off fighting in the east, she had little in the way of military might to protect her city, and near a thousand silver-hungry Northmen hovering at the edge of the place would make any leader nervous. Moreover, that display of pointless violence at the dockside had hardly done their reputation any good. Not that Halfdan had any qualms about killing, of course, for silver, or land, or love, or *revenge*. But killing for no reason was wasteful and risky.

The queen's shadow loomed over the entire encampment, which was another source of concern for Halfdan. The notion that this queen, who was now interfering with their journey, and who now saw Yngvar alone in her fortress most days, might be that shadow of which the Völva had spoken was one that would not go away. Even Gunnhild had nodded sagely when he'd voiced the fear, for she already distrusted the queen in some nebulous way. That the queen could seal the jarl's fate in her own chambers while Halfdan and his friends loitered, trapped among the tents, was not encouraging.

'I hate this tent,' Bjorn grumbled, drawing him back to the now. 'And I hate the queen. And I hate Georgia. And I hate not having women around…' A quick sidelong glance at Gunnhild, which she parried with a glare. 'At least the wine takes the edge off the boredom,' he sighed.

The queen's soldiers had provided great tents not unlike the ones the nomadic peoples of these regions used, and so a large encampment had been set up outside the city beside the river where the ships could be guarded. A fence of wicker and posts had gone up around it, and men only left that fence with the permission of the queen.

How fiercely the rule of non-fraternisation was to be upheld was made clear on just the second day, when six men from Ivar's ship had snuck into the city with the intent to find pliable flesh and perhaps silver into the bargain. The moment they were discovered they had been dragged into the centre of the encampment and Yngvar's men had forced them to kneel. They had begged for their lives, all bar one, who had taken his punishment in a most stoic manner and who Odin may have taken for his bravery. Their six heads now sat atop poles by the entrance to the encampment, a warning against similar infractions. *Those* deaths Halfdan did *not* disapprove of. Stupidity was not the sole province of the jarl and his priest, apparently.

'Go steady with that wine,' he advised the big albino. 'There's no telling when we'll get more.'

The supply situation had not improved as much as they had hoped. In agreement with Yngvar, the queen had provided sufficient foodstuffs and drink to sustain the fleet, though insufficient for any to be put away against further journeys. Supplies in Kutaisi were thin with the ongoing war.

Halfdan had taken to practising with his new sword whenever he could find time. It was much lighter than those to which he was used, but quicker and sharper, and once he had managed to adjust to it, he felt it would give him an edge.

'*Spathi*,' he reminded himself as he held the blade out, testing the reach and the weight once more.

'How do you fight with such a toothpick?' Bjorn grunted, wandering over with wine sloshing from his cup.

'It is faster than my old sword, and lighter, so it saps my strength less. It's a good blade.'

'It's a *midget's* blade. You should get yourself a proper axe and give that to Leif. He's tiny and weak.'

'I'll stick my tiny and weak foot up your backside, fathead,' snapped the Rus from across the tent.

'*Podi*,' Halfdan said, almost absently, looking along the blade. 'Foot.'

'*Opisthia*,' Bjorn grinned through his broken teeth. 'Backside.'

'How you know that worries me.'

From the very first day here Leif had, as requested by Halfdan, stepped up his teaching of vocabulary to the crew. The format was always the same. Three new words every morning, every afternoon, and every evening, each day accompanied by multiple sessions of threading those words into sentences. The length of those sentences was increasing daily, and they were becoming more complex. Indeed, it had become something of a game. Halfdan had managed through Valdimar to source some powerful spirit and sweetmeats, and they could be won by the crew when Leif sprung a question on them if they could answer in passable Greek. All in all, Halfdan was impressed at the speed with which they were improving. Still, Bjorn seemed to be acquiring extra words, often the baser ones.

He sighed. Even Leif's efforts and the prizes were not enough to lift the mood.

The most common thread of concern in all this time was why the fleet had not moved on. Officially, the jarl was seeking information about the land and the path ahead, negotiating, intriguing and trading. Halfdan had harboured his own suspicions of what was truly happening from the start, but it was now becoming general rumour round the camp that Yngvar was under the queen's spell and could no more leave her than a faithful hound could flee its owner. Under the *shadow's* spell? Halfdan shivered.

Due to their enforced isolation, all news came second hand at best, if not third or fourth. Most tidings came from the locals via Yngvar and Valdimar, filtered through Leif, who had acquired something of a role of messenger when he was not a tutor.

The tidings that came were strange and unsettling. It seemed that, far from sailing into a world of unknown lands and open tribal regions where a man might be able to carve out an empire for himself, they were instead in a world that was already one of empires and kingdoms. Worse still, the region was a hotbed of conflict. The King of Georgia was at war with his half-brother, supported by one of the country's most powerful clans, and it was this conflict that had stripped Kutaisi of manpower and supplies.

In a worrying turn of events, it seemed that both the usurping half-brother and Queen Borena herself were of Alani blood, which put that warrior people on both sides of the war. Leif had attempted to make further enquiries but had gleaned only tantalising hints. It seemed there was a distant familial connection between the dragon king Jakulus and the Queen of Georgia, and the Alani were known to pass through the foothills in the north of Georgia unmolested, their presence barely registering in Georgian lands. That raised a shiver from *all* of them. No one wanted to meet that terrible dragon fire again any time soon.

Fotia Helliniki… Greek fire…

'You brood on dark thoughts,' Gunnhild said quietly, moving over and shoving Bjorn out of the way. The big man simply grunted, dipped for more wine and crossed to Leif to begin their latest bout of verbal sparring. She settled onto the bench beside him.

'It's difficult not to,' he sighed in reply. 'I came east with a simple path. I sought to kill a man who deserved that death. Then the gods and the Norns intervened and I found myself signed on to his fleet. I know…' he said quickly, waving his hands at her as she turned with a forceful look in her eye, 'I know. It's how it must be. But things become ever more complicated. I needed to sink a blade into a killer's gut, and now we seem fated to travel through a civil war, possibly to fight for some witch-queen who has enthralled the stupid jarl, and to face more dragons. And if the queen is the shadow seen unravelling my path, then this might be my journey ending in failure. And even if she isn't, if your words are true, then there will be worse than dragons to endure yet at the edge of the world, for who would willingly stand against draugar?'

He sighed and turned a weak, weary smile on her. 'I am in a moment of gloom, but it is a passing thing. I'll cheer up in time.'

Gunnhild nodded. 'It is a common problem. The *Sea Wolf* is the most isolated of all the ships in the fleet, for we are the only one to honour the Aesir and the Vanir. All of the other crews at least socialise with each other and find release and camaraderie there. We cannot, and so your warriors seethe and simmer. And he does not help,' she added, jerking her head towards the doorway of the tent.

Halfdan glanced that way and felt his lip twitch. The jarl's pet priest Hjalmvigi was on his way. The man had become something of a plague over the past week. Having spent his first days in Kutaisi trying to persuade the queen and her court that their cross was wrong and that their weird rituals were the wrong weird rituals, he had swiftly found himself banned from the city with the rest of them, and had slouched unhappily around the camp doing nailed-god things with the other crews until he apparently remembered that they had a pagan ship among the fleet.

Halfdan had sent Leif to intercept the man the last two times he'd come and the Rus, a Christian himself, had managed to turn the priest away, but it was only a matter of time before trouble arose. Realistically, if the priest forced himself upon any other crew in the fleet, they could turn him away, perhaps even tan his hide, and draw at worst a berating from the jarl. But the *Sea Wolf* was a ship of old gods, and Halfdan was under no illusion as to the result of any violence against Hjalmvigi. It would certainly at least mean the end of their part in the voyage.

His fingers once more drifted to the eagle hilt of his sword.

'Don't even think about it,' Gunnhild hissed. 'You'd get the whole crew killed.'

'That bastard is more dangerous than a dozen Yngvars,' he breathed, glaring at the man. 'He is the will behind Yngvar's zealotry.'

'For now, just as with the jarl, you must suffer his presence. And in return, he must suffer yours. Valdimar values you, even if the jarl does not, and Hjalmvigi knows this.'

The priest came on, and the young warrior's gaze took in the men. He felt his spirits sink as he watched their faces slip from boredom and dissatisfaction into anger at the priest's approach. He even saw one man draw his knife and start to play with the tip on a tabletop. The priest might be determined, but he was likely to sport a new hole if he pushed the men today.

'You have to do something,' Gunnhild murmured.

'What?'

'The men simmer, but the pot could boil over at any time, and Hjalmvigi is here to stoke the flames. You have to do something to raise your men's spirits and to deter the priest from his path.'

Halfdan grunted. 'But what? I've not the wit to reason with the man. I don't understand his god. Leif is the man for that.'

'But you have the cunning of Loki and of Odin, Halfdan. Use your head.'

Halfdan nodded slowly.

'Loki and Odin are tricky and wise, but I doubt the priest will even talk to me, other than to spit at me. Even if he does, the man will talk me in circles.' He paused, a thought striking him. 'Maybe there's another way, though. Maybe the attempt to employ wisdom is in itself unwise?'

'What do you mean?'

He shrugged. 'The crew of the Sea Wolf respect strength as well as wisdom and cunning. Many of them carry Thor's hammer around their neck. Where is *strength* in the nailed god and his priests? Where is their power other than in words?'

Smiling, he rose and waved at Bjorn. The big man belched, an impressive, loud and reverberating noise, slammed down the last of his wine, dropping his cup to a table, and strode over. Halfdan jerked a thumb at the priest coming through the doorway. 'How strong are you feeling my friend?'

Bjorn frowned. 'I could wrestle a ship and hold my own. Why?'

'Because it's time we made an example of the nailed god's mouthpiece over there.'

Bjorn's face split into a grin. 'Now *that* I could enjoy. He shits through his mouth daily, and it's stinky shit, not the arty stuff Leif comes out with. What have you in mind?'

Halfdan smiled and turned, striding towards the doorway and intercepting the priest before he could accost any of the crew. 'Greetings, Hjalmvigi. By chance, Bjorn here and I were just discussing your Christ.'

The priest stopped, a suspicious look sliding across his features. 'You were?' he growled.

'You would bring us into your cult, but you have yet to show any of these men what strength there is to be found in the nailed god's world.'

Hjalmvigi straightened. 'Strength is not a matter of base muscle, heathen. Strength is to be found in faith. A man with sufficient faith can move a mountain.'

'Piss,' Bjorn replied scornfully. 'Giants and gods can move mountains, but there is not enough faith in the world for such tricks among men.'

Hjalmvigi gave the big albino a withering look. 'I would pit my faith against your brute muscle at any time, godless dog.'

Halfdan smiled. *Thank you, Loki.* The man had walked straight into his trap. He looked around the large tent. Almost every pair of eyes was turned their way now. This exchange, made at a good volume, had attracted all attention. For the first time in many days, he could see actual interest in their faces.

'It is a contest then,' Halfdan announced, turning to the crew and spreading his arms theatrically. 'Hjalmvigi of the Christ god challenges Bjorn to a test of strength.'

As he turned slowly back, he had to fight not to explode with laughter at the look now gracing the priest's face. His eyes had bulged wide and he had gone quite pale, almost as pale as his opponent. The man swallowed noisily, his throat apple bouncing up and down in his scrawny neck. To give him his due, he steeled himself quickly. The man knew well that he could not back down now.

The priest nodded slowly as Bjorn stepped towards him, holding out a hand to shake. He looked up into the face of the albino giant that towered over him, then back down, staring at the hand as though it dripped with poison. 'I think not.'

Out of the corner of his eye, Halfdan caught Gunnhild nodding gently at him with a look of satisfaction. The idea had been forming for some time as they had spoken, and had fleshed itself out by the time he turned again. 'I need fourteen posts and ten knives.'

As the men rushed around to gather these things, Halfdan watched the two contestants' expressions with satisfaction. He could feel the energy and excitement building all across the tent. For the first time in two weeks the crew of the *Sea Wolf* were interested and alert. Hurrying over, he oversaw the selection of the timbers. Twelve shorter lengths that were left over from the compound fencing and two of the long and strong portage poles were collected. Under his supervision, as the two contestants prepared themselves without knowing entirely for what, the shorter posts were set up as four tripods and tied together at the top with lengths of rope; the longer poles suspended from each pair of tripods some eight feet above the ground. Bjorn was now grinning as he looked in their direction. The priest's expression was pensive, overlaid with his ever-present sneer of superiority.

Halfdan noted Hjalmvigi's eyes widen once more as Halfdan collected up the ten saxes and work knives the men had gathered. He brought them across to the two suspended poles and began to set them in the packed earth, the hilt entirely buried, gleaming blades pointing up threateningly beneath the poles in a slightly zig-zagged line.

'This barbarity is no test of faith,' Hjalmvigi snapped.

Halfdan turned a deliberately accentuated frown on the man. 'A man with sufficient faith can move a mountain, you said. Surely then a man with your faith can hold on to a stick?'

The priest had begun to tremble gently, but even as Halfdan paused, waiting for Hjalmvigi to panic and refuse, he saw the expression of determination settle on the man's face. 'I am prepared,' he said finally.

Bjorn roared with approval. 'Me too, little priest. Let us match our gods, for Thor fills me with his power this day. I can feel it. Would that I had a hundred men to kill to sate my thirst!'

Hjalmvigi gave him a withering look and then walked slowly over to the apparatus. 'We hang from these poles above the blades?'

'For as long as you can,' Halfdan nodded. 'If Thor is stronger, then Bjorn will win. If your faith in your nailed god is stronger, then Bjorn will fall first. And he would regret it in more ways than one, I think.'

The big albino snorted and spat on his palms, rubbing them together. 'Just say the word.'

'The word is said,' Halfdan smiled. 'Let us test our gods.'

Bjorn reached up to one of the poles and grasped it, pulling himself up and wrapping his ankles around it as he folded his arms around the timber. There he hung like a hog awaiting a roasting. A cheer arose from the tent as men hurried over to gather in a circle around the two poles. Halfdan was half expecting to have to help Hjalmvigi up to his place, but the priest gripped the pole and pulled himself up with surprising ease opposite Bjorn. The two men looked at one another.

'Thor, bear me up,' the enormous albino called loudly. Halfdan glanced across at Hjalmvigi. No loud calls came from the priest, though his lips moved constantly as he rattled off silent prayers. Some of the men began to chant Bjorn's name, but Halfdan waved a hand at them.

'Let this be a fair contest,' he announced. 'Show no favour.'

And so instead, the men of the *Sea Wolf* began to drum their hands on tables or benches or knees in a rhythm, the steady beat like a heart pulsing as the two men clung to their poles. Halfdan smiled. The men had not been so positive and animated in weeks, the only diversion they had enjoyed being Leif's lessons in the Greek tongue, which had been taken in with great hunger by the men.

'*Krata gera*,' he said, and while Bjorn ignored him, hanging there like some arboreal giant, the priest flashed him a look of surprise. Being told to hold tight was only to be expected, but being told it in Greek by this heathen Gottlander clearly came as something of a surprise. The priest narrowed his eyes at Halfdan, sweat beading his brow, and then glanced nervously down at the blades jutting from the packed earth beneath him. His arms tightened on the pole. Close by, Bjorn chuckled.

Halfdan watched the pair. Bjorn's grip was effortless. Indeed, it seemed highly likely he could doze off and still remain tightly wrapped around that bar. The priest, however, was beginning to sweat with the effort, his tendons standing out like cords in his soft skin. He was not a strong man, and not made for such things, yet he was doing better than expected. Better by far. He found himself willing the priest's hands to slip with the sweat. There would be repercussions if Hjalmvigi died in this tent, but if he ended impaled on blades by his own zealotry rather than a deliberate attack, they might get away with it. He was musing over the possibilities when Bjorn surprised him.

'*Roufa ta archidia tou Òdin,*' the big man announced, then shut his teeth in a hearty grin.

Halfdan frowned, wondering at the unfamiliar words, though from the shocked and appalled expression that fell across Hjalmvigi's face, whatever it was had been well said. Bjorn turned his head, seeing the frown on the young warrior and his grin tightened. 'Suck Odin's balls,' he translated into their own tongue.

Halfdan snorted with laughter. 'Where do you learn such words?'

The giant laughed. 'Extra lessons.'

Halfdan turned to see Leif with his arms wrapped around his chest, rocking back and forth in silent, breathless laughter. The room had erupted in glee as the crew of the *Sea Wolf* tried to repeat the phrase back and forth among themselves. Halfdan had a feeling he'd witnessed the start of a new oath among the crew, and would be willing to bet his weight in silver this was not the last time he'd hear it said in the coming days.

Gradually the mirth subsided, and Halfdan could see the contest coming to a close. Hjalmvigi had done remarkably well, but now he could no longer talk, his breath coming in laboured gasps as the sweat rolled from his forehead, and his hands and ankles continually slipped free as he was forced to wrap them anew.

When he fell, he did not cry out in alarm, pain or distress, for he was still muttering his Christ-prayers in a continual silent stream. He managed, by dint of luck or unexpected skill, to fall largely clear of the blades, merely scratching a red line across one elbow as he landed. He rose with a defiant air.

'This,' he snarled between heaved gasps, 'proves nothing.'

Bjorn slowly let himself down from the bar and stepped over, grinning. 'Odin is stronger than the nailed Christ, which we all knew, but you lasted longer than I expected, priestling.'

'This is not over,' Hjalmvigi snapped, switching his gaze back and forth between Halfdan and Bjorn. He turned angrily and strode from the tent. At the doorway, he met Valdimar coming the other way and simply barged past him, knocking the Rus prince's shoulder in the process. Valdimar frowned at the unexpected belligerence and turned back to Halfdan as he entered the tent.

'What's got stuck in *his* throat?'

'He lost an argument.' Halfdan smiled.

'That *is* a rarity.' He took a breath and straightened, hands going to his hips. 'I am the bearer of good news, my friend.'

'You are?'

'I am. Gather your things. The fleet sails in the morning.'

Halfdan stepped back, surprised. 'So suddenly? What about supplies? When will the jarl talk to the skippers?'

Valdimar gave him a shrug in reply. 'Yngvar has secured a week's supplies, all the queen was willing to spare. Their last meeting was short, and guards escorted us from her palace. What has been decided I cannot say, but the jarl is filled with purpose. Come, friend. We sail at last.'

Nodding, Halfdan's gaze strayed to the tent doorway and the distant figure of Hjalmvigi marching angrily away. The sun was at an impressively low angle and the man's shadow reached back for the tent, long and narrow. Halfdan shivered. His gaze snapped to Gunnhild and he was unsurprised to find her looking at him.

The shadow...

Part Four

ᚠᛁᚱᛖᛗᛋ ᚩᚠ ᚩᚾᛁᚻ

The Dragon and the Wraith

Chapter 15

'I wonder whether the shadow the Völva saw in our future is not the queen, but Hjalmvigi,' Halfdan said.

Bjorn scratched his head uncertainly. 'Not sure how you see that. He's tied to the jarl so tight you couldn't squeeze a fart between them. How is he likely to hurt Yngvar? The queen might be a threat, yes, but his own priest?'

Ketil shook his head. 'There was no certainty to that, Bjorn. The shadow stopped the woman seeing the end. She said, if I remember right: "It may be that this other is to bring the end about. It may be that this shadow foretells your own end." What the shadow means is uncertain, but almost certainly something bad, and it is tied to Yngvar.' He turned to Halfdan. 'I agree, though I do not think we can rule out the queen. What do you intend to do?'

'I don't know. Gunnhild says that since we've left the queen now, her interference may be at an end, while Hjalmvigi travels with us. She advises I do nothing yet, until we know more.'

Bjorn snorted. 'If he's the shadow, kill him the moment you get the chance. Shit, but I'd kill him just for the fun of it. The man annoys me.'

'Just… keep an eye on him whenever we're near. We need to be alert.'

The other two nodded and went back to their chest-seats while Halfdan stood at the prow of the *Sea Wolf*, drumming his fingers on the carved figurehead as he watched the steep hills slide by to either side and wishing he had a better understanding of geography.

His thoughts circled back to Yngvar. Valdimar had been right. Something in the jarl's manner had changed during their sojourn at Kutaisi, though the majority of the fleet noticed nothing for they were simply glad to no longer be confined in the camp outside the city. The relief at moving on, the freedom of the open river and the knowledge that their quest was underway once more, was a relief to all, and spirits had been high even as the ships slid into the waters of the wide and impressive river to begin their journey once more.

'You told them?' Gunnhild said, seemingly arriving out of nowhere.

'I had to. The jarl's doom is bigger than me now. It affects all of us.'

She nodded. 'You are beginning to display the wisdom of a leader of men, Halfdan.'

'Do you think his path has changed somehow? Is it still possible the queen *is* the shadow and that she does not need to come with us to the edge of the world? That she has already done her work in some way, obscuring his end?'

The shield-maiden frowned. 'How so?'

'The Völva said that Yngvar pulled at his weaving, trying to unstitch it. And after Kutaisi, he is different. I can feel it. Damn, but I can even see it. His manner has changed.'

He couldn't say exactly *what* it was that was nagging at him about Yngvar, but that it was something in the jarl's attitude. Until their stop at Kutaisi and the man's time with the queen, Yngvar had moved forwards each day with a sense of distant focus, of destiny at work, his sight upon that future time when he would find a wild and untamed land beyond the river's source and would settle there, founding a kingdom.

'On the surface nothing has changed,' Gunnhild pointed out.

'But what is happening *beneath* the surface?'

Still they moved along their intended course, towards the source of the great river, but the supplies they had taken on that last day in the white city had been meagre. The queen had been less than generous in that regard, though in fairness the ongoing war had rather diminished her own supplies, and she still had a city to feed. Their food would last little more than a week, but rumour in Kutaisi had said they were no more than a week's hard sailing from the source of the river. It fit. It worked. The jarl had managed to wheedle from the queen sufficient supplies to see them to their destination, where they would be able to forage while they planned it all out. Everything seemed perfectly normal on the surface. But one look at Yngvar's eyes told a different tale.

'I sang the song,' Gunnhild told him. 'Last night, while men slept, quietly I sang the song and I cast the bones. I do not have the clarity of sight of old Mother, but I see things. With Yngvar all I see now is shadow.'

Halfdan began drumming his fingers again. The jarl no longer radiated that vague distant determination. Now, he was all purpose and immediacy, as Valdimar had noted, and it had showed in their departure from the white city. Leaving Kiev had taken a week of planning, gathering supplies and general activity. Leaving Kutaisi had taken just hours. The fleet was alerted that they would be moving on in the late afternoon, and by the time the sun was above the mountaintops the next morning they were in the water. Something Yngvar had learned or decided in the city had changed his plan, though he had yet to inform anyone else what it was.

'Can you send Leif to me?' Halfdan murmured. 'I am lost in this land.'

They had followed the river north from the great city, ever moving against its current in the limp breezes and blue-grey mornings of early spring. Halfdan had understood that they would be following the river east, yet their northerly course could not be denied. If he remembered what he'd been told correctly, to the north lay the lands of the Alani, including that dragon warrior and his warband. North seemed a bad direction to be heading for a number of reasons.

The day wore on, with effort from the men, slight illumination from the knowledge of Leif, and continued fretting over their journey. For a time, the river continued as a wide and lazy flow, though by the end of that day it had narrowed and the current had picked up in both pace and strength, becoming a tumble of powerful black water. By the end of the next day, as the course gradually swung eastwards to Halfdan's great relief, it became a struggle to make headway against the strong flow.

'We have to be nearing the headwaters now,' Ulfr said as they put in to the bank in the late afternoon, the light already waning due to the high hills all around.

'I told Bjorn we would cross mountains,' Halfdan said.

'I don't know about that, but if the shape of the river holds true then two days, maybe three, it will become unnavigable.'

'The Völva told us the path woven by the Norns would take us to the edge of the world, and we would meet wraiths there. The edge of the world cannot be here, in Georgia, or even in the Alani lands, I think. It must be beyond, and that means beyond the mountains.'

'So where are these wild lands the jarl intends to claim for his own? If the fleet is in Georgia and making for the kingdom of the Alani, any lands here will be troublesome to settle.'

Halfdan nodded absently. How would they reach the edge of the world across the mountains? Where would Yngvar seek his new realm? Yet the jarl continued to move with fresh purpose. What had he learned in Kutaisi that now drove him, and to where was it driving him?

Three more days of tough sailing, using the oars almost exclusively for the wind, such as it was, was rarely favourable, and matters only intensified. The river continued to narrow and in places split into channels so that they were forced to choose a path, sometimes with advantageous results, sometimes obliging a retreat and the selection of a new channel.

At the end of the third day of heaving slowly eastwards the river once more began to turn north, springing fresh doubt into the young warrior. They were approaching Alani lands now, a fact confirmed by Leif and Ulfr, working together to determine their position. Camp was made for the night, and the ships' owners were all called to a meeting with the jarl away from the main gathering.

Halfdan took a seat on the ground close to Valdimar in the circle as the shroud of night closed in on them, bringing its chill. He could feel the tension and interest rising in tandem as he took his place. Perhaps they would now finally discover what had changed. He caught the acidic glare of Hjalmvigi opposite, beside the jarl, who somehow seemed to have secured a place meant only for ship owners, and returned the hateful look.

'We are close to the source of the great river,' Yngvar announced. There was something else there, Halfdan could sense, something unspoken. A 'but' waiting to be revealed.

'As close as we'll get,' grunted Nænnir, tugging on his braided beard. 'My ship will go no further. Her draft is sufficient, but we'll start to break oars soon. Unless you intend us to walk our ships with oars as legs, this is our limit.'

'An *unprofitable* limit,' added Æskil in a dangerous tone. 'Promises of treasure were made in Kiev – of silver and slaves – yet so far we have found only hunger and boredom.'

Halfdan nodded. He'd made similar promises of his own to Ketil and the men. If the other skippers were beginning to doubt, how long before trouble sought out the *Sea Wolf*?

Yngvar flashed Æskil an irritated look. 'Treasure will be yours yet. I have a plan, my friends, though not the one to which we have been working thus far. I had left home to seek a throne, for one was denied me there, as you all know, and you came with me to found a new world. Since Kiev, where I learned of these places, I had sought to create a kingdom for myself in the wild lands at the source of the river, for until then we would be in the lands of other kings. Our sojourn in Kutaisi changed things, though. I discovered much there. There *is* a kingdom to be had, but it does not need to be carved out of the unknown after all.'

Now all eyes slid towards the jarl, suddenly interested.

'You no longer wish to find the end of the river?' Valdimar asked quietly.

'The end of the river is no longer relevant. I learned from the queen in Kutaisi many things that opened my eyes,' the jarl said, and a few barked laughs arose among the skippers, earning them sharp looks. 'I learned of *this* kingdom above all,' he continued. 'It is rich, this Georgia, rich and ancient as Miklagarðr itself, and the throne here is already contested. Two men seek to be king here, and both fight for the crown, both with allies from beyond their borders, yet the queen has no love for either of them. She is the king's second wife, a wife of political convenience and no more. The king's brother is distantly related to her, but she dislikes him too, for they are of opposing clans. A wily man in such a world could play one would-be king off against another until there are no kings left.'

Halfdan nodded to himself. There it was. The distant future Yngvar had sought with an uncertain world had gone, to be replaced by the desire to usurp a kingdom already rich and subjected to the nailed god. *That* was what had changed, and that was the purpose and urgency that now drove the jarl. And despite himself, he found that he was nodding. The jarl was planning like a Viking of old, not some Christ-driven lunatic. Best of all, such a straightforward decision suggested no interference from any shadow. Indeed, his path seemed clearer now, rather than obscured.

'The queen wishes us to join her husband's war,' Yngvar said, shattering in an instant Halfdan's relief. It seemed the queen was not yet done meddling, even at this distance.

'She may not love her husband,' Yngvar said, 'but she supports him. I have agreed to lend our steel to her cause.' He held up restraining hands at the shouts of indignation around the gathering. That he should speak for them without any consultation was unacceptable. That he should allow them to labour on along their way under a misapprehension was worse.

'I am your jarl,' he said in cold, steely tones, a quiet voice yet one that brooked no opposition. He sat back for a moment to let them digest that and then, easing the veiled threat, he continued in more conciliatory tones. 'The founding of our new kingdom was never going to be an easy task. There would be blood spilled and hardship for all, and it would take time. As your jarl, I am conscious of my duty to do what is best for us all, and so Kutaisi and its queen have changed things. As any jarl worth his salt would do when he spied such an opportunity, I seized upon it, and I have kept nothing from you by intention. I have been working through the plan before presenting it to you all.'

The gathered skippers settled into a low grumble of dissatisfaction, a few faces, such as the outspoken Æskil and the powerful Valdimar, still radiating disapproval. Yet all were listening now, interested.

'We will join the king, Bagrat, in his war, but we will play the game with care and make sure that we reach the edge of the 'tafl board before we are trapped. We are not here to help other lords, after all, but to become lords ourselves. It would be to our advantage to defeat the king's opponent and secure the support of the queen, but it would be even more so if the king himself were to fall in the war. Accidents happen in the heat of battle, after all, and with all claimants to the throne gone, Georgia itself can be ours. You saw the gold almost dripping from the queen, my friends. Think of the treasure that awaits us when we control this kingdom.'

'Heresy will be stamped out,' Hjalmvigi interrupted, earning a glare from the jarl. The priest seemed not to notice, driven by his inner monologue. 'Their misshapen cross can be torn down, their dissenting rites rewritten. This can be made a *true* Christian land.'

Valdimar cleared his throat meaningfully, and Yngvar looked back and forth between the prince and the priest. The Rus was of the Greek faith which, apparently, was considerably closer to the Georgian one than to that of Hjalmvigi. The jarl waved his hands, casting the entire matter aside.

'The future of the kingdom is ours to write, friends, but first we must claim it.'

Halfdan's eyes, though, were on the priest. A lifetime ago, it may have been Yngvar's order that tore down the Odin stone in a far-off northern village, but it had been Hjalmvigi's will behind it. Now, the zealot had set his eyes on an entire country. Even children of the nailed god were not to escape his zealotry. Yngvar was not driven by his faith, though, at least not currently. Other forces guided the jarl...

'You want their queen.' Halfdan bit down on the words as they left his mouth. He'd been thinking them, but had certainly not intended to utter them out loud. Such things said openly were dangerous. Indeed, Yngvar's gaze shot his way and the colour rose in the jarl's face.

'I have no recollection of seeking your approval, *heathen*, nor your advice. I seem to remember trying to divest myself of your presence, only to find that you manage to cling on like the remnant of a lost world that you are. Hjalmvigi is perhaps correct that we should have left you in Kiev. You saved me from an arrow, and for that you remain a skipper in this fleet, but do not seek to judge me.'

With that he turned his attention from Halfdan, ignoring him further.

'We do not seek the end of this river now,' he reiterated. 'A little further east, according to maps I have seen in Kutaisi, a valley leads off and connects to another with a total of just over ten miles, leading from this river to a second navigable waterway. That in turn pours into a great river that marches east through the rest of the kingdom.'

'A portage of ten miles, across mountains?'

Halfdan nodded to himself. He'd seen as much from their first oarstroke in this land.

'Along a valley,' Yngvar corrected. 'We have each done more in our time. Ten miles of portage is within reason.'

'And at the far end?' Æskil prompted. 'On this new river there is silver? There are supplies? Your people need payment for their service, Yngvar, and we have enough food to see us to your new river, but no more.'

'Somewhere beyond that portage,' the jarl replied, 'the king fights his brother-in-law. Since we have come from his queen to his aid, King Bagrat can hardly refuse us supplies and silver, and until we can find him, we will have to manage with ekeing out our supplies and on forage. I made every effort to secure us greater provender, but what could be spared has already been sent to the war. There was no more to be had. Unless we wish to eat earth and stone, there is nothing for us at the end of this river, but the king has abundant food for us all, especially when we fight with him.'

The jarl moved in his seat. The others seemed not to notice the change, but Halfdan saw that he had shifted uncomfortably. There was another unspoken 'but' coming here. He waited patiently as murmuring among the gathering died down and Yngvar steeled himself.

'There is more. I made a further agreement with the queen, though it pains me to have done so, and I pray that the good Lord will forgive me. The king's cause is dire and even with our aid, the weight of strength will come down upon the side of the enemy, and so the queen wishes me to secure further allies in this war. At the mouth of that great river, at the edge of the world in the east, lies a tribe of dangerous pagans called the Kipchak. The king will not seek their support for he and his Serk allies detest the pagans as much as we—' a quick look shot at Halfdan and then Hjalmvigi '—but the queen believes that the war cannot be won without them.'

'What does this queen know about making war?' spat Nænnir. 'We need no pagan animals, and I find myself surprised that you would consider it.'

Yngvar nodded. 'Such creatures make dangerous allies, yet Valdimar was right about them. Sometimes their support is too important to ignore. The king faces the dragon warriors, and this tribe at the river mouth are known to have fought the dragon's fire and won. Their lands surround the Alani to the north and the east, and if they cause trouble on those borders it will prevent the Alani from sending too many warriors to the aid of the enemy. Any tribe that can face the dragon and walk away are worth seeking out.'

This raised a series of nods around the circle as each man remembered watching Gorm's ship alight, the fire burning even on the water as his men died in agony.

'So,' Yngvar continued, 'I have agreed to seek them out for the queen. We will find this king and resupply, but before we involve ourselves in his war, we must continue down the river to its end and deliver the queen's message to the dangerous tribe that dwell there.'

'So now you are the king's minion *and* the queen's messenger boy?' Æskil grunted. 'I'd seen you falling under her spell, Yngvar, but I'd not realised how *far* you had gone. I came south serving a great jarl and to earn my fortune, not to play support to a bitch queen's lackey.'

'Watch your tongue,' snapped Yngvar, rising to his feet, his hand going to his sword hilt.

Valdimar waved the jarl back down even as his hand clamped around Æskil's arm, preventing him from rising in opposition. 'Calm,' the Rus prince said levelly. 'We are here to discuss and agree, not to fight. This is a Thing, not a *holmgang*.'

The jarl slowly subsided, eyes still on the outspoken karl opposite. 'Everything I do is in careful balance. I have no wish to ally with some godless heathen tribe,' he admitted, 'as much as I have no wish to ally with the Serks as the queen does. But the more sides that are involved in this war, the more confusion and mutual destruction there will be, the more opportunities for the king to fall, and the better the chance of our rising to the top to claim it all. And if we must face the dragon and his liquid fire once more, which is possible, given the Alani's involvement with the war, I will happily place a heathen warband between it and myself. We must look beyond the civil war, too. The queen herself is of the Alani. If we want Georgia for ourselves then we need her favour, lest we find ourselves at war with her people to the north afterwards.'

There were nods at this. No one relished the idea of meeting the dragon again, and if they were going to, having a tribe of misfits to throw at them first was a good idea. Bravery was to be lauded, but there was a point where bravery and stupidity bled into one another.

'It is worth delivering a simple message, when the ultimate prize is a golden kingdom, is it not?' Yngvar concluded. 'And once we have Georgia, once I sit upon the throne and you are all nobles of this land, then such heathen neighbours can be scourged and this land's slanted cross replaced with the true one.'

Now Hjalmvigi was nodding, the fire of zeal in his eyes, though Valdimar looked uncomfortable, doubtful. Halfdan could find a hundred problems with the jarl's plan just at a glance, yet he kept his teeth barred and his lips shut, for something the jarl said had sent a Seiðr shiver up his spine. The end of this next river, and war with the dragon. The jarl's plan was dangerous and daring, and the young warrior had seen that future promised by the Norns coming apart as they neared the end of the river, but now he could see the weave clearly once more, the threads carrying them forwards towards Yngvar's fate. The end of the river. The edge of the world, where the draugar dwelled and where Yngvar's doom would begin.

'Portage it is,' Halfdan said confidently, drawing surprised looks from all. The jarl cocked an eyebrow at him suspiciously, but as Valdimar nodded and spoke, Yngvar found himself swept up once more.

'Aye, portage,' the Kievan said.

Others were agreeing now, and gradually the gathering subsided, settling into a silence that the jarl then filled. Halfdan sat quietly as Yngvar began to relate everything he had learned in Kutaisi, of the geography of this land, of the river Kura for which they were bound, which flowed past the Serkish emirate of Tpilisi and to a sea so vast no ship had crossed it. He spoke of the king's brother and the Alani to the north, and on and on and on, though now Halfdan was paying little attention. His mind's eye was fixed instead upon the mouth of that next river and the uncrossable sea. The edge of the world, where the draugar awaited.

Soon after that the meeting broke up, each skipper returning to his ship with the news, and Halfdan found himself wandering alone towards the *Sea Wolf* deep in thought. Yngvar had plotted his rise to the throne neatly enough, but the man had paid too little attention to each rung on his ladder.

A portage of ten miles could be done in a few short days, but they were already five days out of Kutaisi, and they had managed to stow not much more than a week's food. The supply situation would be of great concern, and soon. Portage was hard and hungry work. Men ate and drank more over land than on water, so there was a strong likelihood that supplies would be gone even before they dropped to the next river.

He shook his head to clear it of doubt, though fresh worries assailed him. They were walking into the middle of a war. Would they manage to reach the endless sea through the heart of the conflict without becoming embroiled in the fight? And they had to do just that. Only there, at the edge of the world, would they find the draugar and the jarl's doom. Surely the Norns had foreseen that?

Returning to camp from the meeting, Halfdan was almost immediately accosted by the crew, barraged with questions. He relayed the jarl's decisions, attempting to put the most positive spin possible upon the words and to gloss over the many holes in the plan. He could see

Ketil and Ulfr looking at him with narrowed eyes, and he knew that they too had foreseen the problems, yet they said nothing and let him conclude. That Gunnhild nodded her agreement helped. Her wisdom was respected by all.

'That we are currently at the rear of the fleet benefits us,' Ulfr said, musing. 'The ground will have been cleared and packed ready by twenty-seven other ships before us. Our way will be clear and much easier than the leaders'.'

Halfdan nodded. 'And we have a little time to prepare supplies. While we wait our turn, we will fish and hunt and gather. There will not be much to be had in this land, but what there is will be ours while the others concentrate on portage. Everything we can find we will salt and store for the coming days. Others may go hungry, but we shall make it through.'

Chapter 16

'My feet are killing me,' Leif grumbled as he settled at his oar.

Behind him, Bjorn snorted. 'That's because you're a midget. You're closer to them, so the pain travels quicker. The rest of us take a few days to notice now that we're on our backsides again.'

Halfdan smiled. It had taken three days from the first vessel leaving the water to the last ship, the *Sea Wolf*, splashing back down into the new flow, though each crew had used five days of rations in the process.

'I can't hear the barking of my feet, anyway,' the big albino grunted, 'over the growling of my stomach.'

'You're more hungry,' Leif snorted, 'because your belly is bigger than any two of us.'

Men nearby laughed as Bjorn glared at the little Rus.

The fleet had begun to run out of supplies towards the end of the portage, and even early on rations had been halved by each skipper to preserve what they had. The *Sea Wolf* was in a better position than most, though, having had an entire day to forage while the other ships began to move. A few hours' hard work with a net in the muddy waters of the river had produced a large quantity of small trout, which had been salted and packed against the coming hunger. Not enough to satisfy Bjorn, though, of course.

'When you think you're hungry,' Halfdan said, pointing ahead at the rest of the fleet, 'remember what it is like for that lot.'

The men of the *Sea Wolf* ate little, yet considered themselves as kings when they saw what other crews had resorted to, some stripping bushes of berries, even tearing the bark from the pines to seek the meagre nourishment of the soft inners.

With no further complaints about food, the *Sea Wolf* set off downriver in the wake of the jarl's fleet. The landscape rolled slowly past, the river widening slightly with every passing hour, Leif teaching them new words all the time.

'*Ypodima*… boot. *Zoni*… belt.' With each word, the little Rus pointed at his clothing.

'Teach us something useful,' a voice called from further ahead.

'And try to keep your oar in time while you fuck around,' Bjorn grunted.

'All right,' Leif said. 'Something closer to your hearts. *Argyros*.'

'Which is?'

'Silver, my friends.'

A cheer from the crew had the men of the nearest ship throwing them irritated looks. Only the *Sea Wolf* seemed to have any spirit that morning. They settled into the rhythm of the oars, making sentences from Leif's new words.

Another day with growing discontent and further hunger among the fleet, and men from the other ships were coming down with stomach illnesses born of eating whatever rotten foods they could find, poisonous berries from the riverbanks and any fungus they could lay their hands on. Even Halfdan's men, better supplied as they were, were now ekeing out their last goods under the jealous gazes of others.

Finally, towards the end of the second day beyond the portage, the eighth out of Kutaisi, the fleet spied their first settlement. There had been small villages and individual shacks higher in the mountains on the previous river, though none had numbered more than half a dozen houses, smaller even than Halfdan's own village. This place, however, looked promising as the fleet pulled up at the bank.

The locals initially refused to trade, citing the fact that winter was only just past and they were ekeing out the last of their stores until the growing season. In addition, three different warbands had passed through this region on the way to fight one force or another, and each had taken what they could find, forcing the townsfolk to keep their meagre stores well hidden. Negotiations faltered as Halfdan and the others watched from their ships, and the jarl eventually resorted to direct threat. Each crew prepared for the worst, but the town's leaders capitulated with poor grace and gave up what they had. Valdimar, a man to whom pity came easily, paid them in good silver, though Halfdan was certain they'd rather have had the food. The fleet left the town unmolested with enough supplies to see them through another day, but no more.

The next morning the river widened considerably, and an hour later the hills to either side lowered to a plain that was wide and fertile. They spent the next three days sailing in a south-easterly direction, making slow but steady progress, halting early each day in order to allow time to forage, hunt and fish.

Despite the increase in available sustenance, the crews were still on short rations, while luxuries such as drink had dried up entirely. The men of the fleet were becoming increasingly restive. It was with a deep sigh of relief, then, when the city came into sight.

'Now that is a welcome sight,' Bjorn grinned.

'Cities worry me here,' Halfdan said quietly.

'Cities mean food,' Bjorn retorted.

'And uncertainty. We're in the middle of a civil war, Bjorn. Last time we were in a city, the entire point of our journey changed. I'd as soon avoid such a place.'

'Pah,' was the big albino's dismissive response as they all took in the vista.

A mass of roofs rose from a busy riverbank just downstream of a confluence of two rivers, up the slope of a huge hill the shape of an upturned merchant ship and fully a quarter of a mile long. The city was sizeable, but it was that which crowned the hill that drew every eye, for a fortress with high walls and many towers rose atop the mound, colourful pennants snapping up there in the breeze.

'Fortresses mean armies,' Ketil noted sourly.

'The jarl says we will put in and trade,' bellowed someone from the ship in front, passing Yngvar's word back across the fleet. Halfdan chewed his lip pensively. The last time the jarl had tried to trade, he'd resorted to threat. As Ketil had noted a fortress meant an army, and an army made threats dangerous.

Sure enough, as the ships slowed and closed on the city, Halfdan could see small groups of armed men moving through the streets and making for the riverside, where a dock serviced a number of small fishing vessels. The overall air was less than amicable and, with a nod to Ulfr,

Halfdan had his steersman guide the *Sea Wolf* between two larger ships, closer to the heart of the fleet than their usual position, and near to Valdimar's vessel, the only one he felt he could count on in times of trouble.

This looked very much like such a time.

He squinted up at the fortress. Flags were flapping up there. They were too far away to make out any detail, but what he could see was that they were red and white in hue. Turning to Leif and Gunnhild, who stood nearby murmuring about destiny and its various perceived divine sources as they peered at the city, he cleared his throat. 'The banners up there, can you see them?'

They looked up at the crest of that great hill, both shaking their heads. 'I can see the colours but no more. Why?'

'We're walking into the middle of a civil war, so it would be nice to know who's in charge here. Red and white were the queen's colours in Kutaisi. They might be allies, though they don't look very friendly.'

Those armed men were converging on the dock, towards which Yngvar's ship was now making. A rough head count put them at perhaps fifty or sixty men, which was no real worry for a fleet of this size, but the question was: were they all the city had to offer? There was a war going on around here, which meant that it was distinctly possible most of the fighting force were away with one side or the other. But the presence of that looming fortress up the slope also offered the worrying possibility that this city remained garrisoned, and if that was the case there could be thousands more up there within those walls waiting to pour down upon them.

As the jarl's ship closed on the dock, the fleet fell quiet, every ear straining to hear the coming exchange, so that the scene became eerie, so many silent men with just the rush and stutter of the water and the groan and creak of timber and ropes on the vessels. Thanks to their central position, Halfdan was close enough to pick up the first words as the jarl stood proud in the prow of his ship, addressing the waiting men on the dock.

He tried to understand the exchange, and was pleased to discover that he could pick up parts of it, and the whole thing felt faintly familiar, though he was as yet too restricted in his words to pick out more than those odd parts. Leif leaned close, understanding.

'The jarl has offered trade. Furs, silver and amber in return for food and drink.'

Halfdan nodded. It was a good approach. His spirits sagged though as he watched a gaunt man in a black robe step forwards. The official rattled off a reply, and Leif continued. 'He says they have no need for such trinkets, and the food they have stored is all accounted for.'

Yngvar's voice took on an edge. To the townsfolk it probably sounded menacing, though Halfdan could detect a hint of desperation in it too. The skippers of the fleet, especially outspoken and powerful ones like Nænnir and Æskil, were becoming fractious and angry, and he had to secure them supplies soon, or he might well be looking at a civil war of his own. Halfdan bit into his cheek in irritation, willing the man in black to acquiesce and feed the fleet. Clearly it was not going to happen.

'The local has told Yngvar to leave. The jarl does not look pleased.'

'I can see that. I don't need the picture translating, Leif.' Halfdan found himself fretting. 'Yngvar would be best served cutting his losses here and facing the anger of his own fleet.'

'What?'

'Our fleet could take the defenders on the dock, but there are two problems. Firstly, only Yngvar's ship is close enough to launch an attack without manoeuvring midstream, and secondly, if that castle on the hill turns out to house a garrison of thousands, we could be neck deep in shit in minutes. Either way, the jarl needs to keep his temper in check and back off.'

His teeth ground together, for he knew the likelihood of that.

'The jarl has given an ultimatum,' Leif reported, a hand cupped to his ear. 'He says he needs three days' food for his fleet and will leave in peace. The locals are defiant. Yngvar has told them that their queen sends us to war and it is their *duty* to feed us. He has withdrawn his offer of trade now in favour of a straight demand.'

Halfdan's hand went to the hilt of his sword and his eyes rose up the hillside. Sure enough, he could see men pouring down the sloping road from that fortress. This was not an easy proposition. The jarl was walking into disaster. No, not walking, jogging.

'The local says that Yngvar does not fool him,' Leif added. 'He knows that the *Varangoi* serve Liparit and the usurper against the king.'

'*Varangoi?*'

'It's the Greek name for Northmen. It seems that the emperor in Miklagarðr has sent *his* Northmen to aid the enemy. That could be a problem. The guard are commanded by Harald Harðráði, and his reputation back in Kiev is fierce.'

Halfdan huffed. Things were about to get nasty. He turned to the rudder. 'Ulfr, can you get us to the riverbank?'

The short Svear frowned. 'Not easily. We're not at the back of the fleet now, but closer to the middle. I'll piss off a few ships doing it.'

'Do it anyway. Get us close to the jarl's ship, close to the bank.'

As Ulfr, complaining, shouted orders to the rowers and the ship began to backwater from between the two larger vessels, Bjorn settled at Halfdan's side. 'Why?'

'There's going to be a fight, and we need to make sure Yngvar doesn't get himself spitted.'

'Why?'

'If some lucky Georgian puts a spear through his gut, my blood debt goes unpaid, Bjorn. Nobody other than me gets to finish the jarl. If that means saving his murderous backside, then so be it.'

Bjorn frowned. 'I meant why will there be a fight?'

'He can't afford to leave without supplies, and these men think we're the enemy. Reinforcements are coming from the hill, and it'll take time for the ships to land. This is going to get bloody and get there quickly.'

Ketil, having apparently either overheard or come independently to the same conclusion, began moving about the boat, telling the oarsmen to be ready for a fight as he adjusted the hang of his sword and the throwing axe tucked into the back of his belt. They backwatered clear of the fleet and as Ulfr expertly guided them off towards the left bank, slipping around the edge of the fleet that remained settled midstream, they began to hear the exchange once more. From the volume and tone of the words, all negotiation had failed and what was being exchanged now were simply insults and threats.

'Why hasn't he given the order for the fleet to land yet?' Halfdan fumed. 'Take us to the dock.'

As they slid towards that stone embankment, finally the jarl's patience cracked and he turned, yelling to his fleet, shouting the call to battle. Ships lurched into motion, struggling towards the bank, vying with one another for the little space there was. Halfdan's early decision had claimed him a place, though, and as the northern army roared their fury, and the ships sluggishly closed on the dock, the *Sea Wolf* slammed against the wet stones, bouncing twice before grinding to a halt with a ligneous squeal.

Two of the men jumped from the ship with mooring ropes, making for the wooden posts that jutted from the ground at intervals. The rest of the men, including Ulfr who usually remained behind with the ship, leapt over the strake, drawing axes and swords, grasping their shields where they sat hooked over the side, and landing reading for trouble.

Halfdan reached for his own shield, which Ulfr had miraculously repaired and which Leif had obligingly and very competently re-painted with the three wolves, Geri, Freki, Odin's wolves, and Fenrir who would swallow the great god at the end of days, and drew that short, gleaming Alani blade. A quick glance along the dock showed that Yngvar's ship had also begun to disgorge its load onto the bank, though it had moored prow-first, so disembarkation was slow. There would be irritation among the other skippers that Halfdan's ship was moored side-on and taking up a lot of space, but he cared not for it allowed his men to disembark much faster.

The crew of the *Sea Wolf* were now jogging along the dockside, making for the jarl and his men, who were disembarking slowly two at a time from the prow as other ships began to reach the bank in stages. Halfdan roared with his men and hurtled for the jarl's growing predicament as the town's defenders moved from the city's streets to stop him. Already there were twice as many of them as there were of Yngvar's warriors, without any reinforcements from the hill. Curse the jarl and his violent impulsiveness.

Halfdan broke into a run, using precious energy he knew he should save for the fight to propel him towards trouble, racing past his own jogging crewmen. Yngvar was lined up with a dozen warriors, roaring some Christian chant that seemed to be a prayer for strength from Halfdan's limited understanding of the tongue. They held their shields up and brandished their weapons, trying to cover the disembarking of the rest of their crew as the soldiers closed on them, heavy boots crunching on gravel and rock as their spears came down like a horizontal forest.

Something drew Halfdan's attention as he ran. Why, he couldn't say, but out of the corner of his eye, he saw further movement back among the buildings at the town's edge. Narrowing his eyes, he squinted into the shadows and was rewarded with clarity for just a moment.

Turning, he waved his arm and then pointed at the houses. 'Archers!'

As he veered away from the riverbank, leaving the jarl and his men to face the spears, Halfdan was grateful to hear the bulk of his crew follow suit, racing after him towards those archers now emerging from the houses. The bowmen settled into a line, a score of men long, and nocked arrows to their strange, elegantly double-curved bows. As the Northmen bore down on their flank, a few faces turned their way, but registered no fear as they returned to concentrating on their shots. The reason for their unexpected confidence came clear with the first volley.

As the bowmen released their arrows in perfect unison, a third group of soldiers burst from the street nearby at a run, shields up, swords out and bellowing in their native tongue, cutting Halfdan and his men off from the archers. The young warrior's eyes slid right to the gathering Northmen on the dockside, pouring from Yngvar's ship. The first volley of arrows had been good, but the crews had been ready, and had dropped to a knee behind their wall of shields. Here and there a gap showed as a man writhed on the ground with a shaft jutting from flesh, crying out in pain, but the spaces were closing up as fresh warriors arrived. The real danger was still to come, though. While they were kneeling and protecting themselves from the arrows, the spearmen were closing on them, and they couldn't defend against this main force. Yngvar's time was almost up. The bastard was in real danger now.

Halfdan grunted at his impotency. The last thing he wanted was for Yngvar to gain a heroic death from someone else, yet it looked very likely that that was about to happen. He was aware of his friends closing with him ahead of the crew, and glanced over his shoulder at them. 'Bjorn, take the crew and kill the footmen. Ketil, with me.'

And with that he veered off to his right and summoned yet more speed, exhausting himself as he sprinted now as fast as his legs would carry him. Ketil, huge and rangy, was keeping up with him, balanced handaxe at the ready and shield up. As the bulk of the crew engaged the newly arriving soldiers, Halfdan and Ketil, racing like the wind, skirted round ahead of them, making for those archers. As the pair bore down on them, the bowmen released their second volley.

'Thor's balls!' roared Ketil as he stooped, pulling back his hand to one side and flinging it forwards to release his throwing axe low.

Halfdan blinked in surprise. He'd seen men throw axes many times, from over the shoulder and adding a flick to spin the weapon in flight, but he'd never seen a throw like this. The axe went underarm at knee height, bouncing from the ground halfway between the pair and their prey, raising a small spray of dust and grit. It then ploughed into the legs of the archers. The first man screamed and fell to the side, his leg smashed as the rear of the heavy iron head crashed into his shin, the weapon carrying on and cracking the bone of another man above the ankle before bouncing a second time and coming to a halt as it smacked blade-first into a third man. The chaos was instant as the wounded men fell into their companions and the whole line of bowmen lost their focus.

Ketil now drew his sword and he and Halfdan ploughed into the block of archers, who were utterly unprepared, their own blades still at their sides, bows in hand, having relied upon the protection of the infantry.

As they struggled to draw swords, Ketil crashed in among them, chopping his blade down into the mass, rewarded with a scream and a spray of blood. Halfdan swung the gleaming, straight, eagle-hilted blade he had taken from the dragon warrior, hacking clean through an arm that had dropped a bow and was reaching for the hilt of a sword. The man hollered his shock and agony, and Halfdan sent a brief silent prayer of thanks up to Odin for allowing him to take ownership of such a fine weapon. Never had he seen a blade cut neatly through a limb before, and he was grateful now that he had taken every chance to practise with it since they had neared Georgian lands. It was a very different proposition to a northern blade.

Indeed, as he and Ketil waded into the poorly armoured and largely unprepared bowmen, cutting them down like a field of wheat, he was further impressed. The blade was considerably shorter than the ones to which he was used, yet that reduction made all the difference in the press of men, for he found that he could pull back and cut and stab much easier than Ketil close by, who was grunting curses as he tried to find room to swing his big, heavy sword.

It was the work of a minute and no more to dismember the archers, and as the last of them fell Halfdan wrenched the blade from a man's gut with a tortuous sucking sound, planting his foot on the man's thigh to aid him in the withdrawal.

Straightening, panting, he looked about him. A trickle of blood ran into his eye from some scratch he'd taken during the fight, and he blinked it away, heedless of such minor damage. He'd escaped without a noticeable wound, and that was more than he could have hoped. Mind you, he was close to critical exhaustion now, the sword heavy in his hand.

His crew were fully engaged with those reinforcements who had come to defend the archers, and among them he could see the big shape of Bjorn, towering above the locals as he bellowed the name 'Thor' over and over again with each sweep and chop of his great axe. He'd either lost or abandoned his shield and was clutching the great weapon in both hands. May their gods help anyone who got in the way of that thing, for no amount of armour would.

The reserves and the archers being effectively out of the fight, his attention turned to the dockside. With the flights of arrows having stopped, the jarl and his crew had been able to abandon their defensive crouch and had risen to face the spearmen. The fight was now on properly. Two other dragon ships had begun to pour their crews out onto the dock, and they were piling in to help Yngvar with his fight. It would be a hard struggle, but with every new warrior that arrived from the water, the result would be more and more certain.

'Halfdan!'

He spun at the familiar voice to see Gunnhild standing in the open, clear of the fight, waving her spear to attract his attention. As he turned to her, she jabbed her finger upwards, away from the river. He followed the gesture and it took a moment before he realised what she was indicating. He smiled grimly at the sight. Whoever was in charge up at that hilltop fortress had apparently decided that defending the town was not worth the potential loss, for those men who had been issuing from the gate and out onto the road had turned and were now pouring back into the great arch, returning to their castle.

They were going to win. Yngvar would survive, the crew would get their supplies, and all would be good.

It was then that his eyes, drifting back down from the hilltop, fell upon the figures. Two men had emerged onto the gentle slope of a stone-tiled roof. That one of them was carrying a bow would not have worried Halfdan unduly, yet with a shiver of Seiðr that crawled across his skin he saw that the second figure was that black-robed official who had exchanged verbal spars with Yngvar at the dockside. The man had retreated when the fighting started, yet his argument was not over, and Halfdan felt certain the official was determined to get in the last word despite the fact that the town's soldiers had clearly failed and all was lost.

He turned to Ketil, pointing up at the two men with his blade. 'Get them!'

The lanky Icelander frowned for a moment, then, spotting the pair on the roof, stooped, laying down his blade and plucking a bow and an arrow from the carnage they had wrought. Still, even if Ketil was that good, he wouldn't be quick enough, for the bowman on the roof was already drawing back the string. Halfdan started to run.

Almost as though the gods had taken against Yngvar, a gap opened up in the rapidly diminishing crowd of spearmen, revealing the jarl standing in the open, heaving in exhausted breaths as he recovered from his exertions. Yngvar was lightly wounded, and his shield had been hacked to pieces, little more now than a dented boss and some kindling hanging from his left hand. The jarl thought himself safe though, his men with the upper hand in the dockside fight, the archers taken down by the *Sea Wolf*'s crew. No one over there had seen the danger from the roof.

The effort burned in Halfdan's legs and the fire of every heaved breath seared his chest as he plunged into that gap. Oddly, and this was something he could only put down to the power of Odin, the world of the battle seemed to melt away into sluggish slow motion, the sounds of furious fighting dulled to a low murmur in his ears. It was in this almost muted quiet that he swore later he had heard the 'thwack' of an arrow released hundreds of paces behind him on a rooftop.

Even as his head turned he leapt, throwing up his repaired and unmarked wolf-shield.

The arrow thudded into the timbers, the tip bursting through close to his wrist, and the jump had been so desperate that he had no time to recover and landed badly. Instead of a neat roll, he struck the ground hard and face first, sliding to a halt with a groan. As he rolled over, spent and aching, the shield jamming awkwardly on the ground as the shaft prevented it from lying flat, he frowned at the strangest of sights. Yngvar was staring at him in shock, and the warriors of the jarl's ship beside him were making the sign of their nailed god's cross over their breast.

Chest rising and falling with burning pain, limbs like jelly and lacking the strength even to rise to a knee, Halfdan let his gaze slide towards that rooftop. The archer had been felled, and even as he watched, the black-robed figure who was making to leave and run for the safety of the castle was plucked from the tiles and thrown back by Ketil's second arrow.

It was over. They had won.

Halfdan collapsed.

Chapter 17

'How do you feel?' Gunnhild asked, passing Halfdan a cup of something strong that he could not immediately identify.

'Like the jötnar have been dancing a war jig on me. What *is* this?'

'Something Bjorn acquired after the fight. A local thing. He says its like drinking sharpened steel. I thought something like that would do you good.'

It was evening now, and Halfdan had only just begun to feel more lively. The crew, and indeed the other ships' crews too, had nodded their respect as Halfdan dragged his exhausted body back to the *Sea Wolf*. When one man, who'd been aboard his vessel the whole time, snorted at the 'feebleness of some youths', he had received a punch in the jaw for his derision, along with the almost legendary explanation that this young warrior had outrun an arrow to save the jarl.

That was the word that was being passed around the fleet now: that Halfdan had outrun an arrow. In truth, he had to give all credit to Odin for somehow granting him the eerie knowledge that the arrow had been loosed, for had he not leapt with his shield at that exact moment, Yngvar would have been pinned by the shot. The Christians among the fleet, everyone save the crew of the *Sea Wolf*, were giving thanks to their nailed god for his using this poor heathen to save Yngvar. They had treated the outcast crew with noticeably more civility and respect since the fight.

'You interrupted your evening just to bring me a drink?'

'No, I came to make sure you did nothing stupid.'

'What?'

'Jarl Yngvar is here.'

Halfdan sat up, though every muscle screamed with the effort. The shield-maiden fixed him with a look. 'Even were I to counsel you to vengeance now, the man has come in good faith. Killing him would only damage your own reputation.'

He huffed for a few moments and then nodded. In truth, the jarl would be fresh, while Halfdan was still bruised and dog tired. The fight would be unlikely to go his way anyway. 'You'd best bring him in, but I think I want you to stay.'

Gunnhild nodded then stepped outside for a moment, returning with the jarl who owed him a life.

'I have spent the day struggling,' Yngvar said quietly. Halfdan did not trust himself to reply, and so simply sat silent until the jarl continued. 'I have made it my goal... *a* goal at least... to bring the light of Christ to those in the darkness. Olof the Svear counsels me to caution and care, while Hjalmvigi urges me to fire and destruction. It is hard to know which path is right. I set stock by my own decisions, though. Against Hjalmvigi's advice, I brought you with us, and had I not, I would likely be facing my maker right now. That cannot be ignored. But neither can the fact that you are deniers of the True Faith. Every time those idols of the demons you worship appear I am minded to leave you behind, and yet...'

Halfdan gritted his teeth. Why had the bastard come? Gunnhild was standing behind the jarl, and her expression was a warning. He nodded, said nothing.

'I recall,' the jarl continued, 'a time when I was young, and I loathed your kind. When I was fresh and saw all the world as an opportunity. It occurred to me only that heathens were enemies of God… Hjalmvigi's teachings, I suppose. Maturity has taught me that the world has more shades of right and wrong than just the two, for all that my old priest friend insists it does not. Age takes the fire from a man's soul, you know? Once, I killed a man and everyone he knew for his heathen idols. It was his unwillingness to give an oath that brought me there, not his idolatry, but the zeal burned so bright, and I…'

The jarl turned his face away. 'What happened was regrettable.' There was a long and sad pause then, before Yngvar turned back to him. 'You and your crew are like them, Halfdan the Gottlander, relics of the past and a reminder of the days when demons guided us. But unlike that old man, you have stood by your jarl. A heathen by my side where my own kind were not.'

'What is your point, Jarl Yngvar?' Halfdan murmured quietly, keeping a careful rein on his temper.

'I am not so sure. I came… I came to thank you, but when I asked myself why I needed to do so, I had no answer. I came perhaps in the hope of understanding. Of trying to see the man rather than the heathen.'

'I have no understanding to give. I am both.'

Yngvar nodded. His expression regained some of its old aloofness. 'Then I will have to reward both of you. It is a tradition as true in the world of godly men as it is in your own that a jarl should give a gift for such an act as yours. I spent some time musing over what was appropriate. You have your heretical shield and a sword of high quality. I found it this evening. I'm not even sure why I have it, and it must be some prize of my own from long ago that never sees the light of day. It is valuable, and perhaps more appropriate than I could ever have imagined.'

The jarl placed something wrapped in wool beside Halfdan and leaned back, silent. Frowning, the young warrior strained, weary and pained, to grip the thing and lift it. It was the size of his palm and had a weight to it. Unwrapping it, intrigued, his eyes widened as the contents were revealed, gleaming in the torchlight. A belt buckle of silvered pewter, fashioned in intricate ringerike style and with an image of Jörmungandr, the world-serpent, worked into it, looping around the buckle to consume its own tail. It was not only a rich thing, but a thing of beauty.

'And now I have given a pagan gift to a pagan warrior, Hjalmvigi will want me to flog myself for my godlessness. Perhaps I will even do so.' He sighed and his expression hardened once more. 'Perhaps I should not have come after all.'

He rose. 'Your deeds were brave, and you have earned my respect. Had you been a man of God, I would even now be lauding you and holding you high. I cannot do so. I will never do so to demon-driven heathens. But know that I am grateful, in my way.'

With that, the jarl turned and left. Halfdan waited until he'd been gone for a while, turning the belt buckle over and over in the golden glow of the torches.

'That was… unexpected.' He straightened. 'So what happened while I slept?'

Gunnhild smiled. 'The garrison of this place – Gori, it is called – have stayed fastened up in their fortress on the hill. The walls are lined with men but they just watch the city below while the fleet ravages Gori. The man in the black robe, who Ketil wounded, was found hiding in the corner of an outhouse. On Yngvar's orders he was sealed in and the building fired.'

'Good,' Halfdan hissed, rubbing sore joints.

'Too easy. In the old days a vengeful jarl would have made a bloody eagle of the man.'

Halfdan shivered. The bloody eagle was not a punishment to commit to lightly.

'All is good, though?'

She nodded. 'The fleet is supplied, there are few casualties, and the men of the fleet have... well, let's just say a lot of children will be born in Gori nine moons from now.'

Halfdan grimaced, then slumped back with a groan of weariness. Gunnhild said she would leave him to sleep. He didn't think sleep would come again, yet the young warrior was snoring before she'd left the tent.

–

For the next two days they sailed lazily down the river, recovering some of their humour and energy, allowing the current and the breeze to do most of the work for them. Halfdan quickly recuperated after a night's rest, during which Valdimar had brought him a few prize takings from the city to celebrate his success. Now, as a gentle drizzle settled in for the morning under a pale silver sky, even the slowly soaking weather couldn't dampen spirits. Halfdan was still a little achy, but was feeling much his old self as he now stood at the prow of the ship, trying to piece together his encounter with Yngvar. The man had almost seemed reasonable. He was struggling, clearly, but away from the vile influence of Hjalmvigi, it was interesting to see how different the man seemed.

'Hoy, Halfdan!'

The call came to *Sea Wolf* last, for the ship once again tagged along at the rear of the fleet despite Halfdan's unexpected celebrity. Vessels had been spotted ahead. The fleet slowed in the wide river and, thanks to the tight sequence of loops and curves the flow took here between hills, Halfdan could see what lay ahead. A gathering of ships larger than Yngvar's own sat motionless across half of the river, moored three deep. On the southern bank, covering a wide, flat area between the water and the slope of the hill, sat an army camp: tents in huge numbers, great fires and storage compounds, horse corrals and all. Halfdan whistled through his teeth. Yngvar could call on twenty-eight ships for a total of more than nine hundred men. Beyond the curve of the river sat twice as many ships, plus an army of thousands. A narrow-eyed squint into the obfuscating mizzle revealed red and white banners across the camp.

'The king's banners,' Ketil announced, pointing.

'We hope. The king fights his brother, and we have no idea what *his* banners look like.'

As the fleet came to a halt in the river, anchors dropping to hold them in place since there seemed to be no movement from the other ships, a small party emerged from the camp. The banners of red and white were in evidence once more amid a group of perhaps two dozen horsemen. As they neared the fleet, three of the riders moved out ahead, each in rich and colourful costume, while the others, clearly guards of some sort, kept protectively close.

Halfdan gestured at Ulfr who had yet to drop anchor.

'Take us out to the right, closer to the bank so we can see and hear.'

He watched as the jarl's ship pulled closer, echoed by the *Sea Wolf*, and came to a halt some ten paces from the turf, the heavy anchor splashing down into the water. A strange silence descended while the jarl stood at the ship's rail awaiting the riders. Into this quiet came the drum of hoofbeats, increasing in volume until the riders halted opposite the ships.

One of the three richly attired nobles threw out a hand in an imperious gesture towards Yngvar, who stood at his ship's top strake behind a row of coloured shields, gripping the rigging like a warrior-sailor rather than a jarl. The rider barked out something that sounded like a challenge in his own tongue, and when no one answered and Yngvar simply hung there on the rope watching him, the man tossed his head to shift a limp, soggy red plume, and tried again, this time in Greek.

Another two days on board had given the *Sea Wolf* yet more vocabulary and, now that they were trying to use Greek aboard ship as often as they could, their fluency was coming on in leaps and bounds. Though the small Rus stood close by, translating for them, Halfdan realised that he was only half listening, for he could get the gist of what was said without aid.

'His Majesty the *nobelissimos sebastos* Bagrat the Fourth, King of Georgia, demands to know the identity of the foreign fleet that has the audacity to sail into his camp.'

Yngvar leaned forwards over the water. 'You are the king?' There was an edge of scorn in his tone and the rider straightened, his face twitching angrily.

'I am Duke Kakhaber, His Majesty's representative. The king does not put himself within bow range of unknown villains. Answer me. Who are you?'

The jarl paused for an insolent moment. 'I am Yngvar Eymundsson, grandson of Eiríkr inn Sigrsæli, King of Svears and Geats, Jarl and Master of this fleet. I talk to men, not their dogs. Fetch me your king and go bark elsewhere.'

The duke bridled, and the men behind him reached for sword hilts.

'The king is of a mind to have your fleet scuttled where it sits and to have each man aboard flayed, salted and nailed to trees as a warning to other criminals. We are not unaware of your exploits, Northman. Riders from Gori have already announced your crimes.'

Yngvar stepped up now onto the rail so that the duke had to crane his neck to look up a little further. 'Gori was given a fair chance to trade with us for supplies. We sought only enough vittles to see us as far as your camp, but they refused, believing us the Varangoi of your enemy. They faced us with spears and arrows when we offered silver and trade. They brought on their own misfortune and I have not a care for a single one of them. We were hungry and they denied us. Find your king and tell him that we bring greetings from his queen, on whose behalf we now sail.'

The duke's face folded into a frown. This, he clearly was not expecting. Taking a moment to compose himself, he straightened and turned in surprise as one of the two other nobles flanking him said something in his own tongue and stepped his horse forwards. This second nobleman, a man of perhaps twenty-five summers with deep-set eyes, a sharp nose and a neatly trimmed black beard, swept off his helmet. One of the other riders had moved up next to him and passed across a pointed crown studded with enough jewels and formed of sufficient gold to buy a city. As the young man settled the crown atop his glossy black hair, Halfdan had to admit to being impressed.

'You have spoken to Borena?' the king said in a calm, sing-song voice.

Yngvar frowned at the man. 'What manner of king hides himself among his warriors?'

Bagrat of Georgia gave a light chuckle. 'A sensible and long-lived one, when civil war rages in his country. So, you are no enemy of my house? When word came that Varangoi had sacked my garrison town of Gori, I feared that Liparit had moved unexpectedly and swiftly and somehow slipped past my pickets. I had even wondered if my cursed brother had somehow sneaked through the mountains unseen. I must admit that my fears diminished when I saw just thirty ships. Such a force I could wipe from the land without breaking a sweat. You have word from my wife, Northman?'

The jarl dropped back down to the planks of the deck, nodding. 'We stayed at Kutaisi for a short while as I sought information about this land. We are not the servants of your Byzantine enemy, King of Georgia, but free men from the North. In return for supplies and the consideration of concessions when this war is over, I made an agreement with the queen. We would lend our swords to your army in the coming fight.'

Bagrat's eyes narrowed. 'Concessions?'

'Land, titles and the like. Nothing you cannot afford to grant.'

Halfdan bit down on his anger. One of the tenets of the Christians they seemed to vaunt was their truthfulness, yet here was Yngvar playing the humble servant while he secretly harboured plans to usurp the very king to whom he offered his sword. He breathed out slowly and calmed himself: this was not his war, just the stage for his revenge.

Bagrat nodded thoughtfully. 'My brother has a small force of your countrymen serving him on behalf of the Emperor Michaíl. They are a feared unit, led by an infamous lunatic by the name of Harðráði. I cannot say it does not appeal to me to field a force of their countrymen to match them.'

The king clapped his hands together and rubbed them vigorously. 'You come at an opportune time, Northman. Liparit and Demetre are massing their forces to the north, in the mountains on the edge of Alani lands. I have garrisons watching every pass to give us warning when they begin to move. They will take perhaps a week and a half, two at the most, to cross the range when they march. Thus you have ample time to settle in and find your place in this army.'

Yngvar shook his head, which raised frowns from the riders and wide-eyed surprise from the king.

'You deny me?'

The jarl shrugged. 'Your queen tasked me with journeying to the river's end and delivering an offer to the Kipchak tribe there. She believes that their intervention will make a difference in the war.'

An explosive rattle of derisive chatter burst from the other two nobles, and the king folded his arms, his gaze focused, scrutinising Yngvar as the jarl stood there at the rail. 'That course of action is not open for debate. I have told the queen on more than one occasion that we will not accept the aid of a people who still sacrifice to unseen spirits and engage in unholy rites. The Kipchak and the

Cumani are given to demonic practices. The moment I accept their aid, the Catholicos and his bishops will turn their backs on me and throw their support behind my brother. Moreover, the Emir of Tpilisi would withdraw his support. No one knows how many Kipchak tribes there are, or their strength. I cannot risk losing the Church and the emirate from my force in return for an unknown band of ravaging pagans.'

Yngvar nodded. 'I am inclined to agree with you, on purely religious grounds, King Bagrat. I follow Christ and the Theotokos Mother with every bit of your zeal, and associating with these heretics does not sit so well with me. However, I have recently learned a lesson in not putting godliness above safety. The Alani who serve your enemy hold the secret of Greek fire, and I am told they can raise thirty thousand riders. The queen was very persuasive in her arguments. She asked me whether a few fat churchmen and a heretical Serk from Tpilisi were worth facing such a threat. I have seen their fire, King of Georgia. It engulfed one of my ships, its crew, and even the water upon which it sat. If there is a chance to remove the Alani then it should be seized upon. I have given the queen my word that I will deliver her offer.'

Bagrat remained unmoved. 'Regardless of what you say, given the events at Gori you will understand if I am not inclined to send a fleet of unknown Northmen downriver through my undefended kingdom and through the lands of my allies. Your fleet will go no further.'

The jarl snarled angrily and stepped up onto the strake once more in a belligerent posture. 'I have given my word, and I will not go back on it. I will deliver your queen's message.'

'Yngvar,' called another voice, and all eyes turned to the new speaker. Valdimar was at the prow of his ship, gesturing to the jarl. Yngvar introduced the Rus prince, who received a respectful bow of the head from the king. 'Yngvar,' Valdimar said again, 'from here we face only a journey of, what, six days to the mouth of the river if we bend every back to it? Leave the fleet here and take only fast vessels. We can deliver the queen's offer and be back before this Liparit crosses the mountains, and just a few ships will give the king less cause to worry for his kingdom.'

Yngvar's face crumpled into a disapproving look. The idea of leaving the bulk of his fleet behind with another ruler did not sit well with him, yet the king was clearly considering the notion. He nodded his head again, this time in thought. 'Six ships. Fast ones,' the king said. 'The rest of your fleet and force stays here to prepare.'

'That is unacceptable.'

Bagrat's expression hardened. 'Listen to your Rus friend, son of Eymund. You may proceed through my kingdom with six ships to deliver your message, a matter I shall discuss at length with my wife upon my return. You will take sufficient supplies for your journey and avoid all settlements in your path, overnighting in the wilds, away from civilised folk who might *bring on their own misfortune*. You will then return to this camp and prepare to fight for the King of Georgia. In return for your fealty and your understanding, your rewards will be great. When the enemy fall, there will be lands and dukedoms suddenly free of incumbents. Obedience and sense reap great rewards, Northman.'

The jarl seemed to muse on this for a while. Finally, he nodded.

'I have no intention of stopping on this journey,' Yngvar continued.

The fire guttered and spat as fat from the carcass hanging above it dripped and ran. Nearby, the fleet bobbed in the flow of the river, its crews encamped on the damp, springy grass of the riverbank. It had been dusk before the rain receded and Valdimar emerged from the gloom and beckoned to Halfdan. The jarl had summoned five of his skippers to a meeting.

'The *Sea Wolf* is the fastest ship in your fleet,' Halfdan said.

Yngvar nodded. 'Hjalmvigi is unrelenting in his insistence that you be left out of this; he thinks your presence will curse us. I remember how... *useful* you can be. I want only fast ships and clever, dangerous men.'

Powerful Nænnir, Kåre the barrel-chested, Sæbjôrn of Märsta and Valdimar of Kiev all nodded their agreement. Troublesome Æskil was now all puffed up with pride at having been handed the rest of the fleet to look after in Yngvar's absence, and so he was not here to argue with the jarl this time. In a moment of defiance, Halfdan had decided to keep his sleeves up to reveal the Loki-snakes on his arm, and his Thor hammer amulet hung from his neck flagrantly. It made him smile to see the five powerful men around him carefully avoiding looking at them.

'We shall row and sail as fast as sense allows, from first light until dark, and camp only for the sleeping hours. Hjalmvigi will come aboard my ship to offer us God's guidance upon our journey. The river ends when it flows into a red sea, it is said, where whirlpools form that eat ships. No sailor crosses that sea, for beyond it is nothing. At the river's end is a spit of land called Siggeum, and it is this headland where the tribe we seek have a seasonal meeting. They are nomads, but certain places they maintain as gathering points. The Kipchak are godless heathens, and that is another reason I have brought our own godless heathens: to meet them eye to eye.'

He threw a strange look at Halfdan and the young warrior couldn't tell whether it was sarcasm or genuine gratitude. He shrugged. 'I will do what must be done.'

In so many ways…

'What do we want from these creatures?' Sæbjôrn grumbled.

'You heard me earlier. The Alani and their dragon can field some thirty thousand riders and they have the secret of the liquid fire of Miklagarðr. Such a force is too much for any army to face, unless the seraphim themselves take the field with us. The Kipchak, though, and their Cuman neighbours, number many thousands, and their lands surround the Alani to both the east and the north. If we can persuade these animals to nip at the Alani's heels, which they are already inclined to do by nature, then the Alani will be unwilling to commit greatly to Bagrat's enemy. After all, no man facing a punch-up wants their opponent to have a friend behind them, do they? Best of all, the more forces we drag into this war, the more confusion there will be, and the more opportunities for us to change in our favour the way things progress.'

Nænnir nodded. 'So what are we offering in return?'

Yngvar uncrossed his legs and rose to his feet. Behind him, a barrel stood in the dancing shadows of the firelight, a wool cloak draped over something leaning against it which all present had assumed to be short spars of timber. Stepping beside the barrel, the jarl stood next to the cloak and pulled the wool aside. The heavy item underneath gleamed and glittered in the firelight, and all eyes around the fire widened. The cross was almost waist high and seemingly formed from gold. It shone like the dream of avarice in the warm light, as men whistled and hissed surprise through their teeth.

'Yes,' Yngvar nodded. 'A fortune in its own right. But have no personal designs on this. It goes to the savages, and when they help us win this war and we can sweep Georgia itself out from under the feet of its own unworthy lords, we shall raise this cross in the Kipchaks' lands for them at the top of a new church, for they will be brought into the arms of Christ. But all that is for after, when we have our new kingdom. For now, we must concentrate on the plan.'

As the jarl went back to detailing what they would face in the coming days, Halfdan's gaze kept wandering to that great, golden cross. *That* was something he was going to have to keep secret from the *Sea Wolf*, for in his mind's eye he could not shake the picture of Bjorn grinning like a madman as he hefted that priceless gold and lugged it off into the darkness.

Tomorrow they would move on, just the six ships, and in a few days they would reach the edge of the world where the draugar lived. The weaving had never been so clear.

Chapter 18

'This is *all* Bagrat's lands?' Halfdan murmured, impressed. Georgia seemed to go on for ever, from the flat lands they had first encountered, across mountains and now down into a landscape of rolling hills.

Leif shook his head. 'Not quite. We left Georgia hours after we sailed, and passed into the lands of the Emirate of Tpilisi, the king's Serkish allies.'

Halfdan nodded. The allies, they said, followed the same god as the Georgians, but in some twisted heretical way that made it almost an enemy. He just could not understand how there could be so many different ideas of what their one god meant. Apparently as well as the Christians and the Serks, there were a people out here called Jews, who had yet another different idea about this one god. This was all just another reason the old ways were better. Odin was simply Odin. Nobody suddenly decided that Odin was something different.

'And the Serks control all the lands to the sea?'

Again, Leif's head shook. 'We camped last night in the emirate's lands but this morning we moved into the terrain of Kakheti, which has long since bent its knee and accepted suzerainty under Bagrat. Between there and the coast, the river flows through another Serkish principality called Shirvan, which also pays tribute to Georgia.'

Halfdan nodded sagely, not at all sure what suzerainty was, though accepting the inference that Bagrat still held control over these lands, for all they weren't his. Thus far they had anchored the ships by the left bank but remained aboard and alert at night, given the apparent proximity of the Alani's own lands that rose, brooding as mountains, to the north.

His gaze slipped to Gunnhild, who was seated cross-legged on the deck, eyes closed and swaying, gently intoning the song of her craft. As she oscillated and her tone slipped gradually higher, her eyes snapped open with a visible hint of irritation, and she cast the contents of her hand to the deck, a few small, bleached bird bones, several amber beads, two coins and three pieces of finely worked silver.

'Well?'

She chewed her lip as she looked at the odd collection and then up at him.

'I am no Völva, Halfdan. I have a sight of sorts, but I was not taught all the secret ways. What I see is vague and unconvincing. I cannot for certain identify the shadow. This coin?' she said, holding it up and turning it. 'It has two faces. One is a bearded man, the other a figure in a robe. The strange thing is I do not remember ever acquiring this coin, yet on this casting, it appears. I think it is you and the shadow. I think you are the two sides of the coin that decides Yngvar's fate. But that shadow could be Hjalmvigi in his priest robe, or it could be the queen, Borena, in her dress. Whichever it is, they continue to obscure the weave so that I cannot see.' She carefully stood the coin on its edge and set it spinning, no mean feat on a gently rolling ship. Halfdan was surprised when it rotated to a halt without falling over. 'You see how odd it all is?'

she murmured. 'Perhaps things will become clear at the edge of the world.'

'Wherever that might be,' Halfdan replied, looking out across the ship into the empty river ahead.

They sailed on for another day, through flat lands of brown and green with distant hills visible to either side. Again and again they saw small towns and villages along both banks, but the jarl was unexpectedly heedful of Bagrat's demand. They would not interact with any of these places, which suited Halfdan, since it meant they would make it downriver and to the edge of the world all the quicker.

It could have been an easy and leisurely sail, for the wind was with them most of the time and the flow of the river carried them ever eastwards with speed and accuracy, yet they pressed forwards hard. Every man was mindful that the majority of the fleet remained with the Georgian king, and of the coming battle. Even those less than certain of the value of being part of this whole enterprise wanted at least to be back in time for it to happen. Thus, despite the wind and the current, each of the six ships rowed as though the ice giants waded after them.

After another night on board, on the third day from camp, they found themselves sailing once more into deep valleys amid high hills. They all kept their eyes on the terrain as they moved, aware that they were in extremely unfamiliar territory, each man knowing that the peaks now drawing close to the river were those same ones that marked the edge of Alani lands.

Around noon on the third day, they sailed past a small settlement with a fortress upon a hill, and though no one could identify the banner that fluttered above it from such distance, its shape and general hue was reminiscent of those borne by the dragon king and his army. The fleet sailed fast from there, moving with fresh energy.

It was late in that day when they encountered a fork in the river. Logic, of course, told Halfdan to continue with the flow. The current that had carried them thus far raced off to the left, while a new channel joined this river from the right. The problem was that the river they followed supposedly flowed to the east, and were they to keep to that general course it would mean rowing against the current into the new, right-hand flow. Theoretically, following the current would carry them down to the uncrossable sea, yet the river turned here and marched off towards the high, misty grey mountains that marked Alani lands, which seemed entirely the wrong direction.

As the *Sea Wolf* waited in the wide confluence for the other ships to reach them and for plans to be made, Halfdan looked this way and that. The rivers were broad here, and the point of their joining so wide as to almost be counted a lake. A small settlement sat at the meeting point, huddled on the riverbank: poor houses and low walls. No flags or banners revealed their loyalties, and likely they were just rude fisherfolk. Five small islands overgrown with bushes and branches sat close to the village, the river cutting and flowing around them neatly. It was almost idyllic.

They could not be more than three or four days from their destination now, yet if they took the obvious course downstream and they had been misinformed, they could very well sail deep into Alani lands and completely miss their goal.

The other five ships slowed as they approached, pulling out into the confluence so that the half dozen were all within shouting distance of one another.

'North,' bellowed Valdimar from his rail. 'We must turn left and sail north with the flow.'

'Yet that takes us in the wrong direction,' Sæbjôrn pointed out from his prow. 'Do we really want to sail into Alani lands?'

'The river must loop back east,' Yngvar said flatly. 'Neither the king at his camp nor the queen back in Kutaisi mentioned moving into a second flow. One portage was all that was said.'

'If we get this wrong,' Nænnir called, 'then we add many days to our journey, even if we do not run into trouble. Remember that there are only six of us now. You should not have buckled under the king's command. We should have kept the whole fleet with us.'

Yngvar snapped some angry retort that was lost beneath Kåre's agreement that they were poorly manned while the king back upriver could count on all their strength. In return, Valdimar began to bellow his support of Yngvar's decision, and in moments each skipper's best men were voicing their own opinions, the whole river erupting in a ferocious argument. Halfdan left them to it. They were fated to their course. If there was one thing he had learned from months of sailing with the jarl it was that the weaving of the Norns was unlikely to be unravelled by argument.

As the quarrel raged between the other five ships, Halfdan rested an elbow on the figurehead, the carved shoulder of the wolf at just the right height, and stood looking at that village. There were a few small, round-bellied fishing boats moored there, but nothing bigger. The sun was now getting low and they would not move far from the confluence before they moored for the night, although if the argument was not resolved soon, they might well be mooring right here.

He only became aware of Bjorn's presence when a big hand bristling with fine white hairs thrust a leather bag of something that smelled corrosive under his nose. 'Let them argue,' Bjorn grinned. 'With luck they'll kill each other and save us all a job.'

Halfdan chuckled. 'If only that were possible. But the bastard has to survive for now. His end will be worse than a blade, I think.'

It could not be a blade. If Odin chose Yngvar to sit by Halfdan's father...

Bjorn wrapped both hands around the ship's rail and turned a curious expression on Halfdan as he took a swig of the sour ale. 'Do you know what that end will be? Gunnhild won't tell me. I think she thinks I'm stupid and will cause trouble.'

'I don't. But I know it will be some end that will turn even the gods away from him, and it is that thought that keeps me going.' He sighed and smiled at the big man, handing the drink back. 'I am forever grateful that Odin made our paths cross, my friend, and that you are still here with me. Gunnhild is with me all the way, and Ulfr at least as long as I have the *Sea Wolf*. I'm not so sure of Ketil and Leif. The Icelander is his own man and a curious one, and the little Rus? Well, I'm not entirely sure why he's with us anyway. How's the mood among the others? Will the crew follow for a while yet? I've hardly given them sacks full of silver so far for their troubles.'

Bjorn yawned. 'They are men of the old world and we are in a new one. As long as Odin favours you, and you show Loki cunning, they will follow. Remember that we have sailed across the world and fought giants and dragons, and yet they all live. When one day we are sitting in a mead hall in Uppsala, imagine the tales we will have to tell the rosy girls. Every man knows that fame is longer lasting than silver. It's harder to earn and it doesn't disappear as you drink. Give the men tales of great deeds and beer to wash them down with and they will not worry too much about the silver just yet.'

Halfdan smiled. 'There are times when you show a surprising level of wisdom yourself, my big friend.'

Bjorn shrugged. 'I'm repeating what Gunnhild told me.'

At that the two men laughed together and gradually subsided into silence, leaning on the ship side as the sound of intense squabbling echoed across the water behind them. 'Would that we had a roof to sleep under tonight, eh?' Halfdan mused, gazing away at the village.

Something struck him, then, and he frowned, turning to Bjorn. 'Have we drifted closer to the village?'

The big albino's brow creased as he looked across the water. 'No, I don't think so. We're still close to the other ships, and the houses look the same size to me.'

Halfdan shivered. 'Tell Ulfr to get the men to their seat-chests again. Get the oars in the water and take us back up the flow a way, behind the others and close to Yngvar.'

Bjorn's frown only deepened. 'What is it?'

'The islands. Those five islands. They're bigger. That means either they've grown, or they're coming towards us. Get us moving, Bjorn.'

The big man, still peering into the late afternoon sunlight at the islands, began to step back across the ship, waving his hand at Ulfr. Alone once more, Halfdan looked at those islands. They were green and bushy, with fronds and trailing flora dipped into the water, but they were definitely bigger. Not *just* bigger, though, they were in slightly different positions relative to each other.

He squinted, trying to confirm his suspicions. Even as he did, something moved on the nearest of them. Just the fluttering of foliage as though in a strong gust of wind, yet it sent a shiver up his spine, for nothing else was moving in the wind, and the motion was localised. Ulfr had started them moving already, but it was slow as yet. The other five ships were still in uproar. What had begun as an argument over leaving the fleet behind had blossomed into a general exchange of grievances and grumbles, and most of the ships' crews were on their feet now, joining in.

'Trouble,' Halfdan bellowed into the argument, but no one was listening.

He turned back to those five moving islands just in time to see something arc up into the air from the same place where the foliage had fluttered. An arrow cut a graceful curve into the indigo sky and disappeared into the water with a gentle plop just ten paces from Nænnir's ship. Halfdan was roaring now, trying to attract their attention even as the *Sea Wolf* retreated, back beyond the arguing mass of vessels.

Even as he finally managed to catch the eye of some crewmen on one of the ships, the enemy revealed themselves. The nearest island shed its foliage in one smooth move, tree branches and shrubs falling away to drift off with the current as the low, wide ship that had been hidden beneath cut through the water towards them, oars rising and falling in a litany of splashes. All five were now dropping their disguises, and each was well-manned with men who gleamed in steel and bronze.

The other northern ships were in chaos now as the argument ended abruptly and each crew grabbed their oars and began to row furiously, the whole thing an unorchestrated disaster as five skippers bellowed conflicting commands and ships turned into one another. Yngvar's vessel finally managed to clear the rest and pulled back up into the riverflow, close to Halfdan's. Without the need for a command, Ulfr directed the *Sea Wolf* protectively close to the jarl's vessel.

Nænnir's ship, *Far-seeker*, was in trouble, though. They could all see it now, for arrows were rising in small clouds from the five attacking vessels, and those clouds fell upon the ship of the powerful, braided skipper. Men fell from the rail into the water, screaming as shafts thudded deep into flesh. The ship was turning still, trying to race back after the rest, though with many of the oarsmen from its starboard side felled by arrows, it was doing little more than limping in a slow circle as the five enemies bore down upon it.

Nænnir himself rose from the stern of his ship, bellowing to the others to come to his aid, but he knew he was done for. The others were regrouping with the *Sea Wolf* and with their jarl so that a fight could be brought to the enemy as a unified force. The brave, doomed Nænnir would not be part of that. Even as the next cloud of arrows hit and figures fell all across his deck, the big, braided skipper himself suddenly jerked straight with a cry and toppled into the water, two shafts jutting from his back.

'What trickery is this?' Leif murmured.

'The worst,' Halfdan replied, pointing at the five ships. A groan of dismay arose from every northern vessel as red and black dragon heads were mounted in the prows of each of those five ships. The red tapering material socks flapped behind them, that eerie howl rising as the wind caught the dragons' mouths. Halfdan was staring in

horror. They had all lived in fear of the dragon warriors'
return for weeks, yet they had felt safe on the water,
for Jakulus and his riders had no boats. Or so they had
thought...

Even as he watched, the five vessels bore down on the
stricken longship, and the lead of those five red dragons
exhibited some strange activity at the prow. As they closed,
half a dozen men in red and black were working at some
sort of apparatus. The other ships split off into two pairs,
similar activity on display, and the leader began to turn
slowly in the current as it neared Nænnir's ship, closing to
ten or fifteen paces and arcing round to come alongside.

'What are they doing?' called Bjorn from his oar.

'Preparing the dragon's breath,' Halfdan shouted back,
and every man and woman aboard clutched their amulets
in dread.

Halfdan watched carefully as a long gleaming brassy
tube suddenly jerked into view over the side of the enemy
ship by the prow. A plume of dark smoke rose into the sky
just behind it, and now he could see the golden glow of
fire.

Despite Nænnir's fall, someone on his crew had
managed to pull together a defence, for men had grabbed
shields from the rail and hefted axes, while others had
produced bows and were loosing shots as fast as they could
at the enemy vessel that so threatened them.

'Nænnir's ship is about to burn,' he said.

'Then Nænnir's ship buys us time to do something,'
Ketil shouted.

'But what?'

The Icelander fixed him with a look. '*You* are our Loki-
cunning leader, Halfdan.'

The smoke intensified, the golden glow flashing into brightness as the enemy ship ran parallel with Nænnir's. As Halfdan had expected, once in range that terrible liquid fire burst from the mouth of the brass tube like a drake of old spitting flame. It came with such force that the fire jetted out in a graceful arc to fall upon Nænnir's ship. Liquid fire engulfed the prow of the *Far-seeker*, covering the crew in golden sticky fire that coated them and then flowed from their crisping, sloughing skin onto the deck.

The enemy ship moved along the length of the stricken vessel, pouring an endless stream of flaming death onto the timbers. All along the rail men turned into living torches, yelling their agony. Though all knew how pointless it was, men threw themselves into the water to stop the burning, but even as they sank and the water engulfed them, the moment their lungs burned with need for air and they broke the surface once more they did so into a lake of fire that wrapped them afresh in its horrifying arms.

Nænnir's ship and its crew burned, screams chillingly audible above the roar of flames and the crack and spit of the tortured timbers.

Even now, the other four dragon vessels were turning, ready to come around the flaming wreck and deliver a similar fate to every other northern ship.

Halfdan stared at the unfolding events. He felt that itch once more on the Loki snakes on his arm. There *was* something. They could not be doomed. It *couldn't* end here. His lip curled in defiance. It *wouldn't* end here. A curse in a thick voice drew his attention and he turned to see Ketil yelling at him, demanding orders.

The Icelander…

Was it possible? He rubbed the still warm Loki serpents on his arm. He had the cunning, they all said it.

It *had to be* possible.

Halfdan gritted his teeth and prepared to give the orders.

Chapter 19

Halfdan threw out a finger urgently, first at Ketil and then at Ulfr. To the former, he yelled 'Come with me,' and to the latter, 'Listen for my call.'

With that he ran forwards once more, weaving around the chests that doubled as seats for the rowers, leaping across the ribs that supported the mast, with Ketil at his heel, the Icelander frowning his incomprehension.

Off to the left, the remaining four northern vessels were trying to form into a united front, keeping the blazing wreck of Nænnir's ship between them and the enemy to buy them time to organise. It wasn't going to work, for there was sufficient space in this wide confluence for the enemy to sail wide around the burning vessel and still engage those hiding behind it. Nænnir's ship remained afloat, but already it was beginning to sink into the water.

Gritting his teeth, Halfdan prayed he was as cunning and lucky as everyone believed. Reaching the prow, he threw himself against the carved wolf once again and looked out ahead. The two enemy ships that had come out around this side were bearing down on the *Sea Wolf* at speed, and the fire crews were hard at work in the bows preparing their dreadful weapons.

Without turning to look back, he judged the distance and direction and held up a hand. 'Ulfr, turn us two paces to starboard.'

As the ship lurched and changed course slightly, Ketil, also at the figurehead, turned a worried look on him. 'That's straight at them. Are you mad?'

'Possibly,' grinned Halfdan. 'But the gods gave me wits, and they also gave me you and Ulfr. There's a reason for that. We're going to take out their fire, my friend.'

'How?'

Halfdan, still grinning, tapped the bow on Ketil's shoulder.

'We'll be in bow shot in a few moments, for a good archer anyway. You *are* a good archer, yes?'

'You know I am,' the Icelander replied with no trace of false modesty. 'I see what you plan. Loki lives in your veins, does he not?'

'I think you'll get two goes at most once we're in bowshot before their own fire tube has range. Then we're done for. No pressure, Ketil. Two attempts, and then we roast.'

The Icelander took a deep breath. 'It's a narrow gap. But I can do it. Straight down the tube.'

Halfdan shook his head. 'Not like that.'

'I can do it,' Ketil snapped quietly, glaring at the enemy prow.

'I don't doubt it,' the young warrior said quickly, acutely aware that they were running out of time, 'but you probably won't block or damage the pipe with an arrow. It's metal. And I don't think your arrowhead will fit down the tube anyway.'

Ketil frowned his understanding and resigned acceptance. 'What do I do, then?'

Halfdan pointed. 'The fire is fed from some metal container, and there's a man controlling it. See the glow? If there's a glow like that the fire is open to the air somehow. Open things spill.'

Ketil's mouth opened slowly into a grin. 'I see.'

'Can you do it?'

'Let's find out.'

'Brace yourself for a turn. I'll buy you a third shot.'

Ketil unshouldered his bow, peering off at the approaching ship, drawing an arrow and nocking it. Training his sight on the figures there, he took a steadying breath and paused. 'Range,' he announced, and loosed the arrow.

The shot was good. Astoundingly so. The arrow smacked into the side of the apparatus that stood behind the metal tube and its crew. Panicked noises arose from the ship.

As Ketil cursed in his thick Iceland accent and jerked another arrow from his quiver, Halfdan held up a hand and took two paces back. 'Ulfr,' he shouted, 'bear left a quarter, but gently.'

The ship began to turn, and Ketil stepped to where Halfdan had been on the right side of the figurehead where he had a clear shot as the ship turned. Steadying, breathing out, he loosed. The miraculous shot clanged against the brass tube itself, raking one of the men wielding it in its passage, and then disappeared behind them.

'Fuck,' Ketil snapped, then bellowed over his shoulder 'Ulfr, *steady*, man!'

The ship *was* rapidly steadying already as it settled into its new heading. Ketil lifted his bow. They could see the flare now as the enemy prepared to jet liquid fire at the *Sea Wolf*. They were out of time. Halfdan heard the Icelander whisper something to Odin as he lifted the shot and turned with the motion of the ship, loosing his arrow without a steadying breath this time.

Halfdan watched in awe. The Icelander had changed his target. Ignoring both fire tube and the apparatus behind it, he had instead targeted the man dealing with the fire. The arrow smacked into the side of the man's head, plunging in through the soft tissue and small bones around the ear and mincing the brain within. In a beautifully orchestrated move, the man never even had the chance to cry out in agony as the shot pitched him sideways and into the metal container he tended.

The pot tipped. It was secured to the deck against such disasters as the ship lurched and moved, but not securely enough to hold against the weight of a man.

The men at the prow loosed their liquid death.

Halfdan braced and winced.

'Loki,' he breathed.

The fire burst from the tube, but there was no pressure to it. Instead, it simply dribbled from the mouth of the brass weapon into the water below. Things aboard the ship were a little more fiery, however. The metal container had been damaged as it fell, and the flaming contents ran in torrents across the timber deck, flooding the ship. Men in red and black cried out in horror, knowing the dangers of their own weapon, and the more alert ones leapt from the sides of the vessel immediately, swimming for it. Others climbed the ropes to escape the rivers of molten fire running across the deck, the burning rivulets changing course with every lurch of the ship.

In a heartbeat the enemy was ablaze. Ketil turned a relieved look on Halfdan.

'That was a good shot, my friend. A gods-given shot,' the young warrior grinned.

Ketil nodded. 'I will owe Odin for that one. But you, you cunning bastard. You turned us out of danger before the danger was even there.'

Halfdan nodded as the *Sea Wolf*, now on its new course, neatly slipped out of the way of the burning hulk's path. 'Better,' he grinned, pointing at the other of the two ships that had come their way. That ship was now directly ahead. The fire crew in the prow were concentrating in the other direction, making for Yngvar's ship. 'Can you owe the Allfather two instead?'

Ketil laughed and nocked another arrow. Raising it, he trained it on the fire crew of the second ship. As that enemy vessel closed on the jarl's ship there were shouts of alarm from Yngvar's crew and the oars began to work, backwatering as fast as they could, yet unable to move out of the way in time.

The two ships closed to fire range. Two cries went up from the enemy vessel at the same time, one an order to send the flaming liquid at the jarl, the other a warning as a crewman spotted the *Sea Wolf* bearing down on them amidships.

Ketil loosed his arrow.

The fire crew released their weapon. The men holding the tube in thick, insulated gauntlets trained it on the port side of Yngvar's prow, the man at the apparatus throwing a heavy lever. Ketil's arrow slammed in somewhere unseen between the apparatus and the tube. Halfdan watched, tense, as the fire burst from the metal pipe at Yngvar's ship. It came with impressive pressure but only as a single, short splash, which struck the vessel and caught an unlucky man at the rail. But that was all that came. Instead, the arrow having done some unseen damage to the mechanism, a jet of golden flame burst upwards from the edge of the apparatus like a molten geyser, coming down as unstoppable burning rain on the ship. The fire crew were engulfed, screaming.

Yngvar's men cheered as they threw bucket after bucket of water at the burning part of their ship, preventing the inferno from spreading as men with axes worked to cut away the blazing strake.

As Yngvar's crew worked, the enemy ship, now fully ablaze, simply slid past them through the water. A number of enterprising Northmen loosed their own arrows in shots of opportunity, taking the few men on the enemy ship who were not either on fire or in full panic.

'Kill the fire crews,' Halfdan bellowed out across the water, hoping to get the message through to the other vessels. Someone on the jarl's ship clearly heard and passed the message on to the other skippers. The whole confluence was a mess of vessels now, both intact and ablaze, and the young warrior pulled himself up the figurehead, climbing the wolf to get a better view.

Another of the fleet, Kåre's ship, was now burning in the water, but even as Halfdan watched, the doomed ship achieved its revenge. The enemy vessel was running alongside, pouring liquid fire onto the northern ship, but their captain had made a mistake and come far too close. Four enterprising Northmen reacted. Two held up shields to try and save them from the fire as the other two swung the great heavy oar, using the dip between two shields as a fulcrum. The blade of the oar slammed into the metal tube even as it threw fire at them. The weapon spun out of control, throwing liquid death up in the air in an arc, before falling back to the deck and spraying its contents across the ship that bore it.

With a roar of fury, the ships of Valdimar and Sæbjôrn began to move, bearing down on the remaining enemy vessel out to that side, and as they moved, huge clouds of arrows rose from their ships, targeting the enemy. They had learned what Ketil had achieved, but no one on those crews was taking any chances. Thirty arrows had a better chance of putting the fire thrower out of commission than one, after all.

Two ships out of Yngvar's six had burned, but in return they had now taken three of the enemy, and the fourth looked doomed. Halfdan's face creased into a thoughtful frown.

'Where is the fifth?'

Turning, he gestured to Ulfr once more, and pointed out into the open water of the confluence, towards the village on the bank. In moments the *Sea Wolf* was turning gently and moving out into the river, away from the struggles of the remaining ships. Just as Halfdan had suspected, the moment they cleared the mess, he spotted the last ship, the one that had launched the first attack and had been ignored ever since as the fleet dealt with the two pairs of hunters flanking them.

The remaining enemy vessel had turned and was beginning to pull away downstream. Halfdan chewed his lip. In some ways it would be far more sensible to let them go. As well as the risk of actually engaging them, sometimes it was worth letting one enemy go to carry word of your victory and deter future incidents.

But there was something about these Alani dragon warriors and their fire. Somehow, Halfdan felt that allowing them to escape was inviting trouble. Letting survivors carry word was not going to deter this *Jakulus* from trying again.

'Full speed,' he bellowed. 'Attack.'

But the enemy were also moving at full speed, and they had quite some distance on the *Sea Wolf*. Halfdan cursed. He didn't want them to get away. He could picture them reporting to their king, and the man's fury reaching new heights. No, they must not escape. His attention was drawn then by activity behind him, and the snap of a sail catching the wind and bellying. He turned and looked at the sail, now picking up a westerly and throwing them forwards and to starboard with the current, Ulfr heaving on his rudder to keep them from veering too far that way. He grinned.

'Ketil, say another prayer and draw another arrow.'

The Icelander frowned and Halfdan pointed at the enemy ship. 'Watch them change course.'

Sure enough, the enemy now matched the activity on the *Sea Wolf*, their sail catching the fresh wind and carrying them forwards faster. Both vessels were now tacking slightly to starboard, coming closer and closer to the right bank. They would have to change course shortly to stay out in the deep channel, but while they could, both were making use of the wind for extra speed. Halfdan had watched Ulfr do this dozens of times on the way down the Dnieper. The wind in the sail would push them to the bank, and the stocky steersman would use his rudder to counter that and keep them in open water.

'The rudder,' Halfdan murmured, and Ketil, spotting the possibility, laughed.

'What would you do without me, young Gottlander?'

'I'd have to learn to use a bow, for a start. Can you do it?'

The Icelander snorted and lifted his weapon in a languid, almost leisurely manner, selecting and nocking an arrow. Sighting, he pulled back the string and held it for a moment, allowing his aim to drift slightly to the left to account for the increased wind. At the last moment, he lifted it a finger-width, and then loosed. The arrow flew in a low arc. Halfdan had been expecting it to aim for the rudder, though he was not sure whether it would have any great effect on it. Instead, as with the fire crew, Ketil had targeted the helmsman on the enemy vessel and not that which he held.

The arrow thudded into the man in his red and black uniform, and the figure lurched away and fell. The rudder spun free, out of his controlling grip, and the wind in the sail took control of the ship's course, turning it further to starboard, making straight for the bank with the strong wind directly abaft. Cries of alarm went up among the crew, and men scrambled to cross the deck and take control of the rudder, but the ship was yawing and rolling in its sharp turn, the deck at an uncomfortable angle, and the sailors were struggling, skittering and sliding to get to the rudder. They reached it in good time, but even as they began to haul on it in an attempt to break their course, they were done for. Some quick thinker aboard cut the sail free, and it dropped to the deck, covering men, taking the wind velocity out of the equation, but it was too late. Their momentum could not be stopped with the oars and they were almost at the bank, prow first. Someone threw out the anchor, then, its flukes slamming into the riverbed and dragging through the muck and rocks.

It was miraculous. The anchor, the rudder, the oars and the lack of a sail finally arrested their forward momentum, and the enemy ship slowed and jerked to a halt a single boat length from the shore. Unfortunately, their peril did not end there. As they stopped suddenly, the fire apparatus in the bow fell and exploded in a golden fireball, setting fire to the prow of the ship. Men leapt from the vessel and swam for the shore nearby.

'Take us in to the bank,' Halfdan yelled to Ulfr. 'Let's do some hunting.'

—

'Thank you.'

Halfdan accepted the flask of drink from Valdimar and took a swig. It was certainly better stuff than the muck Bjorn kept pushing on him. He took another, then handed it back. An evening of picking off running and hiding Alani had entertained the crew, but now everyone needed rest.

'That was an impressive display,' the Kievan said. 'That Icelander of yours has a God-given talent.'

'Not *your* god, though,' Halfdan said, though with no malice and graced with a mischievous smile.

Valdimar rolled his eyes. 'Don't let Yngvar hear you say such things. He continues to accept you in the fleet because you're proving yourself time and again, but he still doesn't approve of what you stand for. And as for Hjalmvigi…'

'Why are *you* here?' Halfdan said finally, after a strange silence.

'What?'

'Well you have your own kingdom, or at least your father does. You will inherit Kiev, so you have no need of Yngvar and his plots. And if this was just about you making sure for your father that Yngvar was safely out of your lands you could have turned back when we reached Georgia. You are closer to being a king than he will ever be. Why are you in his fleet still, Valdimar?'

The Rus gave him a strangely uncertain smile. 'I am not my father's most important son, Halfdan. I am the eldest, but not the inheritor. Demetrius will take Kiev after Father.' He saw the look fall across Halfdan's face, and smiled. 'Oh, I will not be disinherited. I will be given Holmgarðr to rule, which is a powerful land, if not as rich as Kiev. But Halfdan, you are of old blood. You still tell the stories of the gods and the giants, of adventure and battle. You sail the whale road and seek out new lands. It is a fading thing, such adventure. Holmgarðr is peaceful and quiet. When I rule there the most excitement I can expect will be the building of churches and the ratifying of trade treaties. There are not even enemies on the borders to go to war with. You have nothing, my friend, and yet you have everything. This is a dream for me, but at some point I will wake and the world will be administration and ceremony. I envy you the uncertainty of your future.'

Halfdan stared at his unlikely friend. Such a thought had never struck him, but then he was a poor farmer's boy from a village in Gottland. Had he not embarked on this great venture to avenge his father, his own future would likely have involved pigs and the growing of beans and turnips. He sighed. 'There are dark aspects to my life.'

'I do not doubt it,' Valdimar said, giving him a calculating look. 'There has ever been something you have kept from us. Never assume I am stupid, Halfdan. But whatever it is that drove you to join this expedition, I cannot see it being detrimental to me or mine.'

Halfdan nodded. 'No. Not intentionally, at least.'

'I can accept that. Once we have delivered our message and that gold cross to the pagans at the river mouth and we return to fight with King Bagrat, that will be the end of my journey, I think. Either Bagrat will win – in which case Yngvar is stuck, for he cannot claim the throne, and there is no magical land here from which to carve a kingdom as he hoped – or Bagrat's brother will win, in which case Yngvar will likely be dead. Or both will fall as the jarl hopes, and Yngvar will be King of Georgia. If that happens, I will secure treaties with him on behalf of my father. In any case, it will then be time to return to Kiev.'

He narrowed his eyes. 'I somehow have the feeling that you have no intention of ending this as one of his jarls in Georgia, even if he were ever willing to accept a pagan noble in his service. Somehow I think the whale road will continue to call you and, again, of that I am envious.'

'Yet many an uncertain man would give an arm for a rich land to rule,' Halfdan noted.

Valdimar sighed and leaned back, a dreamy look settling into his face. 'We are on the edge of the Serkish world here, my young friend. I wonder what my crew and my father might say if, when we reach the end of the river, I keep going. Sail south and into the heart of Serkish lands. Maybe as far as Bagdad itself.'

He took a pull of his ale, and Halfdan grinned. 'From what Leif tells me, the Serks do not drink.'

'That settles it,' Valdimar laughed. 'Kiev it is.'

Halfdan smiled quietly and settled back against the tree trunk. The end was in sight. They had fought the dragon, and they had won. Dragons and giants and draugar, and then the jarl could fall, and they would be free.

But free to do what? Damn Valdimar and his questions. Until now, all Halfdan had ever cared about was the death of Yngvar, but as that finally drew close, so too came the time to decide what came after.

Chapter 20

'North, then,' Sæbjôrn said sullenly, returning to his ship.

He had been easily shouted down when he proposed to turn east against the flow of that second river, for Yngvar, Valdimar and Halfdan all favoured following the current.

The four remaining ships pulled out into a calm and empty river. They kept to mid-river and were very watchful of their surroundings, always with an eye out for anything that might conceal an enemy vessel: a hard lesson learned. Once or twice over the following days they saw banners which might have been dragons flying over fortresses and towers in the distance, though no one felt inclined to go ashore and check. The ships moved at speed, using the sail and the oars to great effect. To the relief of all, late that first day the river swung back towards the east, carrying them once more on their intended course.

Early the next morning, the river began to wind like the coils of a serpent, looping back on itself again and again, and the jarl became prickly and irritable, aware that they were crawling across the landscape now despite their high speed, moving just a league to the east for every three leagues they sailed. They passed towns and villages more and more often and yet they kept to midstream or close to the far bank, avoiding contact. Their nights they spent in the wilderness, huddled close and dreaming of dragon's fire, or of tipping over the edge of the world into nothingness.

'*Stauros*,' Leif said on one such night during his evening litany of new Greek words for the men. 'Stake or cross.'

'Which one?' Bjorn grunted.

'Sort of both. A stake that someone is tied to for flogging, and the cross that Our Saviour was executed upon.'

'*Your* saviour,' the big man retorted.

Leif sighed. 'Just learn the words and forget the debate, you big white seal.'

Halfdan turned his attention to the figure emerging from the gloom. It was Gunnhild, who had been off on her own as was her occasional habit.

'Things change,' she said.

'Oh?'

'The coin has gone. Do not ask me where. But the clouds are clearing. I think as we approach the jarl's doom, the shadow is pulling back, perhaps due in part to our distance from the queen, if she be the shadow. Things are being revealed, anyway. The draugar are of import. They pull at Yngvar's thread and it is they who hold his doom in their palm.'

'They pull at the jarl?'

She nodded.

Halfdan scratched his chin. 'I had wondered more than once why Yngvar had so readily agreed to visit distant pagans, even with the reasons he gives.'

'Yngvar can no more resist this meeting than he can his doom. Whatever happens in the coming days, the future will lie in your hands, and perhaps the shadow's, but it will be the draugar who provide the path.'

'I am confident now that Hjalmvigi is the shadow of this weaving, but perhaps we can keep him out of the way,' he mused. Hjalmvigi had been barely evident on their voyage thus far. He had spent the first day sulking and trying to persuade the jarl that bringing Halfdan was foolish, but once the *Sea Wolf* had saved the fleet from the fire ships, even the most zealous Christian among the crew would not listen to the priest's bile. Pagans or not, it seemed that Halfdan was lucky. And so, the priest had retreated into himself from them on, appearing only to glower from the ship's rail in their direction.

'Be prepared,' she simply advised, then turned and wandered back to join the others as Leif tried to begin his lesson again despite Bjorn's constant interruptions. Halfdan settled back and closed his eyes.

On the fourth day the coils in the river became wider and shallower. Men were now avoiding Yngvar altogether, if possible, for he had a tendency to take his anger out upon those around him, and in one particularly bad mood he had broken a man's nose for some minor comment about the river.

The fifth day brought hopeful signs. Though they continued to wander with the course of the lazy river, the presence of gulls overhead, wheeling hither and thither, spoke of the sea, and Halfdan was sure he could detect an increasing hint of salt in the air.

Thus it was with improving spirits that they made camp that night, and the next morning they followed an increasingly straight river as it ploughed east, the scent of salt water undeniable. The day was warmer than the previous one, and with no hint of rain, no clouds in evidence. The four ships heaved and rolled as they forged onwards downstream until finally Ketil at the prow yelled the call they had all been waiting for.

'Sea ahead!'

They slowed now, sailing through a flat, brown and empty world, desolate and strange. Somehow, Halfdan had expected the edge of the world to be more impressive. Gradually the sea, which had been viewed at a distance, crawled close, and could be seen both ahead and to left and right beyond the flat brown expanse. They were sailing out onto a spit of dirt that jutted out into the water.

As they neared the mouth of the river, Halfdan felt a shiver of Seiðr excitement crawl across his flesh at the sight of an encampment. Across that otherwise featureless land on the left bank stood an array of large round tents not dissimilar to the ones they had been seeing ever since they first met the Pechenegs, the 'yurts' as it seemed they were called. Though the place looked deserted, the presence of the tents themselves and a corral that was not quite empty of horses suggested at least some small number of inhabitants remained.

Until this moment, Halfdan had not found himself musing over the nature of draugar. The restless dead of ancient legend were known to inhabit their tombs in an eerie reflection of life, ready to lay waste to any who might enter their mound and take their goods or disturb their peace. That the fleet had met a giant was undeniable and, despite the prosaic scepticism of many of the crew, they had indeed met dragons, none would now argue that. This was an encampment of a strange tribe, not a burial mound, yet he had faith in Gunnhild, faith in the Norns, and faith in the fate that awaited the jarl.

As the small fleet slowed and the ships neared the bank ready to moor, he could hear Yngvar ranting once more. That they risked missing a potentially world-changing battle in order to visit what appeared to be an abandoned camp of heathens had further deepened his foul mood, and as a man dropped the anchor too early, Yngvar let out a roar of anger and frustration and tipped the man over the rail and into the water. The hapless warrior cried out and floundered for a moment until he discovered with relief that the river was shallow here, and he could stand with his head above water. Slogging through the current in his heavy armour, he was the first to stumble ashore. From the grim look on the jarl's face, Yngvar had surely intended the man to drown for his incompetence.

The four ships pulled in to the bank and beached in the shallow mud, anchors dropped astern to prevent drifting, and the skippers and a small contingent of their crews leapt ashore. Their arrival had seemingly gone unnoticed, for there was no sign of movement from the tents a hundred paces from the river.

'A handful of men from every crew,' the jarl snapped. 'No less, in case we meet danger, but no more. Watch these locals. They are heathens, but they are a vast people who have managed to contain the Alani, so they should not be underestimated. If they speak a civilised language, then I shall bear the queen's words to them. I have no intention of staying here any longer than necessary. We deliver the offer and the bribe, and then we leave and return to the fleet.'

With that Yngvar selected a few men to join him, including Hjalmvigi and two particularly large warriors who lifted their priceless burden from the ship, wrapped in blankets to keep its true value hidden.

'Leave the priest,' Sæbjôrn called across to Yngvar. 'These are said to be dangerous men. This is no place for a white-robe.'

Yngvar simply shook his head as Hjalmvigi gave Sæbjôrn an acidic glare. 'He goes. In times past I have felt the brush of Satan's shadow, and were it not for Hjalmvigi, I might have strayed far from the Lord's grace. He is God's will here.'

Halfdan noted this as he dropped from the rail to the bank and turned back to the ship. That the priest might have been the only thing saving Yngvar from a destiny as a hero of old came as no surprise, though to Halfdan the man's influence seemed less of a blessing. He tore his gaze back to his own.

'Ketil, Bjorn, Gunnhild, Leif and Ulfr, with me.'

Once Sæbjörn and Valdimar had gathered their warriors, the small party set off with Yngvar at its head, making for that gathering of circular tents. As they reached the edge of the camp and still no inhabitants made themselves known, the jarl gestured to the nearest yurts.

'Search them.'

Warriors from Sæbjörn and Valdimar's crews dipped inside without calling out a warning, and each re-emerged shaking their head. The place was apparently deserted. The corral had space for several hundred horses, and yet Halfdan counted only twelve. The inhabitants of this place had gone. Or at least *mostly* gone. Constantly reminded of the visions of the Völva, Halfdan found himself peering between the tents and looking for burial mounds. Were the population all dead? Was that why there was no one here? But there were no mounds that he could see. Hjalmvigi was making the sign of a cross over his chest as he moved, his contempt aimed at their surroundings rather than at Halfdan, for once.

'This place is dead,' Leif said quietly, looking about.

'*Beyond* dead,' Ketil replied. 'I have never felt an air so drained of life.'

Gunnhild simply nodded as they moved.

Shivering, Halfdan walked on between the empty tents. Beyond dead. The draugar. A grander tent sat at the heart of the eerie, deserted camp, and the small party made for it. As they approached, Yngvar held up four fingers and pointed only to each ship's skipper. Along with those four and Hjalmvigi, the jarl's two big warriors followed on, bearing the gold cross in its wrappings, while the others gathered outside to wait. Halfdan found himself being gestured to enter first, perhaps bait for whatever awaited them.

He stepped to the tent's doorway, which hung closed, a great flap of leather that was heavy when lifted aside. The interior was dark after the morning sunlight, and his eyes took some time to adjust as Valdimar behind him grunted for him to move inside. As the interior resolved itself, Halfdan frowned. The place was grand, for a tent. The ground was covered with carpets and pelts that felt springy and comfortable underfoot, and the edges, though lost in the gloom, must be similarly insulated to keep the place so warm. A narrow aperture in the roof's centre would allow smoke out when a fire was lit, though there was no fire right now, just an empty pit full of ashes.

A grand seat draped with furs sat at the far side, just visible in the dim light, and behind it hung an old, ragged banner that attracted Halfdan's gaze and widened his eyes, for it was remarkably familiar. In blue and gold, it bore the image of a raven surrounded by ringerike work of a sort he had only ever seen at home. It looked very similar to banners he had seen while mooching despondently around Uppsala the day before he had met Bjorn.

He had to tear his eyes from that banner, though, to the only inhabitants of the tent.

'Odin…' he breathed.

An old man in furs and leather tunic and trousers, with a drooping moustache of speckled black-grey, sat cross legged in front of that throne, and close by a boy of perhaps eight summers lay on his back, wrapped in blankets, shaking. There was a strange and unpleasant scent to the room, like sweet flowers and dead animals bundled together, beautiful and putrid all at once. Hjalmvigi crossed himself again as he stepped inside.

'Lord above protect us,' the priest said, quietly.

Valdimar stepped to Halfdan's left, his nose wrinkling, a hand going to his mouth. To his right, Sæbjôrn and the jarl appeared, the former making gagging noises, his features twisted.

'What manner of hell is this?' Yngvar gasped at the tent and its occupants, and indeed at the aroma, and then his eyes fell upon the banner. 'God in Heaven, but that is the flag of Harald the Svear. Many are the theories I have heard of where he disappeared in my father's father's time.'

'He and his fleet were killed and eaten by these savages,' Hjalmvigi hissed, throwing an accusing finger at the seated man. 'As shall we be if we stay.'

'*Savages*,' echoed Yngvar.

Sæbjôrn huffed. 'Allies or not, I'll have no more of this cursed place, Yngvar. Hjalmvigi is right. I am gone. Meet me at the ships and let's leave this tomb.'

With that, the big skipper left.

'Where are your people?' the jarl demanded of the old man.

The wizened, leather-faced tribesman looked up at him curiously, and then rattled something off in a tongue of which Halfdan had no understanding. 'What did he say?' Yngvar snapped, looking this way and that.

'I do not know,' Valdimar replied, 'but it sounds like the Khazar tongue. We trade with them in Kiev.'

Halfdan cleared his throat. 'Leif will know it.'

'Get him.'

Halfdan hurried to the door, leaned out and beckoned to the small Rus, who joined him inside. Even the ever-positive Leif baulked as he entered, his hand going to his nose. Halfdan led him across to the old man. 'You speak Khazar?'

'Passably,' Leif replied.

'Ask him where his people are,' Yngvar snapped, and Leif crouched opposite the old man, rattling something off in a language that sounded very much like the one the old man had used. Without a smile or a frown, indeed seemingly devoid of emotion, the old man replied. Leif nodded a couple of times, and then suddenly rose and stepped back, his hand going to the scarf around his neck and pulling it up over his face.

'What is it?' Yngvar barked.

'This is a place of death,' Leif replied hurriedly, muffled by the scarf. 'The tribe have moved north for a time, while the disease that racks this place burns itself out. Lord above, my jarl, but this place is a tomb, and we shall all share it if we stay.'

Yngvar recoiled from each word as though they smacked into his flesh like arrows. 'A plague?'

Leif nodded, shivering. Valdimar now threw his hand to his mouth to stifle the air coming in, stepping back several paces. Halfdan felt that prickle of Seiðr once more. The walking dead within their own tombs. The draugar. He felt keenly the absence of Gunnhild and her comforting guidance.

'We should not have come here,' Valdimar said. 'There is nothing in this place but death.'

'Yet the old man... he is not ill, I think,' Halfdan said quietly. 'The boy may lie wrapped in blankets and shaking, but there seems to be nothing wrong with the man.'

'They should all be killed to prevent the spread,' Hjalmvigi snapped, his own mouth now muted with a scarf. 'A cleansing death. Kill the heathen animals and burn the place to ash.'

Halfdan's head snapped round, his thoughts once again on his home so long ago, the jarl there on a mission from a king, struggling to maintain order but driven to the worst murder and destruction by the bile of the priest. Patterns repeat in the weave...

'No,' Halfdan said sternly. 'No, that is not the way.' If Hjalmvigi was to be the wheedling voice of poison in Yngvar's ear, then Halfdan would have to be the sound of reason.

'What?'

'These people may be sick, but their tribe is vast. You said it yourself, Yngvar. This man is a priest of some kind himself, and that is a throne of sorts. Kill him and burn this place, and you likely start a whole new war with a people we came to enlist.'

'They are heathen demons,' Hjalmvigi spat. 'No war on earth is worth such an alliance.'

'Isn't it?' Halfdan urged the jarl, meaningfully. In his mind he saw that coin spinning slowly. He and the priest were the two men who toyed with Yngvar's doom. It had to be Halfdan who came out on top.

'Burn them all,' Hjalmvigi bellowed, his voice high pitched with righteous fury, almost a scream.

As the shout echoed away, another noise arose.

Halfdan's hand went to his hip, touching the pommel of his sword, and the tent was suddenly alive with movement. Figures seemingly detached themselves from the sides of the tent, emerging from the shadow all around them. Even Halfdan now felt a chill of panic. Some bore masks of polished metal, their faces hidden beneath expressionless, dead, steel visages. Others were not so covered, and gods, but how Halfdan wished they were. They were the truest draugar he could imagine. Some had lost their noses, the protuberances rotted away to black, sickly flesh, while others sported bulbous growths that gleamed sickly and were discoloured. They wore their sickness clear on their flesh. And yet their hands went to their own swords as the priest radiated violence and Yngvar wavered.

'Leave,' Valdimar urged the jarl. 'Let us depart this place while we remain hale.'

The jarl gripped the hilt of his own sword, but he was stepping backwards towards the tent door already.

'Yngvar,' Halfdan called, 'the treaty. The offer. The gift.'

The jarl paused near the door while Hjalmvigi replied, eyes glittering with hate. 'Give them the cross. Let it be their tombstone.'

Halfdan shook his head. 'The offer stands. They can be persuaded.'

The jarl choked into his scarf. 'I care not what happens to these sick heathens. Let them choke or melt or burst or burn. My task is done.' With a gesture to the two warriors beside him, Yngvar stormed from the tent after the priest. The two men threw their burden down onto the rugs and pelts, where the blankets fell away, revealing the gold cross within. Leif's eyes widened at the sight. Valdimar had now left too, and the jarl's warriors fled at his heel.

Halfdan stood in the middle of the tent, with Leif quivering close by.

'We must leave,' the Rus said, shaking with nerves.

'No. You speak his tongue. I need you, and I need the others.' Crossing to the door he waved the others inside. As they entered, each gagged and covered their faces. All were wild-eyed and afeared, likely having heard the tidings from Valdimar as he left. The only one who seemed composed was Gunnhild, which should not have surprised him. She brandished her arm, which she had decorated with a pentagram surrounded by runes. Looking about herself, she lowered her scarf and took a breath, nodding.

'Cover your face, woman,' Leif said urgently.

Gunnhild shook her head. 'This is elfish work. I am protected. Here.' Grasping Halfdan's arm, she produced a stick of charcoal and swiftly painted the same design on his forearm, opposite the Loki serpents. 'Freyja protects you. Elfish disease cannot touch you.'

Halfdan fought the urge to cover himself regardless, and yet in the face of her calm and certainty, slowly he lowered his scarf and took a breath. Was it just his imagination, or was the sickly sweet smell not half as bad now? In moments she had gone round the others, marking wards on each of their arms to protect them. Leif looked extremely nervous as she dealt with him.

'You know I don't believe in Freyja or elves, don't you?' he said. 'That this is the devil's work.'

'Then be grateful you wear a cross at your neck, and that whether you believe in the goddess or not, I put in a good word for you, and *she* believes in *you*. Breathe. Show the elves, and this devil if you must, that you defy them and you will not be laid low by their works.'

Leif reluctantly lowered his covering. As they crossed to the old man once more, Leif and Gunnhild stood at Halfdan's shoulders, and when he crouched, so did they. The threatening figures encircling them sank back into the shadows.

'Tell him that the jarl wanted to burn them all.'

The small Rus stared at him. 'What?'

'Tell him.'

Leif spoke to the old man rapidly, who nodded, still exhibiting no surprise. When Leif had finished, the old man began to talk and the Rus hurried to translate as he spoke. 'He is a shaman, a sort of priest or magician for the tribe. The Kipchak. He says that the men of the cross are always coming to try and make them turn on their own spirits.'

Halfdan nodded. That sounded awfully familiar.

'He says that this plague was brought by the men of the cross. He thinks they try to destroy the Kipchak with such diseases, because they are frightened of them in war. He is… I don't know what he's saying now. I think it's a spell of some kind. No, a curse. He is cursing the jarl.'

Halfdan felt that prickle once more as Gunnhild laid a hand on Leif's shoulder. 'Tell him that Jarl Yngvar is a wicked man,' she said. 'That he is an enemy of us all. Tell the old man that I see his spirits in this place, all around us, and that they also hate the jarl.'

'I can't say that.'

'You can, and you will.'

Leif stared worriedly into Gunnhild's unblinking green eyes for a long moment, and then nodded uncertainly. Turning back, he spoke to the old man who suddenly looked up at the shield-maiden, his eyes narrowing. He spoke once more, and Leif translated. 'The shaman recognises you as kindred. He asks if the jarl should die.'

Halfdan shivered. Years of waiting and months of work had brought them so close. Could it be about to end? Gunnhild and Leif were both looking at him expectantly. With a flood of tension released, Halfdan nodded. The small Rus turned and spoke to the shaman, who gave the first smile of the day, though it was a far from pleasant one.

As the northerners watched, the shaman produced a woven square of wool and placed it upon the shivering boy's neck, which was misshapen and discoloured with bursting buboes. Halfdan fought the urge to recoil as he watched. In moments something grey was seeping into the material. The old shaman leaned across the boy, murmuring and waving his hands, and then produced a square of leather. Carefully, he slid the wool square onto the leather and then wrapped it up, tight, tying it all with a thong. Finishing, the old man turned to Gunnhild and held out the package.

Halfdan was surprised that she took it, but take it she did, and then turned and held it out for the young warrior. Halfdan stared.

'Take it.'

Still, he hesitated, peering at the leather package, half expecting sickness to drip from it.

'Take it,' she repeated. 'You have spent your life seeking Yngvar's doom. At the last moment, here at the edge of the world, the draugar have given us the path, and you have beaten the shadow to it. It awaits you and you can hold it. The elves cannot harm you. Freyja watches over us all. Take it.'

Gingerly, he did so, gripping it carefully and at arm's length.

'What do I do with it? Yngvar is hardly likely to let me walk up and rub it in his face, and... and I'm not sure I wish such a thing upon him. It is Hjalmvigi who is the bile and the will, for all the deed itself was Yngvar's.'

Gunnhild sighed. Closing her eyes, she began to mutter. Close by, Leif crossed himself as he watched. When she opened her eyes again, Gunnhild seemed filled with certainty.

'The shadow is still there, Halfdan, though currently behind you, and you have a clear path. The decision is yours. When the time is right, you will know what to do, if you still wish to do it. I have guided you all the way, but now the jarl's doom is in your hands. From here it must be you.'

Ketil nudged Leif. 'Tell the shaman we will swap the gold cross for King Harald's banner.'

Leif did so, and translated a swift reply. 'He cares not about the banner and is offended by the presence of the cross.'

With a chuckle, Bjorn suddenly bent low, folding the blankets back over the cross and lifting it with great effort. 'Well, it would be a shame to see it go to waste,' the big albino grinned.

Halfdan could hardly help but smile at the man as he hefted the cross, and the Icelander removed and folded the age-old banner. 'I would say we have prizes here beyond that which we expected,' the young warrior said. 'Leif, please give the shaman my unending gratitude and tell him that the jarl and his cross will never bother them again. Wish him good fortune and thank him.'

And with that, Halfdan followed the others from the tent, Bjorn struggling with his new booty, while Leif and Gunnhild came on behind. As they emerged into the clean air once more, the camp was deserted, the other crews having returned to their ships. As they did the same, Halfdan peered down at the leather parcel in his grip. For the first time, he had the power not only to kill Yngvar, but to deny him a worthy afterlife. Their journey was almost at an end.

Part Five

ᚹᚩᚱᚠᛗᛋ ᚩᚠ ᚩᚾᛁᛏ

The Jarl and the King

Chapter 21

'You are late,' the Georgian king grunted without any preamble.

The jarl's lip twitched dangerously. The journey back upriver had done nothing to improve Yngvar's mood. Acutely aware of the coming battle that might well decide the future of the kingdom, he had fumed, cursed and ranted at the languid coils of the river they negotiated with seemingly endless repetition on the journey back.

'I gave you no date for our return,' he snapped in reply.

Halfdan stood with the others at the jarl's shoulder, nodding. In some ways at least the *Sea Wolf* was doing better than the other three vessels. While for Yngvar the journey had been largely wasted and they had nothing to show for it, the feeling of achievement among Halfdan's crew was compounded by their acquisition of a gold cross that had to be worth more than the ship.

'Was your journey a success, at least?' the king demanded. 'Did you buy the Kipchak? Will they harry the Alani?'

Yngvar's face darkened. 'Nothing of value came out of the negotiation,' he said.

Apart from a rag full of plague, the jarl's destiny, and a large golden cross that now lay hidden in its blankets aboard the *Sea Wolf*, Halfdan thought, trying not to smile. It had taken some misdirection and subterfuge to get the cross back on the ship without it being seen by anyone outside the crew, but they had proved equal to the task. For a time, Bjorn had been adamant that it was his prize and his alone, and had been exceedingly cantankerous when Halfdan had told him to share it with the whole crew lest he decide to give it to the river.

Bagrat leaned back and rubbed his forehead. 'Liparit and his army move through the foothills, taking town after town. They are close. A day, perhaps two, and they will cross the river and come for us. Your attendance is paramount, for your men will not fight for us without you, and we need to move against Liparit before he moves against us.'

Ten days the return journey had taken, and as the four ships slowed, pulling around the last curve of the river and past a high slope on the north bank, it had become clear that Bagrat's army had grown in their absence. Strange banners fluttered above tents in a new enclosure on the edge of the king's camp, and as they closed Halfdan recognised the look of the men and their garb as the same type of Serk they had met at Kutaisi. These, he reasoned, must be the forces of the Emir of Tpilisi, come to aid the king in his fight.

The four ships had slunk past the local forces and their moored vessels and closed on the fleet of Yngvar. Calls of relief and greeting had rung out all across the fleet, along with a number of disappointed cries at the absence of two of the more powerful ships. Still, their return from the mission was a source of thankfulness among the rest of the Northmen, and cheers resounded as they crunched up against the riverbank and anchors were dropped.

Yngvar returned that glare with daggers in his own. 'You have many troops. You could fight your own war without us. Bear in mind, King of Georgia, that I am not your subject. I fight this war for profit, not loyalty.'

'We are outnumbered,' Bagrat replied with open worry on his face. 'I can field some six thousand Georgian troops of good quality and a rabble of a couple of thousand more allies. The emir here has brought three hundred cavalry and six thousand infantry. With your own forces, this brings our entire army to somewhere in the region of nine and a half thousand.'

Halfdan blinked. The idea of ten thousand men in one force seemed unthinkable. A ship full of eighty men still seemed a lot to him, let alone a fleet of near a thousand. Had the entire island of Gottland joined to fight, including the women, the children and the greybeards, they couldn't have fielded as many as Bagrat claimed to have done, let alone just men of fighting age.

'Spies who have retreated in advance of Liparit's army,' the king continued, 'put his forces at some eight thousand Georgians with a vast array of allies. The treacherous Kakheti nobles have supplied him with another six thousand, while the Byzantines have lent him in excess of three thousand, including a thousand Varangians from Constantinople itself under their infamous and redoubtable commander. Finally, my dear brother's cousin, the Alani duke known as Jakulus, has fielded two thousand of his own men, and along with the Byzantines brings Greek fire. We face a battle against a force almost twice our number.'

Halfdan shivered. *Varangians*. Northmen who fought for the Greeks, and they would be taking the field on the other side. And the dragon warriors too, both with that deadly liquid fire.

'I am confident that we can win this fight, regardless,' Bagrat said. 'Much of this comes down to tactics rather than numbers. Liparit's forces include upwards of five thousand horse, while ours contains notably few cavalry. Our relative locations place the coming conflict within a certain area upriver to the west, where we can force the fight into the forests. I plan to bring Liparit to battle at Sasireti, where the woods will negate his cavalry advantage. Moreover, the Byzantines and Alani both bring war machines with the army, which will be of little use in the woods, while we have spent our time constructing weapons that can by deployed in such terrain.'

Yngvar snorted. 'This is not enough to reduce the odds.'

Bagrat leaned forwards once more, folding his arms. 'Much of Liparit's strength lies in his allies. You are a brute northerner and you do not understand the intricacies of politics in this land. Many of Liparit's supporters are only with him because of tenuous connections that could easily be broken. One snap in the chain and they will all break free. All we need do is shock them once, make it clear that we are stronger than Liparit can ever hope to be, and their support will crumble. The Byzantines will not waste their manpower saving someone if there is a chance they will lose with him, for they are a selfish people. If we make a sufficient show of strength, the Kakheti will abandon Liparit, and may even join us in the process. I am convinced, and my generals and allies agree, that one truly brutal display might just win this for us.'

'Are we, by any chance, your brutal display?' Yngvar asked, his tone flat.

The king took a deep breath. 'I am led to believe that there is little in the world that is more fierce than a Varangian charge. Liparit must by now know that we have Northmen in our forces too. He will expect me to pit you against his own, and for his Georgians to contest with ours at the centre while the emir here deals with the Alani on the other flank, like for like across the field. We shall shatter his expectations. We shall do the unexpected. *I* will take the left flank, where he will deploy his Byzantine allies. You will form the centre, Jarl Yngvar, with your men and my rabble in support, and you will make a straightforward attack on their own centre. You may use the untrained levies as you wish, but your remit is to break through their lines and make for Liparit himself and his banners. Shock the enemy. Break their spirit. Once you shatter their lines and attack their master, their allies will begin to question their decisions. With luck you will manage to kill Liparit himself and the chain will be broken.'

Yngvar gave the man a sour look. 'You expect some seven hundred of us to charge an army of eight thousand and try to kill their commander? Even with your thrall spearmen, if their shield wall holds, we will be slaughtered in heartbeats.'

'That is where my new weapons come in. Liparit's forces will approach from the northwest where they will have crossed the river. We shall approach from the southeast to meet them in the Sasireti woodlands. This will give us the advantage of terrain. The slope is only low and gentle, but that is all we require.'

The king swept out an arm to indicate a small group of people among the various courtiers and officers that were gathered in the tent. These figures now stepped forwards, wheeling something from the shadows. It looked like a cartwheel, though much fatter, perhaps a foot wide from

313

rim to rim and four feet across. As it was rolled slowly into the light, they could see that the outer circle of the wheel was fitted with myriad gleaming spikes that dug into the ground as it rolled, leaving a line of puncture wounds in the rough matting that covered the grass. What it might do if it came rolling towards a line of men did not bear thinking about.

'If the woodlands discourage cavalry,' Yngvar said thoughtfully, 'will they not render such weapons ineffective?'

The king shook his head. 'The Sasireti woods are quite open. Perhaps one or two will be impeded, but there will be adequate room to deploy them. You see how their ranks can be broken now? With the slope on our side, you can shatter their line and exploit the gaps the weapons open up with manpower and sheer will.'

'This still depends upon reaching your woods and enticing your brother to fight there in the first place,' Yngvar noted.

'Indeed, and that is why I have been impatiently awaiting your return. We must depart at first light if we are to intercept them at the desired location. Any delay and we will likely meet them in the plain and on the flat, where no advantage can be found. Can your men be ready? We will have to leave at dawn and cover six miles in order to meet the enemy at the perfect spot.'

'We will be there, our ships can bring us close to the battlefield at speed. And we will break your brother's lines for you. Remember your side of this deal, though, King of Georgia.'

With a simple nod, Bagrat dismissed them, as though they were mere vassals and their obedience assumed. Such, Halfdan suspected, was the way kings' minds worked.

They simply could not comprehend a man that did not accept their sovereignty at face value.

Striding from the command tent, the four skippers met with their entourages once more in the open ground and made for the ships. Yngvar held his silence until they passed through the gate of the camp and marched out across the turf towards the northern fleet. Once they were out of earshot of the Georgian sentries, Yngvar slowed slightly, allowing them to gather around him like storm clouds.

'Bagrat hands us our opportunity,' he said. 'He aids his own betrayal with his plan. He wishes us to kill this Liparit, who is a mere duke and no pretender to the crown. But Liparit does control a claimant who dances like a child's puppet on strings in the form of the king's brother. We shall do as we have been commanded, break the enemy line just as Bagrat proposes, but once the main battle has been joined, there our involvement ends. As soon as we break the line, the king will commit. Until then he will be holding back, so we must go at least that far. We will then, however, withdraw from the fight, circle our way to the flank and fall upon Bagrat from behind. We can leave his rabble to keep the fight going at the centre, and I doubt anyone will notice our temporary withdrawal. He will expect nothing like this, and we should be able to fell the king before he realises what has happened.'

Valdimar frowned. 'What of this Liparit, then? Do we kill him?'

The jarl shook his head. 'He is of no consequence. He is just a duke with no claim to the throne. It is the king's brother who can oppose me once Bagrat is dead, and I note that he was not mentioned as being with the army. Likely he sits in some gilded room waiting to be crowned the victor, when Liparit can pull the strings once more and be the power behind his throne. We shall give them all a new figurehead to rally behind, though. I shall rip the crown from Bagrat's cold flesh as I pull my sword from his belly and, wearing it, demand Liparit's obeisance. It is my belief that as Svears, these Varangians and their Byzantine companions will support us. Who in this strange world could they feel more connected to than men from their homeland? That is our plan: break the enemy line to start the battle, then renege on the deal, kill Bagrat and take control of his army. Then we shall seek the support of the Byzantines, force this Liparit to accept my sovereignty, and then we can hunt down the king's brother and remove him.'

Sæbjôrn coughed. 'That is a bold plan and rather reliant on other people accepting you blindly, Yngvar. And don't forget that the dragon warriors will be among the enemy, and Jakulus is unlikely to bend his knee. He has already declared a feud with you.'

Yngvar glanced at Hjalmvigi, striding along behind him and the priest nodded.

'God is with us,' Hjalmvigi announced. 'He wants the true and only cross of the Church of Rome raised over these people – over *all* these heathens, from the queen's corrupt capital, through this warring land and right down to those diseased dogs in their tents at the edge of the world. Bagrat allies himself with heathen Serks, which is an abomination in the eyes of God, so the Lord will not protect him, while Liparit allies with the dragon warriors, who are an affront both to God and to nature. We shall triumph, for we are righteous, and the enemies of God must fall.'

Halfdan watched the gathered men take heart from this zealotry. While it was useful, he simply could not understand how grown men could believe the nailed god's aid would change a battle.

'As for the dragon,' Yngvar said to them all, 'make sure you have your best archers with you and that they have brought their bows. After the events on the river, we know how to deal with the dragon's fire, do we not? Now to your ships and make ready. At dawn we join the army, and by dusk my claim to this land will be unopposed.'

As the four skippers went their separate ways, each to his ship, Halfdan slowed further, allowing his companions to crowd round him.

'He's insane,' the young warrior said quietly, once Yngvar was far enough away to overhear nothing. 'He truly thinks that the commanders on both sides will simply accept him because he is so tied to his nailed god.'

Leif nodded, his face like thunder. 'As a Christian myself I perhaps should be more understanding, but did you hear the priest? The only true cross of Rome? Perhaps he forgets that the Georgian Church is not the only one that does not recognise his Pope, and that some of us in his fleet follow the Patriarch of Byzantium? Would he see us persecuted and pressed into the service of his own Church too?'

Halfdan was impressed. He'd never heard the diminutive Rus so angry and fervent. Leif smacked a fist into his palm. 'And he thinks the Varangians of Constantinople will support him in his campaign to crush all who do not think the same, purely because he too is a Northman? He has no idea, Halfdan. *No* idea. The Imperial Varangian Guard may have come from the North to serve, but they follow the Greek Church and they are led by Harald Harðráði. Do you know of this man?'

Halfdan shook his head. 'I have heard the name, nothing more.'

'Haraldr Sigurðarson,' Leif said again. 'The one they call Harðráði – the *hard commander* in the old tongue. I met him on my last visit to the city of Miklagarðr. He is a lunatic. A truly fearless and dangerous man. He will be as afeared of Yngvar as a wolf is of a sheep. All Yngvar has to do is *look* at Harðráði the wrong way and the Varangian commander will cut him in half with a glance. This battle is hopeless.'

Ketil appeared at his other shoulder. 'In fact this battle is doomed in *every* way,' the Icelander added. 'If we break the enemy and Yngvar *does* succeed in killing Bagrat, then we'll make enemies of every force on that field. If we do this and do *not* kill Bagrat, do you think the king is going to live up to his promises? To give Yngvar and the rest of us lands and titles? Of course he won't. We'll be killed. And that's all assuming that Liparit doesn't win outright and Jakulus doesn't roast us in our boots.' He grunted angrily. 'Halfdan, I agreed to all of this, and I've not argued since we settled the matter back in southern Rusland, but I am uncomfortable following you into all of this. This is not our battle. Not *your* battle.'

'True. But *my* battle is still somewhere in the midst of it.' He glanced over at Gunnhild, who gave a single nod. 'Our sister over there knows it. The end is upon us. When this battle finishes, somehow, Yngvar will fall. Beyond that I cannot say what will happen.'

'Our threads go on from here,' Gunnhild said quietly. 'Do not abandon Halfdan Loki-born, Icelander. This is his time, and whatever happens here, we go on, all of us.'

All present looked across at the shield-maiden and finally Ketil nodded. No matter what awaited them, nothing they had encountered had flown in the face of Gunnhild's predictions. She carried the authority and the wisdom of Freyja herself. If Gunnhild said they would walk away from this, even Ketil was prepared to believe it. Halfdan's hand went almost instrinctively to the leather pouch at his belt that contained the parcel from the draugar with its deadly contents.

The question was, would *Yngvar* walk away from this?

Chapter 22

'All I'm saying,' Leif hissed between the trees, 'is that whether you believe in Christ or not, it can do no harm having him on your side.'

Bjorn harrumphed. 'By your logic we should pray to every god there is, just in case.'

'And that is why I was there when you drew your Thor hammer on your forehead for the battle.'

'But the men we fight are Christians,' the big albino snorted. 'Surely your nailed god is with *them*.'

'He's with all of us.'

'Then why does he make you fight each other? Mind you, that sounds more like Odin, after all.'

'Will you two shut up,' Halfdan hissed, tensing as a figure moved back through the woods towards him, darting between the sparse trees, one of the locals assigned to the duty by King Bagrat.

The forest here was not like the ones at home. Back in the North they were formed of tall spruce and pine, grown to the height of giants, green and thick the whole year round, the forest floor a thick carpet of needles, almost dark within even at midday. These forests were different, widely spaced and with stretches of open ground, the trees of a sort that lost their foliage in winter and were only just starting to green once more. While the terrain would be extremely difficult for cavalry it was surprisingly open and would hardly inhibit any attempt by man to kill one another. The young warrior gritted his teeth. He could not afford to let Yngvar fall in the battle, lest Odin gather him up for his feasting hall.

'Protect the jarl but look after yourselves,' he called, turning to look at his companions and the entire crew of the *Sea Wolf* who stalked through the trees behind him. 'Yngvar must not fall in the fight, but beyond that, no one throws away their own life or that of another crewman. The moment the jarl is out of immediate danger, let the king's rabble take the brunt. We only need to break their line first so that Bagrat will commit.'

His gaze slid to the left, then right. The other crews stretched out to each side. Halfdan did not know the men to his right, but he had contrived to position himself so that Valdimar's crew were to his left, and beyond them the jarl himself. Yngvar had been happy with the positioning, given Halfdan's good luck thus far, though Hjalmvigi, blessing the army before the fight, had argued against the pagans being in the fight at all, let alone so close to the jarl. The Georgian peasant rabble, unarmoured and largely carrying spears, followed on behind the Northmen, a mass of untrained flesh. Far out on the wings, the king and the emir were also advancing, though they were doing so slower, holding back a little to let the Northmen commit first and break the enemy. The whole line was curved in the shape of a bow, with Yngvar at the centre.

'Enemy ahead,' the scout shouted in Greek as they closed.

Halfdan gestured to the scout. 'What do they look like?'

The man, staggering to a halt, breathed deep.

'It's not fucking Liparit, I can tell you that.'

'What?'

'The men ahead are in the red and black of their Alani allies.'

Halfdan's skin prickled and he felt a cold stone form in his stomach. The dragon warriors. Had Bagrat known this? He had told them that Liparit and his usurping Georgians would hold the centre, but had he done so just to pit the Northmen against those dreaded Alani?

Clearly another scout had delivered the tidings to the jarl, for Halfdan could hear him cursing from here.

'How far?'

'There,' the scout replied, thumbing over his shoulder, and then pushed through the ranks of the *Sea Wolf* to safety beyond them. Sure enough, as Halfdan looked up, he spotted men emerging through the trees some way down that gentle slope, clad in black and red. He swore that he could already smell the acrid smoke of their sticky fire. Damn it, but there was no time to shuffle the ranks now, either. They were committed.

'Stop,' bellowed Yngvar. 'Georgians forward.'

In response every skipper called the command, and the Northmen staggered to a halt, pulling tight together to form gaps in the line and pushing and urging the Georgian rabble through those openings out to the front. Halfdan nodded his approval as he followed suit with the men of the *Sea Wolf*. If anyone was going to be wasted here, let it be the rabble. At least it was their country they were fighting for.

The Georgians were reluctant, naturally, and a few had to be slain or beaten to urge them on. Still, their own leaders were pushing them forwards from behind, and gradually the ranks swarmed out to the front line, passing between the Northmen, trumpets blaring as the dragon horns down the slope answered with their own eerie call to battle. Halfdan watched the Georgians pass and march unhappily into the fight, and knew in moments that committing them had been the right decision. With a sound like the roaring of a dragon, fire was launched into the unarmoured ranks, and an explosion of golden heat seared through the rabble. Men screamed as the fire crashed down in delicate pots among them, shattering and spilling out in a fountain of burning agony. Droplets sprayed into the air, raining down upon the Georgians. Trees caught in an instant, the fire racing up the dry trunks.

'Steady, lads.' All across the line, the Northmen had slowed, giving the Georgians time to absorb the worst of the enemy assault.

'Watch over him,' Halfdan begged the gods, looking along the line to Yngvar and gripping his sword and shield tight.

'The trees are burning,' Ketil grunted. 'Bad enough fighting someone else's war, but doing it in a burning forest?'

Close by, Leif shook his head. 'The trees are far enough apart. It won't spread much.'

The Georgians were raising a din of battle, a mix of agonised screams and roars of rage as the ones unharmed ploughed into the ranks of the Alani, spears levelled and lancing into the red and black ranks with spirit, if not accuracy.

In the brief moments Halfdan could see between the heaving and burning ranks, the impression he got of the battle itself was not a good one. Fully half the Georgian rabble were either lying amid blazing undergrowth, crisping and blackened, or staggering this way and that wailing their torment as patches of skin burned endlessly no matter what they did to try and stop it. The leading surviving ranks who had managed to engage with the red-clad Alani were proving largely ineffective. Spears were jabbing and thrusting, and finding a few targets, but Jakulus's ranks were tightly controlled and well disciplined, and were holding off the Georgians with relative ease.

'Are you sure about this?' Ketil called again.

Before Halfdan could answer, Gunnhild had done so for him. 'You doubt my sight, Icelander?'

'No.'

'Then kiss your steel, clench your backside and fight for the Loki-born.'

The battle having been joined properly now, the danger of fire pots had receded. There was little chance of such missiles being used in close combat for fear of striking their own men. The battle now would come down to proper fighting, though they would have to navigate the burning land to get there.

'Wheels forward,' bellowed Yngvar, a cry taken up by the other skippers. Halfdan felt a momentary sorrow for the Georgian rabble, trapped between the brutally efficient Alani and an uncaring ally behind, an ally about to cause them further agony. Nothing could be done about it, though. The spiked wheels they had been given by the king rumbled slowly forth. The slope was extremely gentle, but it should be enough.

'God have mercy on their souls,' Leif said, crossing himself with difficulty, his fist wrapped around a hilt.

'Don't pray for the enemy,' Ulfr called, 'pray for us.'

'I wasn't praying for the enemy. I'm not an idiot. I was praying for the poor bastards we threw at them only to push spiked wheels into their backs.'

Even Bjorn nodded his agreement this time. 'Odin will see their bravery.'

The two wheels allocated to the *Sea Wolf* were carefully trundled out and Halfdan waited, his men gripping the spiked weapons in preparation. Even once they were all out front and ready, the jarl paused, watching the mess ahead. To either flank, the sound of horns and drums rang out as the armies closed. Bagrat and the emir had continued to slow their approach to let the Northmen strike first. Yngvar was apparently not about to disappoint them. The Georgian rabble were thinning already, struggling to make any headway against the Alani, many still burning.

'Let them fly,' Yngvar bellowed, his call echoing across the woodland, and Halfdan nodded to the four men gripping the weapons.

Each pair tensed, muscles bunching, and then hauled the heavy wheels forwards, jogging with them and risking wounds themselves as they tried to increase the pace of the spiked nightmares even as they rolled. As they let go, the same happened all along the lines, and dozens of deadly heavy wheels rolled forth down the gentle slope.

'To battle,' Yngvar called now, sword held aloft. All along the line, skippers echoed the call, some invoking the nailed god, some the name of their ship.

'*Sea Wolf*,' Halfdan cried, raising a roar of sheer violence from the crew as they began to run in the wake of the wheels, racing for the enemy line.

Here and there the new weapons ran into trees and slammed to a halt, or became bogged down in burning corpses and tipped over to slide to a stop, but the majority made it through and Halfdan had to hand it to the king, for his wheels were horribly effective. The Alani lines had managed to hold the rabble without breaking, but there was nothing they could do to stop the spiked wheels. The weapons smashed into Georgian spearmen and Alani soldiers alike, puncturing, crushing, battering and wounding, forcing holes in the line. Yngvar's timing had been perfect. The Alani were struggling to repair their line as the Northmen hit them like a winter tide against a rotten jetty.

'Wolves of Odin.' Halfdan bellowed his signal as the forces met, and he slammed his short, deadly blade into the nearest red form.

That unique call was repeated from places around him, as his five close companions responded, beginning to pull back and letting the bulk of the *Sea Wolf*'s crew continue the fight. The six of them had their own conflict to concentrate on. Along with Bjorn, Ketil, Leif, Gunnhild and Ulfr, the young warrior waded away from the fight and began to push and shove to the left through the press, heaving Valdimar's warriors aside and gaining angry shouts as they made their slow and difficult way towards where the jarl was fighting.

As he pushed and heaved, Halfdan could feel blows landing on his chain shirt and his shield, not from the enemy, who were as yet held back, but from other Northmen irritated at being pushed aside. Finally, he spotted Yngvar in the press, and his heart fluttered. The jarl was out at the front of the fight, climbing on the piles of the dead to get to the enemy and roaring Christian refrains as he stabbed and slashed and chopped, his shield taking blow after blow. The man was fearless, and perhaps believed himself invulnerable with his nailed god in his heart. Halfdan knew better. No man could so invite death without it coming to answer the call. Even now the Alani were thronging around him, identifying the leader of this group and trying to kill him.

'The jarl,' he bellowed to his companions, who were pushing through the press with him.

'The fucking *idiot*,' Ulfr snarled.

'He fights like one of us,' Bjorn said.

'He will not *die* like one of us,' Halfdan reminded them fervently.

Yngvar's crew were being killed with alarming rapidity, the enemy pressing hard to bring him down. In a blurred moment, Halfdan saw Hjalmvigi, his white robe torn and stained, spattered with crimson as the priest fought beside his jarl, cross in one hand, sword in the other. His eyes were burning with violent zeal. In a heartbeat the figure was lost again in the press.

In another flash between heaving bodies, Halfdan spotted the enemy king, bellowing with rage and pushing his own men out of the way to get to Yngvar. Still, the jarl fought like a bear, standing proud on a pile of bodies as he hacked and hewed with wild abandon. He was increasingly pressed, yet continued to survive by some miracle, yelling his Christian dirges as he killed. Halfdan swallowed a bitter realisation. Nailed god or no nailed god, battle glory of that magnitude was the stuff of legend, and Odin sought such men for the final day. Yngvar was going to get himself killed at any moment, and when he did the Allfather would take him, no matter what. Such bravery would be of great value at Ragnarok.

'Protect the jarl,' he bellowed.

They had to save Yngvar, from himself if nothing else.

Halfdan was pushing hard now, making for the jarl, caring not how many fellow Northmen he aggravated in forging his path. The others were with him, for he could hear oaths to Odin, Thor and Freyja above the din.

Then, in one horrifying moment, he realised that the jarl was about to die. Yngvar had turned to his left, where men were pressing hard on him, his shield battered and broken, and he was hammering at them even as his own men struggled to support him. The jarl had not seen the danger coming from the right, though, in his battle madness.

The Alani leader, Jakulus, was almost on him. A sword similar to Halfdan's in each hand, the big Alani with the gold circlet in his hair and the forked and braided beard was enraged. The man was pulling his own soldiers aside to get to Yngvar, who remained ignorant of the approach, slamming his sword and shield out against the warriors at the far side. Halfdan heaved forwards with fresh urgency, and could hear Bjorn at his shoulder bellowing obscenities as the man came on in support, the others undoubtedly close behind.

He was not going to make it, the young warrior realised with cold horror. After everything he had done, Yngvar was going to fall in this last moment. The jarl was going to die a hero. He was going to be the very epitome of what Odin sought among the fallen, a legend in the making. Halfdan watched Yngvar's death unfold. The dragon leader had forced his way to Yngvar's left side, unnoticed by the jarl as he struck out at men to his right. Halfdan could see the gleam in the king's eyes. Men were shouting warnings to their jarl, but they were lost in the din of voices and cries, Yngvar was completely oblivious as Jakulus suddenly rose beside him like the prow of a ship lifting through the waves, both swords raised and ready to fall on the unsuspecting jarl.

'Nooooo,' Halfdan howled in the press, watching his world collapse.

The Alani leader was roaring in triumph, mouth wide like a black-red chasm spraying spittle like spume, muscles tensing for the blows that would end Yngvar.

Halfdan, tense, stared in shock as that open maw spilling out violence and bile suddenly spouted a shaft with black flights. An arrow plunged deep into Jakulus's mouth, slamming up into the brain until only a finger-length of shaft jutted from between his teeth, the flights quivering to a halt. Swords still raised in each hand, the Alani king stopped bellowing. He stood, an expression of confusion and surprise enfolding his face, and then, slowly, he toppled back out of sight among the press of his men.

A cry of dismay went up among the Alani, which melded oddly with the bellows of triumph from the Northmen. Halfdan was not the only man to turn and look back among their own mass for the source of that arrow. The others were still with him, struggling to push forwards, all except Ketil who, immensely tall as he was, stood visible and proud among the northern ranks a dozen paces further back, his bow slowly lowering, his string-hand still close to his ear.

Halfdan swelled with pride at the sight of his friend. The man was truly a marvel. There was no time to waste, though. The king was dead and the immediate danger put down, but they were still horribly outnumbered, and the battle was far from over. At least the jarl was no longer in direct danger. The fall of Jakulus had sent waves of shock through the Alani, and the pressure at the front had eased up, allowing Yngvar's men to get around their jarl and provide more support and protection.

The jarl stopped pushing forwards, with a bellow that cut through the battle as he hurled a dying red-clad enemy and gestured out over the heads of the Alani. Halfdan struggled to see, and what he could catch only came in brief glimpses, but it was enough. The Alani were falling back, but another force behind them was moving forwards to take their place, men who looked rather similar to King Bagrat's forces. The Georgians of Duke Liparit were now moving to hold the centre.

Yngvar was yelling still, though his sword was no longer gesturing at Liparit's men, but was now jutting out to the left. The time had come. The entire army had committed on both flanks, and now Yngvar had his sights set on felling the king and opening up a path to the throne for himself. Indeed, Halfdan lost sight of the jarl then as Yngvar flung away his ruined shield and leapt down from the heap of bodies on which he'd been standing, turning and starting to push to the left.

Head snapping this way and that to take it all in, Halfdan winced. The crews were surging after the jarl, their skippers bellowing for them to follow, but Yngvar had pulled out too quickly. So strong was his urge to plant a knife in the back of the Georgian king that he was abandoning the fight too early.

Even as Yngvar's crews raced away to take on the rear of Bagrat's forces, Liparit's infantry surged forwards into the gap their withdrawal created, bellowing and cheering. As they moved, the freshly arrived Georgians peeled off left and right, half the force following the retreating Northmen, the others falling upon the flank of the emir's Serks. The king's ally was doomed from that moment. He would never hold the field and if he had any sense he would withdraw immediately before he was overrun.

Halfdan could see it all falling apart. The jarl had been too eager to take down the man standing between him and the throne, and in moving to secure that, he had sacrificed the battle. What use was being the new king if he could only claim the crown for a dozen heartbeats before the battle was lost and Liparit stepped on his throat to remove it from him?

Idiocy.

Noticing Halfdan's expression, Gunnhild hissed at him. 'Remember this is not your fight.'

Halfdan nodded. He cared not what happened to Georgia or to most of the people in these woods, as long as the jarl made it through the fight to die the death of a murderer, not a warrior. And as long as those Odin-sent souls who had brought Halfdan this far walked away unharmed, too.

His failure became clear then in a single, heart–stopping moment. Though the press of Northmen surging towards Bagrat with the intent of stealing his throne even mid-battle was thick and multidinous, somehow the laughing gods contrived to open up a path between the heaving figures for Halfdan to watch disaster unfold. He saw clearly for just a moment as Yngvar roared, sword in hand and shield forgotten, running for the rear of the king's forces. He saw the jarl raise his blade and bellow one of his nailed god chants. He saw the spear come from nowhere. He saw it slam into Yngvar so hard that it threw the jarl aside to disappear beneath churning feet, and then the gap closed as quickly as it had opened, and Halfdan lost sight of the stricken jarl.

Then Halfdan was bellowing. He was crying out defiance at this fate, and challenges to the gods. He was yelling his grief for a father doomed to sit in Odin's hall beside his own murderer, sharing mead with the bastard. He was howling his shame and shock at his failure, his horror at this having come to pass at last, when he had the means of a coward's demise in a pouch at his side. Had the opportunity of which Gunnhild had spoken so many times come and gone somewhere without his noticing it, or was Loki laughing now at the greatest trick of all?

He had failed. He staggered to a halt, men pressing past on all sides, knocking him, pushing him out of the way, yet he stood there like a battered and aimless leaf in a winter stream, as stricken as the jarl himself, shattered and lost. The others were with him, then, huge Bjorn and tall Ketil stopping the bellowing Northmen from knocking him down in the press, Gunnhild and Leif and Ulfr rounding on him, demanding to know why he had stopped. What had happened?

The rest of the *Sea Wolf* were coming to a halt now, not sure what was expected of them.

Halfdan looked up through grime and unexpected tears.

All he could do was shake his head.

Chapter 23

'Dead.'

Halfdan hardly noticed what was going on around him. Everything was utter chaos, though he stood hollow and empty, protected from the bustle and shove of men by friends who he could see were shouting at him.

'Halfdan! What is it?'

'*Move*, Loki-born...'

'Halfdan!'

All he could hear, though, was the slow, sedate beat of his own heart, a bitter reminder that other hearts that should be beating were not. The jarl had died a hero, in battle with sword in hand like a Northman of old.

'Dead.'

Men heaved this way and that in the thick of battle, and for a moment Halfdan was pitched forwards. Bjorn grabbed him and hauled him up, asked him something, shook him, looked into his eyes with concern. Gunnhild was shaking him too now. Ketil had left him alone, was taking his place shouting orders to the crew of the *Sea Wolf*.

'Fall back,' the Icelander bellowed.

They were in trouble. Halfdan did not care. They had attacked the rear of Bagrat's own army, and were known for betrayers, yet Liparit's forces that had now broken through the middle and taken the heart of the battle were pressing on the Northmen's flank. Every man on that field who was not from Yngvar's fleet had become an enemy. The jarl's recklessness had cost his army everything. Neither side in this civil war would welcome them, and there was no chance of securing the throne of Georgia.

'Dead.'

The din of battle had become a background rumble, just the muted groan of the world, as Halfdan listened forlornly to his heart beating out a tattoo of failure. Now he himself would have to die a poor death and make sure he never reached Odin's hall, for how could he face his father, who must surely now sit beside his murderer until the end day?

'Halfdan, come on!'

One sound began to insist itself over the muffled din of war. A *kraa* noise, passed back and forth between sources. Despite his self-involved misery, Halfdan looked up. Two black shapes were sweeping back and forth above the press, shouting at one another. Ravens. They had to be. Huginn and Muninn, the ravens of Odin, gathering knowledge for the Allfather. The information they gathered today would be bitter indeed. And they *had* to be Odin's ravens. No birds flew above a battle until it was over and there were juicy pickings among the dead. No, this was definitely the god's birds. Would he see the *Valkyrjur* come for the brave among the slain?

He watched them as something bumped him from the left and almost tipped him over. Something thumped into the back of his shoulder hard, mortality averted by the chain shirt, though it would bruise and it would hurt. A lot. He didn't care. The others were still shouting at him, pulling him on through the chaos.

'Halfdan!'

He watched the ravens and noted with fascination the shadows they cast as they wheeled before the sun. For such small creatures their shadows engulfed patches of seething battle. They moved together, spinning around one another, their shadows almost melding into one, sliding silently across the fighting below. Halfdan's eyes followed the shapes until the shadows slowed, the birds whirling almost in place.

Kraa.

Once again, a gap had opened in the press and as his gaze followed the shadow, he stared. Yngvar was on his feet. He was staggering, but one of his men was holding him upright while he and the priest, Hjalmvigi, exchanged words. The jarl was in a great deal of pain, for he spoke through bared teeth, his eyes scrunched into slits. Halfdan felt that tingling chill of Seiðr magic in the air once more as the shadow of the twin ravens fell upon Hjalmvigi and stayed there.

The gods were at work now.

'Not dead…'

The sounds and activity of the world came crashing back in suddenly, like an unexpected flood from a mountain meltwater. Cutting, hacking, chopping, screaming, iron on wood, iron on iron, wood on wood, iron on flesh. Bellows and cries and the stink of shit and opened bodies everywhere.

Halfdan was moving. The others, taken by surprise at the sudden activity, rushed to join him. He cast his shield to one side. The Norns' weaving was not done. The gods had given him another chance. The jarl had almost been battleworthy, beloved of Odin, but he had betrayed and fallen, and now the Allfather's interest was shaking. It was time. Odin was watching. His father too would be watching from the god's mead hall.

He ignored that nagging voice deep in the back of his mind that railed against this underhand killing. Despite everything, the jarl had placed value upon Halfdan. He had fought Hjalmvigi's urge to zealotry. He had even tried to connect, in his own stilted way.

But he had to die. The blood debt had to be paid. And Halfdan could not kill him an honourable way, in battle, lest Odin come for him. It *had* to be this way, for all it felt wrong.

Hjalmvigi was busily tearing shreds off his filthy white robe and binding the jarl, while the Northmen were ever more pressed. The rear ranks of Bagrat's army had turned to face the betraying mercenaries, while Liparit's forces moved in from behind. Yngvar's army was being massacred. Even as Halfdan began to jog, men were falling all around them, screaming, blood spraying, limbs torn and mangled. The battle was over. Bagrat had lost yet still he fought on, and the jarl's army was now *everyone's* enemy.

'Now is your time, Halfdan,' Gunnhild hissed somewhere close behind.

He nodded. His empty shield hand was at his pouch now. He fumbled it open as he ran, watching Hjalmvigi work to staunch the bleeding of the jarl's wounds. Out came the leather packet, almost fumbled and dropped. With difficulty he loosened the thong and let it slip open. The stink of sick decay blasted at him for just a moment as that woven square was opened to the air, though it quickly dissipated among the other stenches of battle.

Again his view was blocked by a surge of fighting men. Someone came at Halfdan with a long straight blade, and the young warrior parried it almost absently, knocking it aside. Bjorn dealt with the owner, his iron helmet lending a killing weight to the headbutt that cracked the man's skull.

'Now, Halfdan,' bellowed Ketil.

The surging crowd moved aside once more and Halfdan could see that the Northmen were trying to pull back, to flee the battle. Yngvar was being half walked, half dragged from the fight. Hjalmvigi was struggling, wounded himself. His white robe was little more than a shirt now, much of its length used for bandages, and what was left was filthy and blood-soaked. The priest was snarling for material to bandage the jarl as they dragged him back away from the fighting.

Halfdan shivered, looking to the deadly woollen patch in his hand.

The jarl was howling, though it sounded more like anguish and anger than pain. They were almost there. Even as Halfdan reached the scene, a fresh push by Bagrat's warriors surged their way, and the man helping the jarl was struck by a spear point, falling away with a cry. Hjalmvigi was screaming for help now.

The priest's eyes fell upon Halfdan with a sneer of distaste, sliding from his face, down his arm to the patch in his hand.

'Bind him, Heathen.'

But this was wrong. Halfdan knew it. The debt had to be paid, but not like this. Not a sickly, slow demise. It would pay the debt, but how would Halfdan ever be able to look his father in the eye if he'd done such a thing?

'*Bind him*, you swine,' the priest spat furiously.

Even as Halfdan looked down at the material in his hand, Hjalmvigi cursed him, letting go of the jarl, and

337

snatched the square from Halfdan's hand. The young warrior stared. The gods *were* at work.

'Support him,' the priest bellowed, as the jarl sagged without his help, and suddenly Bjorn was past him, grasping Yngvar and holding him up, Ketil, Gunnhild, Leif and Ulfr all about them, the men of the *Sea Wolf* gathering close.

The jarl didn't seem to know what was going on, his eyes rolling. Since that spear wound he had taken three more injuries, each bloody and vicious. Hjalmvigi had bound all but the one on his thigh and was now reaching down with the plague-infected rag to bind the last wound.

Should he stop this? It was the priest now, most surely finally revealed as the shadow of the Völva's foretelling, who was sealing Yngvar's doom. Things seemed to have come undone at the last, for it had been Hjalmvigi, not Halfdan, who had sealed the jarl's fate. He began to move, reaching out, ready to rip the plague rag from the jarl's leg even as Hjalmvigi started to bind it tight. He found himself halted and turned in surprise to find Gunnhild shaking her head.

'No. This is the weaving. It has begun and cannot be stopped.'

'Is he done? Can we move?' shouted Sæbjôrn urgently. Hjalmvigi nodded as he tied off the last of the bandage.

'Back to the ships,' the senior skipper bellowed loudly, an order for all crews.

Halfdan was almost bowled from his feet as two big men from Yngvar's crew snatched up the jarl from his ministrations and all but carried him away from the fight. Halfdan found himself standing free in a small space, his sword in the ground beside him. Ulfr had apparently grasped the shield Halfdan had thrown away in his run, and was holding it up for him, the three wolves painted on the surface scratched and battered now. Odin's Wolves. That was what the Völva had called them back in Hedeby all those months ago, and that was what they had become. Hungry and dangerous, lean and loyal, fierce and proud.

Halfdan took the shield and pulled his blade back from the ground.

The jarl was doomed, infected with that same plague that had destroyed the Kipchak in the east, but yet he lived, and the doom he faced had been written upon him by Hjalmvigi.

He looked back to see the royal banners of Bagrat of Georgia. The king had lost the battle, but he still fought like a lion, despite the betrayal of his mercenaries. Beyond that, Halfdan could just see familiar-looking shapes. Men in gleaming chain and glittering scales, hefting axes and gripping shields, their heads variously shaved or sporting long, braided hair, beards on many faces. The Varangians. The Northmen of Constantinople, fighting for Duke Liparit. The last thing Halfdan wanted was to find himself facing fellow northerners.

'Back,' he called as his crew began to disengage and pull back along with all the Northmen. '*Sea Wolf*... back to the ship.'

And they were moving. Ahead, retreating Northmen had already run into trouble. Duke Liparit's Georgians had overrun the centre of the field and a unit of them had been sent round behind Yngvar's army to cut them off. Halfdan could see men being cut down, some even dropping to their knees, exhausted, the fight knocked from them.

Men in bloodied and dirty yellow tunics with swords and armour of plates sewn on leather were suddenly in front of them. Bjorn bellowed like a bear protecting its cub and ran at them, shield long gone, big axe in both hands. To their credit, Liparit's soldiers held their ground, the big man's chosen victim paling as the huge albino charged him, and that great axe came down with the weight of a mountain falling. The Georgian managed to throw his sword up in an attempt to stop the blow, but Bjorn's axe simply smashed the raised sword aside and slammed down into the man's mailed head. The damage was devastating. The weight and strength of the blow caved in the soldier's head even through the armour, simply driving the chain hood into the man's brain in a welter of gleaming steel and sprayed blood and ichor. The flailing, spasming body of the dying man fell back as, with a roar, Bjorn withdrew his axe, spinning and sweeping it out. The great heavy blade bit into parts of three men in its passage, and Halfdan might at other times have laughed to see how Ulfr and even Ketil moved carefully and gingerly into the attack, watchful and being more certain to keep out of the way of the big man than of the enemy.

As Bjorn continued the dance of bloody violence at the centre of the enemy, wading into their lines as he howled, the others piled in. Halfdan, determined to see things out, bellowed his cry to Odin and leapt at a man, sword swinging downwards and shield up.

As he stabbed and hacked at the man, he could hear calls and orders being bellowed not far behind in Greek, which seemed almost certain to be the Byzantines and the Varangians. He redoubled his efforts, feeling a sword tear a painful line along his forearm. Though his limb burned, it was not debilitating, and gritting his teeth against the fiery agony with every movement he fought on, knocking aside a man's sword with his wolf-shield and stabbing into the man's neck, feeling the blade slide in, grating between bones. Twisting it, he yanked it back out and kicked the man aside, a wash of blood splashing up into the air, some of it his own from his wounded arm.

He pushed through and discovered that they had overcome the Georgians and the way ahead was clear. They were free. The *Sea Wolf*'s crew was running again, heading up the gentle slope into the trees, leaving the Georgian king to his doomed battle.

He could see Yngvar up ahead, moving slightly slower, being helped by his own warriors. They too were free of the fight. A quick glance over his shoulder told him that the enemy had let them go to concentrate on Bagrat and his force. Mercenaries were of less importance in the grand scheme, after all.

On they ran, pounding through the woods, the din of the ongoing battle increasingly muted with distance. Gradually, as they neared the river heading east, they began to slow. Yngvar had gathered his crew about him now, and was limping onwards with help. The entire fleet was coming together, and Halfdan was shocked to see how diminished their numbers were. At least half the Northmen had been left on the battlefield, and possibly many more.

He looked around himself, relieved to count most of the *Sea Wolf*'s crew still present. He had lost less than a dozen men all told, which was good, looking at the other crews. With relief, he finally spotted ahead the shapes of ships at the edge of the woods. The fleet lay at anchor just where they'd left it.

Emerging from the woodland, the men of Yngvar's fleet looked this way and that. Welcoming cries echoed across the ground from the four men of each vessel who'd been left guarding their ships. The calls of joy turned sour and dark when the sentries at the river realised how few of their fellows were returning.

'What now?' bellowed a familiar voice, and Halfdan turned with a relieved smile to see Valdimar emerge from the trees behind them, his men at his heel. The Kievan prince was waving at Yngvar.

The jarl frowned at him. 'For now, back to the queen at Kutaisi,' Yngvar replied in a pained hiss. 'This is not over. Bagrat is unlikely to leave here alive, and the queen will need a new man to lead the fight against her brother-in-law. The battle is lost, but not the war. I will have Georgia yet.'

'You need time to heal,' Valdimar called, his voice weighted with concern, noting the four bloodied wrappings around the jarl. 'You are sore wounded.'

'I will recover speedily with the Grace of God. There will be plenty of time for that on the ships. For now we need to get out into the water and upriver before the enemy overrun the woods and reach the fleet.'

This met with agreement all round, and each crew ran for their vessel. The *Sea Wolf* lay at the rear as usual, and as they reached the boarding plank, something odd struck Halfdan. He looked downstream. The king's army had largely travelled by land with the Northmen sailing alongside them, but some elements of his force had also come by water and had anchored downstream of the *Sea Wolf*. Narrowing his eyes in surprise, Halfdan could see that one Serkish ship had come adrift and had bashed into a Georgian vessel, the two bobbing midstream, tangled in lines. Bodies in several different garbs lay around on the grass near the ship.

'What happened?' the young warrior asked as he pulled himself up over the rail and dropped down onto the deck of the ship.

'We got into a bit of an argument,' one of the four men who'd stayed said, shrugging. 'Half a dozen of our ships and two of theirs. There was a bit of a scuffle.'

'I'll say. It's a good job we'll be gone before any other survivors get back.'

'At least we came out of it well,' the man grinned, and jerked a thumb towards the stern. A small pile of bags, sacks, crates and boxes sat in the centre of the deck.

'Loot?'

The man nodded. 'Good loot too. We all shared it out. It seems Christian sailors have no issue with dividing spoils with us.'

Halfdan laughed. 'Get the anchor up and that line in. We want to be upriver as soon as we can. Every hand that has strength, get to the oars. We make for Kutaisi.'

And with that the *Sea Wolf* began to prepare for the off. Halfdan staggered over to the prow and collapsed against the carved figurehead as men hurried about urgently. Speed was of the essence now. They didn't want to be here when the king or the emir, or worse still, Duke Liparit, reached the river.

As the ship slowly pulled out from the bank and began to move, Halfdan suddenly realised he was not alone. All hands should be bending to the task. One other was not readying to row, though. Gunnhild was beside him.

'You are troubled.'

Halfdan nodded. 'All has come adrift, Gunnhild.'

'How so?'

He turned narrowed eyes to her. 'It is the shadow, Hjalmvigi, who has doomed the jarl. My blood debt will remain unpaid for it is not I who killed him.'

'He is not yet dead, Halfdan.'

His frown deepened. 'What?'

'The Norns' weaving is complex and there is a reason for all things. Yngvar could not die the death of a hero, lest Odin take him, yet you could not stoop to sending him on his way like this. You are not that kind of man, Halfdan. The solution stares you in the face, but it must be you who seizes upon it now. My guidance is past. What remains is your path alone.'

Chapter 24

'I've never lost a battle before,' Halfdan said in a strange voice.

Bjorn shrugged. 'When you fight enough of them you can't help but lose a few. At least this one didn't really matter.'

Leif stared at him. 'Didn't matter? This could change the world in the Caucasus.'

'Didn't matter to *us*,' the albino clarified.

Leif nodded slowly. 'I suppose.'

Ulfr leaned across. 'The fleet is subdued for certain, but the *Sea Wolf* is better than any other ship. We lost the fewest men, with thirty-two still at the oars. And we might have lost Yngvar's war for him, but we have a cross of gold and a small pile of loot to divide. We are far from poor men, now.'

They had moved with slow urgency upstream and managed to pass the first bend and move out of view of the forest before anyone appeared following them. They'd then sailed upriver as far as they could manage in that afternoon, even into the hours of darkness, and had only made camp on the bank when no man could possibly row further.

Decisions had been made that night, hard ones, and crews were combined to form larger, stronger ones. The chests that formed every man's seat at the oars and in which they kept all their valuables, were gathered ashore and those belonging to dead men opened and emptied, split between the living and the empty containers used to keep the fires going. Once the reorganisation was complete, they had twelve crews out of the thirty that had left Kiev months before.

It was a strange night, men trying to make the best of what had happened by focusing on individual feats of heroism or battle skill, laughing about their booty, and generally trying to find the good side. But the knowledge of their failure and the reminders of the fallen were all around them, and the undercurrent of anger, frustration and unhappiness remained beneath it all. Most surprisingly, there was also an undercurrent of anger at Yngvar, the jarl whose personal quest for a throne had led them only to defeat and disaster.

The next morning they had scuttled all the ships they could no longer crew and the remaining dozen vessels of Yngvar's fleet ploughed on upriver in a light drizzle under clouds the colour of a three-day-old corpse. They had moved west once more, until late in the day they camped on the north bank. Halfdan was waiting for the ship to come to rest before disembarking when Leif hurried over and tugged on his sleeve.

'We'd do well to stay aboard tonight.'

Halfdan frowned and the little Rus pointed ahead upriver to where a cluster of houses gathered around a hill crowned by a fort. Halfdan's heart jumped as he recognised the town as the one they had sacked before meeting the king. He agreed with Leif, dropped to the turf and hurried along the bank to Valdimar's ship, where he passed on the warning to the Kievan, who nodded his understanding and thanked him.

Those two vessels passed the evening quietly, the crews remaining aboard, eating cold food and sleeping early and fitfully with men on watch. Further along, campfires burned and men revelled, beginning to feel safe having come so far from the battlefield.

'How's your wound?' Gunnhild said as they settled for the night.

Halfdan looked down at his arm, bound in pale linen and stained with his blood. Leif had stitched the wound with more skill than Halfdan had expected.

'It hurts more than when it happened.'

The shield-maiden laughed.

In fact, the welter of painful bruises on his shoulder was far worse than the cut. He gave her a weak smile.

'Go join Bjorn and Ketil,' she said. 'Bjorn is beginning to get bored of losing games to Ketil, and you know what happens when Bjorn gets bored.'

He nodded and thanked her, then joined his friends for the night, relieved at her reassurances.

The next morning he had an extra reason to thank Leif, for staying aboard and shunning the revels had been a wise course of action after all. It seemed that lusty women had come to the camp along the bank once the ale was flowing, and had been very accommodating for the drunken sailors. They had fornicated with joy and the fleet had felt that perhaps things were not so bad after all.

The next morning revealed scores of men dead in their blankets, throats cut by the widows of Gori for what they had wrought when first they came. Hjalmvigi had harangued them all then for their degenerate ways, telling them that they had brought such disaster on themselves. It was the first time that Halfdan could remember being in agreement with the priest.

It was a sombre fleet that set off again that next morning. They sailed upriver once more for a time, pausing only at a village for food and supplies. Worrying rumours reached them then, for while the fleet travelled at the rate of tired and injured men, news travels faster than an arrow. The battle had been won by Duke Liparit, though Bagrat had escaped with his Serkish allies and was rallying even now. The Byzantine contingent, it was said, had considered their part played and were returning west. They had been seen in the area and may already be ahead of Yngvar's fleet.

'Something tells me that bumping into Harðráði and his Varangians might not be healthy,' Ketil murmured at the tidings.

Leif nodded. 'There are few Northmen in this land. They will assume we were the ones in Bagrat's army.'

The fleet moved on slower, more carefully, watching the banks.

Valdimar and Sæbjôrn between them seemed to be commanding the fleet now, for the jarl had not put in an appearance since they returned to the ships, and his crew remained tight-lipped. Under the joint command of the two powerful men, they reached the site of portage and camped for the night, and it was there that Halfdan's world changed once more.

Sitting with Bjorn and Ulfr by their fire and trying not to breathe as the two men engaged in a farting contest, he had felt his spirits sink at the sight of the pale figure of Hjalmvigi approaching, though the priest was with Valdimar, who held authority here and was less prone to the priest's bile than Yngvar had been.

The young warrior met the priest and the prince on the edge of the firelight, away from the others.

'What is it?' Halfdan said quietly.

'The jarl is ill,' Valdimar replied. '*Badly* ill. He has been trying to conceal it for days while Hjalmvigi here prayed for his recovery, yet he continues to decline, and now his affliction is undeniable and plainly visible. Others who have been close to him are beginning to feel it too. We have separated them out to prevent a spread of the illness.'

Halfdan nodded his understanding. 'There is no sickness among my crew. Freyja protects us from elfish works.'

Hjalmvigi hissed a reply, though his eyes were wild and uncertain, his confident manner absent now in the light of recent events and the fall of the jarl. 'You might think your heathen magics protect you, but all they do is damn you further. Accept God into your heart, you and your men, and you can be saved. Cast away your trust in demonic idols and ancient monsters and seek the light in Christ. I will baptise you in this very river.'

Halfdan gave the priest a nasty smile.

'If I asked you to kiss the hammer of Thor and pray for Odin's wisdom to see you through a tight spot, would you do it?'

The priest's lip wrinkled with distaste. 'Of course not.'

'Yet that is what you demand of us. We are not to be turned to your Christ, Priest.'

'Animals,' Hjalmvigi snapped, turning and stomping away.

'Have a care, Halfdan,' Valdimar said quietly. 'Even without Yngvar, the priest is a powerful man. He has the support of all the jarl's crews and, if I am not mistaken, back in the North he has the ear of the king himself.'

Halfdan shrugged. 'Out here he is a pest and a danger to us all.'

With a sigh, the Kievan prince turned and followed the priest into the night.

Halfdan waited quietly until the pair were out of sight and then turned and walked to the ship, found his chest and began to rummage. His greatest possession was his sword, but he would have need of that. Fretting, he cast aside numerous treasures until he found his spare belt: a plain and unremarkable thing. Slowly, he removed the one he now wore with the elegant buckle in silvered pewter, which bore the world serpent image, his gift from Jarl Yngvar, and replaced it with the plain one. Slipping the expensive buckle from the belt, he departed the ship once more and walked along the bank to the open water, gripping it tight.

Standing alone in the dark, by the river, he prayed to Odin for his wisdom and his protection, for the survival of the jarl until he himself could finish things, and cast the offering into the water, watching as the silver buckle disappeared beneath the surface. It seemed appropriate as a gift. The buckle had been given to him for saving the life of the jarl, and now he gave it to the gods and asked for the same.

'Seeking aid?' a quiet voice murmured at his shoulder, making him jump a little.

'Sort of,' he told Gunnhild. 'The jarl is very ill. If he dies…'

There was a strange silence and then Gunnhild stepped around in front of him. 'The time is almost upon you. You will know what to do. It is woven for you.'

'Have you sung your song and consulted your bones?'

'I do not need to. The path is clear for all eyes to see.'

Halfdan nodded. He hoped so. He had to end this still, and time was running out.

'Prepare yourself for what comes after, also,' the shield-maiden added.

'What?'

'Revenge leaves a man hollow, I have heard. You have lived your whole life for this, with no thought of what happens beyond. But you no longer have just yourself to think of.'

'I don't?'

'You are their jarl now, Halfdan. These men. Not just the crew. Even Ketil, who once saw you as an opponent, now looks to you for orders. Bjorn is a weapon, but he needs someone to wield him. Ulfr is a good ship's master, but he will only take us where he is told to do so. Even Leif, I think, will not go home. He too is your man.'

'And you, Gunnhild? You only came because the old woman insisted. And now I fear we are at the end of that journey.'

'We have reached a *stop* on that journey. It is far from ended. The whale road goes on for ever, Halfdan. But you need to have a plan. When your vengeance is complete and we are free, and all the crew look to you, you need to know what comes next.'

He thought about that as she turned and went back to the fire. He thought about it all night, and was still thinking about it the next morning when the fleet began the tortuous portage back over those valleys to the western river. The jarl put in a surprise appearance that day, and even Halfdan was shocked to see Yngvar. His face had gone grey and already there was discolouration about his nose and mouth. His forehead had a waxy sheen and sweat ran constantly. He burbled meaninglessly until finally others took him back to his ship and wrapped him in his blankets. Halfdan prayed once more that the man survive long enough for a truer ending to be made possible.

–

The portage was difficult but in another day they were within sight of the great river once more. That night, Valdimar moved among the crews with the tidings. The jarl was close to his end. Another nine men from his crew were showing signs of the same illness. Only the priest now visited him, but Yngvar had called all the skippers to him. Eleven men who led eleven ships, summoned to the court of a dying jarl.

Once again, Halfdan felt the Seiðr crackling in the air as he nodded soberly and followed the prince. He was somewhat surprised as they approached the ship where Yngvar lay wrapped in blankets that only he, Valdimar and Sæbjôrn had attended the summons. Clearly most of the skippers were not willing to risk such close proximity to the plague.

Yngvar had deteriorated noticeably in little more than a day. He looked like a draugr already, like he should be stalking his burial mound in the dark recesses, keeping thieves away from his afterlife treasures. He was on the edge. An hour, Halfdan thought, no more. Hjalmvigi stood off to one side, praying, and periodically glaring at Halfdan.

'A prince...' the jarl wheezed painfully, 'a detractor, and... a pagan. Such is my legacy that none other will come?'

'Say your piece, Yngvar,' Sæbjôrn replied, with little in the way of kindness.

'I will not reach Kutaisi, but I would have my wishes known. Take me home. Back to the northlands. Bury me there as the grandson of a king, if I can claim no crown myself. All I have here, you will split three ways. One third of my wealth will go to the Church, one third towards my burial, and the rest to be split between my crews.'

'I don't want your treasures,' Sæbjôrn grunted. 'I want my crew back and the last few months to live again. We should not have followed you here.' And with that he turned his back on the jarl and stalked away. Yngvar watched him go, a look of fear suffusing him.

'I will do as you ask, Yngvar,' Valdimar replied. 'Rest now.'

The jarl choked for a moment, then gave a weird, rattling cough. 'I shall rest within the hour. The rites?' he asked, looking across at Hjalmvigi, eyes rolling wildly. 'I am slipping.'

'I gave you the rites an hour ago, my jarl. You are the Lord's child. He will welcome you.'

Yngvar gave a painful nod. 'Leave me now. Let me die in peace.'

The priest gave the jarl a sympathetic look, threw a hateful one at Halfdan, and walked away. Valdimar gestured at Halfdan that they should leave, but the young warrior shook his head and motioned for the prince to remain. The end was upon them and the time had come. A feud had to end, and to do so properly, it must be witnessed. Valdimar hovered, uncertain why for some time, Yngvar seemed to be oblivious to the pair's presence, then finally, hissing in pain, he turned in his blanket and a waft of sick corruption flowed over the young warrior standing nearby. Yngvar's eyes fluttered open. His face twisted.

'I told you to go. Leave me.' The voice was little more than a whisper now.

'Not quite yet,' Halfdan replied, taking a step closer. 'I am no skald, but before you die, I have a story for you.' He cast a brief glance at Valdimar. The Kievan prince could easily take against him with what he was about to reveal, but somehow, for some reason, Halfdan did not believe it would be so.

Yngvar hissed. He was trying to wave Halfdan away, to voice his refusal, but only breathy gasps emerged, and his weak hands flopped to his side.

'Once there was a good man,' Halfdan said. 'A father and a dutiful husband was Vigholf, son of Njal, a man of the land, who farmed and who fought when called upon. A man who did his duty by his king and who raised a fine son. Like his father before him, and *his* father before that, all the way back through the line of his forefathers, he had respected the gods. He had maintained the Odin stone in the village and he had seen to the sacrifices when they were required to keep us safe. A good man.'

Yngvar was frowning in incomprehension now, Valdimar was rapt, looking back and forth between the two of them.

'Then, one day, along came a rich man. A man who thought he knew best for everyone, and with him came a priest who was a monster in disguise, who poured words of bile and ideas of hate into the rich man's ear. The pair would not allow the good man to live as his people had done for many generations. They tore down the Odin stone, and because the villagers would not worship his nailed god, the rich man had them butchered and burned, as though they were nothing. Vigholf died in the dust, defiant to the last.'

The jarl's frown had deepened. There was something in his eyes. A glittering. Was it comprehension?

Understanding? Halfdan hoped so. Here at the end the man had to know the truth, just as Valdimar was finally learning what it was that Halfdan had kept to himself all this time.

'Yes, you remember it, don't you?' the young warrior breathed. 'I remember it too. I was just a boy, hiding under a house, watching my world burn, but you cannot have pulled over so many Odin stones, and torn down so many sacrifices, and burned so many farmers, that you cannot remember that day. He was my father, the one who defied you in the village square. And I want you to go to your afterlife knowing that I have spent years in my vengeance. That I wandered and learned, and I found you in Kiev. That I followed plans the gods laid down for you years ago. That the weaving of the Norns has brought us to this place. That among the ashes of my family and my world I swore a blood debt before the gods and that finally I come to claim that debt.'

'You... did this?' the jarl managed, eyes wide.

'No. Strangely, despite everything, I would not sink this low. I had the means, but it was your own priest who bound the sickness into you. I would not have had it so at the last. I owe you a blood debt, Yngvar Eymundsson, but not like that. Gunnhild tells me that your suffering will be beyond human endurance at the end. That even agonised as you are now, the worst is yet to come. I cannot have Odin see you for a heroic warrior, but it is not in me to watch you crumble from the inside.'

The jarl tried to move, but Halfdan simply shook his head. 'You are too weak to fight. You may think this cruel, but what I do now is a kindness.'

With a quiet rasp, he drew that eagle-headed Alani blade from its sheath. He half expected a shout of warning from Valdimar, or the prince's hand to close upon his own and stop him. Nothing came. As he hefted the blade, he turned and looked at the man who had become a friend over these past difficult months. Valdimar's face was bleak and drawn, understanding vying with distaste for control of his expression. Perhaps he understood it all. Perhaps he sympathised. Whatever the case, Valdimar knew that what was about to happen was not murder, nor even an execution, but rather a mercy.

Placing the tip of the blade over Yngvar's heart, Halfdan whispered his father's name once, and then put all his weight onto the sword, driving it deep through bone and meat until it passed through even the blankets below and thunked into timber. Yngvar gave a single gasp, nothing more, and sagged.

Halfdan waited a moment and then withdrew his blade, picking up one of the spare folded blankets and wiping the sticky corruption from his sword before sheathing it once more.

Yngvar's lifeless eyes stared up at him, and he took a deep breath. It was over. The blood debt was paid, and Halfdan's honour remained intact. His father would not have to face the jarl in Odin's hall, and would wait for Halfdan on the day he joined the throng. The young warrior stepped back to the edge of the boat and turned.

'You understand?'

Valdimar nodded slowly. 'Whether it was deserved or not I cannot say, but it was done the old way, and God will accept him into Heaven. You saved him great pain. Hjalmvigi will be incensed, but I shall speak to him, will proclaim it a mercy.'

Halfdan sighed. 'Thank you.' He stood there for a moment longer as the Kievan prince turned and strode away, back towards the camps. Then, alone once more, the young warrior looked down at the body of Yngvar and closed his eyes.

'It is not finished, though,' he said, quietly. 'No. You were the blade, Yngvar Eymundsson, even the hand, but you were not the *will* that killed my father. That man still walks and spouts his hatred. A debt is still owed, Yngvar, and perhaps this one is for you as much as my father.'

With an expression of settled resolve, he turned and walked away.

And unseen by all, except Gunnhild, standing with the crew near the ship and looking upwards with a thoughtful frown, two black shapes winged their way north to the Allfather.

Epilogue

'He is mine. Do not kill him,' Halfdan reminded the others as they approached the great church of the nailed god on the hill of Kutaisi beside that fortress of the Queen of Georgia.

As Halfdan passed into the great building, his friends close behind, he heard Leif making uncomfortable noises. The small Rus had protested strongly against any violence in a temple of his nailed god, yet when it had come down to it and the decision had been made, he had sided with Halfdan after all and was one of the five that accompanied him.

As they moved into the huge hall, a space larger than any Halfdan had been in, with lofty arches and columns and high windows, all glowing with white marble, his friends spread out. Bjorn was at his left shoulder and Gunnhild at his right, his strength and his wisdom. Ulfr and Leif, his skill and his intellect, paced out to his right. Out to the left walked Ketil, his... friend?

There were priests here, lesser ones, lackeys, as Leif had said there would be, yet at the sight of the six armed northerners, they melted away with the slamming of doors, disappearing into hidden places. There remained only two figures in the great temple now.

On a bier at the centre, beneath the high dome and before some sort of altar lay the still form of Yngvar, wrapped in white. Behind him, Hjalmvigi stood at the altar in a fresh and dazzling white robe, groomed and tidy, looking almost regal except for his expression, which carried the same sizzling fire of hatred that it habitually bore.

'You owe a debt, Priest,' Halfdan said clearly as he paced slowly towards the centre. He didn't want to get there too fast, for he wanted Hjalmvigi to understand everything before he was struck down.

The priest sneered at him. 'I have no idea what slight you feel I owe you for, nor do I care, heathen. This place is strong with the Lord, for all their quirks, and I am master here. Even the queen would bow her head to me here.'

'But I will not,' Halfdan replied calmly, coming to a halt. 'You are a corruptor, Priest. A spreader of lies and hate. I have watched Yngvar Eymundsson on this voyage, for I have spent a ten-year and travelled many leagues to pay him back for the death of my father.' *A slight twitch of understanding there?* 'But I have come to know the jarl, and while he always had to die to pay the debt, I now realise that he could have been a great man – a hero like the legends of old – were it not for the poison you poured into his mind. *You* are the illness that has brought him low. Not the plague.'

Hjalmvigi snorted. 'Bold words. So, you are the scion of some long-dead heretic, seeking revenge? Be off with you, boy. I have no time.'

'I will not leave without the debt paid.'

'But you will,' the priest replied. 'And you should be grateful that you can. Without the jarl's restrictions, I am free to follow my own path, and with him dead I would have seen you impaled and burned like the stinking heretics you are, but for a fresh injunction from Valdimar of Kiev. The man seems unaccountably taken with you in spite of his piety, and he has made it plain that you are under his protection. Be very thankful of that in this place, pagan, for I wield more power now than you could ever hope to.'

Halfdan looked about. 'Yet you share a hollow tomb with the corpse of your master. You are no draugr, protecting your grave. You are but a man, and this grave you will share with Yngvar.'

With that, he began to step forwards again, and the others with him.

He halted in an instant, startled as, with a series of thrums, arrows sailed through the air and clacked against the flagstones near the feet of them all. As he stared down at the missiles and then up, searching for their source, Hjalmvigi laughed. 'You think me a fool, heretic? I learned many things in Kiev, not least the value of archers in the upper galleries. Were it not for Valdimar, I would have had them aim higher, but do not test my patience. I may become angered enough to forget my fealty to Kiev for a moment.'

Halfdan stared. Shadowy figures lurked high in the gloom of the upper reaches. He was under no illusion that any one of those arrows could have struck home had they been aimed so, and there would be more ready, waiting, should he take a step forwards.

'Run away, little heathen,' the priest cackled. 'Your world is shrinking fast and soon there will be nowhere for you to go. And when Valdimar is gone home, you will not want to be near me.'

Halfdan set his features in a hard frown. 'I will find you, Hjalmvigi, for a debt is owed. We shall leave this place, but remember my words. There is no prince, priest or king you can shelter with, no land you can run to, where I cannot find you. I waited ten years for the jarl. I have become a patient man.'

With that and a gesture to the others, he turned and strode away. He felt his pulse racing as they emerged into the light once more. It had been a fool's errand, but he'd had to try. Out in the open square before the Christ-temple, the other skippers were gathering, having emerged from the palace.

Valdimar spotted them and strode over, concern written across his face.

'I warned you, Halfdan. What have you done now?'

'Nothing,' he replied. 'You were right. The priest is out of reach... for now. His time will come, though.'

'I feel I should disapprove of you planning to kill a priest.'

'Yet you know this priest, and you know what he is,' Halfdan muttered, and changed the subject swiftly. 'You've finished with the queen?'

The Kievan prince threw back his cloak and rubbed his face with both hands, a weary gesture. 'The queen is somewhat bitter. She laments the failure of the expedition, though the apportionment of blame seems yet to occur. Only Hjalmvigi appears to be in her favour, for the man ever manages to inveigle himself into the counsel of the powerful. There is a sense among the others that it would be best to be gone from here before that happens.'

Halfdan nodded. 'Without Yngvar's grand plan, what will we do? What is the next step?'

Valdimar shrugged and looked around at the gathered faces, each of which readily displayed that same question. 'We will secure at best a few days' supplies here. The queen is in no easier a situation than on our last visit, so we must look to provision ourselves downriver. I am no explorer, though. While I would love nothing more than to sail the whale road, I am the son of Jarisleif of Kiev and I have duties. A life awaits me in *Gardariki* and so I am bound for Kiev, but it is the task of each man here to make his own decision as to the future.'

Sæbjôrn snorted. 'We have wasted half a year and more chasing the dreams of a delusional fool, and all we have to show for it is death and failure.'

'And silver and tales of adventure,' reminded Halfdan, receiving a bitter acknowledgement of the point from the older man.

'Still,' Sæbjôrn went on, 'we left Kiev with a thousand warriors, and we wallow in strange lands with not much to show for it and little over two hundred survivors. I for one am returning to the northlands. I yearn for the clear crisp air of my home and to be surrounded by my own people. I have a wife with a sharp tongue, but even her foul moods look like a balm now.'

This met with a chorus of nods among the others. They had been away from the North for a long time, and many had families. Valdimar looked around. 'I will give you one piece of advice, friends. Wherever you are bound, sail there with haste. The queen could take against us at any moment, and Harðráði and his Varangians have been reported less than four leagues north of here in the last two days. They travel west, likely with the rest of their Byzantine allies. I fear we would be unlikely to be greeted warmly by them, either. Sail fast, get ahead of them and make for your destinations before you are identified as men who fought for Bagrat.'

The skippers nodded and exchanged a few words of farewell with the prince. As they broke up once more and returned to their ships, many in small groups and making plans for their passage onwards from Kutaisi, Halfdan reached up and placed a hand upon Valdimar's shoulder.

'Thank you.'

'For what?'

'On a voyage where almost every soul was set against us, you have been a good friend and a staunch ally. For all your Christian faith, when my day comes and Odin sweeps me from the field of the fallen for his mead hall, I shall commend you to him.'

Valdimar laughed. 'Heavens, man, but you never cease to surprise me. God willing I will see you again. You are assured of a warm welcome in Kiev, my friend.'

And with that, Valdimar shook his hand, slapped him lightly on the shoulder, and strode off back to his own ship. Halfdan turned to see the others looking at him expectantly.

'And where are *we* bound, pray?' Ketil said, eyebrow arched.

Halfdan glanced towards Leif. 'I cannot speak for all men, but I have no desire as yet to sail through Pecheneg lands and return to the North. I have a debt to collect from Hjalmvigi, but he is beyond us for now. Soon, he will return to the North, and probably to Svear lands, for he is a friend of the king. I will find him when the time is right, but until then other lands await us. I have had a taste of a world of which I had no idea. Some here might wish to head north, however?'

Leif rolled his shoulders. 'If you mean me, then think again, Halfdan. I'm for your whale road a while yet.'

Bjorn laughed. 'The little thief will not leave you, Halfdan. Not until you carve up that gold cross and he gets his share.'

This raised raucous laughter across the ship, and earned a kick in the kneecap for the big albino from the little Rus. Once the fuss had died down, Halfdan looked about them. Of almost all of them he was certain, though his eyes settled upon Ketil the Icelander.

'Once, this could have been your ship. You owe me nothing and this has not been a glorious journey. Will there be a challenge?'

Ketil held his gaze for a while, and finally he gave a strange smile. 'I am a strong man, a fast one, and even a bright one, Halfdan Loki-born, but you travel with gods in your heart and at your side. We have faced dragons and giants, met draugar, fought battles and seen a plague that kills without remorse. Yet we are still here, healthy and proud, we have lost few men and they died well. We have no small loot for our pains, and stories that will enthral generations to follow. You say this has not been a glorious journey? I say otherwise. There will be no challenge. Where will we go next, Jarl Halfdan?'

A thrill ran through him then. He looked around their faces and caught that of Gunnhild. She gave a slight nod, and he recalled that night before the portage, while Yngvar lay dying and the bright, beautiful and dangerous maiden of Freyja had warned him of this very moment. He straightened and gave them a smile.

'Valdimar tells me that the infamous Harðráði and his men pass by to the north, returning to Miklagarðr and the service of the Byzantine Empire. He warns all to move fast and avoid them. I am of a different mind. Our countrymen serve in that city, and Harðráði is a man of reputation. I don't know about the rest of you, but while I've met kings and queens and princes and dukes, I've never met an emperor.'

Leif, a twinkle dancing in his eyes, nodded excitedly. 'Miklagarðr is the mother of all cities. She is beautiful and fascinating, rich and dangerous. There is nothing like it. Fortunes and names can both be made there. I'm for Miklagarðr.'

'At least we speak their tongue,' Ulfr added with a nod to Leif.

'Let's just hope the Varangians didn't get a good look at us on the battlefield,' Bjorn chuckled. 'Or our visit might be short.'

'Miklagarðr it is, then,' Ketil announced. 'I'll take some silver and gather supplies quickly before everyone else bleeds the markets dry. With luck we can get a few leagues from here before nightfall.'

Halfdan looked around at the others. Odin's Wolves. Hungry and greedy, for silver and for fame. The old Völva had named them well. He sighed. So much done, yet so much still to do.

Gunnhild laid her hand on his arm. 'Take charge and get them moving, Jarl Halfdan. There is much to do if we are off to meet an emperor. First of all, stop Bjorn from punching Leif's nose off his face.'

Halfdan frowned and looked past her to see the big man busily shaking the small Rus and bellowing into his face. He smiled.

'All right. Let's get ourselves set for the whale road.'

Historical Note

After years of focusing on Rome, of avowing my disin-
terest in the 'Dark Ages' and with several ongoing series
still to write, what is it that led to this story? Initially,
of course, it was the urging of my editor at the time,
who really wanted me to write Dark Age stuff, while I
continued to be resistant. But as with anything outside
my Roman comfort zone, I was only interested in tackling
this genre if I could find something different. No Anglo-
Saxon blood and guts or Vikings burning monasteries for
me. I wanted it to be something different. Something
new. This tale was born from two entirely separate ideas.
One of these is the character of Halfdan. The other, the
Icelandic saga of Yngvar the Far-Traveller (which I have
described in brief at the end of this note).

Having discovered the saga through something of a
back door and decided that I wished to explore and
rework the tale of Yngvar, I was presented with the question of my protagonist. I did not wish to tell Yngvar's
tale directly, from his point of view, partially because he
is far from a sympathetic figure, but also because it is
always good to see important figures from the viewpoint
of others. Other than the jarl himself, the only characters mentioned by name in the saga are Valdimar, Ketil,
Hjalmvigi and Soti. But then there were thirty ships in the

fleet, and that leaves a good number of powerful Viking leaders unnamed. I was free to go my own way.

Though my focus has always been Rome and Byzantium, there has always been a slight fascination with Vikings for me, possibly due to my northern connections to their blood and my proximity to their legacy. One Viking name in particular has fascinated me for the past dozen years. Halfdan, you see, was a real man. Oh, we know next to nothing about him that we can't get from his name, that he was half Danish, that is. But we know one other thing. We know that he spent time in Constantinople, because he left us a reminder. In the Aya Sofya, on one of the upper balconies, the visitor can find scratched into the marble a line of graffiti a thousand years old. In Scandinavian runes, it essentially reads 'Halfdan was here'. Given that from the ninth to the fifteenth centuries, Vikings were to be found in Byzantium in the form of the emperor's Varangian Guard, we can assume that Halfdan was part of that fearsome unit. Not long after the Norman conquest of England (1066), the Varangian ranks are more commonly Saxons that have fled their Norman overlords than Scandinavians, and so we can assume that Halfdan was around before 1066. I have wanted to tell the story of Halfdan since the first time I saw those scratch marks. This was my chance.

Just before 1066, we are told in the Icelandic saga, Yngvar sailed to Serk lands (Serk being a Viking term roughly equivalent to Saracen). Here, then, was my second source for the story. In the early thirteenth century an Icelandic monk, probably one Odd Snorrason, wrote the saga of Yngvar, noting that the hero's death was in 1041. The saga itself is a fantastic tale, full of monsters and magic, all overlain with an odd combination of awe for

Odd's Viking forefathers, and monastic disapproval of the world they inhabited. Yngvar was Christian, we are told, but everywhere he goes they are heathen (though Odd here shows a distinct lack of detailed knowledge, for all the lands in the region were either Christian, Islamic or Jewish and with little or no paganism in evidence). The saga seems to be oddly divided in that the first half is quite prosaic, full of history and realism, while the second half is magical and strange.

It would, in fact, be very easy to write off the whole saga as fiction, were it not for one thing... or in fact, *twenty-six* things. All across eastern Sweden one can find what are commonly called the Yngvar (or Ingvar) Runestones. It was common practice to raise a runestone in memory of someone, and they are a common sight across Scandinavia. These twenty-six in particular, though, lend support to the historicity of the tale of Yngvar. Just to take three examples, we find their dedications to be:

> *Andvéttr and Kárr and Kiti and Blesi and Djarfr raised this stone in memory of Gunnleifr, their father, who was killed in the east with Ingvarr. May God help their spirits. Alríkr, I carved the runes. He could steer a cargo-ship well.*
>
> *Klettr and Bleikr raised this stone in memory of Gunnviðr, their father. He travelled away with Ingvarr. May Lord God help the spirits of all Christians. Þórir carved the runes.*
>
> *Spjóti and Halfdan, they raised this stone in memory of Skarði, their brother. From here he travelled to the east with Ingvarr; in Serkland lies Eyvindr's son.*

Twenty-six memorials exist to commemorate those who sailed east with Yngvar, as far as Serk lands, and died there, never to return. It is almost unique to have archaeological evidence to support a saga in this way. Given that Yngvar therefore plainly existed, he clearly sailed with a fleet far to the south and east, and many died there, then the story starts to look intriguing from a historian's point of view. I acquired the only English translation of the saga and began to read it, picturing the routes and the peoples encountered. And when we came to monsters and magic, I started wondering how they might be explained in a worldly way, and yet preserve that Norse mystique.

As an aside, speaking of Norse mystique, clearly my protagonist was going to have to cling to the old religion if I wanted this to be in any realistic way a Viking tale. At this time, Denmark had been Catholic for some time, having taken on the new religion quite peacefully, almost by osmosis. Norway had become Christian through forced conversion, courtesy of its king. Sweden, however, remained a strangely mixed world, with many Christians, including the king, and yet pockets of pagan life still bubbling away. If I had a pagan protagonist, and Yngvar was a devout Christian, there was always going to be friction. Yngvar had already looked villainous to me from the way he treats people in the saga. He bears all the hallmarks of the violent zealot, and having Halfdan now as a pagan, it was clear that the jarl was not going to be a sympathetic character. The two men began to form the central core of the story, which would thread through the saga and bind them together. It was only through the editing process and the invaluable insight of my editor that Hjalmvigi shifted from being a harmless side character to the truly nasty villain he has become. In doing so, Yngvar has perhaps retained more of the depth and humanity that formed a saga-worthy character.

Given a recent review I received that labelled me essentially a Catholic-hater, I would like to take this opportunity to point out that this is not only a work of fiction, but of *historical* fiction. Attitudes portrayed are appropriate for their time, and do not reflect modern wishes and outlooks. No hatred is intended in this book, and hopefully, though it is centred around ancient religions, the characters of Valdimar and Leif display an open acceptance of many viewpoints. Remember, I am a storyteller. This is a story...

On a more academic note, I am grateful for the work of Mats G. Larsson, who has spent years attempting to divine truth in the saga and who is the one who proposes the route I have used in this tale. Some historians prefer to see Yngvar as having sailed south and reached the Holy Land, while others see Constantinople and the Byzantine world as his end. Larsson sees him reaching the Caspian Sea, and sees the battle in which he becomes embroiled as the civil war in Georgia. That he would sail through the Abbasid Emirate of Tbilisi, and the battle is close by, nicely corresponds with the Serks mentioned on the runestones without the need for Yngvar to have reached anywhere like Jerusalem. Detractors of Larsson's theory cite several years that separate the battle of Sasireti and Yngvar's presence in the region, though given the presence of dragons and giants in the tale, the mistaking of a date by a few years is hardly a 'big whoop'. Simply: the battle of Sasireti fits more closely with the saga than anything else.

Indeed, there are a number of factors in the tale that I have bent with remarkable ease to meet the historical record. Jakulus and the other dragons, for example, I have made the Alani, and with reason. The Alans were by this time a Christian nation to the north of Georgia, but they had a fierce history. As well as being infamous enemies of Rome and Byzantium, they had also been used as mercenaries by both before this time. Though the Byzantines are known to have guarded the secret of their 'Greek fire' jealously (so much so in fact that its precise composition remains a mystery to this day) it is not vastly far-fetched to have it fall into the hands of a sometime ally close to their own borders and with whom they remained in contact. This neatly explains the dragons' fire. The Alani also belong to the same racial grouping as the Sarmatians, and these are the people from whom the Draco banner, so infamous in the later Roman empire, first came. Again: the Alani and dragons. To have this particular group of Alani organised more like the ancient empire than the surrounding feudal armies was not too much of an imaginative leap, as was having swords that bear a resemblance to late Roman and Byzantine blades in their hands. Once I started to make all these connections, I found it very easy to explain away the dragons. The fact that later in the saga they meet pirate ships who spray fire through metal tubes only added weight to my connection. I had to make them part of the Alani, and the description of those fire tubes matches seamlessly with Byzantine naval weaponry.

I had my good guy. I had my bad guys. Now I even had my dragons. Giants are more easily explained away. To the Vikings, the gods looked like men, and the giants looked like gods. The three were closer and more interconnected than in any other theology. As such, having giants who were merely astonishingly tall and powerful men makes a lot of sense. Since the saga already gave me what looked to be a clear encounter with the Pechenegs along the Dnieper, they were going to be my giants.

There are, I admit, some aspects of the saga I have simply left out. A house collapsing on a giant and Yngvar having his leg salted and taking it with them is a prime example. There is also a scene of cliff-side portage, which I am fairly sure was the source for that famous episode in the *Vikings* TV series. That, along with the digging of a canal over several months, two winters spent chatting in cities, and other events too, I have left out. No one wants an exciting Viking romp where they spend an entire chapter digging a canal. No one would care about what it was like for an entire winter stuck in a hall in Kutaisi.

The draugar, though, I had to include. The demons Yngvar encounters in his saga at the end of the river are too intriguing not to portray. Moreover, I needed a way for Halfdan to secure a death for Yngvar that was totally inglorious, humiliating and far from noble. The saga tells us he died from disease. It does not illustrate where he contracted that disease. Turning the demons that Yngvar meets into my draugar who will be the cause of his downfall was easy and satisfying. The spit of land I describe that now juts out from the Azerbaijani coast into the Caspian would actually be a little south for the Kipchak/Cuman peoples, one of the few pagan groups left in that part of the world, but this nomadic people were close to the north in the lands of the collapsed Khazan Empire, and their influence would be felt by about this time.

While we are on the subject of mysticism and wraiths, I shall explain an aspect of the Norns' weaving for Halfdan. We have no real way to know how things worked between those who still followed the old ways and those who had become Christians. For me, though, it became an interesting question. When a Christian Viking and a pagan Viking died in battle, what would they assume of each other? Would the pagan presume Christianity was wrong and that Odin would come for him anyway? Would he assume that both were valid and that neither would meet beyond death? Would he think that Odin would shun the man? What the Christian thought of the Viking afterlife is probably easier to imagine.

But this left me with the idea that perhaps Yngvar could still be taken by Odin from a pagan's viewpoint, which gradually unfolded into this convoluted foretelling where Yngvar's illness is a consequence of his zealotry and a pagan way of making sure the jarl died in some way that ensured the Norse gods would not want him. After all, it seems strange that in a saga of high adventure and heroics, the hero dies unpleasantly of disease after being kicked about a bit. The inclusion of a little Viking magic was too much to resist, since it was still part of everyday life among the pagans, and I wanted to portray these people as more or less the last throes of pagan Viking. It was important to me also, just as I sought to explain the giants and the dragons in a realistic way, to make the magic as vague and unconfirmable as possible. There is clearly magic in this book, and yet when you look at it, there's no real *actual* magic.

In terms of identification, Odd Snorrason assigns names that seem to have been plucked either from earlier texts or from his local dialect. The saga's Queen Silkisif seems to be named 'Silken Wife' in Icelandic. I have used the name of the Queen of Georgia at the time, Borena, instead, which at least is a proper name and not a description. Likewise, her city is known as Citopolis in the saga: the capital of Georgia at this time was Kutaisi, which in ancient times had been the capital of the land of Colchis. The connection between these names was not too great a stretch, so I went with Kutaisi. The king they meet who is Jolf might refer to a man other than Bagrat IV of Georgia. He might indeed be the half-brother who actually won the battle of Sasireti. Or he might be a Kakheti king. For the smoothness of the tale, I made him the queen's husband, based at the ancient city of Mtskheta, and so I used his historic name, Bagrat.

The battle of Sasireti is not well documented. Apart from the coverage in Yngvar's saga, if that indeed *is* Sasireti, it is only briefly mentioned in the Georgian chronicles. We have little detail to go on. Bagrat lost the battle, though he would go on to win the war and become one of the most important figures in the unific-ation of Georgia. The Georgian chronicles tell us that three thousand Varangians (Vikings) landed at Bashi, close to the mouth of the river in western Georgia. It tells us that Liparit took seven hundred more men and the Varangians engaged Bagrat at Sasireti. The Varangians win and Bagrat's army flees. That is more or less all of it. So we have Varangians fighting for Liparit from one source, and seemingly Vikings fighting for Bagrat in another (the saga). I simply had Vikings on both sides to satisfy both sources. In 1041 the great Harald Hardrada led the Varangians in Byzantium, and I am not the first person to have speculated his presence at Sasireti.

This tale is not one of the Georgian civil war. The war has started before our friends arrive in Georgia, and it will end long after they have left. We learn from sources that Vikings were captured in the battle of Sasireti, but that Liparit essentially worked them to humiliate them and then sent them home. This clearly cannot refer to the

Varangians that served in Liparit's army, lending further weight to there being Norsemen on both sides of the fight. So our Viking heroes limp away, having achieved remarkably little and lost many ships and men. They split up, one ship heading for Kiev and one for Constantinople, the others unaccounted for.

Oddly, in the saga it is Ketil who heads north and Valdimar who makes it to the great imperial capital. This is strange, given that Valdimar is often identified with a Kievan prince, a son of Jarisleif, who later rules Novgorod and who, incidentally, is also a grandson of Olof Skötkonung of Sweden, by his daughter. That the Kievan should not go home is strange, but we are told that it is Ketil the Icelander who makes it back north to tell the tale. I have tweaked this to send the prince of Kiev home, while Ketil goes on to other adventures.

And yes, there will be other adventures. One day Ketil will have to make it back to Iceland to tell the tale that will become Yngvar's saga. Halfdan still has some graffiti to carve. And we know where he's heading now, where the man known as the Last Great Viking is leading the Varangian Guard. The crew will return in book two.

—

In the meantime, here is a potted version of the events of Yngvar's saga as related by Odd the monk:

Yngvar's saga begins with four passages of an exploration of the history and connections of some of the characters, through to the death of Yngvar's father, his relationship with the Swedish king and his son Onund, his rise to prominence and his service to the king as he moves across subjugated lands and collects taxes and punishes those who have incurred the king's wrath. It is only with the fifth passage that his tale joins with ours, for, at odds with Olof of Sweden who will not grant him the title of king, he takes thirty ships to Kiev to visit the court of Jarisleif (known more often to history by his Slavic name of Yaroslav).

In the fifth passage, Yngvar spends three years at Jarisleif's court, learning many languages and studying the geography of the east and the south. There he learns of three rivers that flow through Rus lands from the east, of which the central is the largest. He determines to follow this river to its source. Bishops bless him as he leaves and the adventurers depart as a sizeable fleet along the Dnieper. Yngvar refuses to let anyone set foot on land, though one night Ketil is on watch and decides to break the rules and go ashore. There he finds a giant's house and steals a silver cauldron. The giant gives chase and the cauldron falls apart so that Ketil escapes but only with the handle. Though Yngvar is not pleased, Ketil gives him the loot and all is well.

They sail on once more and on one night it is Valdimar's turn to keep watch when he spots a glow on the horizon. Deciding to check it out, he goes to investigate, only to discover that the glow is from a great number of sleeping dragons. He tries to steal a gold ring, but that awakens the dragons, including their leader, Jakulus. Valdimar races back to the ships and the dragons follow him. Yngvar has just enough time to get his ships out away from the shore before the dragons arrive, yet they manage to burn one ship and its crew to nothing with vicious fire.

They sail on, and up a river, encountering towns until they reach a city of white marble. Here they meet a queen named Silkisif (which is likely an Icelandic appellation that means Silken Lady) who speaks many languages. Here the ships are lifted into the city, and a great hall given over to the Vikings. Yngvar forbids any interaction with the local heathens and allows only the queen to visit the hall. Once some of his men ignore the order and he has them put to death as an example. They winter in this city while Yngvar and the queen hold many discussions. He tells her all about God and she falls in love with him and offers him her kingdom. He says that he would love that but he must reach the end of the river first.

In spring they sail east once more, coming to a narrow gorge with a waterfall. They have to haul ships up the cliff and portage them to the water once more. Shortly thereafter they meet the fleet of a king called Jolf from a city called Heliopolis. The king insists that they winter with him, and so they do. Once again their ships are brought into the city. Again Yngvar and his men stay in a hall and do not fraternise with the heathens. Again Yngvar spends the winter in discussions with the king, who tells him about whirlpools, springs and the red sea (note: not the 'Red Sea') and importantly about pirates who disguise their ships as islands and attack with fire. The king asks Yngvar to help him fight a war against his brother, and again Yngvar says he will but only once he's reached the end of the river.

Winter over, they sail again. Soon they reach a massive waterfall and then find footprints eight feet long. They have to spend months in a marshy area digging a canal so they can move on. Finally they find a devilish house with a roof held up by a single pillar. A giant leaves the house to go to the river and they hide until he returns. Then when he is asleep they hack through the pillar and the roof collapses, killing the giant. They cut his leg off and salt it to preserve it.

Sailing on, they meet five islands at a fork in a river, which suddenly move and hurl stones at the ships, throwing off their disguises. They launch fire out of brass tubes, burning one of Yngvar's ships. Yngvar looses an arrow into the fire tube and blows up the pirate ship. This process is repeated until the pirates are beaten. They sail on and find the source of the river, where they meet a dragon. They only escape by feeding the dragon the salted giant's leg.

They then explore a headland, find a fortified city with a great hall which seems to be deserted. One of them hides in the hall and a demon visits him at night and tells him a tale of princes and princesses, of dragons and magic. The banner of King Harald is revealed to him. The demon tells the man to give the banner to Yngvar to take home. He also tells the man that most of Yngvar's men will die on this expedition. That man dies, but Yngvar returns with the banner.

They then sail back to meet King Jolf, who takes them to fight his brother, Bjolf. The two armies meet on a battlefield. Yngvar launches spiked wheels at the enemy, breaking the line. Yngvar then charges the enemy and breaks them. The enemy leader runs, and Jolf pursues, while Yngvar keeps his men back. Yngvar and his fleet are busy looting when Jolf returns and turns on them, and they flee.

That night they make camp and devilish women come to them. Yngvar stabs one and many are put to flight, but some of the men are beguiled and sleep with them. Eighteen men die that night. The next day they set off back west, but sickness strikes the fleet. Yngvar himself is sick by the time they return to Silkisif's lands, and he calls his men together and tells them his will, dividing his spoils up and asking that he be buried back in Sweden. He dies in days.

The fleet returns to the queen who goes to pieces. She has Yngvar buried in her city and builds a new cathedral over him. We are told that when the rest leave, there are only twelve ships now. Ketil makes it back to Russia, and Valdimar makes it to Constantinople. Of the others there is no word and they are all presumed lost. Thus ends the part of Yngvar's saga with which we are concerned for this story.

The text goes on with a second expedition carried out by Yngvar's son Svein, who follows in his footsteps, also visiting the queen, fighting cyclops and so on. The only part of the ongoing tale that concerns us is the moment when Svein meets the Jakulus dragon. Svein shoots an arrow straight into the dragon's mouth and kills it.

So ends our saga.

Simon Turney
26 November 2020

Acknowledgements

I would be remiss were I to leave out a small list of people to whom I am indebted in the writing of this book. Firstly, I would like to thank Mike Bhaskar at Canelo, who continues to test my limits as a writer and historian by dragging me out of my comfort zone and throwing interesting challenges my way. It was at his instigation that I delved at all into the world of the Vikings. Also at Canelo, I am ever-grateful for the masterful editorial skills of Craig Lye, who, as well as this book, applied his considerable talents to my Damned Emperors novels. Without Craig's guidance, this would have been a very different, and distinctly inferior, book.

I am grateful for the assistance of my friend Fotis Karyanos in Athens for helping me with the authenticity of any Greek phrasing in the book. His reaction when I asked him to help translate 'Suck Odin's balls' was magnificent. I am also indebted to Lesley Jolley, an aficionado of Viking fiction to whom I turned at the very start for confirmation that I was writing something readable, and who worked through the original draft as I wrote, supplying me with helpful comments and much-needed reassurance.

I am grateful to my wife Tracey for putting up with around a year of being barraged with facts and titbits about Vikings, for watching Viking films and documentaries with me, and for generally not knocking me out and locking me in a cupboard for the rest of the year. I would like to thank Prue Batten and Gordon Doherty in particular for their ongoing support as friends and fellow authors, who are ever-important to me. Thanks are due in particular to Giles Kristian and Robert Low, whose own ground-breaking Viking epics weaned me on the subject and without whose work I would never have even considered this.

Finally, thank you to the readers whose ongoing support and messages of thanks make this the best job in the world.

Glossary

Aesir – one of the two groups of Viking gods, including Thor, Odin, Loki and Tyr

Årsgång – a form of divination, where walkers tread a forest at night on the eve of the new year, seeking knowledge of what is to come

Blaand – an alcoholic drink made of fermented milk whey

Draugr (pl. draugar) – the restless dead, occupying graves and guarding their treasure jealously

Fólkvangr – a great meadow that is the domain of the goddess Freyja

Freyja – the most powerful goddess of the Vanir, whose realm includes magic, fertility, war and the gathering of the slain to her land of Fólkvangr

Gardariki – the Viking name for the lands of the Rus

Geat – one of the three peoples of modern Sweden, the Geats occupied the southern tip of the peninsula

Goth (also Gottlander) – one of the three peoples of modern Sweden, the Goths occupied the island of Gottland

Hel – a daughter of Loki, Hel rules an underworld for the sick and powerless

Hirð – the companions, retinue, or guards of an important man

Holmgang – an official, ritual form of duel between two opponents

Holmgarðr – the city and domain of Viking Novgorod

Hrimgrimnir – a frost giant (see also *jötun*)

Jarl – a noble of power (the derivation of the English 'earl') who receives fealty from all freemen of a region

Jörmungandr – the world serpent, a child of Loki, which encircles the earth and grasps its own tail. When it lets go, Ragnarok will begin

Jötun (pl. jötnar) – the giants, who have been at war with the gods (the Aesir and Vanir) for all time

Kakheti – an independent principality in the Caucasus annexed by Georgia in the late eleventh century

Karl – a free man. Neither a noble, nor a slave

Khazar – a Turkik people of the Russian steppe whose power was broken by the Rus in the tenth century

Koenugard – the land ruled by the Rus prince of Kiev

Loki – a trickster god, a shape-shifter, who is destined to fight alongside the giants against the other gods at the end of days

Lørdag – weekly bath day for the Scandinavian peoples of the time, falling upon a Saturday

Miklagarðr – Viking name for Constantinople, the capital of the Byzantine Empire, now Istanbul

Mjǫllnir – Thor's hammer

Norns – the female entities who control the fates of both men and gods

Odin – most powerful of the Aesir, the chief god and father of Thor, who gave an eye in return for wisdom and who has twin ravens and twin wolves, and an eight-legged horse

Pecheneg – a nomadic Turkik people who occupied the land south of the Rus

Portage – the lifting of a ship from the water and its transportation overland to be returned to a different water

Ragnarok – the end of the universe, including a great battle between gods, giants, monsters and the slain who have been gathered by Odin and Freyja

Ran – the goddess of the sea, who is implacable

Ran's daughters – the waves that claim ships and men

Ringa – Viking name for a Semgall settlement that is now the city of Riga in Latvia

Ringerike – a Scandinavian style or design, formed from intertwined loops and swirls, often found upon runestones

Rus – the descendants of the Vikings who settled Kiev and Novgorod and areas of Belarus and Ukraine, from whom the name Russia derives (Rusland)

Sax – a short sword or long knife of Germanic origin, known to the Saxons as the Seax

Seiðr – a form of magic that flows around men and gods, which can be used and understood by few, the source of divination (Seiðr-woman)

Semgall – the tribe who occupied the region that is now Latvia

Serk – a catch-all term, perhaps derived from the word silk, which is variously applied to all Islamic lands or to the exotic lands south of the Byzantine Empire

Sessrúmnir – the mead hall of Freyja in Fólkvangr, where, like Odin, she gathers the fallen for the final battle at Ragnarok

Skald – a poet or bard

Sleipnir – Odin's eight-legged steed

Svarthaf – Viking name for the Black Sea

Svear – one of the three peoples of modern Sweden, the Svears occupied the northern regions of Sweden, around Uppsala

Thing – a parliament, or political gathering, where oaths are made, deals are struck and feuds and disagreements are settled

Thor – son of Odin, the god of thunder, one of the most powerful of the Aesir

Thrall – a slave with no will beyond that of his master, often a captive of war

Tyr – a god of law and of justice

Urðr – the concept of fate as is spun by the three Norns

Valhöll – the mead hall of Odin, where he gathers the fallen for the final battle at Ragnarok

Valkyrja (pl. Valkyrjur) – the Valkyries, handmaidens of Odin, who select and retrieve heroes upon their death

Vanir – one of the two groups of Viking gods, including Freyja and Njord

Völva – a wise woman or witch or seeress with the power of prophecy and the ability to understand and manipulate Seiðr

Wends – Slavic peoples who inhabit the southern shores of the Baltic